# A STARTLING TALE OF TERRORISM THAT *COULD* BE TOMORROW'S HEADLINES

The President awoke to find himself alone and bound. He was lying on a bed on his back. He looked around. It was dark and hard to see, but in the gloom he could make out bare walls and a single window that looked out on a gray predawn. He tried to stretch his legs, and found they were tied to the sides of the bed. His hands were also bound, taped at the wrists. He scratched at the tape but couldn't dislodge it. He called out once, twice; the second call dissolved into a fit of coughing, and he lay gasping for breath. Finally he gave up, exhausted from the ordeal and the struggle, wondering what had happened and where he was....

---

"Sudden turns of plot, lively pace...and authentic in-the-air scenes."
—*Publishers Weekly*

"[A] big, ambitious thriller...The authors offer an intricate build-up to the pay-off moment."
—*Kirkus Reviews*

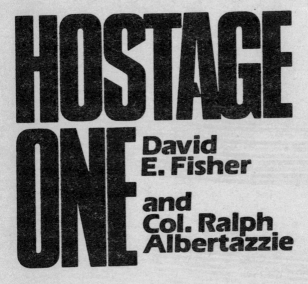

# HOSTAGE ONE

David E. Fisher

and Col. Ralph Albertazzie

SMP

ST. MARTIN'S PAPERBACKS

HOSTAGE ONE

Copyright © 1989 by David Fisher and Ralph Albertazzie.

Library of Congress Catalog Card Number: 89-3792

ISBN: 0-312-92144-6

Printed in the United States of America

Random House edition/July 1989
St. Martin's Paperbacks edition/October 1990

10  9  8  7  6  5  4  3  2  1

This book is for Matthew Scott DiLalla,
a master of suspense and timing

ACKNOWLEDGMENTS

I am grateful to Jose "Pepi" Garcia of the Miami Air Route Traffic Control Center, Federal Aviation Authority; Lieutenants June Green and Tom Barth, and Major Bob Dulaney of the U.S. Air Force; David Caldwell of the McDonnell Douglas Aircraft Company; and the staff of the Imperial War Museum.

# Contents

## Author's Note

Anyone can kill the president of the United States. There is no trick to getting within rifle range—even handgun range—undetected. The chances of getting away again alive are small, but there is no shortage of people for whom that is not an important consideration. Then why have there been so few attempts at assassination? For the same reason that all attempts so far have been by crazies rather than by political entities: there is nothing to be gained by the death.

On the contrary, there is much to be lost. Presidential policies are no longer—as they were, for example, in the days of Wilson or the first Roosevelt—the policies merely of the president; rather, they result from long discussions and arguments among his advisers, and in fact are frequently contrary to the president's own wishes. It follows that the death of a president will have little or no deleterious effect on the policies one wishes changed. The result may even be positive, as witness the Great Society that blossomed under Johnson after Kennedy had been unable to get the same programs through a recalcitrant Congress; that same Congress fell all over itself to comply when Johnson made the same demands.

In the field of foreign relations there is even greater danger. Nothing makes a people as angry as the murder of their leader, and so if, for example, the PLO were to assassinate a president as a protest against American support of Israel, the result would surely be increased rather than diminished support of that country.

On the other hand, the taking of American hostages has proved to be a viable method of obtaining concessions, arms and money.

# I
# Preparations

# 1

David Melnik left his hotel room and walked down the hall. His trench coat was slung over his left shoulder, and he twirled his hat in his hands. The hallway was dimly lit, but he didn't bother to remove his sunglasses. There was a cart piled high with towels and sheets beside an open door to room 1418. He stepped inside and smiled at the maid. "Are you nearly finished?" he asked in French.

"Oui, monsieur," she said. "Just let me put the towels in the bathroom and I'll get out of your way."

"No hurry." He unslung his coat, dropped it and his hat casually on the chair, and stood looking out the window until she left. Then he turned around, took off his sunglasses, and carefully surveyed the room. He stood motionless, tall and slim; only his eyes moved at first. They were a cold blue, their intimidating effect heightened by the absence of eyebrows above. After they had covered everything in front of him, his head began to move slightly to the right, then to the left. The unblinking eyes and his hawklike nose gave him a curiously animal air. It was only after he had seen, really *seen*, everything in the room that the rest of his body was able to move.

He walked to the telephone and studied it for a moment, then lifted the receiver. He unscrewed the earphone, took from his pocket a plastic wrapper and from that a speck of small whitish clay. He pressed it behind the wires and inserted a small electrode, barely larger than a pin tip, into it; then he screwed the earphone back and replaced the receiver.

He was finished now, but instead of leaving he stood where he was and took another look around. He had been following al-Kuchir for five days now, and though the Libyan's routine was less than compulsive it was reasonably predictable; it was unlikely he would return right away. Melnik walked around in the footsteps of the maid, touching nothing. In the corner was a solitary suitcase. He stopped and studied it, his hands at his side as he bent and peered. He immediately found the short wire extending out of the handle, but couldn't believe that was all. He was right, but it took another five minutes before he saw the thread lying along the lower zipper. When he found nothing else, he decided to take a chance and open the case.

Carefully removing the wire and the thread, then laying them precisely on the bureau, he lifted the lid. Again he stopped, touching nothing inside, scanning everything with those cold eyes until he found it: another small thread lying halfway under a pair of socks. He removed it and placed it next to the other two, then began to riffle through the clothes. Beneath the shirts was an Iraqi passport and an airline ticket. He opened the passport; it was for another face and name. The ticket startled him: it was for the name on the passport and was from here in Paris to New York.

Melnik was glad he had taken what might have been an unnecessary chance. Sometimes a man had to go with his instincts. He replaced the inner thread, then the documents, put the shirts back in place and closed the suitcase, putting the outer thread and the wire back in precisely their previous locations. Then he put his sunglasses back on, picked up his coat and hat and left room 1418.

Melnik didn't go back to his own room, but walked down to the end of the hall, turned the corner and waited. Every time he heard the elevator door open he walked briskly toward it, turning the corner and passing al-Kuchir's door. Sometimes the emerging passengers would turn the other way and walk away from him; then he would simply return to his position. If they came toward him he would pass them and continue on around the corner; when he heard them enter a room and shut the door behind them, he would return.

Finally al-Kuchir came out of the elevator. He was not alone. As David passed them he saw that the other man was the face in the passport. They reached their room and went in just as David put the key in his own lock and entered without looking back. He left his door open a crack. He wished he'd been able to leave a bug in al-Kuchir's room, but he didn't have one with him. Al-Kuchir would probably have found it anyway, but Melnik didn't think he'd notice the tiny spot of plastic, which looked like nothing more than a bit of adhesive to hold the telephone wires in place.

He was jeopardizing his mission by waiting, but a sixth sense told him that something important was going on. They didn't go to the United States; they simply didn't do it. They understood American psychology too well. So what did the ticket mean?

He dropped his hat and coat on the bed, put away his sunglasses, lifted his hand to his head and pulled off his hair. Sitting on the bed, he rubbed his long fingers over his totally bald head and waited.

It seemed like hours, but only a few minutes later Melnik heard al-Kuchir's door open. Quickly he shut his own and held his breath, releasing it with relief when he heard only one pair of footsteps going by. He waited till he heard the elevator doors open and close, and then had to decide again whether to wait some more. It was 9:00 P.M. and he thought he could afford to. Al-Kuchir had never yet gone out at night, and he might have calls to make confirming to his superiors that he had passed the ticket on without any problems. If he didn't call they would know something had gone wrong.

Melnik waited till nearly eleven. He couldn't be sure, but probably everything that al-Kuchir had to do had been accomplished by then. He had to decide. He took a little pack that looked like a Walkman radio out of his pocket, extended the antenna and laid it carefully on the night table. Instead of a tuning dial it had only a single button. He lifted the receiver and dialed al-Kuchir's room directly. It rang four times, five—had al-Kuchir gone out without his noticing?—and then it was picked up.

"Oui?" al-Kuchir asked sleepily. The phone must have awakened him.

"Monsieur al-Kuchir?"

"Oui. Qu'est-ce que c'est?"

Melnik held the telephone away from his ear and pressed the button on the Walkman. The line went dead and he replaced the phone.

He had heard nothing. He went to the door and opened it, looking out into the hall to see if anyone else had been disturbed. Not a sound. He closed the door quietly, walked across the room to the bed and lay down. He didn't bother to undress; he knew he wouldn't sleep. He lay on his back with his hands under his head, listening for any sound of commotion in the hall, staring at the ceiling until the first light of morning came.

Then he got up and put on his hair and a pair of lightly tinted eyeglasses. He took his hat, coat and suitcase and left the room. The night had been quiet; no one had come banging on al-Kuchir's door, which meant that no one had tried to call him and become nervous at discovering his phone was out of order. The maid would find him—he felt a moment's compassion for her, walking into the room to find a man with the side of his head blown off, but it couldn't be helped—and then the death would be made public. But the man with the passport would report to his superiors that nothing had been disturbed at the time he was there, and they would probably decide that the person who had planted the bomb in the telephone had not found the tickets and passport. David guessed they would probably rely on their precautions and go ahead with the trip to New York, perhaps changing the schedule as a safeguard. It would be interesting if one could find out why the other man was going to New York.

Melnik checked out of the hotel at 7:30 A.M., patiently joining the early morning line of tourists anxious to catch their flights to London, Brussels, Rome or Tel Aviv.

## 2

The corridor was long, brightly lit and bare, with office doors set regularly in the walls every twelve feet. It was lit by overhead neon lamps set flush in the ceilings, and by a single window at the end of the hallway. This early in the morning the sun reflected off the white stones outside, and the glare of the window hurt Julian Mazor's eyes as he stood outside his door and stared down the corridor, smoking his last cigarette of the day. It was 9:12 A.M. He wondered how he was going to get through the rest of the day without another cigarette. No, he didn't. He knew damn well he was going to finish the pack before lunch, but he pretended to wonder.

He looked down the corridor, squinting against the glaring sunlight, and sighed in vain regret as he did whenever a tricky problem came up. If only he was working for Scotland Yard, he told himself at such times, things would be different. In Scotland Yard, he was sure, the corridors were dark and convoluted, and the offices had fireplaces, heavy rugs and old portraits on the wall and heavy polished furniture.

He knew this wasn't true, of course; he had asked too many Scotland Yard people about their workplace. But he had read all the old thrillers, and he liked to pretend that somewhere such a world existed. Here in Mossad headquarters in Israel everything was sterile, functional, efficient and depressing. He longed for a Victorian ambience, for hidden nuances instead of direct orders, for muffled shapes moving silently through shadowed corridors. He sighed again, then entered his office, closed the door, crossed to the desk, took one last, long suck on the cigarette, nearly inhaling the filter, stubbed it out, sat down and read the report again.

He buried his head in his hands and shook it wordlessly. Where was it written, he wondered silently, that an operator should have "intuition"? Where did these idiots pick up such notions? He tried, Lord knows he tried, to teach them that the proper way to carry out orders was *to carry out orders*. Intuition belonged only at the higher echelons of headquarters, where people had time to indulge in it because they had nothing better to do. There one could sit back in one's chair with one's hands clasped behind one's head, think about one's youth and fantasize about what might be in the most improbable of worlds. Then one would flush the fantasies down the toilet and get on with the realities of this most businesslike of worlds.

That's where intuition belonged: at headquarters, in the toilet. In the field it was only another word for guessing, and guessing is not the proper way to make a nation secure. But how do you teach a crapshooter he is bound to die broke when he beats the odds on his first roll of the dice?

Mazor sighed. He was fantasizing again; it was not Melnik's first roll of the dice. He was fantasizing that Melnik was one of the young ones straight out of school, and that all he had to do was whack him on the ass and teach him not to pick his nose in public. But Melnik was thirty-eight years old, nearly as old as Mazor himself—older really, since Melnik was a first-generation Sabra, which meant he had been born twenty-five years old. They were the worst, those first Sabras. The young ones today seemed to be little different from young people anywhere, but those first Jews born in Israel in the first years of the new state were different creatures, a different species of humanity. Had God created them that way because such people were needed in a nation besieged by hatred on all sides? Or were they molded by their mothers, who saw them as the first true Jews in more than two thousand years?

He smiled, remembering the old joke. Question: How do we know that Jesus was a Jew? Answer: He lived at home till he was thirty-five, he went into his father's business, and his mother thought he was God.

Mazor's smile faded into another sigh. He took out the pack of cigarettes, struggled briefly with himself, lost, and decided it was Melnik's fault. How could a man stop smoking when he had operatives like Melnik?

Melnik had been after al-Kuchir for nearly four months. It was his third assignment in just over a year for Mazor, and he had finished the other two as ordered. He had tracked a Libyan terrorist to Istanbul and dispatched him there, and he had found a PLO murderer in Italy and ended his career. He was a good choice for al-Kuchir, who was responsible for an airplane bomb that had killed fifty-six Israelis in 1985, and who had organized a military strike against a busload of tourists last year, killing seventeen.

Such men were nearly more trouble captured than free. If their arrest was announced, it would be followed, as surely as the sun by the moon, by the taking of hostages. Some innocent men and women would be kidnapped and their lives offered in trade. One could not deal with such scum, but as the weeks of trial progressed the pressure by the kidnappers would increase, the torments of the victims and their families would multiply, and finally all would die, both the convicted and the hostages.

It was Mazor's job to avoid such confrontations. His squad worked on a list of known terrorists, and when they found them they killed them—simply, without fuss, without retaliation. Israel never acknowledged knowing anything about it. It was playing the terrorist game of murder, Mazor admitted, but because of terrorist retaliation it was the only game in town, and Israel had learned to play it well.

Mazor picked up his ashtray, held it a moment and then flung it across the room. It hit the wall, shattered, and fell tinkling to the bare wooden floor. He reached into his desk drawer, took out another ashtray, placed it carefully in the center of his desk and lit another cigarette. As he shut the drawer he noticed that he was running low on ashtrays.

He mustn't think about his job on such levels. That was what usually happened to his agents: they began to think too much about what they were doing instead of why they were doing it, and then they were useless. He let his breath out in a long, slow sigh. It was the hypocrisy of the world that overwhelmed them all, but this hypocrisy was based on principles originally formulated by Judaism, so who was a Jew to complain? *Thou shalt not kill. . . . Vengeance is mine, saith the Lord. . . .* So no civilized state could admit to murdering murderers without formal trial. Hence Mazor's group was not only unofficial but totally anonymous, providing total deniability. The Knesset had never heard of them; the Prime Minister would be shocked if confronted by the world press; the Mossad itself would wash its hands of them.

Mazor's agents were sent off with a list of people, with money, equipment and instructions to disappear. They contacted headquarters only with problems they could not handle on their own, and those agents who could not handle problems on their own did not last long; they were terminated either by Mazor or, more permanently, by the murderers they stalked. That was the usual end of an agent. Occasionally one lasted long enough to begin having attacks of conscience, and then he retired to an office job. But Melnik? Mazor had had high hopes for him, and now this! Intuition!

His head began to throb. He glanced at his watch. It wasn't yet 9:30 A.M., too early for a headache. He massaged the bridge of his nose between thumb and forefinger and tried to relax.

Melnik should not have opened the luggage, should not have waited before carrying out his assignment. He had taken a chance on losing al-Kuchir, which would have meant four months of wasted effort and who knows how many lives destroyed by that murderer before they had a chance to pick him up again. Melnik's intuition—his arrogance, really—could have filled the hospitals and morgues of Jerusalem or Tel Aviv. And for what? A glance at a passport, an airline ticket? Mazor shook his head. He would have to bring in Melnik, break that arrogance and discipline him. But how?

The telephone rang. It was the Director. Mazor stood up, stubbed out his cigarette and walked quickly down the hall.

3

Fazal Abdul Nissar shifted in his chair, bit on his mustache and looked around nervously. Inwardly he laughed at himself: *What do you expect to see?* In any event, the boulevard was normal. Automobiles sped up and down and people walked on the sidewalk and in the street, ignoring the cars as the cars ignored them. Fazal did not wonder that there were not more accidents; he was used to traffic even more chaotic than this. But he did wonder about everyone sitting at the tables in this sidewalk café: were they looking at him? When he looked at each in turn, of course they were not. But when his head was turned, what then?

Paranoia, he told himself, nothing but paranoia. Then he looked down again at the newspaper folded in his lap, and the nervousness crept once again up his back and scratched the closely cropped hair on the nape of his neck.

The paper reported that a M. Wadir Nagoorni had been murdered on the fourteenth floor of the George Cinque Hotel, his head blown apart by a bomb planted in the telephone. It smacked of a political assassination, but no terrorist group had claimed credit, nor was M. Nagoorni a known political activist. His passport was Algerian; nothing else was known about him.

Was it al-Kuchir? Fazal wondered. He didn't know what name or nationality al-Kuchir was traveling under in Paris. He hadn't even bothered to notice the number of the room last night. It was high up; the fourteenth floor seemed about right, but he hadn't noticed. *Idiot!* He must learn to notice such things.

But never mind that now. There wasn't time to waste on self-recrimination. What was he to do now—that was the question. He had no instructions to cover such a situation; he had no one to ask. Suddenly he remembered al-Kuchir opening the suitcase in his room, and the memory calmed him. He remembered al-Kuchir pointing out the one thin hair lying on the handle, the second one lying on the zipper, and the third lying under the socks. Surely no one had opened the suitcase, so even if the dead man was al-Kuchir the murder had nothing to do with him. He must not panic. He must stay calm, and . . . and *what?* What should he do now?

He had no choice, Fazal realized. No provision had been made for such an eventuality. He had no way to contact anyone, no way to change plans even if the murder *did* concern him. He had his instructions, and he would have to proceed with them to the letter. He would report to Orly on Saturday in precisely the clothes specified, carrying the prescribed suitcase, and take the flight listed on his ticket.

Fazal shook his head angrily and finished his coffee. He was only a simple pilot: he wasn't used to all these machinations. Then he reminded himself that he was no longer the Syrian boy Fazal Nissar; he was the Iraqi Mohammed Asri. And no, he wasn't just a simple pilot anymore.

4

"Julian, I want you to call your ferrets off one of the rats," the Director said without preamble.

Mazor's face immediately took on a worried look, and the Director laughed; Julian was always suspicious of anyone making a deal with terrorists. "Not to worry, old son," the Director said, his speech reflecting his Oxford education, "we simply have more important things to do with him than bury him. Something very big is going down, and we've finally got a lead. You have someone after this man al-Kuchir, don't you?"

*Oh, Jesus,* Mazor thought. He nodded.

"Of course you do. At the last meeting you reported closing in on him, didn't you? Results to be expected soonest, as I recall; that's what you said, isn't it?"

Mazor nodded. *Why, God? Why me?*

"Good. Excellent. But don't kill him. We want him trailed to see who his contacts are, then pulled in alive for questioning. After that you can kill him, I promise. All right?"

The Director was puzzled that Mazor's worried look did not relax; indeed, it seemed to intensify. For his part, Mazor was having trouble swallowing.

"Something wrong?" the Director asked.

"Yes, sir."

The Director looked at him. "Don't tell me—?"

"Yes, sir."

"Damn!" The Director pounded his fist into his palm, stared at Mazor as if he wished he could pound him as well, then spun his chair around and stared at the wall. Mazor concentrated on trying to swallow his saliva. The Director turned back to him. "When?" he asked.

"Just yesterday. Received the message a few hours ago."

"Where?"

"Paris."

"Confirmed? No chance he was merely wounded?"

Mazor was insulted. His men never merely wounded. "None. Blew off his head with a telephone bomb."

"Has the body been found?"

"I imagine so."

"Don't imagine! Get somebody there right away. If the police aren't there yet, check his pockets. Check his room, wherever he was living. We've got to find some lead that will move us forward."

Mazor thought of Melnik's intuition and blessed it. "May I ask—"

"No, you may not! Not anything! Just get on this right away before the blasted French flics screw everything up. We never get anything from them. Why couldn't you have killed him in Germany, where they know how to cooperate?"

"May I suggest—?"

"Nothing! I don't want to hear anything from you until you find something that can lead us past al-Kuchir."

"I think we may have that," Mazor said.

The Director stopped his tirade and looked at Mazor warily, then became aware that he was tipped forward on the edge of his chair and was pointing a finger in Mazor's face. He settled back, folded his hands, looked suspiciously at Mazor and asked, "What?"

"Our agent Wizard—that's David Mel—"

"Not his name. I don't want to know his name."

"Sorry. Wizard took the chance of searching al-Kuchir's room before the hit. He—"

"Isn't that unusual?"

"Very unusual, sir. I'm afraid Wizard is one of our more imaginative operators."

The Director lifted his eyebrows and Mazor went on. "Evidently he found a passport and an airline ticket from Paris to New York for a Mohammed Asri."

"That's it!" The Director literally jumped out of his chair and walked around it several times in excitement. "That's what we're looking for. Do we know this man—what's his name, Asri?"

"Haven't had time to check yet, but it's not familiar to me."

The Director sat down again. "Take care of it right away." He leaned back and beamed at Mazor. "Hot damn," he said, a phrase reflecting the two years he had spent with the CIA twenty years ago. "Finally a bit of good luck."

5

Damn, David Melnik thought. What rotten luck. He sat morosely in the window seat, looking down thirty-seven thousand feet at the Atlantic Ocean. In the distance the blue of the waters merged slowly into a gray haze and then emerged again as the blue of the sky, with no definable border between atmosphere and ocean. He thought of the words of Genesis: And God made the firmament, and divided the waters which were under the firmament from the waters which were above the firmament: and it was so.

He wondered what in hell he was getting into now. Whatever it was, he didn't like it. He liked what he had been doing. He liked being on his own, not even having to report in for weeks or months at a time. He liked murdering murderers. He didn't like working in a group— No, he thought, be honest. It could be all right if they were good groups. What he didn't look forward to was working with a group of Americans.

Americans. That's what they called themselves, ignoring the Canadians, Mexicans and all of Central and South America. They called their country America as if those other countries didn't exist. They were loud, arrogant and boorish— No, he stopped himself again. Be honest. Those words were used for caricatures of Americans; he didn't know any Americans himself. But he knew enough about them to know he didn't want to work with them.

On October 7, 1973, David Melnik had been twenty-one years old, wearing newly commissioned wings in the Israeli Air Force, living for six months far from home in the Norfolk village of Coltishall on extended loan to the Royal Air Force, learning to fly Hawker Harriers, the vertical-take-off jet fighters that the IAF was planning to buy. His father, Albert Ben-David Melnik, was a construction engineer in Tel Aviv and a reserve captain in the Israeli armored corps.

During the preceding weeks Israeli intelligence had reported mounting evidence of a combined Syrian and Egyptian attack designed to push the Israelis into the sea, to destroy every one of them, to exterminate the Jewish state. But when the prime minister, Golda Meir, asked for the American government's opinion, she was told that the CIA's information was that the Egyptian and Syrian governments were only trying to goad the Israelis into launching a preemptive strike, which they would then claim was evidence of Israel's expansionist policies. Their military buildup was nothing more than a political move on the game board of world opinion.

In Tel Aviv, Albert Melnik went to work each day, came home for lunch and worked until a late supper. He wrote his son a letter every Friday. Golda Meir wanted to announce an emergency, to call up the reserves and mobilize Israel's forces. But the American ambassador warned her to be cautious, and she bit her lip and held her tongue.

On Wednesday, October 3, 1973, Israeli intelligence reported Syrian tanks moving up to the forward lines along the Golan Heights, and Egyptian tanks moving up to the edge of the Suez Canal. They also reported that the Syrian and Egyptian air forces had been put on a war footing, prepared to attack at a moment's notice, and that there were massive troop concentrations along the borders.

On Thursday, October 4, Israeli intelligence warned that a massive synchronized invasion was slated to take place on both the northern and southern borders at 6:00 P.M. on October 6. Now Golda Meir telephoned President Nixon, who told her that America's drive for peace in the Mideast was approaching a successful climax, and for her to hold on a bit longer. In response to her entreaties, so the story went, he sent his secretary of state, Dr. Henry Kissinger, directly to Egypt. On Friday, October 5, Kissinger met with Mohammed el Zayat, the personal adviser to the Egyptian president, Anwar Sadat. In a stern manner Dr. Kissinger warned him that the United States and Israel had received information that an Egyptian attack was slated to begin the next day at 6:00 P.M. Was this true? The United States would not look kindly on such an event, and he, Kissinger, would be personally disappointed if his Egyptian friends were to violate the renewed spirit of peace in the Middle East. In a friendly and relaxed way el Zayat assured Dr. Kissinger that President Sadat agreed completely with Kissinger's widely publicized peace initiatives, and that if only Israel would relax her military buildup there could be permanent peace in the region.

When Kissinger left his office, el Zayat picked up the telephone and said, "Yes, he just left. The Israelis are expecting us at six P.M. No, I don't know how they found out. I suggest we move up the attack hour to noon."

And Kissinger called Nixon, and Nixon called his ambassador to Israel, Kenneth Keating, and on the morning of Saturday, October 6, Mr. Keating met with Mrs. Meir to urge her to take no warlike preparations, to trust the United States. Mrs. Meir asked if President Nixon himself would talk directly to Anwar Sadat. He would, Mr. Keating replied. So Golda Meir went to her Cabinet meeting at noon and refused to order the Israeli army on full alert. At that precise moment the Syrian and Egyptian armies and air forces launched the Yom Kippur War.

It wasn't until late that afternoon that Albert Melnik was called up and sent to his battalion of tanks, not until early the next morning that he was in combat trying to turn back the Syrian hordes below the Golan Heights with less than a dozen tanks manned by crews still dressed in everything from pajamas to tuxedos. It wasn't until after 11:00 A.M. on Sunday, October 7, the second day of the war that the United States had promised would never happen, that Albert Melnik died burning alive in a mangled tank while the Syrians passed jubilantly by, cheering his flaming tomb and wiping out the Golan kibbutzim to the last man, woman and child.

*Trust me*, Kissinger had said. *Believe in us*, Nixon had declared. *Fools*, came back the whispered word of God.

David Melnik shook his head violently. It didn't do to remember such things too often or too well. But it also didn't do to forget. *Not again*, Melnik thought. *Not ever again*. Then he thought, *Enough*. There were other things to think about. He stared out the window at the Atlantic Ocean speeding by in slow motion seven miles below.

It was his own damn fault, anyway. Nobody had told him to go into al-Kuchir's room and take a look around. Curiosity killed the cat, and it never had done an intelligence agent much good either.

He hadn't really thought it was very important: a name on a passport and an airline ticket. But he had reported it for the same reason he had opened the suitcase in the first place. That's what intelligence is, little bits and pieces of information that mean nothing by themselves but eventually fit into a larger pattern, pointing in directions, giving indications, finally leading to something concrete.

So Melnik had been only mildly surprised when Mazor had flown to Paris the next morning with a portfolio of photographs. They had been the normal variety, from mug shots taken on arrests to long-range telephoto shots of people scurrying in or out of doorways. There had been hundreds of them, and it had taken him hours to go over them. They had covered a wide range: terrorists, suspected terrorists and people who had simply been walking too slowly past houses in which a suspected terrorist might once have lodged. Still, it hadn't surprised him that the face he had seen walking down the hotel hallway with al-Kuchir was not among the photographs.

"Look again," Mazor had said.

"If he was there, I'd have seen him," Melnik replied.

"Look again," Mazor insisted.

At times like these you had to humor chiefs. He pulled the books of photographs back across the table, opened the top one again, took a pack of cigarettes out of his shirt pocket, extracted one and stuck it between his lips. It was dark and French, a filthy weed, but when he had to think or was bored he liked to chew on one. He had stopped smoking years before.

After several pages of pictures Melnik glanced up and noticed Mazor staring at him, chewing his upper lip. The cigarette, he realized. Of course. Poor Mazor. Somehow he couldn't quit. He must be past his quota for the day already. Innocently, studying the pictures, he patted his pockets, then looked up at Mazor. "Got a light?" he asked.

Mazor swallowed twice and passed his lighter across the table. David lit the cigarette, trying not to choke on the obscene taste, blew out a thick cloud of smoke and returned to studying the pictures. Twice in the next five minutes he noticed out of the corner of his eye Mazor making a sudden, aborted movement toward him. He said nothing. Finally Mazor exploded. "Give me a cigarette!"

"I thought you'd quit," Melnik said with surprise.

"I *am* quitting. I just feel like a smoke."

Melnik slid a cigarette across the table to his superior, feeling pleasantly revenged for being made to go over all those photographs again after he had stated clearly that the man was not there.

It was well after midnight before Melnik had again finished the last of the terrorist books and started on the subsidiary set of exchanged prisoners. It was nearly another hour before his forefinger paused for a moment in midair.

"What?" Mazor asked, immediately alert.

"Nothing," Melnik said. "I just thought for a moment—" He was exhausted; he had looked at faces until they all blurred into a mélange of swarthy, ugly noses, teeth, eyes and . . . Still he hesitated; then his forefinger moved backward, turning the previous page open again.

"Is that him?"

"No," Melnik said, but even as he said it he wasn't sure. He stared at the picture from the military prison file book. It was a full-face mug shot of a Syrian fighter pilot shot down and captured during the Yom Kippur War seventeen years earlier. Fazal Adbul Nissar, the caption read. The face was thin and arrogant, with a thick mustache and long, unkempt hair, none of which the man he had briefly seen walking down the hotel corridor possessed. But with fifteen years of aging the face naturally would be thicker. . . .

"Well?" Mazor insisted. "Do you think it's him?"

"I can't be sure. The man had dominant lips and a weak chin; here I can't see the lips and the chin is obscured. But take away the mustache . . . He had large ears, swept slightly forward, and here the hair is long and covers the ears, but . . ."

"But? But?" Mazor urged him on.

"The eyes. The eyes and the nose . . . I can't be sure," Melnik said finally.

"But maybe?"

"Maybe? Oh, yes, certainly 'maybe.' " He grimaced, frowned and studied the picture for several long seconds. "I *think* it's him. I can't say more than that."

Mazor leaned over his shoulder and stared at the picture. "A Syrian fighter pilot sent to New York by our Libyan al-Kuchir with an Iraqi passport," he mused. He stood up, stretched, leaned over, snapped the book shut and handed Melnik an airline ticket to New York. "Find him."

That wasn't so bad. David had half-expected it; after all, he was the only man who knew what "Mohammed Asri" looked like. But then Mazor had told him that he was being reassigned to quasi-permanent liaison duties with the American FBI. "You leave tomorrow," he said. "Pick up some new clothes."

"What's wrong with these?" Melnik protested.

"Too European. Buy some things that look American."

Melnik started to ask what this meant, but then realized what Mazor had said previously. "Quasi-permanent?" he asked suspiciously. "What does that mean?"

"Until this business is cleared up."

Melnik protested. He would go to New York and pick up Asri when he came through customs; certainly he would do that. Or he would follow him and pick up his contacts in America; he would follow through as thoroughly as Mazor could wish. But he didn't need the FBI. Why even tell the Americans he was coming? What was the point? He didn't need them.

"Don't be stupid," Mazor said. "We must assume the man is a trained operative. You can't follow him on your own. Can even the great David Melnik follow a man who doesn't want to be followed?"

"Of course not," Melnik answered irritably. He didn't like having his intelligence doubted. "But why can't we put together an Israeli group? What does it have to do with the Americans, anyway? Just because Asri's going to New York?"

"He doesn't just *happen* to be going to New York, he's not simply passing through America, not going for a visit to Disneyland. Something big is going down," Mazor said, echoing what the Director had told him. "We don't know exactly what it is, but it involves a strike against America. Almost certainly *in* America."

"You don't know exactly what it is?"

"No."

"Perhaps you wouldn't mind telling me *approximately* what it is?"

Mazor shrugged.

"If I'm going there to work on it, perhaps at least you could tell me everything you *do* know."

Mazor smiled. "I just did," he said.

Oh, well. There were many perks to being a Mossad agent, Melnik thought. How else could a poor Israeli travel all over the world, staying sometimes, it was true, in the dingiest of hotels, but also sometimes in the grandest, depending on where his target was or what his mission might be. How else could a man see the world, experience its pleasures, dangers, fleshpots, symphony concerts and grand restaurants, and put it all on an unlimited expense account? There were many perks, as when after wandering around a lovely city like Paris for weeks, one could terminate a murderer who had killed without mercy a score of Israeli citizens. Yes, there were many perks in this business, but choosing your assignment was not one of them.

So. America.

6

Charles Werther arrived at his office at 7:45 A.M., fifteen minutes before his secretary, took off his hat and hung it on the hook behind the door. He was one of the few FBI agents who still wore a hat; most of them had taken to sunglasses instead, trying to suggest a CIA look, but Werther was a traditionalist.

He was a thickset man in his mid-forties, with close-cropped hair turning gray. He had the gentle look of a professor or a pediatrician, which fooled a lot of people. He crossed the outer office and went into his private room; sitting at the desk, he began to look through the late memos that had been left there.

At 8:10 A.M. his secretary brought him a cup of coffee; she was a traditionalist too. At nine o'clock she reminded him it was time to leave for the airport. It was early, but the roads would be more crowded than usual, if that was possible. Werther thought again briefly of simply taking the subway, but it wouldn't give the right impression. It was always best to start on the right foot with these people. He walked out to where the car was waiting, got into the right front seat and was driven out to JFK. Coming back he would ride more formally in the rear.

They got to the airport in plenty of time and stood waiting in the lounge watching the television set. The camera was right outside; looking out the large windows he could see the same view, though not as close up or in as good color. Air Force One was coming in to land, its wings stretched out like a hawk's, its wheels extended like primeval feet reaching out to touch the ground as it balanced on the wind. The President was visiting New York this spring of 1990 as a preliminary to the fall congressional elections. With a puff of smoke the wheels touched down and the cameras panned away to the welcoming crowd. They didn't focus on the airplane again until it stopped and the door was opening.

For a moment Werther had a waking nightmare, telescoped in time and space. He saw someone in the crowd step forward and throw a grenade. As it exploded at the President's feet the scene dissolved in the smoke. He saw the President's limousine pulling away out of the gates, speeding down the expressway into the city, where a man and a woman kneeling by the curb extracted a short rocket tube from a baby carriage and in one quick movement leveled it, aimed it and pulled the trigger. As the limousine exploded in flames the scene dissolved again to the President walking jauntily into Madison Square Garden, his Secret Service guards surrounding him as he moved between throngs of people held back by heavy rope barriers, and as he waved, someone in the crowd reached into his jacket pocket—

"The El Al flight's landing," the driver said.

Werther turned around and glanced up at the announcement

screen. "Thanks," he said. "Let's go." The President, after all, was not his concern. He hoped.

The customs agent turned around and nodded at them, and Werther studied for a moment the man being handed back his passport. The first thing he noticed was the hideous blue plaid sport jacket; if it was any indication of character or taste the man was going to be a trial. He wore tinted glasses, was an inch or two over six feet and carried his slim frame easily. His hair was thick and brown but closely cropped. As he came through the customs gate Werther moved forward with hand outstretched.

"Mr. Melnik, I'm Charles Werther. I've got a car waiting out front," he added, guiding him away from the crowd. "Do you have luggage?"

"Only this," Melnik said, indicating his overstuffed carryon. "Identification?" he asked as they walked away.

Werther tried not to smile as he handed over his wallet. If he weren't the proper person, how would he have known who Melnik was? Amateurs, he thought, but more with condescension than irritation; small-country amateurs were always so self-important.

Melnik tried not to sigh as he read the ID closely. It was just as he had thought it would be. The Americans were so insulated from the real world by their oceans and military power that they had no concept of security. It was going to be like working with a spoiled child.

"So," Werther said as they entered his office. He gestured Melnik to a seat and slid in behind his desk. "Tell me all about it."

Melnik looked at him expressionlessly. "It was my understanding that I was coming here so that you could tell *me* about it," he said.

Pause. They stared at each other. Then Werther tried a smile. "Our whole professional training," he began, "is based on the concept that we shouldn't trust anyone. We don't completely trust our CIA or Secret Service, and I guess you don't trust your—what do you call it—your Institution. The Institution for Military Intelligence, right?"

Melnik nodded.

"But I think this situation is serious enough for the two of us to realize that we can't afford *not* to trust each other. Am I right?"

"Of course," Melnik agreed. "You start."

Werther stared at him for another long second. This isn't going to be an easy man to work with, he thought. Then he said, "Certainly. Right." He nodded. "I'll start."

He got up and began to pace around the room. "I'm probably wrong," he said. He considered this, then added, "I'm probably crazy, is what most people around here think. But something big is going down, and we don't know what's up. In a nutshell, that's it."

He stopped and looked at Melnik, who stared back at him, not saying a word, waiting. "I want to be honest with you. What I'm talking about does not have the unanimous backing of the United States intelligence organizations. But I *smell* something out there, and I've been around long enough so they humor me and let me see what I can find." He smiled. "And I found you."

Still Melnik didn't react. Werther pulled a chair over to him, sat down and said, "Look, the United States hit Libya in 1986. It was a personal attack on Qaddafi and his family, no matter how it was presented in the press as a military attack. Qaddafi and the entire Arab world know it was a direct attempt at political assassination. Qaddafi swore to unleash a holy war of terrorism in retaliation. Late that same year he sent a squad of hit men to the U.S. to get Reagan, but we picked them up and kept the whole thing quiet. When Reagan visited England in '88 there was a 'coincidental' upsurge in Arab tourists with false passports, but Scotland Yard took them off the streets, held them until Reagan left the country and then deported them. Since then what's happened? Nada. Nothing. Now, that would appear to be a bit worrisome. Certainly the absence of any evidence that he is doing anything should not be taken as evidence that he *is* doing something, on the theory that he's so clever that we wouldn't be able to find out what he's doing. If he's really doing it. You follow?"

Melnik nodded, and Werther continued. "But it's also just as certain that the absence of evidence is not evidence of absence. Do I make myself clear? So what we have is the expectation of some kind of attack coming from Qaddafi, and we wait for it and all we hear is a big loud nothing. So first Reagan and now Bush act like big shots to the world press: Qaddafi is afraid of us, he's powerless, there's nothing he can do. But you know and I know that's a lot of bull. The man is crazy, and crazy people aren't afraid of anybody. And with all his money and all the people in the world who will do anything for a petrobuck, he's anything but powerless. Which means there's *plenty* he can do. So when he does nothing, Reagan and Bush can bluster all they want but people like me get very, very nervous.

"Add to that the beginnings of a few whispers. We begin to hear about money flowing in and out of Swiss accounts. As far as we can ascertain, this money is coming from Libya. Now, you know the damn Swiss; that money flows in and it flows out again, and it's very hard to keep track of where it comes from and where it goes. It's hard, but it's not impossible, and some of it has been funneling here into these United States, and that scares the hell out of me. It looks like that son of a bitch is in fact working on something, and is managing to keep it quiet. When a loudmouth braggart like him keeps things quiet, it's either because he's not doing anything at all or because he's beginning something very big.

"Then just a few days ago the CIA picks up a tip that your friend and mine al-Kuchir is involved with this in some way. He's the middleman in hiring somebody to do something unpleasant, and I happen to know somebody here and somebody there—I've made a few friends in my twenty-five years in this business—and I find out that the Mossad is looking for al-Kuchir for some other nasty business during the past few years. But before we can get the word out that we'd like to talk to him you kill the bastard. Then it turns out that you found a United States visa, an Iraqi passport and an airline ticket to New York for a Syrian ex-pilot, and I begin to imagine all *kinds* of possibilities, among which is *not* the possibility that Bush is right and Qaddafi is scared of the power of the good old United States. Now you can take your choice as to which of those possibilities is the actuality. I guess I've made it pretty clear which side of the fence I come down on. How about you?"

Melnik thought for a moment. "I can tell you how Israel feels," he said. "Israel is scared to death of the United States. Yes, it's true. We're afraid that you will feel we've let you down. The Mideast is supposed to be our sphere; we're responsible there and are supposed to know everything that goes on there. You say you're scared. Well, I can tell you we are frankly terrified that the Arabs will pull off some tremendous coup against you, and you'll be ticked off that we didn't find out about it for you. You expect your CIA to fail; you expect the Mossad to succeed.

"That's the atmosphere back in Jerusalem," Melnik continued.

"Then when we find this Mohammed Asri being smuggled into the United States, everybody panics and they yank me off my assignment and send me here to find him for you."

"Okay. You've told me how everybody back home in Israel feels," Werther said. "How about you? What do *you* think?"

"What do I think," Melnik asked, "or what do I feel?"

Werther was impatient. "Think, feel, intuition, intelligence. Never mind the verbiage. Just give me the whole schmear. What's your estimate of the situation?"

"Remember the old song from *The Music Man?* I say we've got trouble, right here in River City." Melnik smiled for the first time, pleased with his knowledge of Americanisms. "Something *is* happening," he went on. "I have no idea what. I don't know if it's an outlandish operation that Qaddafi's dreamed up in the middle of the night or if they really have some plan that's concrete and workable, something they can put into play. I think you shouldn't panic, but it would be well worth your while to find out what it is that's happening."

"Right," Werther said. "Let's do that, shall we?"

"How do we start?"

"We start with your friend Asri. We follow him when he comes in, and we see where he leads us." He paused. "To be honest—"

"Which is the American way," Melnik prompted.

Werther looked at him. He couldn't tell if this was a wise guy or not. He nodded. "Right," he said. "Anyway, like I say, this Asri is all we've really got. Aside from him, what is there? There's the money trail, which is like a smell of smoke in the middle of the night; it tells you there's a fire out there somewhere, but it doesn't tell you where, or how big the fire is, or anything worth a damn. We know that some of the money has gone into banks in Miami and New York, but then we've lost track of it. This country is goddamn paranoiac about letting us keep track of things. Kennedy died twenty-five years ago, but you'd never know it by the way people keep bitching about civil rights, privacy and all that crap. Anyhow, aside from the money, about all we have to go on is a name: Dallas."

"The city?"

Werther shrugged. "The city, or a man, or just a code name. We don't know."

"Not many Libyans named Dallas," Melnik observed.

"Very good," Werther replied. "I can see you're going to be very useful to us here. We hadn't thought of that." No, he stopped himself, don't be sarcastic; give the guy a chance. He came around his desk, sat on it and swung his legs. "Not many Libyans of *any* name in this country. We're not exactly on friendly terms with Libya—"

Melnik's expression had not changed, but inwardly his attitude stiffened. The sarcasm hit him like a wet slap in the face. He had expected no better, he told himself; he had expected nothing but smug superiority from the all-powerful Americans. So what else is new?

"—as you clever foreign intelligence types may have picked up from the newspapers," Werther continued, riding quickly past his sarcasm and forgetting it, as the Israeli didn't seem to pick up on it. "The advantage of this is that they can't come and go here as they please; they're easy to pick up and it's easy to know where they are. Which means if they're going to pull anything off they have to work through other nationalities."

"Perhaps American," Melnik suggested.

Werther nodded. "Exactly. Like maybe somebody using a name like Dallas."

"Or the city."

Werther kept nodding. "We don't know," he said. "Or maybe it's the code name for the operation. We don't know much, and we're not exactly clamping iron bars all over the border, but when you tell us about this Syrian trying to slip in with a false passport picked up from this guy al-Kuchir, we begin to get a little worried. We'd like to know more about this guy Mohammed Asri. So now you tell me."

Melnik nodded, leaned forward and began to tell Werther about his assignment in tracking down and eliminating al-Kuchir, and how he had opened the suitcase. "And that's it," he finished.

"No more background?"

"Everything Israeli intelligence knows was covered in what you said. There's obviously a feeling that something big is happening, but you know how it is at this stage. It's more intuition than fact." In his own mind Melnik thought it was something else entirely. He could see Israeli intelligence reacting with a certain scorn, but also with the fear he had mentioned, that the Americans must be placated somehow. What a terrible thing if a terrorist should actually be trying to sneak into *their* holy country!

He leaned back, took a pack of cigarettes out of his pocket, began to chew on one and continued. "So far the Arabs have understood well your American psychology—" He stopped and smiled, realizing his own chutzpah. "This is just *my* interpretation of *their* understanding of *your* psychology," he explained, "and perhaps it's all wrong. But as I see it the Arabs have always been careful not to make the Americans angry, and they do this by staying away from your majestic purple shores. Killing Marines in the Near East, killing American passengers on a liner in the Mediterranean, hijacking an American airplane from an airport in Greece—that's different. It gets headlines, it gets your attention, but it doesn't actually get you angry because it happens half a world away. You're still safe in Kansas, in Wyoming, even in New York. If a few Americans are foolish enough to travel to Israel or the Near East, what can they expect but trouble?

"So they've been careful not to hit anyone *inside* the United States. But perhaps now they feel it's time. If it is, it will have to be a hit big enough to do more than annoy; it will have to be big enough to convince you at one stroke that you're helpless in this struggle. It should be big enough to turn your anger not on the attackers but on those *responsible* for the attack—their allies, the Israelis, us; big enough to convince you that, as in Vietnam, you're in over your heads for a cause you don't really care about, and that you should get out and forget what's going on over there on the other side of the world. Just as Pearl Harbor was intended to do: knock you out of the war before you really entered it. So what do you think?"

Werther nodded. It was possible. More, it was roughly what he had been thinking. But how? A military attack? Impossible. A missile attack? They had no nuclear warheads and no ICBMs, but they could mount a large number of short-range missiles on merchant ships and fire them as they approached the American coast. Still, the damage would be limited to coastal cities. Much better—and easier—would be a series of attacks with planted bombs on airlines all over the country, or directly within the cities. It was as easy to blow up department stores in New York, Wichita or Salt Lake City as in Paris. Thanks to the National Rifle Association, guns were freely available anywhere in the country, and dynamite was just as easy to obtain.

"Of course we're both just guessing," Werther said.

Melnik shrugged. "As long as we're just guessing," he said, "have you thought about Dallas as a code name, but picked *because* of the city? It's been a long time, and maybe you've forgotten in America, but in other countries Dallas is still remembered as the place where your President was assassinated."

. Werther was quiet for a moment. Then he said, "No. No, we haven't forgotten."

7

He intended to leave Melnik at the hotel where his secretary had made a reservation, but at the last moment his compassion betrayed him: instead of dropping him off at the curb, he made the mistake of walking him in. Unless you are rich, New York hotels are incredibly dreary. The lobby of this one, selected by his secretary for the visitor with an eye to Israel's per diem allowance, was so depressing that Werther simply couldn't leave him there. He looked around while they waited for the room clerk; as they waited the brown walls and floor seemed to rise up to suffocate them, and suddenly Werther found himself urging Melnik to come home with him instead. He could stay overnight, have a drink and a good meal, and tomorrow they'd find him someplace better to stay.

Melnik saw nothing wrong with the hotel. It wasn't bad by one-star European standards, which was all he expected on an assignment like this. He had never seen a normal American Howard Johnson's or Marriott. This place wasn't his idea of gracious living, but such a thought never occurred to him. It was dry, warm and seemed reasonably clean; it would do. He tried to decline graciously, and then almost to the point of rudeness. He had no wish for anything more than a strict business relationship with this American. But the more he declined, the more Werther insisted, obviously feeling that Melnik was as distressed by the hotel as he himself was. *We're going to have a communication problem*, Melnik thought wearily as he gave up the struggle and went home with Werther.

"Lori? I'm home," Werther called as they entered the Village flat, but there was no response. "Working late," he apologized to Melnik. "She wasn't expecting me to bring you home."

"I understand," Melnik said. "Look, I can catch a bus back to the hotel and we'll do this some other night, all right?"

But every obstacle only made Werther more stubborn, and he insisted on Melnik's taking off his blue monstrosity of a jacket and relaxing on the couch with a martini. Melnik would have preferred a beer, but he accepted the drink and sat down while Werther searched the refrigerator for some leftovers to use as hors d'oeuvre.

He came out with half a chicken in a roasting pan. "Had this for dinner last night," he explained. "We can nibble on it till Lori comes home, then go out for something to eat."

"What sort of work does she do?"

"Lawyer. Makes more than I do. Works harder, too, but she loves it, so what the hell."

"Children?"

Werther shook his head, swallowing a large gulp of his martini. "That's the problem. We've got it made, except for kids. She's younger than me, but she's in her thirties, and if we're ever gonna have them it's gotta be soon. But right now she's in one of those critical points in her career. The problem is, it seems like as soon as you finish one critical point you move into another, so when are you gonna be able to sit down and take a few years off to have a couple of kids? Well, it's a common problem nowadays. Another drink? Come on, it's been a long day."

It had been, and finally it was letting up. Melnik felt more relaxed with Werther, and wasn't sure whether it was because he'd had a martini or because Werther had. Either way, it would be smart if they both had another.

They were relaxing with their third when the front door opened and slammed shut again. "Oh G-a-h-d!" came a tired wail, and a moment later Lori Werther fell into the room, throwing her briefcase in one direction and kicking her shoes off in two others. She grabbed her husband's drink, swallowed it off, and as she spun and fell backward spread-eagled into the huge armchair she saw Melnik on the couch.

She recovered magnificently, bouncing up as soon as her bottom touched the cushion, taking a deep breath to cool off the martini that was burning its way down into her abdomen, and held out her hand politely as Melnik rose to meet her. "I'm sorry to burst in like that, but it's been a hell of a day," she said. "Charlie didn't tell me he was planning to bring anyone home. I'm Lori Werther."

"David Melnik," he said, shaking hands.

"The Israeli? He looks rather normal," she said, turning to her husband. "He was afraid you'd be more . . . well, *primitive*," she said, turning back to David.

"You haven't seen his jacket yet," Charles said, gesturing over his shoulder.

"Oh," she said, considering it. "Well, don't worry, we'll get you something suitable. You're a bit thin for one of Charlie's but we'll find something. Have you had dinner—Oh, my God!" She noticed yesterday's chicken in the roasting pan sitting on the coffee table. "Charlie, you didn't— Well, I guess you did. Couldn't you at least have put it on a plate? Never mind, it doesn't matter." Knowing when she was beaten, she reached over and picked off a piece of chicken with her fingers.

Werther smiled to himself, unaware that nothing of his pleasure showed on his face. He was not a man to fawn over his love, but he took great satisfaction in his wife and in their life together. "Pretty good chicken," he said.

"It's very good," Melnik said, staring at Lori as she chewed. She was young, as Werther had said, lovely, slim but buxom, with thick waves of cascading red hair and wide red lips that opened easily. She seemed trusting and open; for the first time in the U.S. he thought that someone might be a friend. With this thought came the realization that he had been holding himself in, feeling himself a stranger in an alien land, uncomfortable, stiff, hoping for nothing better than to leave soon. The feeling faded away.

"There isn't enough here for dinner," she said, picking at the remains of the chicken.

"I thought maybe you'd whip up something," Werther suggested.

She blew him a kiss. "We're going out," she said. "Are you starved? Give me just a minute. Have another drink and I'll be ready."

Two drinks later they all decided they didn't need any more food and that it was too much bother to go out. Lori put her feet up on the couch and suggested that David make himself more comfortable.

"Take off your glasses and tie and shoes," she suggested. "Or even your shirt." She smiled wickedly. "Take off anything you like."

"All right," David replied, feeling totally relaxed and a little drunk by now. "I think I will." He reached up and took off his hair.

Lori gasped and sat upright. It was as if he had taken out his teeth. David sat there with his lovely brown hair dangling from his fingers, smiling at her. When he took off his glasses, it was as if he were an alien from another planet. It took a moment to realize why: he had not a single hair anywhere on his head, not even eyebrows or eyelashes.

Normally he would have been embarrassed at this point, but in his martini-altered state he was amused. "Did I startle you? *Alopecia universalis.*"

"What?"

"*Alopecia universalis.* It's a virus, picked up God knows where. It's rather like Agent Orange: it totally defoliates one."

"Totally?"

"Totally," he repeated seriously.

Now that the shock was over, Lori found herself intrigued. He didn't look *bald*, he looked . . . different, lean and unencumbered. She had a quick flash of him sitting next to Charles naked, looking the way the first human must have looked sitting next to a gorilla. Yes, she was definitely intrigued. "Don't you have any hair . . . anywhere?"

"Not a single follicle," he answered. "Not . . . anywhere. That's why I wear glasses. I don't really need them, but they hide my lack of eyebrows and lashes. The same with the wig. The last thing an intelligence agent wants is to stand out in a crowd."

"Then we'll have to do something about your jacket," she said. "Is that what they're wearing in Israel these days?"

"I haven't really been in Israel for nearly a year. I've been working in Europe, and my chief thought my clothes looked too European. I bought that to look American."

"Dear God, what a notion you must have of Americans! Well, we'll fix you up first thing in the morning, if you have time. What's your schedule?"

"We're not due at Kennedy until nearly eleven," Charles answered for David. Turning to his guest, he said, "We haven't really discussed your assignment yet. What I want you to do is—"

"Just a minute," David interrupted, his temper flaring unreasonably. He closed his eyes for a second, admonishing himself. It *was* unreasonable; he mustn't be so touchy. But he must let this American know where they both stood; he must draw a line in the dirt. "Let me tell you about Israeli traditions," he said.

"Later," Charles said, with a quick but obvious glance at his watch. "What I want you to do is simple enough—"

"*Now*," David said, and a hint of the anger burning in him came out, so that Charles gave a short sigh and a long look at Lori and leaned back in his chair. "I understand that the U.S. has shaken itself free of traditions, perhaps because you are a young nation," David began, and then smiled at the absurdity. "Israel is, of course, even younger, but perhaps our roots are stronger, for we are firm believers in tradition. The Mossad in particular relies heavily on tradition for its strength."

"I think that's nice," Lori said. She wondered what he was getting at.

"I too think it is nice," David said. "Our foremost tradition comes directly from our founder, Isser Harel. It is said that from the day he created the Israel Secret Service no one ever told him what to do; no one once gave him an order. Except of course," he added, "Ben-Gurion and Rivkah."

*Prickly*, Charles thought. It was what everyone had told him about working with the Israelis: they had to be treated gently. "All right," he said. "I take your point. We'll discuss together what should be done, okay?"

Melnik nodded.

"I know who Ben-Gurion was," Lori said, "but who is Rivkah?"

David smiled. "Rivkah Harel. Isser's wife."

She smiled in return and glanced at Charlie. He didn't think it was funny. They would have a hard time getting along, these two. They had the wrong things in common. She looked at the Israeli's fingers holding his glass, folding around it like a pianist's, long and slender, strong and gentle. He fascinated her. "If you don't mind," she said, "it's been a long day and suddenly I'm rather tired." She stood up, and they scrambled to their feet. "Do you have things to discuss?" she asked her husband.

"Just a few. I'll be right up."

"Then I'll leave you," she said, putting her left hand on his shoulder and kissing him on the cheek while at the same time reaching behind with her right hand and touching David lightly on the thigh, drawing her fingers up his leg so lightly that he trembled, and so softly and quickly that she had turned and left the room before he realized what had happened.

8

It was not the first time this sort of thing had happened to David Melnik. Something about being totally hairless seemed to arouse women. Not all women, of course, but not all that few, either. It happened so frequently that he was renowned as the luckiest guy in the Mossad. The succession of quick, painless affairs suited him: they left him without remorse or even memory. They also suited the life he led, which had no room in it for any sort of permanent relationship. Usually, that is; in his present circumstance such an affair was decidedly awkward. One does not fool with one's partner's wife, and like it or not Charles Werther was his partner, at least temporarily. He hoped *very* temporarily. Perhaps one day when this business was over, if he met Lori Werther under different circumstances . . . But not now. Not tonight. He decided firmly that if she came tiptoeing into his room he would explain the facts of life to her.

With this decision firmly made, Melnik turned, pulled the sheet over his shoulder, closed his eyes and was more than a little discontented when the night passed and morning came, and Lori had not.

Not only had Lori not come slipping silently into his room in the dead of night, but when she did appear in the morning she was totally Charles's wife, entering the kitchen with him, dressed properly in slim jeans and a loose shirt, making breakfast for them all. She was silent until after she had brewed coffee and drunk her first cup; then she chatted pleasantly but properly.

The only moment of personal involvement came when they were about to leave; she insisted that they stop at Barney's on the way. She would call and have a proper jacket waiting for them. It wouldn't take a moment, and would save their mission, because with that blue-plaid monstrosity David wouldn't be able to tail a blind man through a thunderstorm in the middle of the night without being spotted. "Be sure to ask for Carlos," she called as they left, and when they pulled up at the curb and David entered the store he found Carlos waiting for him with a brown tweed jacket in two sizes, the first of which fit him perfectly. He was back in the car within two minutes, and they arrived at Kennedy in plenty of time.

Werther introduced him to several members of the group, and they took up their positions. Werther and Melnik would wait in the cavernous luggage-claim area just beyond passport control. They could stand there indefinitely without arousing anyone's suspicion; they would look like two more lost souls waiting endlessly for their luggage. Each passport agent had a foot button in his cage, which was routinely used to notify security agents when anyone suspicious or on the lookout list came through. Today it would be used to notify one of Werther's men when Asri checked through. The agent would immediately walk through into the luggage-claim area to let them know he was coming. Melnik would be on continual alert, however, in case Asri had managed to pick up a passport in another name.

As he waited, Melnik let his mind wander, thinking about this man Asri. He had been a fighter pilot during the Yom Kippur War; he might have been the man who killed his father. Standing in Kennedy Airport, he saw the rocks of the Golan Heights, heard the rumble of tanks and the staccato bark of gunfire, saw the hills erupt with black cockroaches that grew and turned into Syrian tanks as they came nearer, felt the earth tremble with the rumbling of their charge, saw the sudden flames and heard the terrible roar of a flight of Sukholev fighters zooming over the crest of the hills, anti-tank rockets slung under their wings, alone in the skies for one more day because the Israeli Air Force had not been mobilized in time to meet them. . . .

His father had died burning alive in a tank, and he had to live with that knowledge. He didn't know if the missile had been ground- or air-launched, but he knew that Asri had been in the air over the Heights that day and had been shot down three days later when finally the Israeli Air Force had managed to recapture the skies from the enemy.

Werther tapped him on the shoulder. Turning, Melnik saw the first agent walk through the door from customs. Asri was coming. He shut his eyes for a moment in relief; he wanted Asri very much. He had been prepared to wait for weeks here at the airport, to have the man never show up. It had been almost too much to hope for that he would keep to his original schedule, though in reality Melnik knew that this had always been the most likely option. He walked over to the carousel next to the one on which the TWA luggage was scheduled to come in, and stood there with the tired, resigned look of all the others who had flown across the Atlantic and were now waiting for their luggage, only half believing that it would show up.

Melnik wasn't afraid that Asri might recognize him. He was wearing a closely cropped brown wig instead of the thick black one he had worn then; together with different glasses, he was not the same man. Like all Israelis, his technique was to turn innate disadvantages to advantages, and he delighted in his ability to change his appearance like a chameleon.

The door from the passport check-in was opening and closing continually, and in another moment Asri came through. He stood looking around for a moment, then moved to the TWA area. Melnik studied him easily enough; it was the perfect place to do so, with everyone simply standing around with nothing to do but wait. It was Asri without a doubt. He had tried to change his appearance slightly; he had a haircut and different hairstyling, and had begun to regrow his mustache, but none of it made any difference. He looked around calmly but continually, trying to see if anyone was looking for him.

He wouldn't know, Melnik thought, giving grudging credit to Werther and his men. Werther was near the exit, talking uninterestedly to one of the luggage inspectors, looking perfectly normal. Several agents were in various acts of picking up luggage. When Asri's head was turned, Melnik nodded to Werther, confirming that this was their man. By the time Asri's luggage came and he started through customs, Werther and most of his agents had already left the room.

Asri picked up his suitcase and went through customs without incident. He had been terribly frightened. He hated to admit it; to himself he had used the Syrian equivalent of words like *nervous* and *anxious*, but he had been *frightened* by the al-Kuchir murder. To know that they were so close, that they might even have been watching as he and al-Kuchir walked into that hotel together, that even as he had been talking with al-Kuchir in his hotel room there had been a bomb there waiting to go off . . . It *was* frightening.

He looked around now, trying to be casual. If they were on to him they would either pick him up here or try to follow him, depending on how much they knew. He saw no one that seemed to be paying any attention to him, so he walked out through the big doors into the lobby crowded with people bearing signs, pressing against the ropes, looking for relatives and friends coming into the United States of America.

Asri relaxed just a bit for the first time since leaving Paris. Perhaps they didn't know anything after all. Perhaps no one knew he existed. He moved into the crowd, pushing his way between them, and was lost in comforting anonymity.

Melnik and Werther watched him get on the bus to the subway. They got into a waiting car and drove there, easily beating the bus, which made several stops at other airlines on the way. An agent was on the bus to make sure Asri didn't leave it at any of these stops.

When Asri disembarked with the other passengers and walked to the subway platform, he paid no attention to the people already waiting there.

As the subway pulled away from Kennedy Asri felt safer. There really was no reason to think that anyone knew or cared that he was here. But he was a born fighter pilot, and he wasn't comfortable unless he was continually looking around to cover his rear. He carefully noted the faces of the passengers in his car, checking them off and out of his memory as they left at each successive station. When he reached Fourteenth Street most of them were still aboard; following his instructions, he got off the train there, jumping from his seat at the last second and dashing out.

He got his first fright then. Two other passengers jumped at the same time. One shouted, "My God, is this Fourteenth Street?" someone answered yes, and they both hurried to get off the train. The doors nearly closed before they made it, but Asri held them open. As important as evading any phantom followers was determining if they in fact existed. They thanked him; he nodded, stepped aside and stood there watching as they walked down the platform, talking and laughing together, then disappeared up the steps without looking back. He settled himself to wait for the next train.

Werther had twenty officers in his group, including himself and Melnik. Now that he and the Israeli had jumped off the train with Asri, that left eighteen down in the subway system and the two of them high and dry on the street.

Melnik took off his jacket, tie and hair, put on another wig, rumpled it casually, and went back down into the subway. Werther stayed up above to pick up their target if he left the subway after all.

Melnik spotted the Syrian still waiting. He wandered down to the other end of the platform, and as Asri took the next train he got on a different car and spoke into a small radio.

Werther heard the message and relayed it to the eighteen other agents who had got off the original train at several different stops up the line. Then he flagged a taxi and headed for Rockefeller Center, hoping to catch up there.

Two women and one man had come down to the subway platform as Asri waited, but none of them had shown any interest in him. He didn't see how the Americans could have had agents waiting at each stop for him, so he probably had eluded any effort they might have been making to trail him. He took the next train just one stop, getting off at Thirty-fourth Street and transferring to the N train heading toward Times Square.

Quite a few people joined him, but he had been expecting this. As everyone knew, Times Square was the center of the world.

Christ! Werther hadn't panicked, but he was thinking furiously and barking out orders over his walkie-talkie system. Looking out the subway door as the train pulled into Thirty-fourth Street, Melnik had seen Asri get off. With so many people leaving the train, he had taken a chance and done so too. Milling around with the crowd, he had been able to call in to Werther, who realized that this probably meant the target was headed for Times Square. It made sense: the more crowded a place, the easier it was to lose surveillance.

Werther had two other people waiting at Thirty-fourth Street, which gave him three agents still in contact with Asri. He himself was in a cab speeding north on Sixth Avenue, just passing Thirty-eighth Street. He yelled at the driver to head for Times Square instead and, mentally checking all the points on the subway map he had in his head, began bringing in his other fourteen agents from their scattered spots along the way.

By the time the N train had pulled into Thirty-fourth Street and picked up Asri, Melnik and the two other agents along with a surging crowd of Saturday shoppers, five more agents had arrived at Times Square and taken up position near the several exits at street level. Werther himself pulled up at the Seventh Avenue entrance. He had just jumped out of the cab and dismissed it when his radio crackled and Melnik reported that the train had reached Times Square. Anticipating Asri's move, one of the agents had risen and gone to the door, while he and the other agent thought it wiser to stay on board in order not to arouse suspicion.

But Asri had not got off the train, which was now rattling north toward Central Park with just the two agents still in contact.

Much of the train had emptied at Times Square, and Asri now looked around casually at the remaining passengers, trying to remember if any of them had been with him at Kennedy. He didn't think so, but it was hard to be sure. At any rate, he had his instructions and would follow them to the letter. It was comforting to follow intelligent instructions; it gave one confidence in how the mission was being planned. He sat quietly as the train passed Fifty-seventh Street.

Werther decided that now was the time to panic. There was no cross station with the N train before Lexington and Fifty-ninth, and after that Asri would be out in Queens with too many stations and possible exits for his men to cover.

He managed to grab a taxi by actually pushing a woman laden with packages against the curb. Out of the corner of his eye he saw her trip and fall, scattering her bags, as he lunged into the cab and slammed the door. "Fifty-ninth and Lex," he shouted, and the cabbie, indifferent to the poor lady, whirled out into traffic. Thank God for New Yorkers.

Werther directed two agents onto the F train to pick up the N at Queens Plaza, and put the four agents left waiting at Times Square onto the No. 7 train; two would ride it out to Queensboro and try to catch the N there, while the other two would switch to the 4, 5 or 6 and try to reach Lexington in time.

They didn't. He himself was just passing Fifth at Fifty-third street when the radio crackled and Melnik told him that Asri had left the train at Fifty-ninth and Lexington. The other agent had got off with him, but Melnik had thought he'd better not. He would get off at the next stop and double back. Unfortunately the next stop was across the East River in Queens.

In the meanwhile the target was on the streets with just one agent in contact.

Asri came up out of the subway onto Lexington Avenue at Fifty-ninth Street and paused to take his bearings. A pushcart vendor was on the corner, and he thought this would be a good time to have his first American hot dog. He put down his suitcase and stood eating it, looking back at the subway entrance to see if anyone coming up after him would fail to move on. Nobody did. The people who had got off the subway with him came loping up the steps and set off without a backward glance. *So*, he thought, *I am really safe*.

He did not realize that there was another subway entrance diagonally across the street; from this the last of Werther's agents had emerged and, spotting Asri standing on the corner, walked immediately into the lobby of a bank. He stood invisibly behind the glare-reflecting darkened windows and watched Asri finish his hot dog, pick up his suitcase and walk west toward Park Avenue. He called in on his walkie-talkie, then casually and unobtrusively followed.

By the time Asri crossed Fifth Avenue and Fifty-ninth Melnik had managed to change to an inward-bound subway train and was hurtling back toward Manhattan. In his cab Werther had reached Sixth Avenue and Central Park South and told the driver to pull in to the curb and wait. His agents, scattered and lost in the subway system in the chase, were now beginning to regroup in the area. One had reached the Plaza Hotel, directly in Asri's apparent path, and Werther contacted him and told him to wait by the front entrance, where there was bound to be at least a small crowd among whom he could loiter.

Asri crossed Fifth Avenue onto Central Park South, eased his way through the group of people waiting at the Plaza entrance and walked up the stairs into the hotel. He looked around for a moment, blinking to accustom his eyes to the soft lighting after the bright sunlight, and saw a most peculiar sight. . . .

The agent following Asri up Fifty-ninth Street made eye contact with the one waiting in front of the Plaza and continued on his way. The second agent had started up the steps into the hotel when suddenly he saw Asri emerging again. His reflexes were quick, however, and after the first glimpse he turned aside and backed into the crowd haranguing the doorman for a cab. He saw Asri turn west on Central Park South and stride quickly down the street, apparently without further fear of the possibility of pursuit. He stepped out of the crowd and followed.

"It looks good," Werther said on the radio. "Where are you now?"

"Coming out of the subway at Lexington," Melnik replied. "Where is he?"

"Perfectly safe," Werther answered. He was standing at a line of telephones in the lobby of the St. Moritz, hunched over his walkie-talkie as if he were talking on the phone. "He's clearly convinced he's shaken off any followers. He left the Plaza and walked down a block to an outdoor café here at the St. Moritz, Central Park South and Sixth Avenue. He's sitting at a table nursing a beer, obviously waiting to meet somebody. My men are back on station now." It had been a close thing, Werther reflected; for those few moments when he'd had only one man in contact he was afraid they might lose Asri, but now everything was okay. "I've got an agent at a table close by, two others across the street, and I'm in the hotel lobby. Can you find your way here? Head west on Fifty-ninth till you see the St. Moritz. It shouldn't take you more than ten minutes. I don't think you have to hurry. It looks to me as if we have time now."

"I'll be there in five minutes," Melnik said.

Just four and a half minutes later he came into the hotel lobby, looked around and saw Werther seated in the restaurant. He slipped into a chair beside him. "Where is he?" he asked.

They were at a perfect vantage point, allowing them to see clearly the outside café while being hidden in the darkened interior. Werther gestured out through the window toward the sidewalk tables. "Where?" Melnik asked again with a sinking feeling.

"Right over there," Werther pointed. "That's my agent two tables down from him."

"I see your agent," Melnik said, his voice rising in agitation as he leaned forward, "but where is Asri?"

"Right over *there*."

There was no mistaking the direction of his pointing finger, nor the stocky Arab at whom it pointed sitting calmly at a table. Melnik's heart dropped. "That's not Mohammed Asri," he said.

## 9

"Tell us again," Werther said.

"I told you."

"Again," Werther said.

The Arab shrugged and tried not to be frightened. He had his legal residence card and he had broken no law, he kept telling himself. Just be a poor, dumb Arab and they can't do anything to you. He wasn't back in Lebanon, where the secret police would have cut off his fingers out of frustration. "They paid me two hundred dollars," he said. "To be a double," he added. "For the movie," he finished.

"What movie?"

"I don't know what movie! The gentleman offered me two hundred dollars to walk out of the hotel lobby. What do I care what movie?"

"What man?"

"I told you!"

"Tell me again."

Rasheed Amon sighed. "I was having coffee. It was in the Moroccan coffee shop on Eighty-seventh Street and Amsterdam, where I have coffee every morning. This man came up to me—"

"What man?"

"I don't *know* what man! He said his name was Halim Shadmi, and—"

"An Arab?"

Amon smiled softly and lowered his eyes. "A gentleman of Middle Eastern heritage, I believe. Yes, what you would call an Arab."

Melnik sighed. That was the problem. To the Americans everyone from the Mideast who wasn't a Jew was an Arab, and they all looked alike. Good God, he thought bitterly, this man doesn't look at all like Asri! He tried to put himself in the Americans' place: this man was swarthy, yes, and about the same height. Certainly he was dressed identically and carried the same suitcase. His hair was cut in the same style, and he had the same two-day-old mustache. But— Oh, well. To him every cockroach looked identical, so he supposed to the Americans every Syrian, Lebanese, Palestinian, Saudi Arabian, Iraqi, Iranian, Libyan and Kuwaitan did, too. It couldn't be helped now.

"So this Arab, Halim Shadmi, offered you a part in a big Hollywood movie?" Werther asked. Amon sighed. "I didn't say a big Hollywood movie. I only said he told me he'd pay two hundred dollars to dress in the clothes he would give me and carry the suitcase he would provide and walk out of the hotel lobby and down the street to the café."

"When?"

"When what?"

"How did you know when to do it?"

"I told you. I was to report to the hotel this morning at eleven o'clock, dressed and carrying the suitcase. I was to wait there while they set up—"

"Did you see anyone 'setting up'?"

"No, they would be outside, wouldn't they? I was told to wait until I saw the real actor, the person I was doubling for, walk in the door. Then I was to walk out the way he came in."

"Then what?"

"Then nothing. I was to walk to the café and take a seat. If the scene went well, that would be all. If they needed me to do it again, they would come over and call me back."

"Which they didn't do."

"No," Amon said, "you came instead."

"When were you paid?"

"Half when he hired me, the other half today when I showed up at the hotel. He also said I could keep the clothes and the suitcase."

Werther stared hard at him. "You want us to believe you thought this was for a movie?"

"I did! I was told!"

"Where did you think the camera was?"

"It was a long-distance camera, hidden in a car somewhere on the street. They always take street scenes this way, Shadmi said, so people on the street won't be staring at the camera."

Amon tried to look innocent. He tried to *feel* innocent. In a sense, he *was* innocent, he told himself. He didn't know anything; he hadn't done anything wrong. He hadn't believed what the man had told him, of course. Undoubtedly it was a ruse to distract the police; probably the man was smuggling cocaine. But no one could prove he hadn't believed the man, and what had he actually done? Carried a suitcase out of a hotel lobby. He'd made sure there was nothing illegal in the suitcase; he opened it when the man gave it to him and assured himself there was nothing but clothing in it. So where was the harm? He had done nothing illegal.

Except lie to the police, of course. But how could they know he was lying? Unless they already knew that the man who had hired him was an American. . . . He began to sweat.

Werther looked at him in silence for a long time. "Describe this man, Shadmi."

"I did!"

"Again." He glanced at Melnik. What else could they do?

10

When Asri had walked into the Plaza lobby and looked around in the dim light, he had been surprised to see a gentleman dressed just like him. The man had picked up a suitcase like his and had walked right past him, out the way he had entered.

Asri had not been told of this, but once over his initial surprise he had realized the purpose. Following his instructions, he crossed through the lobby and down the hallway, emerged from the hotel through the Fifty-eighth Street door, walked quickly down to Fifty-second Street and back into the subway system. He emerged again at 168th Street and Broadway, where he was picked up by a young woman in a red dress driving a Ford Escort. He got into the backseat, and while she drove to the George Washington Bridge he concealed himself under a tarpaulin on the rear floor. After they had paid the toll and crossed the bridge along with hundreds of other cars, he sat up again and looked with interest out the window at the New Jersey Turnpike. He was dropped off at the Thirtieth Street Station in Philadelphia, where he caught the five o'clock train to Baltimore. From there he took a cab to the airport, and at eight-thirty boarded a United flight to Tucson.

In Manhattan, FBI agents combed bus and train terminals. In Newark and Queens they patrolled airline check-in counters. Over the next three days they picked up nine Arabs that matched Asri's description, but all were soon released.

Finally Werther had to admit that Asri was gone.

## 11

Freddy Mason wheeled himself out of the house, down the ramp, spun the chair expertly around against the side of the car, opened the door, backed off, pulled the door wide open, rolled in again and turned the chair around so that it was parallel to the front car seat. With his left hand he grabbed the top of the doorframe and with his right he pressed against the car seat and shoved himself out of the wheelchair and heavily over its arms into the car. Reaching back into the wheelchair, he extracted a small, heavy bag, then pushed the chair away, closed the door and fastened the seat belt. Using the special hand controls, he started the car and drove into town.

He pulled up at a Seven-Eleven that had outdoor telephones at window level and dialed a long-distance number. When an automated voice told him to deposit the correct amount, he reached into the bag at his side and extracted a handful of quarters.

The phone rang for a long time before it was answered. When it was, he asked to speak to Rasheed Amon.

"Just a minute."

He waited patiently, feeding quarters into the telephone at frequent intervals. Finally he heard through the telephone the sound of running steps, and then a woman's voice answered in a breathless, worried tone, "Hello?"

"Is Rasheed Amon there, please?"

"No, he's not here," she said. "I don't know where he is."

"Ah," Freddy said.

"Who is this? He didn't come home last night. Do you know what happened? Who is this?"

"My name's Adams. Just a friend of Rasheed's. No, I don't know where he is. Sorry. Good-bye."

He hung up and drove home again. As he wheeled up into the driveway of the house the kitchen door opened and a man came out and stood there sipping a cup of coffee. He watched patiently as Freddy hoisted himself out of the car and back into his wheelchair, then asked, "Well, kid?"

"They've got Rasheed."

Gee Hardy lifted his eyebrows. "How about that?" he said. "So they were following Asri."

"How do you think they caught on to him?" Freddy asked. "It worries me."

Hardy laughed. "It doesn't matter how they caught on to him," he said, "since now they've lost him."

"And Rasheed?"

Hardy sipped his coffee and smiled softly. "Oh, they can have Rasheed," he said.

12

Mohammed Asri, as he now thought of himself, spent the night in Tucson at a Quality Inn, resting for the first time since he left Paris. Though he had eaten nothing beyond the hot dog on Lexington

Avenue, he went to bed without supper. This was not because he was afraid to go out on the streets and find a restaurant; once out of New York he was sure he had evaded any possible surveillance. No, he simply ignored hunger and any other demand of his body beyond that of minimal sleep; it was part of his regimen and self-imposed training, part of the price he was willing to pay.

Though his FBI pursuers thought of Asri as an Arab, he was not one in the original sense. His family had never wandered the desert, but for generation upon generation had been city people, born and bred in Shaba, a city founded by Alexander the Great and named by him Philippopolis, after his father. The city lies at the center of the great Jebel Druze basalts that constitute one of the world's great outpourings of ancient volcanic rock, over five thousand feet high.

Lying in bed now in Tucson, surrounded by an American desert and with the air conditioner blowing cool streams over his naked body, Asri was reminded of the mountain breezes that flowed through the sun-baked streets of his home. He thought of the boy he had been, playing games in those crowded streets as if he and his friends owned them; indeed, it had never occurred to them that they did not. He felt sad now thinking of his father and his father's father, and of the knowledge that neither he nor his father nor any of his people had ever truly owned those streets since the first days of Philippopolis. The city had been built by a conquering stranger from another world, and in all the centuries that followed it had never truly been ruled by the people who lived there.

He remembered the stories his grandfather had told of the Turks, and of the local revolt spawned by the great Turkish revolution in 1908. Twenty years later it had been the people of the Jebel Druze themselves who had rebelled, rising up and overthrowing the so-called Kingdom of Syria, which had been set up by France after Turkey's fall in the Great War, and which was nothing but another foreign state in Syria, disgraced by the puppet king Feisul.

Those were wonderful times, but in the succeeding years the people lost by sloth, corruption and lazy indifference the great gift of independence that their fighters had given them. Treaty by treaty, lie by lie, the French had taken back the land, the cities and the wealth of the country, and had given them nothing for their freedom.

*We have sold our birthright,* Asri thought as his skin chilled in the air-conditioned breeze in the motel in the American desert; *we have sold it for a mess of pottage.*

Would it never end, he wondered? His city rested on foreign rock, rock that had come millions of years ago from the center of the earth, erupting through the native soil, pushing it aside and arrogantly forming a mountain in the midst of the desert. His city had been founded thousands of years ago by a warrior from across the sea. Yet those were his rocks and his city, and he would have them for his own. First the Greeks, then for untold centuries an ebbing and flowing tide of conquerors from east and west, an unending flow that became in the stories of his grandfather the Turks and the French, that continued in the stories of his father the French, British and the Jews, that remained today in his own memory the Jews and Americans.

He himself had fought for the first time in the great war of 1973, when Syria and Egypt had united to drive the invaders into the sea and make Syria free for the first time in its ancient history. But they had failed. *He* had failed; he had been shot down by an Israeli jet he hadn't seen sneaking down on him out of the sun, and had languished three years in an Israeli prison.

Before then he had been an idealist, living in a fairy-tale world of great warriors and noble causes, of chivalry, honor and mighty battles. He had learned about the real world in an Israeli prison in Haifa, in a tiny cell crowded with starving, stinking people. He had learned that in this real world a nation like Syria could not compete militarily with a country like the United States, and that Israel was nothing but its sharp wedge sunk deep into the heart of Syria. He had learned to fear and to hate, and when finally he was released he returned not to the Syrian military forces but to the worldwide Arab revolutionary movement and to its terrorist armies.

So he lay in bed that night without eating or drinking, and ignored the demands of his body. He needed nothing but a few hours' sleep every few days; otherwise he was strong, independent, determined. He would eat and drink when it was offered him; he would do without when it was not. He would be strong; he would be ready.

He woke in the morning at first light, splashed cold water on his face, dressed and left the motel. He took pleasure in walking past two restaurants on his way to the bus station, where he caught the 5:30 A.M. Trailways to Dallas. There he changed buses, arrived in Wichita, Kansas, ten hours later and took a taxi to the airport.

Asri had not thought it would be difficult for his hosts to recognize a Middle Eastern man in a small Midwestern American town, but as he walked through the terminal he saw several people like himself. He appreciated now the instructions he had been given. Stopping at a newsstand, he bought a local paper, then walked out through the main doors and stood idly looking at the several parked cars by the curb, his weight on his right foot, his left crossed in front, absentmindedly tapping his right cheek with the folded paper. Immediately one of the car doors opened. He walked to it and looked inside. A Middle Eastern man said with a small smile, "Mr. Asri, I presume?"

Mohammed nodded and got in. They drove in silence for forty-five minutes, cruising along a straight, narrow highway through the flat plains to the north. Finally they turned into a small private airfield. Asri got out of the car and walked toward the solitary building that served as both hangar and office. Looking at him now, his mother would have said he was happy; no one else would have noticed the slight smile lurking at the corner of his lips or the expectancy in his eyes. He himself did not know he was happy; he no longer thought in such terms. He knew only that finally he was about to learn what his mission was.

13

Hardy stood at the window watching Asri walk across the tarmac in the shimmering sunlight. He puffed on his cigar and nodded: right on time. He didn't bother to express satisfaction beyond the brief nod; he expected things to happen as he had planned them, and to happen right on time. When he was in charge, they always did.

Hardy was a tall man, but he gave the impression of massiveness rather than of height. Broad-shouldered and muscular, he resembled the type of statue carved in Russia out of Siberian granite to idealize and memorialize Soviet Heroes of the Soil. He was in his early forties, but he never thought about his age; growing old was for other people. His thick, wavy black hair was cut short in a relaxed military style, but it gave the impression of luxuriance. Luxury was an impression that permeated the air through which he moved, trailing in his wake like the gown of a queen. It was his size, his dark blue eyes that had a brilliance beyond that of reflected light, and his assumption of quiet authority; he dominated his surroundings without ever bothering to try. It had always been that way, from kindergarten through the Marines, and even, in a strange way, in the Cong prison.

It certainly was true here, where the only other person in sight was Dr. Wahid Mahouri, the small dark man who had driven Asri from the airport and who now followed him to the building as Hardy walked over and opened the door.

"Welcome," Hardy said to Asri, introducing himself but ignoring Mahouri. "Have a good trip?"

"Thank you," Asri said. "It was pleasant enough. No complications."

"Put your suitcase down there by the door. No complications at all?"

Asri shook his head. "I don't believe anyone even attempted to follow me from the airport. You heard about al-Kuchir?"

Hardy nodded. "We were afraid it might have some relation to us," he said.

"So did I." Asri nodded. "I would have liked to change my travel plans, but I had no way to contact you, so I had no choice but to follow through as planned."

"I'm glad you did. I was confident that our precautions would be sufficient to throw off any pursuit. At any rate, here you are. Tired, hungry?"

"I am fine, thank you."

"Have a piece of pizza?" Hardy asked, gesturing to the box lying on the desk.

"No, thank you. I would prefer to get down to business."

"Right." Hardy smiled. "You'll be living and training here in Wichita for the next few months. We've got a place to live where you'll be comfortable enough, if that's important to you."

Asri didn't bother to reply, and Hardy went on. "You'll blend easily into the social milieu here. Wichita is a center for Middle Eastern students; they've got a big program at the state university in town. You'll find that most of the people in your apartment building aren't Americans. But let me show you what you're here for." He turned toward the door, then stopped, opened the box of pizza and took a piece for himself. "It's still warm," he offered again.

"Thank you," Asri said politely. "If you insist." He took his first bite of food in nearly thirty-six hours, but thought of it only briefly. His eyes were on Hardy, who was gesturing him through the door toward a hangar as Dr. Mahouri trailed behind.

The hangar, big enough for several airplanes, housed only two. One was an ancient DC-3, squatting on its tail-dragger gear like a dinosaur. In front of it stood a sleek dark-blue jet fighter. Hardy walked up to it, turned to Asri and paused expectantly.

Asri laughed. "Where did you dig that one up? A World War One museum?"

Hardy smiled, but without humor. He didn't like to be reminded by young fighter pilots that suddenly he was a generation older than they were. He remembered vividly the Spitfires and Mustangs of World War II; one of his earliest memories was of being startled as a Mustang suddenly flashed low over his house while he was playing in the yard. And this plane in front of them was as far beyond the Mustang as he was beyond an orangutan. It was a Grumman F9F Panther, the first Marine jet fighter to see action. It had been the Marines' favorite fighter over Korea; it had dominated the skies, a beautiful machine, a joy to fly. Even today it was fast and maneuverable enough to hold its own with anything but the most advanced jets, and was a favorite among civilian air racers. Yet Asri laughed at it.

"It's neither a Camel nor a Spad," Hardy said, and was disgusted when Asri looked blankly at him, not even recognizing the names. "It's a Panther. A Marine fighter."

This didn't impress Asri. "How did you get it?" he asked. "And why?"

"We bought it for racing. At least that's the cover." He didn't answer the second question. Instead he said, "The guns are gone, of course, but that's not a problem. You can buy almost any kind of gun you want legally in one state or another, and what you can't get legally is almost as easy by other means—just a bit more expensive." He smiled. "We don't have the original twenty-millimeter cannon, but we're replacing it with fifty-caliber machine guns. More important, we've got two Sparrow missiles."

Asri looked blank. *Jesus*, Hardy thought, *it hasn't been that long*. The Sparrow was the best weapon in Vietnam. Did this kid know *anything* about fighters? "Heat-seekers," Hardy explained. "They'll home right in on a jet's exhaust gases."

It was beginning to sound interesting, Asri thought, but he was still puzzled. He was starting to ask more when a motion out of the corner of his eye caught his attention. He turned as a self-propelled wheelchair came rolling out from the other side of the Panther. "Let's meet the rest of the team," Hardy said, gesturing as the wheelchair rolled up to them. "This is Freddy Mason."

The man in the wheelchair was, if anything, more muscular than Hardy—as far as his muscles went—which was down to the bottom of his torso on the left side and to the knee on the right side. Below that he had lost both legs. On his lap and hanging around his shoulders was an assortment of wrenches, pliers and other tools.

"Freddy is our mechanic," Hardy explained.

Asri lifted his eyes slightly and Hardy smiled. "Don't let him fool you. The wheelchair is only a disguise." He laughed at Asri's expression and jumped back as Freddy wheeled the chair around and nearly ran over his toes. "Just kidding," he said. "But Freddy gets around okay. He can pick himself up by one hand and hang upside down while he's screwing something into the cockpit, can't you, kid? Only thing he can't do is screw the one thing that counts, right?"

"Screw *you*, man," Mason replied good-naturedly. "What do you remember about screwing anyway? A man your age?"

"I've got a couple of years on him," Hardy explained to Asri, who wasn't quite following the conversation and wasn't really interested. He wanted to get back to why he was there, and was relieved when Hardy took him by the shoulder and started to walk him around the airplane, with Mason rolling behind. "We're putting in a small fighter radar," he said. "Old war surplus from our side, but it fits well enough. You probably won't need it, but we don't stint on anything. The main thing is the aircraft itself. It's not supersonic, but it can top six hundred fifty knots at fifty thousand feet, with a range of over a thousand miles. Of course that doesn't allow you to get home again, but you won't care about that."

*I won't?* Asri thought, but didn't say anything. At this point he wanted only to listen.

"We're attaching a couple of rocket assists under the wings, which will give you a thirty-second boost when you need it. That'll take you up quickly over any airliner," Hardy was saying, "and with your nose down just a bit you can catch it easily enough. Then you squirt the Sparrow up her nozzle and Bob's your uncle."

Asri didn't understand the English expression, but he was more worried about what he *did* understand. He seemed to have gotten himself mixed up with a bunch of idiot amateurs. He should have known better when he was told that he was needed for a mission in the United States. He had thought he would have an opportunity for something daring and different, a breakthrough in the war against the real enemy, those fat and complacent ones who stood out of danger far behind their paid peasants in Israel. Yet here he stood looking at an old jet fighter being secretly renovated to shoot down an airliner. His grandfather would have muttered *Merde!* Now he himself softly said the word.

"What?" Hardy asked, pausing in his explanation.

"I said *merde*," Asri answered quietly. He shook his head sadly, wondering how he would get the money to fly home again.

"What's wrong?" Hardy asked.

Asri looked at him for a moment, then at the fighter and sighed. He looked down at his shoes. Didn't these people read the papers? Didn't they know how things were done? "It wouldn't be as romantic and daring," he said, "but it would be simpler just to put a bomb on an airliner instead of shooting it down in a dogfight."

"It's not easy to get bombs onto the airliner we're after," Hardy said. "Which is?"

"Air Force One. The airplane of the President of the United States."

Mohammed looked stupefied for a moment, then broke into a wide grin. He turned around and looked down at Mason, who nodded and smiled back at him. Well, this was more like it! Maybe they were crazy, but they had an idea! "Tell me about it," he said.

"The details are all-important but very intricate. We'll go over them in the fullness of time. Basically the plan is to intercept the President's plane during one of his congressional campaign trips this fall, which fortunately are made public in advance, contrary to most presidential travel. You will simply intercept the flight and shoot it down. We'll guide you right to him; you'll come in on a reciprocal course a few thousand feet under him, and then switch on your rocket assists." Hardy used his hands to illustrate, as all fighter pilots the world over do. Asri followed the hands with enthusiasm as he had listened to his friends tell their stories since his first days with the Syrian Air Force.

"As you pass him you'll chandelle up and over, and come down behind him," Hardy said. "He won't be expecting anything, and even if he is there's nothing he can do about it. You can't dogfight a Panther with a Boeing. You'll slip right down on his tail and squirt the Sparrow right up his anus. If anything goes wrong, you still have the machine guns."

"Escort fighters?"

"There won't be any. This is a free democratic society, not a military dictatorship, remember? And there isn't a hostile country within four thousand miles."

"But surely they'll have it on radar surveillance?"

Hardy nodded. "You won't be able to escape afterward. But simultaneously with the attack there will be a declaration of war by your government. In the meantime our cover story here, in case anyone comes around asking, is that we bought the Panther for racing. The guns and missiles won't be installed until the last minute, and then the insignia of the Syrian Air Force will be painted on this fighter. Yours will be the first and at the same time the culminating attack of that war. You'll land at the nearest airfield, where you'll be treated as a prisoner of war, and as soon as peace is arranged you'll be repatriated. Now, if you'll come back to the office we'll go over your cover story with you, and tomorrow you'll begin flight training."

When Mohammed left in the car they had provided him to find his apartment in town and settle in, Dr. Mahouri turned to Hardy and said, "That was a fascinating plan, but it's not what you're being paid for."

"Don't worry," Hardy said. "That's not what we're going to do."

14

It was late that evening before Mahouri left to return to his hotel in town. The next morning he would catch the commuter flight to Kansas City, and from there to New York and Paris. Freddy took two beers from the refrigerator and threw one across the room to Hardy. "I don't like it," he said.

"Tell me about it," Hardy said, opening his bottle on the corner of his desk.

"I don't like Mahouri coming here," Freddy said, opening his beer on the arm of his wheelchair. "Every contact is an added risk."

Hardy took a long swallow of his beer. "What you're saying is they should trust us, right?" He looked up at Freddy and smiled. "Would *you* trust us?"

Freddy thought about this for a second and then laughed. "Well, I still don't like it," he said finally.

"I don't either," Hardy agreed. "But what can we do? You have to admit there are people in this wicked world who wouldn't hesitate to screw their Arab brethren out of fifty million dollars if they could. This is not a perfect world we live in, Fred, old buddy. Perhaps you never noticed that before?"

Mason nodded. "It's been brought forcibly to my attention once or twice," he admitted. "But what's the goddamn point, anyway? They try to get you to tell them what we're going to do, and you never *do* tell them, so why do they keep bugging us?"

Hardy shrugged. "They come and they look around, and they don't find out what we're up to, but they see we're doing *something*, right? They see we're not just fooling around, that we've got some kind of plan, that we're not just hustling them along for their money. I think maybe they even like it that we won't tell them what we're doing; they think we must be smarter than they are, which God knows is the truth."

"And God knows ain't saying much."

"*Nevertheless*," Hardy said, "it reassures them." He smiled across the room at Freddy.

"I suppose," Freddy said. If Gee said so, it was probably all right.

* * *

Robert "Gee" Hardy was not the smartest man in the world, not the richest, not the strongest or the handsomest. But all his life he had been *one* of the smartest in his group, one of the richest, one of the best athletes, and always the one who got the best-looking girl. Sometimes there had been someone who was smarter, but in order to be smarter than Hardy somehow you had to wear glasses and be either very fat or very skinny, and spend all your time alone with your books. And there was always someone who topped two hundred and fifty pounds, played nose tackle and could lift people off the ground with one finger, but mastodons like these had crushed noses and no necks and grunted when they tried to talk, while Hardy played quarterback and could laugh as he outran you, and the girls fainted when he passed by.

Hardy's family wasn't rich in the style of the old gentry, but he was one of the first in high school to have a car, and of course it had to be an MG, used but gorgeous, noisy and sexy. He was never in trouble in high school, not because he didn't do the things that got others in trouble but because he seldom got caught—and when he was, no one had the desire to punish him; he was all their dreams, standing there with a smile like Errol Flynn when he had done something naughty but clever, and they would smile too and clap him on the shoulder and tell him he really, *really* mustn't do that again. Then he'd nod sincerely and turn and run off to the library or the football field, to college, to the Marines.

Hardy was above it all. He soared through life like Superman, swooping higher than everyone else, looking down on them protectively. He took what he wanted because—well, being Superman, he was entitled to it.

He had picked up the nickname Gee in his senior year in high school, when they all read *The Great Gatsby:* immediately, spontaneously, everyone recognized that he was Gatsby. (In the Marines, no one knew how the nickname had originated, and they began to tell the story that it had started like the nickname of the Air Force's B-1 bomber, the "Savior." When visitors were brought to the production plant and saw the fantastic, droop-nosed, swept-back futuristic monster, their jaws would drop open and they would mutter, "Jesus Christ . . ." It was said that when a Marine introduced his wife or girlfriend to Hardy, her jaw would gape and she could only mutter, "Gee . . ." Both stories, of course, were exaggerations, but neither was much of one.)

Hardy took no special pleasure in this; he never thought about it. No one had ever told him he was different, and he never claimed it, but he was. He was as different from ordinary men as a bird is from a snake: somehow he had taken the next evolutionary step; metaphorically speaking, he had wings on his heels. Hence, without thinking about it and without taking advantage of it, he had known all his life that ordinary laws were not for him. He never intentionally broke them; he simply ignored them.

The world was his. Whatever Hardy wanted was given to him; if not, he took it, and people smiled when he did so, whatever "it" was: money, girls, whatever he liked. It was an honor to lose your girl to Gee Hardy; it was an acknowledgment that she was someone special, and so you were too. It was a pleasure to loan him money, which he always returned eventually. Above all, it was a pleasure to follow him wherever he led.

The Marines had been the perfect path for Hardy after college. One could easily visualize him flying a jet fighter over mountains and oceans, protecting this nation and the unfortunate of the world, punishing evil-doers and rescuing lost maidens in far-off lands, someday sitting in strategic councils in a resplendent uniform deciding the fate of nations. He would be the ace of aces, Eddie Rickenbacker, Joe Foss, Pappy Boyington, Dick Bong, the Great Gatsby, his wife the glamorous—not Daisy—Zelda, his life a perfect mixture of reality and fiction.

Then had come the Cong prison.

"What's the matter?" Freddy asked as they sat in the farmhouse kitchen.

Hardy shook his head, rubbing his fingers hard over his eyes. A cloud had just passed over him, its shadow chilling him. He didn't like thinking about it. "Nothing," he said. "Throw me another beer."

# II

# Origins

## 15

When William Casey became head of the CIA, he knew that the world had changed since his exhilarating World War II days with the OSS, America's first venture into professional spying. He realized that his most important role would be in fighting a long-term cold war with the Soviet Union, and that the hot wars would employ terrorism rather than formal military actions by the host of small undeveloped countries that considered themselves America's enemies.

The two threats raised different responses. For the Soviet Union, surveillance of known KGB agents carelessly disguised as political employees, together with technological spying, would be useful: satellites, U-2 overflights and bugs in embassies would form the basis of his global network. But for the smaller Third World countries, the threats would be from individual actions and counterintelligence, and would necessarily require a more personal approach.

Casey was delighted. This sort of work had the romantic flair of *real* spying. He envisaged a network of agents infiltrating every hostile two-by-four nation that sprouted up anywhere in the world, reporting by secret radio or invisible ink every conversation in every tent or tenement on hostile ground.

It didn't work out quite that way. The main problem was that America's enemies not only were not American, but weren't anything *like* Americans. Basically they were neither black nor white: they were Arabs, Afghans, Pakistanis, Indians, Sikhs, Libyans. Half-castes, they had been called with scorn in the old days, treated with contempt if they were noticed at all. Today they were the enemy, and Casey did not have the human resources at his disposal to pass through their lines. The agents recruited from college campuses in the United States could never pass as native Sikhs or Libyans, could not slip unnoticed into these countries and set up businesses with Agency money and melt into an inconspicuous life as they could in England, Germany or even Central America.

At first Casey tried to turn the natives into friendly agents, but this ended in overwhelming failure. The governments of those countries hostile to the United States were largely of a fundamentalist religious nature, and few of the people involved in the governments or terrorist organizations they spawned were vulnerable to offers of money or sex, the two baits of intelligence infiltration since time immemorial. Increasingly, therefore, William Casey turned his attention to spying on friendly countries.

This was not as unreasonable as it might sound. First, it was possible: agents of friendly governments could be convinced that the United States was their friend, and that spying for America was merely a way of circumventing red tape and making sure that their friend was most able to help when help was needed. This was particularly effective because Casey was clever enough to ask each friendly agent to focus on *other* nations. A minor member of the Chad government, for example, would be asked to supply any information he might come across that related to Libya or to the Sudan; in time he might come to volunteer Chad secrets as well, but no effort was made to induce him to do anything he might consider a violation of his loyalty to his own country. In this way, throughout the seventies and early eighties, Casey built up a wide network of spies throughout the developing world, surrounding each hostile nation with informants in countries that were on friendly terms with both sides.

Still, it was an imperfect system, and it worked imperfectly. Rumors would filter back to Washington, and as they came in from various countries they would be collated and correlated, and slowly a picture of impending danger would develop. The problem was that the pictures all too often developed all too slowly. Thus, in 1983 stories began to circulate in Washington that a serious terrorist effort was being set in motion in Lebanon, but nothing concrete was discovered before the truck filled with explosives ran into the Marine compound in Beirut, killing hundreds of Americans.

On the other hand, reports that Libya was preparing a military incident in 1981 were specific enough that the United States military forces in the Mediterranean were put on full alert, and when in the early morning hours of Wednesday, August 19, Libyan fighters attacked two United States Navy F-14 fighters, the Tomcats were not caught by surprise. With their pilots warned of a possible threat and their radar sets fully operational, they were able to shoot down the Libyans without loss.

Libya's leader, Colonel Moammar Qaddafi, was furious. Within a week Casey received a secret report from his agent in the neighboring country of Ethiopia: Qaddafi had announced to Mengistu Haile Mariam, leader of that country, that he was going to have President Reagan killed. One month later a report came in from a Palestinian, one of a group convinced that his people's future lay with efforts to pry American support loose from Israel by convincing the Americans that the native Palestinians could be better allies than the Israelis. He reported that a Libyan effort was being made among dissident PLO terrorists to mount an action against the American President. Further confirmation came in from agents in Afghanistan, Pakistan and India.

A few weeks later counterintelligence agents in Italy arrested a ring of Libyans who confessed that they were under instructions to assassinate United States Ambassador Maxwell Rabb. Then early in October Casey heard that Qaddafi was in Syria organizing a combined terrorist attack against the United States; details were lacking. Two weeks later an Italian source reported that a Libyan hit team had arrived in Rome and gone into hiding. Several days later it was reported that the team had left Italy.

On November 12 an attack was made on the American chargé d'affaires in Paris, Christian A. Chapman. Luckily he escaped the gunshots.

A number of fragmentary reports followed in the next several months, indicating that Qaddafi had decided on a series of attacks on American personnel, to be climaxed by the killing of the President. In a television interview on January 27, 1982, President Reagan was asked about the reports, which by then had leaked to the press and public, that Libyan hit squads were infiltrating Western Europe and even the United States. Reagan answered that the rumors were true, and that appropriate countermeasures were being taken.

For months that stretched into years, nothing more was heard. Then at the end of 1985 reports began once more to accelerate, culminating in March 1986 with the information that an attack on American personnel in Europe was imminent. By early April the location of the attack had been narrowed to East Germany, but before the CIA could locate the exact place, time and nature of the attack, a bomb exploded at 1:50 A.M. on April 5, in the LaBelle dance hall in Berlin, killing or wounding more than two hundred people, most of them American military personnel. Within two days Casey had confirmation that the bomb had been planted by Libyan agents.

Throughout the early months of 1986 reports began to filter into Washington from CIA contacts all over the world about an operation code-named El Dorado Canyon. Casey did not encourage such reports; he did not even seem to be interested. Small wonder, for this was in fact an American operation. For the three years preceding the Berlin attack, the United States had been preparing a counterstrike against Libya. Plans were made for individual terrorist actions and for full-scale military options. Security was tight, however, and though counterintelligence agencies around the world did their best to uncover the plot, not much more than the code name was known. On April 14, at 18:36 hours, Greenwich mean time, eighteen U.S. Air Force F-111 fighter-bombers took off from Lakenheath in England on a fourteen-hour five-thousand-mile flight. Each carried four times the bomb load of the famous World War II Flying Fortresses. They had two targets. One was a single camouflaged tent flapping in the breeze inside the El-Azziziyah military compound, inside which, they hoped, would be Colonel Moammar Qaddafi himself. The other target was Qaddafi's home, where they hoped to kill his family.

Operation El Dorado Canyon was a failure. Although one of Qaddafi's children and a few dozen other Libyans of no consequence were killed, Qaddafi and the rest of his family escaped.

Qaddafi ordered immediate revenge. If he didn't have the high-technology capabilities that would enable him to send a flight of jet fighter-bombers or missiles across the Atlantic to the city of Washington, he had something just as good: men of loyalty, devotion and a burning fanaticism.

When Naji abu Hijazi, chief of Qaddafi's palace guard, received the summons, he thought he was being called to die. Although he was not responsible for Libyan air defenses, and in fact had no authority over them, he was responsible for the safety and sanctity of Colonel Qaddafi's home, family and life, and he had failed in this responsibility. The palace had been bombed and the Colonel's daughter had been killed. Qaddafi himself had escaped by the grace of Allah, not by the strength of the palace guard. If Hijazi had been Qaddafi, he would have ordered his death on the spot, so now he stood enduring his leader's stare in what he assumed were the last moments of his life.

Instead Qaddafi said, "I want you to kill the President of the United States."

Hijazi didn't even blink. He simply turned a corner. He had come to the command tent to die, he left it to kill. Either way, he would obey his orders.

Though he set to work immediately, it took some time before he had the right men. There was no shortage of warriors in Libya eager to carry out such an assignment, but it was necessary to pick precisely the right ones. Men who had never missed a target once it was within the sights of their rifles, that much was obvious, but other characteristics were necessary as well. He needed men unknown to the Western intelligence agencies, yet men who had traveled enough to feel confident when alone in the devil's lands, for he intended them to travel independently to their destination. He needed men who combined the cold flame of their religion with the desert tradition of silence, for secrecy was clearly paramount.

To ensure that precise details of the assassination site and date did not leak out, Hijazi told no one the exact details. Instead he summoned the band of men he had chosen later that summer of 1986, and told them for the first time what their objective was. They were to travel one by one to the United States; they would be given ample funds to enable them to go to ground there, and wait. They would travel not only independently but at intervals, so that there would be no sudden surge in Arab tourists noticeable to the American passport control authorities. They would hole up in certain cities throughout the United States until the evening of November 15, when they would converge at a room reserved in the name of Abdallah Nasu at the Hay-Adams hotel in Washington, D.C., a hotel frequented by international visitors, among whom they would not be conspicuous. At that meeting they would receive their final orders.

Twenty-five years ago President Kennedy had been killed by one assassin with one rifle. It had been a ridiculously amateurish attempt; if the man had missed, that would have been the end of it. Naji abu Hijazi did not intend to take such a chance. There would be fifteen men with fifteen rifles, and they would not miss.

They probably would not have missed had they ever got the President within their sights. But Bureau Five of Israeli Intelligence, the Foreign Ministry Directorate, picked up word of the operation and managed to subvert one of the assassins. When he flew to New York he was picked up by the FBI and whisked off into comfortable seclusion. There he provided them with every detail, and they provided him with an amount of money exceeding his fondest hopes, with a new passport and a new name, and with an airline ticket to Pago Pago.

Armed with his information, the FBI quietly picked up most of the remaining Arabs as they entered the United States one by one, finishing off the operation on November 15 by rounding up the residue, together with Naji abu Hijazi, at the scheduled meeting.

The assassination attempt was over, though no one in Libya knew it. For both strategic and political reasons the American authorities made no announcement of the arrests. Strategically, why give information to your enemies? Even more important was a political consideration: the American Air Force had attacked Libya, and though they had not attained their objective they had achieved a great propaganda victory. Indeed, since they had never announced their intention to kill Qaddafi, they could claim the mission a complete success: they had spanked the Colonel's bottom, and the man would now behave. But an assassination attempt by Libya on the American President would not be seen as correct behavior; it would necessitate further admonitions, perhaps even leading to outright war, and this the administration was not eager to attempt. It was much better, the reasoning went, to present to the world and the American public the image of a dictator vanquished, or at least publicly humiliated, a petty tyrant helpless before the power of the United States.

And so the winter days vanished into spring, and nothing happened. The aerial attack on Libya was viewed by everyone as a lesson administered and learned, and in the United States fears of Arab retaliation disappeared from the press, while in Libya Qaddafi alternately sulked and stormed until he finally accepted the fact that his mission of revenge somehow had failed.

16

Not much was known in the West about Ayn Allah Ja'far. According to records at Cambridge University, where he was admitted to the study of law in 1952, he was born in 1930. His father, who paid for his English education, was a wealthy businessman in Tobruk, to which Ja'far returned after taking his degree. Friends from his Cambridge days reported that he was rather well liked for a foreigner; he was remembered chiefly for being wildly enthusiastic about Shakespeare. Aside from this one passion, he appears to have been unremarkable. Evidently he kept to himself, for only a few young men of those days, and no young women, remember him at all.

After returning to Tobruk, Ja'far dropped out of sight; apparently he had settled into the life of businessman-lawyer. But when Colonel Moammar Qaddafi seized power in 1969, it turned out that the middle-aged Ja'Far had been one of his earliest supporters among the civilian population. He quickly rose to one of those positions of power in a dictatorship that are noteworthy to outsiders mainly by the degree to which the occupants disappear from public view. Ja'far's name was occasionally heard; one occasionally caught a glimpse of him in the corridors of power; one heard whispers of a certain amount of authority. In the West those whispers were greeted with relief that at least one person with a good Western education—indeed, a person "wildly enthusiastic" about Shakespeare—was one of the unruly Qaddafi's advisers. It was hoped that he would prove to be a moderating influence on the dictator.

In fact Ja'far first came to Qaddafi's notice when he informed the secret police of a plot on the Colonel's life. Qaddafi was particularly impressed when it turned out that one of the conspirators was Ja'far's younger brother. Qaddafi also noted the impassiveness of Ja'far's face when his brother was sentenced to death by beheading. (In fact, it is not at all clear that the brother was a conspirator. There is evidence that he was an innocent victim, used by the real villains without knowing what was happening. There is also evidence that Ja'far was aware of this.)

Far from being a moderating influence, Ja'far rose to a position of power in 1972 as the founder and organizer of the National Arab Youth for the Liberation of Palestine, a group he put together from outcasts of the Black September and PFLP (Popular Front for the Liberation of Palestine). The people he chose were outcasts because they performed acts of terrorism too extreme even for those murderous organizations. Though the provisional leader—the man known to the West as its leader—was Ahmed al-Ghaffour, Ayn Ja'far was the true brains of the group. It was he who quelled the wills of the psychopaths who gathered under its banner, he who sent them out to firebomb the Pan Am flight i͏        me and to machine-gun the TWA flight in Athens. From this         est beginning he rose in the inner circles of Qaddafi's council of          r. so that when the Colonel decided that his own initiative had fai        ͏   ͏at he must seek further advice, it was to Ayn Allah Ja'far that

Ja'far shook his head sadly a                   dafi told him the story. "It was a mistake," he said. "Hija                        " he added quickly as a sudden glitter swept into Qaddafi's                    ng no doubt as to whose fault it was.

"A military retaliation must not merel                  ective, it must *be seen* to be effective," Ja'far went on, "and                end it must follow immediately upon the provocation. Had th         rican president been killed within days of his cowardly air force's                justice would have been seen to be observed. But coming mont          r, what would have been accomplished? Any one of America's           ess enemies could have done the deed. Who would see it as             evenge, unless we publicly claimed it? And we could not do tha            'far added quickly before the Colonel could announce that this            ed had been his intention, "because that would force the Amer            devils to escalate their response, and one must admit that our sk           ave proved to be open and permeable to their weapons. Though th          vils failed in their cowardly attempt on your life, it must be admit         that our military defenses were helpless against them. Our radar was jammed by their countermeasure aircraft, not a single attacking aircraft was shot down, and we lost four of our own fighters. We must reluctantly admit that we cannot defend our people against further military attack by the United States."

Ja'far paused. "I am honored that you seek my advice. It is this: our response must be one of political terrorism, it must be overwhelming in its devastation, and it must simultaneously both reveal us and conceal us."

Qaddafi waited. Ja'far closed his eyes and was silent. He had no idea what should be done, but he could not let this opportunity pass. He emptied his mind, waiting for a revelation to sweep in. He knew Qaddafi would be patient; he was a Bedouin. The minutes drifted by, like grains of sand on the desert beyond the tent, flickering grains, with an infinite desert of time feeding them. Then slowly, at first in hesitant words, phrases, ideas, the answer came to Ja'far. What was required was revenge combined with preemptive precaution. In essence, hostages would have to be taken. But what hostage would be important enough to protect Libya against American wrath?

Eventually the answer arose from the shimmering desert air: the American president himself would be the hostage. Neglecting for the moment the question of how this was to be accomplished, Qaddafi and Ja'far played with the result. They could question the captured President about the failed assassination attempt; he would deny everything, of course, and they would have his denials on videotape. Then, as a condition of his release, they would publicly demand the firing of all those who had planned the attack and insist on full public revelation and apologies from the American government. When this had been accomplished, they would release the tape showing the President denying what his associates had already admitted. When they finally released him, they would be returning a destroyed symbol of the ineffectuality of American power, and Qaddafi would emerge as the most powerful man in the world. Untouchable!

Perhaps he would even *not* return the President. Perhaps he would put him on trial for terrorism!

The concept was so pleasing, its magnificence so overwhelming, that Qaddafi allowed it to go no further that day. Realizing how difficult the plan would be to carry out, he refused to allow himself to think about it, unwilling to dispel his hypnotic trance of exultation. He would not permit his joy to be punctured by the dreary details of planning such an operation himself. Instead, as he rode high on a manic crest, all the implications of the idea suffused his imagination. He could not bear to force himself to plan precisely how it could be done. The planning would surely be strenuous, the details would be dreary—but the monumental magnificence of the idea itself!

Qaddafi called for pen and paper, and in his own hand wrote that all the resources of the Libyan empire—that largely imaginary but incredibly wealthy entity—were to be placed at the disposal of Ayn Allah Ja'far for the purpose of planning and carrying out the abduction and transportation to Libya of the President of the United States.

Ja'far in turn consulted with his own personal council. Immediately the question of how to implement the operation asserted itself. To make the attempt within the borders of the United States seemed out of the question. Even if they should somehow break through the President's personal defenses and capture him, the borders would be closed and there would be no way to get him out of the country. For days that stretched into weeks Ja'far and his advisers conferred on how to attack the President when he left his own country for a visit overseas. Then, in April of 1987, it was announced that the President would visit Venice in June for an Economic Summit, and would stop in Berlin on his way back.

For a hectic two weeks Ja'far and his group tried to put together a hasty plan, but clearly there was no time, and reluctantly he called a halt. They would have to be patient, he told them; there would be another time. The President had been averaging two foreign trips a year, and they would be ready for the next one. Better a successful job later, he explained to Colonel Qaddafi, than an unsuccessful one immediately.

Unfortunately Reagan stayed in his own country for a full year while Qaddafi kicked the sand and Ja'far fretted, until finally in the spring of 1988 it was announced that the President would visit Mikhail Gorbachev in Moscow at the end of May and would meet with Margaret Thatcher in London on June 2 and 3.

Russia was out of the question. Internal security was too tight there, and Moscow was insulated from the outside world by a thousand miles of Russian territory. But England was another matter. It was a country that luxuriated in its people's freedom to move around without internal permits; it had a capital city within a hundred miles of a long and open coastline; there was access to the sea and half a dozen other countries within a few hours' voyage. Yes, Ja'far thought, it could be done there. They could take the President and disappear on the European continent before anyone knew what had happened and the borders could be closed.

Easier said than done. Ja'far divided the operation between two groups, one of which would gather the necessary information about the President's itinerary in London while the other would carry out the attack and abduction. To ensure secrecy and avoid the mistakes Hijazi had made, the two groups were kept small and separate.

To no avail. The English are not quite as free from security police as they appear to be, they are merely more circumspect about it. The streets of London were in fact filled with secret agents for the President's visit, and when Ja'far's intelligence-gathering group went into operation they asked a few wrong questions of the wrong people and soon attracted the attention of these officers. Within weeks of their arrival they were picked up by Scotland Yard as security risks. Their passports, issued in different nationalities, did not withstand close scrutiny; the diplomatic representatives of the countries whose passports had been used were consulted, and in return for not protesting the incarceration of the men who were supposedly their citizens, no protest about their connivance with an obvious terrorist group was made by Her Majesty's immigration authorities. The arrested Arabs were kept in isolation until President Reagan left the country, and were then deported. Meanwhile the members of the attack group waited helplessly in their assigned hotel, and when the President departed, they went forlornly home.

The lesson was clear. Though Ja'far and his advisers spent another several months studying films and reports from every Western nation, it slowly became clear that the precautions taken against any attack on a visiting head of state—and particularly on the President of the United States—were enormous: no nation dared incur the slightest risk of the President being attacked in its territory.

Eventually Ja'far's thinking regressed to his first plan of attacking the

U.S. leader in his own country. Ignoring for the moment the question of how to spirit him away once captured, they tried to think how they might mount an assault, but ran up against the unyielding reality that had sabotaged Hijazi. Arabs stood out like a sore thumb as they went through passport control in entering the United States; it was impossible to bring in and disperse a large group, at least without help from friends already resident in the country. Moreover, Libyans in particular were persona non grata in the United States; there were only a few thousand in the entire country, and the only organization of any size was the People's Committee of Libyan Students. In this organization there were indeed several men and women on secret payroll, but they were amateurs whose only function was to keep Libya informed of student attitudes, and of no value for an operation of this kind. Indeed, Ja'far suspected that the FBI had more informers in the ranks of the People's Committee than Libya did.

Given the nature of relations between Libya and the United States, there was no hope of importing the necessary team under a diplomatic umbrella, and smuggling in the large number of people needed would be such a complex operation that it must necessarily fail. Reluctantly Ja'far and his advisers were forced to agree that such an attempt precluded their doing it themselves; they would have to rely on others.

Once this sank in, Ja'far took the next major step. While his aides were still noisily discussing the relative merits of a PLO versus Iranian hit team—and realizing not only that the groups they trusted most they did not trust much, but also that these groups themselves suffered from the same deficiencies as their own in operating within the boundaries of the United States—Ja'far was letting his mind roam freely. If they were forced to employ outside help, this at least allowed them to consider the best people in the world. If it was not possible to rely on Libyans, there was no need to rely on Arabs at all.

Immediately the next step became obvious. Ja'far rose to his feet and stood towering over the low table around which they were arguing. The sudden movement caught their attention, and the squabbling discussion died down as they turned to him. He nodded curtly. "Enough," he said. "We will do it ourselves or we will not do it at all. Already, we have talked too much, for 'enterprises of great pith and moment with this regard their currents turn awry, and lose the name of action.' " He paused and smiled, but no one appeared to recognize the quotation. He closed his eyes for a moment, irritated with the barbarians he had to work with. No matter. "Discuss this no further," he said. "Explore the recesses of your own minds. Come to me with any new ideas; otherwise forget we have ever talked. No word of this must leave this room. If I do not call you back together within one month, the project is dead. And so, of course"—he smiled—"is anyone who mentions it again."

When they left, Ja'far went to a corner of the room, reclined on a pair of cushions, closed his eyes and began to think. He would have to travel, he realized; he would have to talk to people who knew people. He would be like a spider, exploring a worldwide web; like Diogenes, searching the world for an honest man.

## 17

Ja'far wasn't sure precisely whom he was looking for. A mercenary warrior king would have been perfect, if only there were still some around. At the time of the great Catholic schism, he remembered from his days at Cambridge, Europe had been crawling with such creatures. Unfortunately, the species seemed to have become extinct. A common mercenary warrior would have to do. There was no shortage of such people, but he was worried about their background and experience. He could probably find someone capable of leading a commando raid on the New Jersey coast and capturing a lifeguard; he could find many people capable of planting a bomb on an airliner or in a crowded pub or synagogue; without moving from Libya he could have put his finger on a score of people who could smuggle drugs into and out of any country in this world.

But what he needed was someone who combined all these capabilities, and who could be bought. It would do no good to find such a person only to discover that he was a patriot of some country or a religious zealot. He needed someone he could trust, and since the only thing he could offer was money, it had to be someone who understood and appreciated its value. Someone who could take orders and follow them unswervingly, and yet could think for himself, for Ja'far did not delude himself: whatever plan was devised would of necessity have to be modified as it was implemented in this less than perfect of all worlds.

He shook his head sadly. As the list of qualifications grew longer, the list of possibilities shrank alarmingly. As he flew from Tripoli to Rome he added one more qualification to the list. No, not a qualification, he thought dreamily, for it was not likely to be fulfilled: it was more of a wish than a requirement. Wouldn't it be lovely if the mythical mercenary warrior king was an American?

Ja'far spent two days in Rome wandering about the city, musing in the Colosseum, gazing at the Sistine Chapel, sitting by the fountains, putting his thoughts in order before he contacted the Red Brigades. He couldn't tell them what he was looking for: there was not an organization anywhere in the world without its complement of plants, moles, spies or simply men and women of something less than an overwhelming sense of mission—men and women who might feel a need to talk to people who should not be talked to, people who would pay a good deal of money to find out why Ja'far was wandering the streets of Europe searching for who-knew-what.

It was not easy to phrase his questions correctly, to draw out of his contacts names that might be suitable, to check with them on the suitability of names he himself had placed on the list. The one thing that made security possible was the sheer magnitude of the objective. It was clear that he was trying to set up a terrorist mission, but no one was likely to guess the target. None of these people had the imagination of Qaddafi, Ja'far realized; none of them were within light-years of his dimension as a world revolutionary leader. Most of them, in fact, were nothing but scum: intellectuals of subnormal intelligence, illiterate theoreticians, uneducated teachers, frightened soldiers, incapable organizers who found solace and relief from their frustrations in such acts of heroism as leaving a briefcase bomb in a railway station. They drank red wine and dark beer, and spent their days telling one another how brave they were.

But some of them rose above the crud at the bottom of the sewer. A few of them knew their business and were worth talking to. By the end of two weeks in Rome he felt he had the beginnings of a list.

The list changed day by day as Ja'far made his way to Catania, Milan, Marseilles, Munich, Salzburg, Brussels, Amsterdam and finally London. It had taken him nearly two months, but he thought he had come up with at least three good possibilities.

On the other hand, he couldn't be sure. In Salzburg, for example, he had thought that he had finally learned to appreciate Western chamber music. During his years at Cambridge he had learned to respect Western culture, and had come to understand and love Shakespeare and a scattering of later English poets. He appreciated the slightest gesture of Laurence Olivier and Vanessa Redgrave. But he sat in befuddled silence and enduring boredom through seemingly endless hours of Mozart, Haydn and Beethoven. Then in Salzburg he had gone once again to an evening of Mozart. He went because he knew in his mind that there must be something to this music; it had endured too long to be only a fad like Warhol or the Beatles. He went as if to a final confrontation, because after all this was Salzburg, and if he didn't find Mozart here he would never find him.

But find him he did—or at least he thought he did. The concert took place in a small room in a dingy castle in the old town, lit by candles, shadowed by the centuries. The music seemed to soak into the cold stone walls and reverberate from them, and he was transported back hundreds of years and held motionless while the music of the spheres washed over him. He was overjoyed; it was like the ending of a search. He'd had faith and it had been rewarded.

Then tonight in London he had gone eagerly to another Mozart concert, and had been appalled to find that in the brilliantly austere hall the music had lost its charm, had become once more nothing but a series of disconnected noises of an alien culture. Evidently the night in Salzburg had achieved its effect more from the surroundings than from the music. He had been unable to separate the mood from the atmosphere.

This worried him now as he walked back to his hotel. Was he doing the same with the names on his list? Had he been talking to too many people, gathering too many impressions? How could he be sure?

He decided to stop collecting names and to begin interviewing the people at the top of the list. He hesitated, because he wasn't sure what to ask them or how to divine their capabilities. Never mind, he decided, he would have to rely on his intuition. He might not understand Western music, but he did understand its poets and playwrights, and so he felt some confidence in his understanding of its people—particularly the violent ones.

Ja'far left most of his luggage in the hands of the chief porter at the Dorchester, packed only a small valise with a few changes of underwear, socks, shirts and a stack of papers, and checked out.

He took a series of underground trains and went through several hotels and pubs, entering by one door and leaving by another, until he was sure he wasn't being followed. Then he took the train to Stratford-upon-Avon.

He walked from the train station into town. It wasn't the season yet, and the streets were empty. There had been only two other passengers that traveled all the way from London to Stratford; even at the height of the season most visitors came by car, since the trains are infrequent and don't run on Sundays. Both passengers took taxis and disappeared quickly from view. He turned down a side street and walked along rapidly, pleased that he seemed to be remembering the way, not quite sure that he hadn't taken a wrong turn, and then suddenly he saw it.

It was an ordinary house in a long row, with a small plaque identifying it as the Mar-Lynn Hotel. He used to stay here when coming up from Cambridge several times each year. He rang the bell, and it was soon answered by a tall, gray-haired man who smiled and asked him in. Ja'far was pleased to see him; it was the same man who had run the place in his student days, and he was saddened that the man hadn't recognized him. Had he changed so much?

It was better this way, he consoled himself as he was led upstairs to a room on the first floor. Closing the door, he walked around the small room, touching the bed, fingering the violets in the vase on the bureau, noticing the bedraggled copy of Shakespeare that took the place of the standard hotel Bible. He opened the pair of French doors onto a small stone balcony overlooking a lush garden. First thing in the morning he would pop down to the theater and pick up a ticket for that evening's program. He wasn't worried about getting one; even at the height of the season they held fifty tickets for sale on the day of the performance, so that one could always come down for the day without planning months in advance. The British were a civilized people. He smiled and sat down on the bed, breathing in the cool air that wafted in from the garden. He was home.

Ja'far had planned his itinerary carefully ever since leaving Libya. He couldn't be sure exactly what day he would arrive in England, and when he would be ready for Stratford, but he had been determined to get here in time for the Roses plays, the histories that together depicted the Lancaster-York rivalry.

He picked up his ticket the next morning, then returned to the Mar-Lynn for breakfast, passing the several large and established hotels, the Shakespeare, the Falcon and even the new Hilton. He shuddered as he passed them. In every city of the world he normally stayed at the best hotels, but here in Stratford it would have been out of place. Here one stayed at a bed-and-breakfast like the Mar-Lynn, a family place run by people who loved Shakespeare and scorned the commercial establishments and the rich tourists staying in them who were disappointed if anything but *Hamlet* was playing.

He spent the morning sitting in the sun on his balcony with the papers from his valise spread over the small table. He lunched on local beer and sandwiches at the Dirty Duck on the river's edge, remembering when he finished to sweep up the leftover crusts and wrap them carefully in a paper napkin, which he put in his pocket. In the afternoon, the sun having left his small balcony, he strolled through the parks carrying his valise, going over in his mind what he had read in the morning. Periodically he stopped by the Avon to sit on a bench, take from his pocket the crusts that he had put in his pocket and feed the swans while he looked again through his papers.

That night he saw *Henry IV, Part One* and, the music of the language still reverberating in his ears, slept more soundly than he had in years. In the morning he bought a ticket for *Part Two* that evening, and spent the day as he had the previous one. By the morning of the fifth day he had seen all the plays, culminating with a magnificent *Richard III*, and had come to a decision. At the local post office he placed a single call to Libya, then checked out of his hotel and returned to London, being as careful on the way in as on the way out to shake any possible followers.

He checked in under another name at the Savoy, a hotel he had detested ever since its purchase by an Arab group several years before. It was no longer *English*. However, it had the advantage that he was not known there, and indeed he found himself left alone during the next two days.

On the third day there was a knock on the door, and a short, fat man with sleek hair and a thin mustache stood nodding, nearly bowing, as Ja'far opened the door. It was Yusuf al-Banah, the man among his council he most trusted, the one man he felt it worthwhile to have summoned here to help him come to a decision.

Ja'far presented a summary of his thoughts on the problem, and spread the papers out on the desk for al-Banah to look over. He had already decided on three names out of the many he had gathered, and now he asked his friend's advice. Two of the names were of assassins who had shown in their work an uncommon degree of imagination and organizational ability. Al-Banah agreed on these two, questioning only the third. This was a man of different background, a mercenary soldier and drug smuggler rather than a terrorist.

"Agreed," Ja'far acknowledged. "But since we're not sure of our precise plan I thought it might be useful to talk to somebody a bit different. Perhaps we will get a different slant on what is needed." He did not mention a minor point, which was included in the résumé he had put together on the man: he was an American. In the back of his mind Ja'far continued to consider the advantages this might confer.

After discussing it, they agreed that it could do no harm to talk to the American along with the others.

Taking normal precautions, the two Libyans rented separate hotel rooms in various parts of London for each of the interviews. The first, which took place in Chelsea, was with Peter Morency, an Englishman who had worked both sides of IRA terrorism. The second, in Bloomsbury, was with Pierre Voule, who had gained his experience and renown in Algerian liberation movements and in internal French criminal circles. Both interviews were much the same, producing neither surprises nor insights. The gentlemen interviewed gave a sense of competence without imagination, which presumably was precisely the quality the Libyans were looking for. Al-Banah was pleased with both of them, but Ja'far was hesitant.

"What do you want?" al-Banah asked. "What we are looking for is essentially a nondescript robot, a man unknown to the police, a

Westerner who can enter the United States and travel around it without exciting notice. A man who can follow orders, whom we can depend upon. Both these men seem eminently qualified. Our only problem will be in deciding between them."

Ja'far nodded. It was true. "And what orders will we give the one we choose?" he asked.

Al-Banah shrugged. The plan was not yet worked out in detail, but that, of course, could not be done until they'd gotten a report from the man who would take charge and investigate conditions in America. Basically the plan involved attacking the President with a small force of men when he was protected by an even smaller force.

"And when is that likely to be?" Ja'far asked.

Al-Banah spread his hands wide. "Be reasonable," he answered. "Our man will discover that. Perhaps when the President is traveling by limousine, perhaps at Camp David; how do we know? He can't be fully protected all the time; there must be some weak link in the chain. That is precisely what these men are good at: learning their subject's habits, finding the weakest point in their protection."

Again Ja'far nodded. "But what they are not good at is organizing a group of attackers," he pointed out. "They work alone, and this is not a one-man job. Let's talk to our soldier of fortune before we decide."

Al-Banah shrugged. Why not?

Late in the morning of September 13, 1988, Gee Hardy entered the lobby of the Hotel Ebury and glanced around. He had already taken the precaution of finding out which room the Arabs were in, but when the desk clerk looked up at him helpfully he walked over and dutifully asked. The clerk told him their room number, adding that it was on the third floor and that there was an elevator to his left.

Hardy walked up the stairs instead, inspecting the halls carefully as he went. He knocked on the door and was admitted to a small room overlooking a rear garden, which, he could see through the window, was bounded by similar small hotels and flats.

Hardy turned his attention to the people inside the room. One was short and fat, the other thin and of medium height with a sprinkling of gray in his hair and an air of quiet authority.

"Good afternoon, Mr. Ja'far," Hardy said.

One eyebrow raised slightly. "Khadim," the man said. "Aswan Khadim."

Hardy considered this, shaking his head sadly. "If you say so," he said, "but that sure disappoints me."

"Why should that be?"

"Because when I got your message I thought you might have something interesting to say, so I flew across the Atlantic Ocean just to talk to you. And now I find you're nothing but another dumb Libyan with too much money and not enough sense to know when to talk and when to bullshit. So why don't you just give me my expense money and I'll leave right now, Mr. Ja'far."

Silence. Then, "How did you know who I am?"

"I sure hope you don't really have to ask a dumb question like that."

Ja'far studied the man, not sure if he liked what he saw. Of course he hadn't needed to ask that question. In the course of the past several months he had been talking to people in a multitude of terrorist and criminal organizations throughout Europe, putting together his list of names. It would have been naive to think that none of these people would in turn talk to others. Clearly, word had gotten back to Hardy, and he had made his own inquiries. "What else do you know?" Ja'far asked.

"Not much. You're looking for a man to carry out some kind of mission, and for some reason you don't want your own men to do it. That's kind of interesting."

"Does anything else about us interest you?"

"Your reputation, I have to admit. Not yours personally—I mean the reputation of the Libyans."

Ja'far smiled politely. "I am afraid I do not know what our reputation is in your country."

"The same as it is anywhere else: money. Qaddafi bankrolls more than half the terrorist operations worldwide, and he's not known for penny-pinching. On the other hand, I'm not a terrorist, so why do you want to talk to me?"

"Then what are you? How would you describe yourself?"

"You know already."

"I know *what* you are. I do not know how you would describe yourself. I am interested in your self-image."

Hardy shrugged and sat down for the first time. He stretched his legs out in front of him and considered his toes. "I'm a fighter pilot," he said. "Ex, but once a jock always a jock. I flew Phantoms in 'Nam. Now I run my own business."

"Smuggling drugs into the United States."

Hardy looked at him without comment.

"Before that, when you returned from Vietnam—from a bamboo cage in Hanoi, I believe—you flew attack jets for Chad against Libya."

Hardy nodded.

"Why? Surely they couldn't pay as much as we would have."

"I wouldn't fly for Qaddafi," Hardy said. "The man is crazy."

The short, fat man started to answer, but Ja'far silenced him with a casual wave of his hand. "But you *are* willing to work for me?"

"I'm willing to talk to you. I'm assuming that what you've got in mind is a one-shot deal that pays well. It might or might not be worthwhile. I guess I'm never going to find out if all you want to do is sit here and chat about my life-style."

Again Ja'far smiled. "You would like to get down to business."

"I would."

"Very well. We are thinking of asking you to kidnap and deliver to us the President of the United States."

There was a moment's silence. Then Hardy's mouth broke into a wide grin. He leaned far back in his chair, put his arms behind his head and stretched. "Tell me about it," he said.

It didn't take long, and then they sat in silence for a few moments as Hardy digested the information, a smile still flitting around the corners of his mouth. He took off his jacket and dropped it on the bed. The idea was better than he had imagined; it was bigger, more intriguing. Whether or not it was possible was another matter. "Am I the first person you've contacted?" he asked.

There was a moment's hesitation, and Hardy shook his head angrily. "If we don't have perfect honesty and cooperation between us, this plan hasn't a chance in hell. You either trust me or you don't. If not, you've wasted a couple of thousand dollars getting me here, but I guess you can afford it." He rose, picked up his jacket and slung it over his shoulders.

"There have been two others," the fat one said.

"Who?"

The fat one glanced at Ja'far, who nodded. He named them.

"They're terrorists," Hardy said. "Which means you're stupid. Which means I'm not sure I want anything to do with you."

"But you're not sure. You're not walking out yet," Ja'far pointed out.

"You're stupid, but you're also rich." Hardy smiled. "Filthy rich. And you're not stupid enough to think this isn't going to cost you a bundle."

"And money intrigues you."

Hardy unslung his jacket and sat down. "It does that," he said.

"Why are we stupid for having talked to two eminently successful terrorists?" Ja'far asked.

"If you want to kill the President, you go to terrorists. If you want him alive and delivered to you, you're not talking about a single man getting within rifle or bomb range; you're talking about a military operation. You're talking organization, equipment, planning, logistics. You're talking words those two other creeps don't understand. You're talking me."

Ja'far nodded. Even al-Banah was frowning in concentration, he noted. This American was speaking as if he were repeating his own thoughts. "You can do it?" Ja'far asked.

"I don't know. You've just presented me with the problem. I haven't thought about it yet."

Both Ja'far and al-Banah shook their heads. "No, your thought is not necessary," al-Banah said. "We will do the planning. What we are looking for is someone to carry it out."

"Good-bye," Hardy said rising again. "Lots o' luck."

"Just a moment."

"One moment is all you've got. I may be a dumb soldier, but I'm not stupid. If I do it, *I* do it. Everything, beginning to end. The only possible hope you've got—and I'm not sure yet if it's possible at all—is for someone familiar with the American military establishment and presidential procedures to work it out and carry it out. A bunch of goddamn Arabs squatting in the desert are worth diddly-squat. Period. End of discussion."

They were silent. Al-Banah was too embarrassed to look at Ja'far. He would gladly have slit this man's throat; all he needed was a glance and a nod from his superior. Instead Ja'far said, speaking directly to Hardy, "How long do you anticipate it will take to develop your plan?"

"If I knew that, I'd know what the plan was. Maybe a week, maybe a year. I don't rush these things."

Ja'far smiled. "*If* we decide to employ you, we will expect a complete plan within a month. It is now mid-September. Let us say by the end of October."

"Why the rush?"

"Though obviously you are not politically inclined, even you must know that the American elections will soon take place. Reagan will not be president much longer."

"So what? You don't want Reagan, you want Bush."

Ja'far merely raised his eyebrows.

"Look," Hardy explained, "your interest in this is undoubtedly due to the American strike against Libya two years ago, right? So it's taken you two years to find the right man for the job. You think the rest of it can be done in two months? No way. Besides, if you take Reagan, Bush simply takes over. Since it's almost certain that he'll be elected president anyway, there'll be just a smooth transition from acting president to new president, and what will you have gained? Reagan's so old and frail he'd probably croak during the kidnapping, and you'd be left with nothing but a corpse that nobody wants. But if you wait and grab Bush after he takes office next year, that leaves Quayle as president of the United States." He laughed. "The government will come to a standstill in confusion. You'll have them just where you want them; they'll agree to anything to get Bush back. Washington will be Panic City."

Ja'far inclined his head, thinking it over. "You are not as politically naive as you appear," he said finally. "But how do you know Mr. Bush will win the coming election?"

Hardy snorted. "I'm willing to bet on it. A very clever American once pointed out that no one ever went broke underestimating the intelligence of the American public. They'll go for the no-new-taxes and pledge-of-allegiance and no-abortion and prayer-in-the-schools issues every time. He'll win, believe me."

Ja'far nodded and rose to his feet. "If we decide you are right, we will contact you."

."That won't be necessary."

"Then how will you know that we have decided to employ you?"

"I'll know that when I read in the papers that Morency and Voule are dead."

The Libyans raised their eyebrows.

"We're not playing games here, gentlemen. Secrecy is the name of any successful military operation undertaken against odds, and three people contacted are two too many. I'll meet you here in this same hotel at noon precisely four days after the *New York Times* carries the stories of their deaths. At that meeting we will discuss money. Good afternoon."

"You realize, of course," al-Banah said, "that by your own standard you yourself are at risk—if we should decide to go with either of the others, that is."

Hardy picked up his jacket, then paused on his way to the door and nodded. He took a pack of cigarettes out of his jacket pocket, stuck one between his lips and said, "On the other hand, you don't want to fool around with guys out of your class." He crossed to the window and opened it. "Would you like to put your hand here?" he asked, gesturing at the table in front of the window. "Right here?" He waited, looking first at one man, then at the other. "No? You're not as dumb as you talk. That's a good sign." He picked up a coffee cup, put it on the table and stepped back. Five seconds later the cup disintegrated, flying apart and splattering them all with tiny shards of pottery.

They had heard no sound from the rifle that had fired the shot; there hadn't been enough noise to alarm anyone in the hotel or passing by outside, but clearly if Hardy had wished it they both could have been murdered. In the commotion they didn't notice him take the cigarette out of his mouth and break it apart, with his other hand take another one out of his pocket, breaking it apart as well, and drop the two cigarettes beside each other on the bed. He crossed back to the window and shut it again.

"How did you know which room we were in?" al-Banah asked.

"I did my homework before I showed up," Hardy said. "This is a small hotel. How many Arabs do you think are staying here? Just you, actually." He smiled and sat down again, casually holding his breath.

The two Libyans began to talk to each other in their native tongue, but in another minute they were unconscious. Hardy got up, opened the window again, leaned out and breathed deeply. He opened it wide, and a nice breeze swept through. He picked up the two Arabs and dumped them crumpled on top of each other in the corner, then sat down again and waited.

"What happened?" Ja'far asked when they woke up a few minutes later.

"Binary nerve gas," Hardy explained. "While your attention was on the rifleman across the way." He stood up as they staggered to their feet. "Don't get in over your heads, guys," he said over his shoulder as he walked to the door. "I'll be watching the papers."

"How'd it go?" Freddy asked.

"Like clockwork," Hardy said. He laughed. "You should have seen their faces when you shot that cup on the table. Good thing you didn't miss; it wouldn't have been quite as impressive. Then I gave them the cigarette trick. Cheap stunts, but they worked. Come on, let's go home."

"What was their proposition?" Freddy asked as he rolled his wheelchair out of the room and down the hall to the elevator. "Anything interesting?"

"Yeah, I think you could say that," Hardy said. "We're going to have to give it some thought, but it's definitely interesting. Let's grab a cab to the airport and I'll tell you."

18

At his first meeting with the Libyans, Peter Morency had given them a month to make up their minds. He told them he would await their decision at the small seaside village of Seacottages, on the Northumbria coast just above Tyneside. It was one of his favorite places, consisting of a few dozen cottages, one street that led down to the sea and a pub that carried Newcastle Brown Ale. He spent his mornings walking on the beach, his afternoons and nights in bed with his popsie, and his evenings in the pub arguing politics and football, and singing.

Three weeks after the meeting he went to the pub as usual, just after evening opening. The barmaid told him he had a message; someone called just before three o'clock closing and she had told the caller that Morency would surely be in that evening; was that all right? The message was simple: "Agreed."

Seacottages lies on the Newcastle–Berwick railroad line. It is a small stop, the trains hardly pausing before they move off again. The station is unattended; passengers buy their tickets on board from the conductor if they don't have a round-trip ticket from one of the larger stops. Thus no one at the station noticed a passenger getting off the train the next evening, and since the villagers spend their evenings either in the pub, the church or at home in front of their televisions, no one saw the man as he walked down the long road from the station into the village, nor later as he walked back to the station, waited on the empty platform and boarded the next train to Newcastle.

The following day Anne Gillian, Morency's popsie, told the police she didn't know anything. There had been a knock on the cottage that night; Morency had told her he was expecting someone and she should keep her bloody nose in the telly. He had put on his jacket and left, and after a while she had gone to sleep. He often acted mysterious like that; she was used to it. Well, to tell the truth, it *did* piss her off, but he was just like that, wasn't he? And she had to put up with it, didn't she? Because they're *all* like that in one way or another, aren't they?

She had slept late, and hadn't really missed Morency until the police came knocking on her door and said they were sorry to bother her, miss, but a walker on the beach had found a body and the village policeman had said it was the visitor who had rented this cottage, and could she please identify it for certain? If it wasn't too much bother?

On the same day Pierre Voule was gunned down on a small street in Montmartre as he was leaving a porno show, two men and three women, live onstage, acts of love.

The *New York Times* reported in a small article the apparently unrelated deaths of two suspected terrorists. Most readers said "Good riddance," turned the page and sipped their coffee. Gee Hardy simply said "Good," sipped his coffee and nodded in satisfaction. They'd had enough sense to dispatch both men simultaneously, so that neither one had time to hear about the other and begin to think unsavory thoughts. Perhaps they weren't too dumb to work with after all.

\* \* \*

"How will you do it?" Ja'far asked at their next meeting, but Hardy only shook his head and waggled an admonitory finger. "We have a saying in our country," he told them. " 'Who knows what evil lurks in the minds of men? Only the Shadow knows.' " He smiled. "Only the shadows will know what is in my mind."

That was unsatisfactory, al-Banah argued while Ja'far looked on in silence, but Hardy was adamant. Finally they were reduced to the assurance that he indeed *had* a plan. His smile was infuriating, but of course they were too polite to show their fury. "May one perhaps merely ask *why* you are agreeable to performing this mission?" Ja'far asked. "You have lived most of your life as a soldier of the United States, and now you tell us you are willing to kidnap your president and turn him over to those who are surely enemies of your country."

"Marine," Hardy said. "A Marine, not a soldier. Don't ever confuse the two." Ja'far sat stolidly, his expression unaltered, waiting patiently; he was not willing to argue the point. Finally Hardy returned to the question, but just barely. He looked away. "My reasons are my own business. Let's just say I've seen enough of the way governments operate not to live my life in awe of them. They take what they can from you, and there's no reason for anyone else not to do the same. Besides," he said, and his smile returned, "who wouldn't do it for fifty million dollars?"

They stared at him. "We have not yet discussed money," al-Banah said.

"We just have," Hardy answered, leaning forward now. "Fifty million American dollars. Ten million deposited in my Swiss bank account within five days, the rest upon completion."

"I do not think—"

"That does not include expenses, for which a separate account of another ten million will be set up at the same time. The expenses may grow; I don't guarantee keeping to a fixed budget."

"But—"

"There will be no delay permitted in the setting up of the accounts. I want to know whom I'm dealing with. If you boys can't arrange that kind of money in a few days, you're not the representatives of the government you say you are. If you are, then you can."

There was a long silence. "We also have a saying in our country,"

Ja'far said. "A good try, as you call it in your country, is what we call total failure. Understood?"

"Understood. We guarantee success."

"*How* do you guarantee?" al-Banah protested. "We don't know your plan or your timetable. How can we trust you not to take the twenty million and run?"

Hardy shook his head sadly. "Every time I begin to believe I'm conversing with a couple of shrewd operators," he said to Ja'far, "you let this one"—pointing to al-Banah—"open his mouth and I realize what a couple of *shleps* you are."

He sighed and took a cigarette out of his pocket, then laughed when he saw their reaction. He raised it to his lips, lit it, sucked in the smoke and blew it out again. "Look, buddies, in the normal world there are business contracts and laws to enforce them. In our world there are no contracts and no law, but if I took your money and ran I'd be looking over my shoulder the rest of my life—which I guess wouldn't be very long. I could kill you two right this second if I wanted—" He hesitated while they struggled to keep their eyes rigid, not looking out the window or at his fingers to see if he had some other weapon that hadn't been detected by their guards before he entered the hotel room. They had taken that precaution at this second meeting, but they had already learned to have more faith in Hardy than in their guards. "—but you could do the same to me. You could hide from me by spending the rest of your lives in Libya if you cheated me, but I wouldn't have anywhere to hide from you. We both know this, and that's what will keep us both honest. That's one of the two things that will keep me from deciding not to turn the President over to some other group instead of you when the operation's complete, and that's what will keep you from not paying me the rest of my money at that time."

"And what is the other thing?"

"The amount. Fifty million dollars is as much money as I figure I can possibly spend in this life, so anyone else offering me more would constitute no temptation at all."

Hardy told them that the plan would be put into operation during the congressional elections of 1990. They objected to the delay, but he said he needed the time to make the necessarily complicated arrangements. Besides, in the congressional campaigns the President's schedule would be forecast: there were certain cities he simply had to visit, and as a matter of public relations the visits would be announced some time in advance. Knowing that the President would be in a specific place at a specific time, they could make their preparations and simply wait like a spider for him to come to them.

They agreed finally, shaking hands on it, after once again asking him for his personal guarantee of satisfaction and staring deeply into his eyes as he answered, looking for any residue of doubt. Hardy had no such doubt; though his plan was not yet formed, it was clear to him already that if he failed to deliver the President it would only be because he was no longer alive, so he had nothing to lose by an ironclad guarantee.

"In our country," Ja'far said, "a handshake is a binding contract. It is the same in Britain, and I trust also in the United States. We are agreed on that? There is now no turning back?"

Hardy nodded. As they walked to the door he remarked that in the future they would refer to the operation as "Dallas."

"But why?"

All operations need a code name, he explained.

"But why Dallas? What does it mean? Is that where you intend to carry out the abduction?"

Hardy smiled and shook his head. "Of course not," he said. "That would be stupid; if they picked up the name, they'd know half the plan. No, the name means nothing at all. That's the first prerequisite for a good code name: it should mean nothing at all, just in case the enemy happens to come across it."

That was the second time Hardy lied to them.

19

The first time had been just minutes before, when he told them his reasons for agreeing to kidnap the President of the United States. The fifty million dollars was a part of it, but the real reason was more complex and more personal.

In a sense it had begun more than twenty years ago, when he went to Vietnam as pilot of a two-seat McDonnell F-4 Phantom fighter-bomber. Originally the F-4 had been developed as an all-weather air-to-air fighter, and the Marines felt it was the best in the world. They argued for a role in wiping the skies clear of North Vietnamese MiGs, in doing what fighter pilots were born to do, but the Air Force felt that this role belonged to them, and the Air Force called the shots in Vietnam. Hence the F-4s in general and the Marines in particular were relegated to a ground-attack role.

Gee Hardy flew with a shore-based squadron in the south that specialized in two types of mission. The first consisted of low-level attacks on antiaircraft positions, suppressing ground fire to allow the Air Force's high-level bombers to come in and destroy military targets. The Phantom jocks would zip in at treetop level, depending on their speed to avoid ground fire, and at a distance of two miles would go into afterburner and zoom straight up to three thousand feet, pull over on their backs, look "up" through the canopy to spot the gun emplacements, then pull the stick back into their bellies and dive onto them at 30 degrees, drop at two thousand feet, roll away and head for home.

Which sounds okay. The problem was that the sites were usually protected by radar-directed SAMs—surface-to-air missiles that could jump out of an overcast ground cover and hit you nearly before you saw them—while at the other end of the spectrum was the low-caliber machine-gun fire which blanketed the air at the drop point and which you had to fly through without flinching, because if the plane zigged the bombs zagged and you might get home safely but the Air Force bombers wouldn't because the antiaircraft guns would still be firing.

These missions were dangerous, but the second type was even worse. It consisted of hitting small targets of opportunity or targets too small for an all-out Air Force attack. The idea was that the aerial reconnaissance guys in their high-flying Crusaders would photograph the whole damned country every day, north and south, and bring back pictures that some joker in air intelligence would search for "anomalies." An anomaly was anything that didn't seem to belong. In theory anomalies were indications of enemy activity; in practice they were often just shadows or blurs on the photographs that might not mean anything at all. If an ROTC-bred lieutenant back at headquarters thought a shadow under a tree looked more like a truck tire than a tree branch, a flight of two Phantoms would be sent the next morning to destroy that shadow and the surrounding neighborhood.

The good part about these missions was that there was hardly ever any SAM activity around, because the shadow on the photo that looked more like a tree branch than a tire to everyone except the ROTC lieutenant turned out most of the time to be nothing but a tree branch after all. The bad part was that the Phantoms were flying four or five hours over enemy territory—*all* of Vietnam was enemy territory, no matter what you read in the papers—and just as many aircraft were lost to malfunction and accident as to enemy fire, since the Phantom, like any other fighter, had been built more for maximum speed and firepower than for getting there and back every time. Also, to hit the targets, which were too small for the high-flying Air Force to bother with, the pilot had to go right down on the deck where any Charley with a machine gun or even a slingshot could take a shot at you as you passed. It didn't take much of a hole in the fuel tanks for enough of the stuff to stream out to keep you from ever getting home again.

Once in a while the bombs would set off secondary explosions in the bombed area, indicating that the ROTC lieutenant had been correct and Charley had hidden a fuel or ammunition dump under the trees. More usually, the Phantoms would see no result other than a few more Vietnamese trees blown into shredded matchsticks.

That was bad enough. Sometimes it would be worse.

One morning the anomalous spot was near a "suspected Cong" village. "Suspected Cong" meant that the intelligence types at head-quarters for one reason or another had decided that the villagers were likely to be Cong sympathizers. (One likely reason might be that the village was located near the demarcation line, in an area that belonged as much to the Cong as to the South; any village of intelligent people in that part of the country *ought* to be Cong sympathizers.) At any rate, it was thought that this particular village might be harboring the enemy or providing them with a storage point for ammunition or food supplies. Twice in the past few months ground troops had been sent in by chopper on surprise raids, but the grunts had found no positive proof. Why intelligence continued to suspect the poor villagers after failing to find such proof was anybody's guess.

Signs of activity had now been detected around the "anomalous spot" near the village, and intelligence had concluded that this was what they had been looking for: this must be where the Cong forces the villagers were hiding would be found. The village was at a strategic location, just above Quang Tri: if Charley built up a secret force there, he'd be able to strike with devastating effect.

Hardy and his radar intercept officer, the other member of his crew, loaded up with napalm canisters, since they were after people rather than supplies. Just before dawn Hardy looked out through the locked canopy, checked his wingman, rammed the throttles home to the first step and released the wheel brakes, and the two F-4s began to accelerate down the runway. In a few seconds they were rolling well and he pushed the throttles outboard to clear the first stop and shoved them into afterburner.

With a rush the speed began to pick up. At 125 knots Hardy's nosewheel began to loosen and extend, and at 135 he rose off the ground and the bouncing and shaking stopped; the Phantom was in its element. Holding its nose high, glancing around to be sure his wingman was with him, he climbed to a few hundred feet and then trimmed off. They'd cruise in at this low altitude to within a few miles of the encounter point, then swoop in at treetop height.

They hit the checkpoint right on the button. Hardy pushed the throttles to full again and dropped his nose; they'd zoom in as close to sonic speed as they could, trailing their noise behind them, giving no advance warning of their coming. They sped over the trees, passed the village in a kaleidoscopic blur, keeping their eyes fixed on the clearing that would soon open. . . .

Hardy spotted it with just over half a second to spare. A moment before actually reaching the clearing he pickled the napalm and felt the Phantom jump as the canisters fell away; the forward motion of the plane would carry them along so that they'd hit the ground right on target.

He zoomed over the clearing while the canisters were still tumbling through the air. He was traveling at over six hundred miles an hour as the Phantom's nose cleared the trees that ringed the clearing, and he looked down and saw in that moment that for once intelligence had been right: there was indeed human activity there.

And it sure as hell was anomalous. It was kids.

He cried out in horror. The moment froze in time. At more than six hundred miles an hour it couldn't have lasted more than a tenth of a second, but it was an instant that would haunt him all his life. The villagers, afraid of another surprise attack by American helicopters, or perhaps afraid of the Cong forces, had moved the children out of the village into this area around the clearing. The children looked up wide-eyed as the two Phantoms came blasting over the trees, flying as fast as their sound, appearing without warning, zooming over them like pterodactyls from some prehistoric time.

To his eternal damnation Hardy had the precise vision of a jet fighter pilot. In that one eternal moment he focused on one child squatting in the dirt, dribbling little streams of it between her fingers; a girl maybe ten years old, with long black hair and eyes that opened as wide as her mouth, staring up at him, screaming in the silence as he flashed over her head.

He screamed too, at the falling napalm canisters to stop—at least, please God, to *miss*. Just this once, he prayed in terror in that one everlasting tenth of a second, *let me miss!*

Then he was banking sharply, looking back over his shoulder, seeing the napalm fall into the forward edge of the clearing, seeing the canisters break open, seeing the flaming red and orange jelly spurt out and cover the whole clearing with the fires of hell.

He should have gone home. He should have put his nose straight and level on the treetops and scooted for home, leaving the sight behind. Instead he pulled up and circled around, hoping against all hope not to see what he knew he would see.

It had been just a small clearing in the overgrown Vietnamese jungle, nearly covered by the canopied leaves of the surrounding trees. Now it was invisible, hidden by a sulfurous black plume of smoke, lit from within by a horrible red glow. Everything for fifty yards in every direction was on fire. The fire at the center of the blackness was more intense than anything Dante had ever imagined Hell to be. Through the smoke he could see nothing; in that smoke he could imagine everything: the dark, twisted shapes blackened and charred, the empty eye sockets with viscous fluid vaporizing from them, and the empty-eyed, black-haired, open-mouthed little girl of ten with the burning flesh and the twitching body screaming silently.

Hardy was the best fighter pilot in the Marine Corps. He was the best fighter pilot in the goddamn world. He had always known it; he never thought about it consciously, he just knew it. Someday the Air Force would wise up and turn the Marines loose on the MiGs and he'd end up with the highest number of kills in the war. He'd be top ace, like Rickenbacker in the first war and Bong in the second. He was a professional warrior and proud of it, but he was not a murderer. He'd shoot down enemy airplanes, he'd bomb aircraft positions and even anomalous targets of opportunity, but he didn't burn children alive.

Yes, he did. *Oh, Christ,* he thought, *yes I do.*

Had he been set up all his life for this? Was his whole life nothing more than a preparation for this moment? Like most pilots, he didn't believe in some personal god who could be manipulated by prayer and phony concessions and hypocritical self-recriminations. But without thinking much about it, he had passively accepted most of what he had been taught as a child. Now it all came flooding in on him. Had he been fortune's child all his life only as a ghastly joke? Had he been set up only to be knocked down, to be shown that he was no better than the worst of men?

There but for the grace of God go any of us. Suddenly the grace of God had been withdrawn from him. Hardy saw himself, and he could not stand what he saw.

Hardy circled one more time, floating like a hawk on the wind one time too many. Suddenly he heard the tiniest *clink-clunk,* almost like the patter of small hail on the roof of a car. That was all. He felt nothing; there was no cataclysm, no explosion, no fire, nothing but the quiet voice of his wingman several minutes later as they formed for the trip home. "Fox One, Fox Two," he heard in his earphones. "You're streaming fuel."

No. Hardy checked his gauges. Everything looked good. "Fox Two," he called. "Say state."

"Fox Two, state six-seven."

Oh Christ! Hardy's own fuel gauge indicated only 5,200 pounds left. Their flight time was identical, and in maneuvering the wingman always used a bit more fuel, so if he was 1,500 pounds lighter he had to have lost a hell of a lot. Now, even as he stared at it, he could see the needle flickering and lowering. Mentally he calculated the fuel remaining, its estimated loss rate, his position and the distance to Da Nang, and then he calculated it again. Then he calculated the distance at least to the DMZ, and then he calculated the distance to the refueling tanker. None of the numbers came even close to working out. He got on the RT. "Marblehead, Fox flight off target, heading home at angels two. Fox One losing fuel, no chance of rendezvous. Estimate ten minutes remaining. Request Jolly Green."

Acknowledgment came, and he settled down to fly as best he could, using full power to get as far as he could because his life's blood was leaking out faster than the engines could eat it. He was five minutes short of the DMZ and at least marginally friendly country when the needle bounced on the peg, and seconds later the engine flamed out. Suddenly the Phantom was a 29,000-pound junkpile dropping through the air at two thousand feet, its short, stubby wings incapable of keeping it up. Hardy informed his radar intercept officer that it was time to go. Then he reached up and back with both hands, grabbed the ejection handle in the seat top and pulled it out and down. The canopy blasted off and a hurricane-force wind smashed him in the face. In the next instant the seats blew and he was flying up and away from the falling Phantom, tumbling, strapped in, totally blown away in every sense.

Then the chute opened and the tumbling stopped. He was jerked upright, and for a few moments he hung relatively stable in the air. He even had time to look around, and to see the Phantom dive into the ground and erupt in a fiery explosion. But that was all he saw. He spun in his seat, looking for his RIO's chute, but there was none.

He was all alone, dropping through enemy air. For one second he felt a terrible fear rising from his gut. Then he caught himself and forced calm into his bowels just as he fell through the thick green foliage into the darkness below.

20

"Fox One, Jolly Green feet dry at ninety-five for ten, angels two. Say state." Freddy Mason was flying a rescue helicopter—a Jolly Green Giant—from a carrier offshore, and had just crossed land 95 degrees from the two Phantoms and ten miles away.

"Jolly Green, this is Fox Two. Fox One has just ejected, and we have one good chute."

"Repeat."

"Just one chute, Jolly Green, but he looks okay."

So they had lost one man already, Freddy thought. Breaks of the game. "Estimate eight minutes to contact," he called in. "Can you stick around?"

"Affirmative."

Freddy was about to switch off but he was curious. "Fox Two, you're out of Da Nang?"

"Affirmative."

"VMFA 319?"

"Affirmative."

"How's old Gee Hardy doing? Keeping sober?"

There was a slight pause, and Freddy thought, Christ, that's it. Then the voice came in again and said, "That's Hardy in the silk."

Well, he hoped it was. And some mother somewhere, if she knew, would be hoping it wasn't. Because either Hardy or his brother officer was already dead. Freddy switched off and concentrated on the terrain ahead. There was nothing but trees out there, and under those trees would be nothing but grass if he was lucky. On the other hand, if he wasn't lucky, there could be a Cong with a machine gun under every damned one of those trees. He'd soon find out. The nice thing about the problems associated with this job was that there wasn't a damn thing you could do about them, so why worry? On the other hand . . .

Freddy had grown up in the fifties and sixties with Gee Hardy in Ternville, Virginia. He was one of the few kids in high school bigger and stronger than Hardy, and he was nearly as smart, so they became best friends. He played offensive tackle on the football team and was good enough to get several scholarship offers, but he never went to college. Hardy tried to talk him into it, but he was too gentle for college football. High school had been all right, but when he visited the college campuses and talked to the coaches, he realized he'd never fit into the high-intensity, bone-breaking regimen they described. His father had been angry, telling him that he was damned if he was going to pay for his kid's college education when the damn fool could get it free just for playing a game, and the next day Freddy joined the Marines.

Well, that's what kids do. He hadn't really thought it out, but once he got through boot camp and had a few moments to think about it, he decided he liked it. He had liked football in high school, but what he had really loved was his car. He had liked taking it apart and putting it back together again even more than he had enjoyed trying to do much the same with girls in the backseat, although he'd never admit that to any of his buddies. The Marines quickly discovered his mechanical aptitude, and by the end of his first year he was in hog heaven, an aircraft mechanic taking million-dollar jets apart and trying to put them together again.

Freddy was brighter than the other grease monkeys, but they were good old boys and he had a good time with them. It was like professional high school, like never growing up. All he had to do each day was learn more about the innards of these incredibly complex, beautiful pieces of machinery, and occasionally throw a salute or two. The Korean War was over, the Marines had become democratic, there was almost none of the spit-and-polish crap of his boot camp days; all in all, it was sort of like belonging to a country club where you could do just what you liked.

He still liked to read. He was going through Gibbons's *Decline and Fall* a little at a time. He didn't spend much time on it, but he did enjoy it. He also enjoyed the reputation it gave him around the base. If he'd been short and skinny and wore glasses, he wouldn't have dared read a book like that on a Marine base, but standing six foot two and topping one ninety, nobody teased him.

When the Vietnam "police action" started, however, and the Marine Corps suddenly needed a whole lot more helicopter pilots, Freddy's battalion commander called him in and told him he was too smart to spend his life covered with grease. The commander had expected an argument from him, but actually for the past year Freddy had begun looking up a little wistfully as the airplanes he put together lifted their wheels off the ground and climbed into the wild blue. So when the commander suggested he go into chopper training, he saluted briskly and said, "Yes, sir."

It turned out to be perfect for him. He would never be a true zoomie; he lacked that instinct for strapping a plane onto his back and soaring up into space, flipping over and turning the world on its ear. He lacked even more the killer instinct necessary to find the target, press the button and kill him before he killed you, or to straddle a ground position with a string of bombs and blow antiaircraft guns into the air. But he liked pulling up the rod and feeling the gooney bird lift off the ground; he liked feeling the earth separate and fall off below. He didn't understand the concept of motion sickness, and whether he was skewed forward, backward or sideward, whichever direction the horizon below was tilting he always knew exactly where he was and where he was going.

When they shipped him off to Vietnam, Freddy's one fear was that he would end up flying a gunship, holding it steady while his gunners killed people on the ground below. He had trained in the States to fly rescue and ambulance missions, but there was just one thing about the goddamn Marines: you could never trust them, you never knew. So when he ended up as a Jolly Green Giant, skimming low over the Viet jungles to pick up downed fighter pilots and bring them home, he was as content as a young man facing death every day could be.

His electronics man tapped him on the shoulder, and he flipped the mike. "Fox Two, Jolly Green. We have you on the scope now. Any activity below?"

"Fox Two. Negative."

There were two ways to run an operation like this. One was to bring in the Spads, Douglas A-1 Skyraiders, propeller-driven gun-planes that would circle around the downed pilot's position, try to spot any Cong below and blast them to hell before the Jolly Green made his pickup. The other way was to slip the JG in as quickly as possible, not giving Charley time to locate the downed man and send troops to the vicinity.

The problem with the first method was that you couldn't see Charley in the dense jungle below, so you didn't know he was there until he started shooting at you. Giving him the first round of shots often meant giving him another downed aircraft. The trouble with the second method was that the goddamn Cong were all over the goddamn country, and you never knew if they were already there or not. So the chopper might slide in nice and slow and come to stop fifty feet in the air right over a Charley patrol. All they had to do was lift their guns, close their eyes and pull the triggers. They couldn't miss.

Today someone had decided on the second method because Fox

Two had happened to go down so close to the carrier's position that they felt they could get the chopper there quickly enough to minimize the risk of the pilot being found by the Cong first. So now Freddy leaned forward, peering through the Plexiglas, searching inside Fox Two's wide circle high above while his radioman scanned the instruments for signs of the downed pilot's emergency transmissions, trying to locate him, wondering if the trees down there hid a Cong ambush or not, wondering if at any moment the trees would come alive with the sound of machine guns.

And old Gee Hardy was down there, either dead of a failed parachute or alive and waiting for him. Hang on, old buddy, here comes the United States Cavalry! Freddy smiled nervously. Was this how those cavalry jokers felt as they charged across the desert into the Indians? His hands were sweating as he nudged the chopper lower, slower, just over the trees in a searching circle.

Hardy had crashed through the trees nearly to the ground. His harness caught on the branches and he found himself swinging wildly at first, gradually slowing, finally nearly motionless. It was bright daylight above the treetops, but down here all light was cut off; it was a primeval twilight, as if he'd suddenly been cast back four hundred million years in time.

As his eyes adjusted to the gloom he saw that he was hanging ten feet in the air. He hung there quietly for a while until the swinging stopped entirely, listening to the jungle and for the sound of men.

When he heard nothing he slipped out of the harness and fell to the ground, landing easily. Again he lay listening and heard nothing.

He turned on his emergency radio and called his RIO several times, but got no answer. He must have gone straight in with a faulty chute. You'd think the goddamn U.S. could afford decent parachutes! But he had other things to think about; he'd get angry later. He switched the radio to rescue frequency and found that the Jolly Green was already on its way.

Thank God for them. He counted off the number sequence and they zeroed in on him; in another moment he heard the rumbling overhead. It quickly grew to a locomotive chugging away right overhead and then he saw the canopy of leaves above part and a small black object come winding down right on the button, not fifteen yards away. It was a penetration seat, a heavy cone-shaped object let down from the chopper on heavy steel cable; it hung now just over the jungle floor, swinging back and forth with the motion of the helicopter hovering above.

He crashed through the leaves and tree branches toward it, climbed aboard, strapped himself in and called out on the radio. Immediately it began to pull upward, slicing through the trees and lifting him away. At that instant, Charley appeared.

Looking down, Gee saw him: one lone soldier, stepping through the thick wall of green below, appearing suddenly out of nowhere, silent and unreal below in the chattering noise of the chopper above. He saw him unsling his machine gun, he saw others materialize beside him—two, three, suddenly a score or more.

Then he was through the treetops and blinded by the dazzling sun, swaying sickeningly in the empty air as they hauled him aboard. "Cong!" he shouted. "Get the fuck out of here."

They were already moving. Hardy strapped himself in as the chopper tilted forward and began to accelerate away just as the bullets came spewing up out of the foliage below, spattering and clanging against the armor. But they were moving, they were on their way!

They almost made it. Ten seconds later the engine went *clunk-clunk*; that was the only warning, and the end of it all. The blades stopped rotating, there was a burst of flame and Freddy dumped her down into a small clearing. He and Hardy were held tight by their seat belts, but the copter's radio/medic was thrown clear and landed on his head, snapping his neck. Hardy climbed out and began to run, afraid of fire, but then saw that Mason was still inside. He went back for him and found that he was jammed in, his legs caught under the seat, crushed by the engine when the mountings had snapped on impact. Hardy started to pull him clear, desperately trying to get him out before the ruptured fuel lines ignited, but Freddy screamed with agony at the first hard yank and he didn't know what to do. The fuel was streaming out of the lines and the wreck could go up any second, so he yanked again; Freddy gave one last terrible scream and, thank God, fainted. Hardy pulled him loose and dragged him across the ground until he heard a *whoosh*; he threw himself over Freddy's body as the chopper exploded, showering them with flaming debris.

Hardy brushed the fiery shards off them and sat down for a moment beside Freddy's unconscious body. Then he saw the jungle foliage part on the other side of the clearing, and Charley stepped through. For one moment his instinct was to run, but he couldn't leave Freddy. He couldn't run anyway, he realized, as he struggled to his feet. Then Charley raised his rifle, aimed it at him and pulled the trigger. It made such a small noise, and then he heard nothing at all.

He woke up in a bamboo cage, jouncing from side to side as they carried him along a jungle trail. He thought at first it was the pain in his shoulder that had woken him; at every bounce he fell against the hard bamboo railings of the cage, and the pain shot down from his shoulder and through his side. He saw the blood soaking through and felt sick.

Then he realized that it wasn't the pain; it was the horrible screams and cries that were coming from the other body in the cage. Freddy was bouncing against him and against the bamboo rails, his legs twisted around under him, pointing out at impossible angles. He was semiconscious and still screaming.

When Hardy called out to the men carrying them, one shoved a heavy stick through the bars and knocked him back. When he tried to shout again they pushed the stick back in, jammed it against Freddy's legs and shoved hard. Freddy's head jerked up and he screamed.

They laughed.

## 21

Hardy gritted his teeth, shut his eyes tight and forced the memory down below the thin line between conscious life and the stinking hole underneath which held the thoughts that could not be thought. After a while he realized that he was not breathing and that his facial muscles were clenched so tight they were hurting. He looked around the plane and saw with relief that nobody was paying any attention. He waited another moment, then looked around inside his mind, glanced fearfully into its corners, and saw that the succubus had submerged to where it lurked unseen, buried somewhere in there. Slowly he began to breathe again, stretched his shoulders and came back to life.

It was the morning after the meeting with the Libyans, and he was now being carried at five hundred knots across the Atlantic. Everything was all right. Everything was A-OK.

After the war, when they finally took Hardy out of the cage he had come to think of as home and gave him back his flying coveralls with the blood washed out in the stream behind the village, when they sent him down to Saigon and the government had shipped him home, he found he was still lost. He was back in the United States of America, but it was as if he had never been there before. He was frightened of the strange land.

An officer came and stood beside his hospital bed, holding a clipboard in his hands, to tell him they had been unable to locate his wife and son. She had moved from their last recorded address, and with everything confused because the POWs were returning in an anonymous jumble, there hadn't been time to locate them. Hardy's records had barely beaten him across the Pacific. But not to worry, the officer said, the Marines would find them; the Marines take care of their own. Hardy turned away, pulled the sheet over his shoulder and stared at the hospital wall.

He was unreasonably afraid of everything. He lay in his bed, afraid to leave it, terrified not only of the country that lay beyond the cracked, plastered hospital walls but of everything beyond his own sheets. Lying there in the cranked-up bed, afraid to get out to go to the bathroom, he would break into a sweat. He would lie for hours while his kidneys ached for relief. For nearly the whole of the first week he wet his bed rather than get up. Finally, on the sixth day, he forced himself out of bed and to the toilet.

In the movies that would have been the breakthrough; from then on everything would have been easy. It was not. Back in bed, he would lie trembling, trying to force himself to think what was out there waiting for him. In his imagination he walked down the street of Ternville, Virginia, and saw his parents' home and the movie theaters and restaurants. He told himself he had been there before, he had lived there, but it was like *Alice in Wonderland*.

He was afraid of his wife, and she was afraid of him. When he was shot down in Vietnam in the fall of 1968, he had been listed as missing in action, and then there had been no further word. The Cong had never informed the International Red Cross of his capture, and the months and years had passed by.

Their son had been three years old in 1968. Two years later he remembered his father only from the framed picture in the living room and the model of a Phantom jet fighter he played with in bed. Hardy's wife clung to hope at first and waited for him. But the very nature that had attracted him to her, her vibrant and passionate extroversion, made it impossible for her to live a solitary existence for long. When the Marine record officer finally found her, she was living with someone else.

It was the Red Cross who told him. While he was still lying on his bed in the naval hospital in San Diego afraid to go to the bathroom, a pleasant, sad-faced middle-aged lady told him his wife had been located living in New York with a successful lawyer.

He didn't care, he said. He wasn't psychologically ready for involvement with another person, he said. He wanted to be alone. He wanted nothing more than to be left alone.

"Your son—" the Red Cross lady began, but he rolled over and faced the wall. He didn't even want to *think* about his son. He couldn't take the responsibility. He couldn't take care of himself, so how could he take care of a kid?

The Red Cross wrote his wife and told her that he was a sick man and needed help. He wrote his wife and told her that he was all right and that he didn't blame her; in fact, he was relieved to find she had someone else. He asked her to take care of the divorce details; he would sign anything she sent him.

His wife cried for two days and then filed for divorce. What else could she do? Leave the man she had learned to love for the sick shell of the man she had once loved? Give up her life to nurse him back to health? Would he ever come back to health? Did he even want to try?

The answers were all negative. Their son had accepted that the father he never knew was dead and was beginning to accept the lawyer she lived with as a father. She wanted more children, and she was reaching the end of her childbearing years. If she returned to Hardy she would have to forget about any more children; even if he did recover, it would take years. What was the point of saving his life—if she could, which she doubted—at the cost of the lives of her unborn children?

She wrote Hardy a long letter explaining all this, asking for his understanding and forgiveness. He didn't finish reading it; midway into the second paragraph it dropped from his fingers. The nurse put it on his night table, but he never picked it up again. Finally an orderly threw it away by mistake. The nurse was angry. Hardy didn't care. He never heard from his wife again. When the papers arrived from her attorney he signed them without reading them.

Eventually they dismissed him from the hospital. He had recovered from his injuries.

Hardy didn't know what was wrong. Everyone told him he was lucky to be alive and without any disabilities. His shoulder had healed. Not that the Cong had given him any medicine for it; it had just healed. The bullet had gone clear through, and it had been a toss-up whether it would become infected or not. The Cong doctor who had examined him told him straight out: they weren't about to waste any of their pitiful supplies of penicillin on a murderer like him. If it got infected he would die. The doctor walked away; he would probably die anyhow.

But he hadn't. He had come home, which was the cruelest punishment of all. After long arguments, which he never heard, the Marine Corps decided that his mental state made him no longer fit for military service. He was of unsound mind, they decided. From the way the Medical Corps major told him he knew what they were thinking: he had given in; he didn't have the guts of a true Marine.

Hardy didn't even have the energy to curse them. He took his discharge and walked away. He looked for an airline job, but ex–military pilots were a drug on the market; the only ones the airlines were interested in were the MATS boys, who had built up experience flying military air transports.

So he left the U.S. He went off to Africa with the first group that contacted him, and for the next five years he fought in a series of little wars over there. It was crazy; it didn't make any sense. He wasn't afraid in the jungle; he wasn't afraid of flying and fighting. It was home he was afraid of. It didn't make any sense, but it was the way it was.

He did well, building quite a reputation for himself. What the hell, at least the people he fought for were trying to win their wars, unlike the good old U.S. of A.

Slowly he healed—enough, finally, to want to come home again. Enough to realize that America was a country as blanketed in hypocrisy as Los Angeles was in smog, but that it was still his country. Fuck 'em, he thought, they think they can take it away from me, but fuck 'em. He went home with a plan.

He visited Freddy Mason's folks back in Virginia and was told that Freddy was alive but not well; he was living with his sister in a rented trailer on the outskirts of a little town nor fifty miles from home. Hardy wrestled with himself for a long time before he thought he could look at Freddy again. Driving down to see him, he could think of nothing except the days and weeks of constant screaming when they had lived together in that cage in the village square, with the kids reaching in with long sticks to poke Freddy's fractured legs.

Hardy found Freddy sitting alone with two bottles of beer left in the refrigerator, so he drove back into town to get a couple of six-packs, and then they sat around and talked. Freddy was beginning to let himself go. He had tried awfully hard. He had been in the hospital for nearly a year when they'd brought him back and amputated his shattered legs. Since then he had been living on his disability and working out like a madman. From the waist up he was poster-strong, but he was finally about to give up. He had found that without legs there wasn't much he could do. Yes, he could have gone to college and even law school, something like that; everyone told him he could. But he couldn't. He had gotten as far as collecting a bunch of applications; they were still around the trailer somewhere. He was just beginning to feel sorry for himself, losing control, with nowhere to go.

Hardy began to tell him his idea, and Freddy perked up. Not right away; at first he just stared at Gee with dead eyes, shaking his head. No, he couldn't do it; he couldn't do anything. But slowly, as Hardy talked, his head stopped shaking, his ears began to really listen and his eyes began to sparkle.

Just then the screen door had banged open and his sister walked in.

"Do we have visitors? There's a car parked outside— Gee!" she screamed.

Alison still looked like a kid. Cutest damn kid he had ever known, he remembered. Freddy Mason's kid sister. She'd always wanted to be one of the boys, was always following after them, trying to get into their games. They'd put up with her because she was so damn cute and good-natured, always smiling, always happy. He shook his head and laughed. "You still hanging around, kid?"

He calculated rapidly. She had to be twenty-five at least. Still cute as ever. "Isn't it about time you went off and got married?" he asked. "Make yourself a bunch of kids?"

Alison smiled self-consciously. "You know me, Gee. Still trying to play with the big boys."

Hardy looked around the trailer. "You live here?"

She nodded.

He understood, but he didn't like it. A girl shouldn't give up her life for her brother, no matter how much he needs her. If wives don't do it, sisters shouldn't.

"We're just talking some business," he said. "You want to go take a walk around the block and give us a little more time?"

"I'm still not big enough to play?" she asked.

"Not with the big boys," Hardy said. "Go take a walk, kid."

She looked at her brother and saw the excitement in his eyes, the eyes that had tried so hard but had begun to die moment by moment over the past long months, and she nearly cried right there and then. Quickly she walked across the trailer to Hardy, put her hands on his shoulders and reached up and kissed him quickly on the cheek. "Bless you, Gee," she whispered, then turned and left.

For a moment there was silence. They waited until her footsteps had died away; then Hardy started talking again about his idea.

It was simple enough, and though Freddy wasn't convinced he was willing to try. What did he have to lose? So with part of the stake Gee had brought back from Africa Freddy flew down to Florida, where he rented a paraplegic-control automobile and toured the lonely stretches between the Everglades and the East Coast until he found a bankrupt airport. They leased it for fifteen hundred a month and Hardy flew down with the twin-engined Beech he'd bought in Kansas. With Gee taking care of the flying aspect and Freddy the ground duties, they began flying marijuana in from Mexico.

It was a piece of cake. Mason had to haul himself around the airplanes hand over hand like a monkey, but he got around fine. He could fix anything, anything at all. He could pull the motor apart, put it back together purring like a kitten, and have enough parts left over to make another motor. Hardy had learned to fly in any kind of weather under any kind of conditions, and neither the locals nor the Florida cops were anywhere near as tough as the Cong. It was like a vacation. Business grew rapidly until the Bush task force began operations a few years later, whereupon they simply moved their base to Louisiana and continued as before. But though the risks were small on each flight, the odds were cumulative; they were beginning to think it was time to get out.

Flying back from his second meeting with the Libyans, Hardy thought about this now. They had started their smuggling business nearly ten years ago, and now here he was coming back to Freddy with another idea—a much better idea. It was what they were looking for, their way out: a one-time shot that would put them on easy street for the rest of their lives.

Freddy met him at the airport, and as they drove home Hardy told him all about it.

At first Freddy blanched. This was too . . .

"Too what?" Hardy asked.

"Too big."

Hardy smiled. "You're right," he said. "You are goddamn right: it is big. It is awfully damned big. But you're also a little bit wrong, because it is not *too* big. Not for us, not for you and me together. We can do it, Freddy."

Freddy didn't notice that Gee was talking at him, but not *to* him. Hardy was looking inside the dark crevices of his own mind, talking to the demon that was cowering there and tormenting him in its own agony. He was looking at the photograph. Freddy didn't know that; he thought Gee was still sitting there sipping his beer, talking to him. But Hardy was a long way off, ten years off, looking at a photograph.

It was datelined 1971, and it had come from Saigon. It was grainy, and it had appeared in virtually every newspaper in the civilized world.

It showed a naked Vietnamese girl in Tra Nang, her clothing burned off, her naked skin on fire, screaming in terror and running down a bombed-out street, trying in vain to escape the napalm that clung to her wasted skin and bones. Looking at the picture, you knew the girl was a running corpse; she must have died moments later.

Hardy had seen the picture before, but he had never really looked at it until the day it arrived in an envelope from his son.

He had been back from Vietnam for six years, the last five of which he had spent in Africa. At last he was getting a grip on his life. He was well enough now to get to know his son again, to be a father for the first time.

It was 1978, and his boy was thirteen years old. He had left him in 1967 to go to Vietnam, and had not seen him since. He wrote to his wife and she replied, inviting him to visit. When he got there they all said a few polite words, and then she and her husband left and he sat down to spend the afternoon with his son.

He should have waited before trying to explain. He should have slid into it gradually and easily, should have talked about his life before the war. Maybe then they'd have gone up to the boy's room and he'd have seen the pictures of Marine Phantom jets thumbtacked to the wall, and the model of the Phantom dangling from the ceiling as if in full flight. Maybe then he'd have understood the hero worship of a thirteen-year-old boy for his mysterious, glamorous father.

But he tried too soon and too hard. He thought he had begun to be normal again; he didn't understand the depth of the guilt that still racked him. So, too soon, he tried to explain to his son why he hadn't come to see him as soon as he'd returned, why he hadn't become his father again, why he had disappeared again for another five years. He tried to explain what he had suffered. If he had talked about the Cong prison and the tortures he had endured, it would have worked; the boy would have been wide-eyed, even worshipful. Instead Hardy talked about the real pain, about the nightmares. He told his son about the child seen for one split moment as he flew over the jungle clearing, the child whose face he would never forget.

The boy was thirteen years old. Until that moment he had blamed himself for having a father who didn't love him, for being so inferior to a man who couldn't be bothered to be his father. He had thought he understood perfectly; he himself wouldn't want to hang around with a pimply, nothing sort of kid if he was a famous jet fighter pilot.

Now suddenly these complex rationalizations crumbled, and life was different and even more terrible than he had ever imagined, and he didn't know where he fit into it. He never took his father up to his room to show him the model and the pictures of the Phantom jet. Suddenly it was nothing to be proud of. He never said a word about his dreams and his life. He sat there stony-faced and silent, until finally Gee gave up and left before his wife and her husband came back and saw him humbled, sweating and nearly begging this stony-faced thirteen-year-old boy to simply *look* at him.

Then the boy went up to his room and looked through the collection of war books until he found that photograph he had once seen but never paid attention to. Carefully he cut it out, folded it, put it in an envelope and sent it to his father. Then he took down the pictures from his walls and the model from the ceiling.

Hardy never saw his son again. In 1983, when the boy was eighteen, he spent a year in the Peace Corps in Africa just a couple of hundred miles from where his father had fought as a mercenary a few years before. When his enlistment was up he went with a Quaker group to Nicaragua. He was living in a peasant village, teaching them about sanitation and sewage, when a group of Contras burst into the village clearing with machine guns ablaze to reconquer the villagers' hearts and save them from the Sandinistas.

The attack killed twenty villagers and one American boy. The machine guns they used had been bought with money obtained from Iran, funneled illegally to the Contras.

Hardy sat now holding the beer, staring out beyond Freddy's head, seeing the photograph of the burning Vietnamese girl and the dead bleeding body of his son.

They were all the same: Johnson who had sent him to Vietnam; Reagan and Bush who had sent weapons to Nicaragua. Bush in particular: the hero, the all-American boy, the consummate politician, the hypocrite. The kid who had played baseball at Yale and grown up to fly an Avenger for the Navy; the vice president who had been "out of the loop" when they discussed selling arms to Iran for money to send guns to Nicaragua in order to kill American kids who only wanted to help the peasants; the hypocritical President, who now said it was "time to put that behind us and go on." The man who wanted to forget the past.

Forget, hell. His hands dripped with blood—Hardy's blood, and the unknown girl's, and the blood of the son Hardy had never known. So when the Libyans told him they wanted him to kidnap the President of the United States, he hadn't been able to breathe for a second, as suddenly it all came home to him. Would he kidnap him? Would he take the bastard? Oh, yes. By God, yes, he would.

"Gee?"

Hardy blinked it all away. Freddy was leaning forward, his face wrinkled in apprehension.

Hardy smiled at him, leaned over and put his arm around his shoulder. They could do it, he told him; they could do anything. They could shake the world and hear it rattle!

They went into the house still talking, still arguing about it. Freddy kept rolling his wheelchair around in little circles, instinctively pulling away, turning his back to Hardy. But as they talked he gradually made shorter circles, and finally he stopped. He shook his head, but he shook it tentatively. Attacking the President of the United States was a lot different from sneaking grass past borders, he argued. Then Hardy knew that he had him. He was talking operational details now, and while they didn't know the answers yet, Hardy had a basic idea.

He went to the refrigerator and pulled out a couple of beers. They sat around and talked about it, and finally Mason began to nod. It was dangerous, of course, but it was a one-time operation and it looked good.

"Alison?" Freddy asked.

Hardy shook his head. "She doesn't have to know anything about it. She's used to our traveling around and she won't see us doing anything different. We can tell her about it when it's over."

Freddy nodded, Gee smiled, and they clinked beer bottles together.

The next day Mason would fly down to Florida, concentrating on the west coast from Tampa on down, looking over their old airports, the ones they'd used when their smuggling operation was based down there. Something with an unpaved grass strip, nothing that would attract attention. With the Bush task force most of the people in the business had switched operations to other states, as Gee and Freddy had, and it wasn't likely that all of their old airfields were now occupied. "I'll head out west," Hardy said, "and find us a 707 we can lease."

None of the grass airstrips would be able to land a giant four-engined Boeing 707, but that wouldn't matter. Their 707 wasn't going to land there. Or anywhere else.

# III

# The Phantom

## 22

Charles Werther had a disgusted look on his face. David Melnik sat in a corner, not taking part, his face a careful blank, but in his soul was more than disgust; there was despair. How did Israel ever get saddled with such incompetents as allies? The Americans seemed to take a national pride in screwing up the simplest things. How could they assign people to trail an Arab who couldn't tell one Arab from another?

He knew this was unfair—the switch had been masterfully arranged—but he nursed his anger because subconsciously it fed his ego. Yet not quite subconsciously; deep down in some recess of his mind he was aware of it and ashamed of it. Now he put all such thoughts out of his head and listened to what was going on.

Which was, at the moment, silence. Werther was staring at Rasheed Amon, who was licking his lips and looking around nervously at the others in the room, hoping for some help or a sign that they believed him. It was, Rasheed told himself, a perfectly simple and believable story. Why didn't they believe him?

In fact they did, but as Werther had explained to Melnik when they were walking into this session a couple of hours earlier, they had nothing to lose by leaning on this man. After all, they had nowhere else to go. So Werther stared at Amon with disgust and finally said, "There's not much point in your continuing to give us this bullshit."

"I swear by almighty God it's the truth!"

"Whose God?"

"Yours! I mean mine! Both! I swear—"

"And which truth?"

Rasheed paused. "I don't know what you mean. There's only one truth—"

"Ah. I didn't know you understood that. Then stop giving us the truth you've cooked up for us and tell us the true truth." He held up his hand before Rasheed could answer. "Enough!" he suddenly yelled, so that Rasheed jumped. "I know you're lying. Don't you have enough brains in your head to understand *how* I know?" He paused, then spoke quietly again as Rasheed struggled to understand. "Because I know part of the story, and it's not what you're telling me."

Werther let this sink in, then got up and turned his back, walking away from Rasheed. "I don't really give a damn. I doubt you know any more about it than we do already. I don't know why I'm wasting my time on you. We know you're lying; we have proof that this wasn't set up by some goddamn Arab pretending it was a movie, so to hell with it. I've got the deportation order signed already"—he turned around suddenly, took a sheaf of papers out of his jacket pocket and slammed them down on the table—"so the hell with you. By tomorrow you'll be back in Lebanon, and good riddance."

"My family—"

"Fuck your family. I've got no quarrel with them; they can stay where they are. You can write them from Lebanon and tell them what happened to you."

"You can't—"

"I can, and I'm doing it, buddy. I've got no more time for you." He turned and started for the door. Melnik rose and followed him.

Rasheed held out until they had actually opened the door before he called out. "Wait! I'll tell you—"

Werther whirled and pointed his finger at him. "I've got no more time to waste! You understand that? I know part of your story—shit, I probably know it *all*—so if you give me just one more lie you'll find your ass in Lebanon within twenty-four hours. Do you read me, mister?"

Rasheed nodded violently and began immediately to talk. "It was all the truth, I swear," he began, and then as Werther turned to leave again he shouted, "except for one thing!"

Werther stopped, still facing the door, and waited.

"Maybe two things," Rasheed admitted. "He did tell me it was for a movie, but I didn't believe him. He said it with a smile, you understand? To tell me that it was what I could say when you arrested me. He said you couldn't prove anything else, so you'd have to let me go. But I didn't know what it really was, I swear! I still don't know anything!"

There was a pause, and then Werther said, "You said there were two things."

"Yes. Well . . ." Rasheed paused. "He wasn't an Arab. He told me to tell you he was; he said that it would sound more like the truth. But he was American."

"Name?"

"Dallas."

Melnik and Werther exchanged glances, and Rasheed added, "That wasn't his real name, but he said that was what I should call him. I don't know his real name."

"Describe him," Werther said.

"He's a big man," Rasheed answered, telling them everything now. "Very strong. Taller than me—about your size"—he pointed to Melnik—"but bigger, stronger. . . ."

23

Teaching Mohammed to fly the Panther turned out to be easy enough. The method Hardy used was the standard technique employed by the military to teach any pilot to fly a new single-seat fighter. First you sat him down in a comfortable chair someplace and handed him the flight manual. Then you came back in a few hours and quizzed him on it. Then you sat him in the cockpit while you kneeled on the wing, and went over the instrument layout with him. Then you left him alone for a couple of hours, and when you came back you blindfolded him and had him touch every instrument and control lever as you called them out while you were kneeling on the wing. Then you held on to the open canopy as he fired up and taxied back and forth on the runway. Then you went over the tricky bits with him again: how the plane could climb like an eagle and turn like a sparrow, but if he tried to turn it too tightly it would suddenly snap-roll, and before he knew what happened he'd find himself spinning into the ground.

But of course by this time he wasn't listening; he was nodding, but he was doing so before you'd finished your sentences, and you knew he wasn't listening because he was a fighter pilot and he had his hands on a new toy and all he wanted was for you to get the hell off his wing and let him fly.

So you tried a bit harder. You told him that the Panther's fore and aft stability was a bit like a drunk's on roller skates, and that directional snaking was likely to creep up at high speeds. But he knew and you knew that these were just details that a man had to find out for himself, and there was only one way to do that, so finally you gave up and slid down off the wing and jumped out of the way of the exhaust as he gunned the bird off into the Kansas sky.

Hardy stood watching as it climbed steeply, steering it with his shoulders and body until it disappeared from sight, and then walked back to the hangar. Freddy was sitting outside in his chair; Hardy flopped down on the ground beside him and they sat there with the sun on their faces and their eyes closed.

Twenty minutes later they heard the first faint scream. They opened their eyes at the same instant. Shading their gaze with their hands, they looked out over the airfield. Hardy saw it first, and pointed. There it was, just a speck against the deep blue, its jet exhaust screaming at them as it came from infinity and passed high over them. Then it turned over on its back, hung there for a moment and came roaring down, straight down toward the ground, moving nearly as fast as its scream now, pushing the speed of sound. Freddy leaned forward on his arms and began to curse as it hurled down inverted at slightly over the vertical. For a long moment it looked as if it would auger right in, but then the nose began to lift and it pulled out over the edge of the field and came racing right at them, trailing its roar behind like the tail of a tiger. At ten feet it swept across the field, and they sat there and watched it hurtle right at them and the hangar. At the last possible moment the nose lifted and it roared over their heads and the hangar roof by inches, and the building shook and rattled with the force of its passing.

"Goddamn fool," Freddy cursed.

Hardy smiled. "He's a fighter pilot. He'll do."

There was nothing more for Hardy to do but let Asri get acquainted with the ship and the surrounding terrain, so he was glad when the message came from Philadelphia. It sounded as if his contact might have found what he was looking for, so he flew up there on Thursday.

Alfredo San Medro was all things to all men. To his father he was an honest and loyal son. To the children growing up in his North Philadelphia neighborhood he was a role model, a living example of how to escape the poverty of the ghetto and be a man in a stinking, dishonest world. To the virgins of the neighborhood he was the apotheosis of the glamorous, mysterious macho male. To the girls in his stable he was a brutal, callous, possessive son of a bitch. To the local mafiosi he was a soldier climbing out of the ranks: honest enough, strong enough, ambitious enough—just enough, not too much. He looked like a comer.

To the patrol car police cruising the neighborhood San Medro was a punk, a pusher, a pimp. They looked forward to the day they'd catch him at something serious enough to warrant clubbing him over the head with a .45. They didn't worry about it; they waited for it calmly, for they were sure it would come.

To Hardy, San Medro was a merchandiser. When he walked into the tavern in the Logan section of Philadelphia, Alfredo was waiting for him at a table in the far corner. Hardy walked over, put the briefcase he was carrying on the table and sat down. "So," he said, "what have you got for me?"

"Everything you want, man. How about a beer?"

Hardy shook his head, but San Medro gestured over his shoulder to the bartender, who brought them two bottles and took away the empty that was sitting in a wet ring on the table. He didn't bother to wipe away the ring.

"You got it all?" Hardy asked when they were alone.

San Medro spread his hands wide. "Sure, man. No sweat. Wasn't nothing complicated on the list."

"Where is it?"

San Medro smiled, looking at Hardy's briefcase like a raccoon impressed with its own cunning. "Where's the loot, man?"

"Outside."

"So let's go outside."

Hardy pushed his chair back, but San Medro held up his hand. "Hey man, I didn't mean like *now*." He gestured at the beer. "My mama always say 'Waste not, want not.' " He laughed. "Things were different for the old ones, huh?" He looked insultingly at Hardy, who was probably almost as old as his mother, he thought.

Hardy waited for him to finish off his beer, not touching his own. San Medro drank it down slowly, enjoying the moment. As soon as he finished Hardy started to get up, but San Medro reached across the table toward Hardy's bottle. "Waste not, want not," he said again with the same feral smile, which disappeared abruptly as Hardy clamped his fingers around the wrist of his outstretched hand. Holding him stretched across the table without apparent effort, though San Medro tried with all his might to pull away, Hardy lifted the bottle of beer with his other hand, leaned across the table and slowly poured the beer into San Medro's lap.

He held the bottle until it was empty, then set it down. "Waste not, want not," he said, and then released San Medro's hand. "Let's go outside."

San Medro unlocked the back of his truck and they climbed in. He handed Hardy a flashlight, locked the door behind them, and concentrated on trying to stand so that his wet pants didn't cling to him while Hardy checked out the merchandise. As he had said, it was all there: the bazooka, grenades, rifles, Uzis, handguns and cartons of ammunition.

When they got out of the truck, San Medro locked it again and Hardy held out his hand for the keys. San Medro took a step away from him and waited. Hardy walked around to the driver's door, got in and placed the briefcase on the seat beside him. San Medro slid into the passenger's seat and opened the briefcase. Hardy waited patiently while he counted the money. Finally he looked up and smiled. "A pleasure doing business with you, man," he said.

Hardy held out his hand for the keys to the truck, and San Medro handed them over. While shutting the door behind him Hardy started the engine and drove away.

## 24

"Could I speak to Rasheed Amon, please?" Freddy asked again. It was his sixth call. On his second call Rasheed's wife had been in tears; Rasheed had been arrested, and she didn't know what to do. On Tuesday, Wednesday and Thursday the information had been much the same. Each time she asked whether he had anything to do with Rasheed's trouble, but each time Freddy just hung up.

Today was different. After a similar long wait—the telephone was evidently in a tenement hallway, and the Amons had to be summoned—a male voice said, "Hello."

"Rasheed Amon?" Freddy asked.

"Who is this?"

"I'm calling for Dallas. Is this Rasheed Amon?"

"Yes."

Freddy couldn't be sure, but there seemed to be a trace of nervousness in that one syllable. "Is everything all right?" he asked.

Silence.

"Your wife said they'd arrested you."

"Yes. Yes, they did." The voice was definitely nervous. "It's all right."

"They believed your story?"

"Yes. Finally."

"You stuck to it?"

"Yes! Yes, of course I did! They couldn't prove anything. . . . I have to go now. Don't call me again, I don't want anything to do with you." He hung up.

Freddy smiled at the dead telephone.

"He talked," Freddy said.

"You're sure?" Hardy asked.

Freddy nodded. "He was as nervous as a cat. Scared to death. Hung up on me."

"So now they know everything Rasheed Amon knows." Hardy smiled. "Good."

25

The DC-3 in the hangar was Hardy's excuse for his occupation of the airfield, as well as being an intrinsic part of his plan. Under the name of Privatair he ran a charter flight service, covering most of the country at one time or another, although mostly within the adjoining states. Today he had a contract to fly a high school band from a small town fifty miles away to a national competition in New Mexico. He had filled out the contracts and insurance forms a month ago, signing and countersigning what would have been a bewildering array of government-required paperwork—that is, it would have been bewildering if anyone bothered to pay any attention to it beyond the requirement of signing everything in quadruplicate.

Among the papers, for instance, was an assurance that he had insurance liability up to one million dollars per passenger, which was enough to make a frog laugh. One of the benefits of having a Republican administration that cut funding to all federal agencies was that officials like the FAA people no longer had the manpower to check on such paperwork for all the tramp charters in the country. Nobody cared, anyway. The school district was satisfied as long as they had Hardy's signature to relieve them of all liability, the parents were satisfied that the school district was taking care of their children properly, the kids didn't give a damn because they couldn't possibly imagine dying, and Hardy was satisfied because he knew he had nothing to worry about. Although the DC-3 looked no better than the other tramps flying the airways, inside the engine nacelles were two beautifully maintained engines, with hydraulic lines and control surfaces to match. He wasn't taking any chances, and neither, though they didn't know it, was the school board.

As copilot Hardy chose a local flyer who wanted to build up his multiengine time in order to qualify for an airline job, and they flew the band to Taos, New Mexico. Telling the copilot to take the rest of the day off, but to be ready the next day at noon for the return flight, he then flew on alone to San Francisco. After arranging for a tie-down and to have the gas tanks topped off, he stopped in at the airport manager's office. Bud Malcolm was an old Marine buddy of his, and every time he was in the area he stopped in to renew old ties and to hear the same old stories. Bud was always good for an hour of relaxation and a few laughs.

Hardy took particular pleasure in learning about the operation of the airfield. He was interested in all the problems, from the politics involved in stroking local officials—"And their wives once in a while too, huh, Bud?"—to those of dealing with union bosses who were little better than outright thieves and con men, from technical details such as the best filler for tarmac cracks to the problems of cleaning rest rooms. Bud was always happy to discuss such kitchen detail with an old buddy, and the two of them usually, as they did today, wandered around the airport while Bud pointed out just where he was having trouble with what. In the last month or two, Hardy had become a familiar figure around the airport. Most of the workers recognized him, although they didn't know exactly who he was; somebody official, they would have said if asked, since he was always with the boss.

It was late in the day when Hardy left the airport in a borrowed official car, but it was summer and the sun would be up for several hours yet. On the way into town he stopped at a gas station and made a phone call to make sure that his appointment was understood. Fifteen minutes later he picked up a man at the Mark Hopkins, then drove over the hills into the wine valleys beyond.

Hardy's passenger had been in town for a week, spending his time seeing the city and becoming familiar with it. He bore a passport in the name of Matsuo Nakaoka, which was the name Hardy used to address him. Previously he had worked for the Black June movement of the PLO, the most recent job being two years before, when he and a companion had driven a truck laden with explosives to within a few hundred yards of a Marine compound outside Beirut. Two of them had been necessary up to this point: in case of challenge along the way, they had planned to fight their way through. Nakaoka, acknowledged as the better shot, was riding as passenger with an Uzi submachine gun hidden at his feet.

They pulled to a stop just beyond a full curve in the road. Fifty yards around the curve was the steel fence and barbed-wire topping that marked the edge of the Marine compound. It was guarded by a pair of

Shore Patrol with shiny helmets and white armbands who had a machine gun set off to the side. From this point on, they knew they had already succeeded. Nothing could stop them now, and it would be wasteful for them both to go. According to the plan they had previously devised, Nakaoka reached into the glove compartment and withdrew a pack of playing cards. Without a word he placed them on the seat between them, then cut and showed the card he had drawn to his companion. He didn't look at it himself, but waited while the other man did the same.

His companion drew a ten of clubs. Nakaoka looked at his own card: the queen of spades. He nodded; it was as close as either of them came to speech. Opening the door, he stepped down, walked to the rear of the truck and from under the tarpaulin pulled down a small motorcycle. Then he crept into the back of the truck and, working easily in the dark under the tarpaulin, armed the fuses for explosion on contact.

Nakaoka jumped down, kicked the motorcycle into life and drove away back down the road. The sound of his motorcycle engine was the signal for the truck driver, who shifted into first, then second; by the time he rounded the curve he was in third and roaring at full speed for the guarded gate. He crashed through it before the two guards had time to reach the machine gun, and by the time they swiveled it around toward him he was already bouncing up the two steps and into the heavy oak door.

Nakaoka was nearly half a mile away when he heard the explosion behind him. He continued on his way, threading along between the horse-drawn carts and slow automotive jalopies. In a few minutes sirens began to be heard, and soon ambulances began to stream past him. He pulled aside to let them pass, visualizing as in a distant movie the survivors stunned and panicked, standing around helplessly staring and crying as the building collapsed and burned with their friends and brothers inside. He felt nothing more than a sense of a difficult job well done.

It was not easy to find a competent pro who was willing to risk his life, and Hardy had brought Nakaoka into Operation Dallas as soon as he found him in order not to lose him to someone else's project. But he wanted to see if the Japanese was as good with a rifle as had been claimed. After half an hour's test-firing in an empty field with the rifle he'd brought along, there was no doubt. Then he spread out a picnic lunch and told Nakaoka the plan. He had expected at least surprise, or perhaps a smile, but Nakaoka simply sat through the recital without a change of expression. Were there any questions?

Nakaoka stared at him for a moment. "It seems simple enough. There will be crowds lining the route, of course. I will enter earlier an office that you will have rented in advance and I myself will have had a chance to investigate?"

Hardy nodded, and he went on. "The gun you provide will presumably be in a briefcase of some sort?" Again Hardy nodded. "When will I have it for practice?"

"At least two weeks before the event. I will then take it back from you, but all this will be coordinated later."

"What do you mean, take it back from me?"

"Just in case something goes wrong, we don't want you walking into the office with the gun in your possession. The gun will be delivered to the site by someone else. If he's stopped and the gun is discovered, you will still be safe."

"What is the point of being safe without a gun?"

"There will be a second gun that someone else will get to you."

Nakaoka shook his head violently. "A second gun is useless! The gun must be tested and adjusted by me personally or I haven't a chance of hitting him at five hundred yards."

"You will have *both* guns to practice with and to adjust as you like. You yourself will pack them into two briefcases, and you have my word that no one will touch them thereafter until one of them is delivered into your hands at the site." Hardy smiled placatingly. "After all, I am not an amateur. The simple fact is that if you are stopped and are carrying a gun, everything is lost. So we do it my way." He paused, and this time did not smile. "We do *everything* my way. Nothing is negotiable."

Reluctantly Nakaoka agreed. They finished their lunch and drove back to San Francisco in silence.

# 26

It sounded like the kitchen of a fashionable restaurant, the dominant noise being the clatter of steel upon steel. You could close your eyes and imagine knives sliding against sharpening rods, except that the odor was one of human sweat.

The room was wide and bare, lit by unshielded bulbs in a high ceiling. Two parallel three-foot-wide rubber strips ran lengthwise down the room, and on each of them a pair of figures was dancing back and forth, lunging, parrying and striking again. David Melnik stood in the entranceway, squinting to see better. The lights were bright on the dancing figures, but faded into darkness around the edges of the room.

He shouldn't have come, he was thinking. It was stupid to raise unnecessary complications. He was a professional, and there was a job to be done. But it didn't matter; none of that mattered. He had been saying it to himself all the way down Fifth Avenue and across town. He had heard the reverberations of those warning words as he walked up the dimly lit stairs, and now he heard their echo as he stood in the entrance. Anyway, he was probably wrong; probably nothing would happen. He was just curious. He stepped into the room.

A dozen or so people dressed in white canvas jackets and tight-fitting pants were scattered around the hall, doing bending and stretching exercises or lunging at one of the two dummies in a corner. They were about evenly divided in sex, though with the similarity of uniforms and hairstyles the only clue was the slimness and hip shape, and neither of these was conclusive. He walked over to the nearest man and said he was looking for Lori Werther. The man straightened up, looked around and finally pointed to one of the figures fencing on a mat.

Anyone unfamiliar with the sport would have wondered how the man could have known who she was; in the dim light her red hair flowing from under the fencing mask had lost its distinctive color, and the only bit of flesh that showed was the nape of her neck and the fingers of her left hand. But Melnik knew that each fencer's style is distinctive, and anyone familiar with it could identify her from the lunges, parries and footwork as easily as by the shape of her nose or the curl of her mouth.

He stood watching her for ten minutes, until with a sudden shout of "E-yah!" she skipped two steps forward, disengaged her foil from her opponent's, lunged and scored a hit just under the bib. They took off their masks, shook hands and stood talking together for a few moments, catching their breath. When they parted, she saw Melnik.

"What a surprise," she said, coming up to him, taking off her fencing glove and shaking hands. "I thought you'd be in Washington with Charlie."

He shook his head. He had offered to go, of course, but Charles had turned him down. The trip was one of the necessary evils of government service, he had said, and there was no need to inflict it on an ally. He had to report in to headquarters on their progress in the investigation, to keep the other two departments—the CIA and the Treasury Department—up to date, and to fight off the attempts they would certainly make to take over jurisdiction as the lead agency for the Dallas investigation.

"Standard procedure," Werther said. "Whenever any two or three government agencies have to cooperate, we're always bickering over who takes the lead and the final credit. The CIA always tries with anything like this, where it's clearly an effort from outside the country, but they know and we know and they know we know that we have jurisdiction over anything that happens within our borders, and it's pretty clear that if anything is going to happen, this is where it will be. So it's just to show how keen they are in case anyone's looking."

"I understand. But why the Treasury Department?" Melnik asked.

"They operate the Secret Service, which is responsible for the President's safety. If Dallas should turn out to be an attempt on the President's life, they could claim authority, so of course they're looking at everything we find out to see if they can construe it that way. Don't worry; they can't. I'll be back tomorrow."

*So what am I doing here tonight?* Melnik asked himself.

Lori asked him the same question, and then immediately answered it herself. "Oh, that's right," she said. "You're a fencer too, aren't you?"

The three of them had had dinner together the previous weekend, and when Charles had mentioned Lori's fencing, David had said that he himself had fenced for the Israeli national team. "You said épée was your weapon, didn't you?" she asked now, and turned to look around the room. "I only fence foil, but let me see if there's anyone here. Would you like to work out?"

"I don't have any equipment."

"That's never a problem. We can dig up something for you. Oh, look, there's Tommy Halpern. He's very good. Are you in shape?"

"Enough to hack around," Melnik said, and Lori took him over to meet Tommy and to fix him up with some borrowed equipment.

Lori watched Melnik, at first with curiosity and then with pleasure. He balanced easily on the balls of his feet, his left hand held high behind him for balance. His right hand was extended but not stiff, the point of the épée floating nearly motionless, barely quivering from side to side above his opponent's blade. His whole body gave the impression of a snake—no, a panther—ready to strike. Then there would be a feint and a slash, his left hand slapping down backward hard and tight, his right leg sliding forward like a shark through water, the épée extending in a deadly stroke, and the action would be over.

She could see that he was out of practice; the accuracy of his point was not as adept as the sinuous measure of his motions, and half the time he would miss the evading target and lose the point. But *he* would win it or lose it; his opponent—who was really quite good, she reminded herself—had little to do with it. If his point had been accurate, he would have dominated the match.

When they finished she allowed him to rest a minute, sitting on the bench with the sweat pouring from his face and soaking through his jacket, and then asked if he'd like to try the foil.

"With you?" he asked. "I'm not really a foil fencer, and you're good. I'll be a little clumsy."

*No,* she thought. *You would never be clumsy.*

They touched swords, and then she initiated a one-two attack, feinting hard to his left and immediately disengaging and lunging forward to hit him on the chest. With the first motion his right arm shot out and he caught her square as she came in. Then he stepped back and lifted his mask. "I'm sorry, that was your point. You had right of way."

It was the classic blunder of the épée man fencing foil. In épée, which is a re-creation of the old dueling sword, all that counts is to hit your enemy first. Foil is a more stylized weapon, and the rules are formal; with her initial feint she had established right of way, and he had to parry her sword before he could riposte, so she had won the point. In real life, of course, she would be dead. *But this is not real life, is it?* she thought. *Is it?*

They fenced off and on for another hour, as gradually the *salle* emptied around them. When someone called, "Lori, I'm leaving now. You lock up, all right?" they stopped, lifted their masks and looked around, surprised to find the room nearly empty. "Okay," she called, and waved as the last member walked out and left them alone.

"Should we go?" David asked.

"It's all right," she said. "We're very informal. The last person always locks up. Let's go a few more minutes, shall we?"

The slipped their masks back into place and went at it again, till finally she flèched past him, catching him squarely in the ribs as she left the mat, then continued across the room and collapsed on a bench, her chest heaving. "Oh God, that was good," she said, pulling off her mask, "but I'm exhausted." She lowered the tip of her weapon to the floor, her head thrown back, her face toward the ceiling. "I can't move a muscle. I'm totally defenseless," she said. "Skewer me if you will. I can't resist."

He walked over, stood in front of her for a moment, then touched her lightly on the breast with the tip of his sword. "Touché," he said, and sat down beside her.

He was glad it had turned out this way. He must have been mad, he told himself, to have wanted to start anything with her. When she had touched him that first night at her house, it must have been an accident and she had been too embarrassed to apologize. He was glad he had misunderstood, though, for otherwise he wouldn't have come here tonight, and it had been fun.

He took off his mask and they sat together on the bench sucking in air deeply, feeling their blood pound and their sweat drip, leaning back against the tiled wall, feeling the chill of the tiles seep through their wet canvas jackets into their shoulders and necks. After a while she said, "The men's locker room is over there," pointing to a door on the far wall.

"Yes, I know," he said. "That's where I changed."

"There's a shower in there, too. There should be a pile of towels just inside the door." She added, "Bring out your clothes and I'll take them home and wash them."

They sat another two minutes as their breathing calmed; then he said, "Meet you out here in ten minutes?" and she nodded.

The shower room was large and brightly lit. He stripped, left his uniform in a wet pile near the door, and walked to the first nozzle. A heavy stream of water spurted out and he luxuriated under it.

In the women's locker Lori walked naked into the shower room and stood in front of one of the cubicles unable to decide, ashamed of her boldness in even thinking such thoughts. But sometimes she felt so stifled. She knew Charlie loved her, but she wasn't sure *he* knew it. Just once she would like him to look at her with honest lust, to let loose the passions she knew were in him. . . .

No. That wasn't his style, she thought. Nor had it been hers. She couldn't imagine how she'd had the nerve for what she'd done that first night when she'd met David. She closed her eyes involuntarily as she remembered standing with her back to him talking to Charles; and then swiftly—so swiftly she could try to pretend it hadn't happened—reaching behind her and brushing her hand across the front of David's trousers. . . .

Oh, God. She opened her eyes, wiped her hand involuntarily on her hip and found herself looking into the mirror across the room. She saw herself standing naked and alone in the neon whiteness of the institutional shower room, and somehow the impersonal light emphasized her smallness, femininity and nakedness. Her skin was nearly pure white, the white body topped by a cloud of red hair and touched below by a barely visible puff of reddish hair that hid nothing. Looking at herself, she couldn't help imagining him standing now in the men's shower room even more naked, without even the slightest shielding of hair.

Then, without coming to a conscious decision, she saw in the mirror her naked body turn away and walk out of the frame, back toward the door. She walked through the locker room, and without hesitating opened the door to the *salle* and stepped naked through it. Her bare feet padded across the wooden floor; it seemed to take an hour to cross the gigantic room. Glancing neither right nor left, she walked straight to the door to the men's locker room, opened it and walked to the showers.

He was under the water, slightly turned away from her, and she stood watching him. He was as beautiful as she had imagined: strong, clean, streamlined, looking like nothing so much as a mysterious, exotic android. Then, as if he felt her eyes on him, he turned and simply stood there, looking at her.

She nearly ran back through the locker room, through the *salle*, to the safety of the women's shower. Nearly. But then, still without deciding, she moved forward instead.

He watched her little feet slap against the wet white tile floor. Aside from that flaming crown of hair on her head she was nearly as hairless as he. He had never felt so naked in his life. He nearly closed his eyes as he started to swell and protrude. Then she was nearly but not quite touching him; she raised her eyes to his face and put both hands lightly on his shoulders. The water from the shower was still spraying over him, splattering onto her, droplets catching her eyebrows, glistening in her glowing red hair.

"I wanted to see what you look like," she said simply. "I've never seen such a really naked man before." Without taking her eyes from him she reached over, picked up a bar of soap and rubbed it lightly across his chest and shoulders. With both hands she began to rub his skin, working up a lather, washing him lower and lower. He put his left hand behind her neck, touching the cool skin just under her hair. With his right hand he reached up to his chest, lifted off a handful of white suds and spread them across her breasts. He pulled her gently closer and began to rub the suds over her skin as the hot water bounced off them both. His right hand slid wetly over the tips of her breasts as her hands lowered on his body and their heads bent forward and their lips gently opened and met.

27

"Okay, gentlemen, listen up, please." Werther clapped his hands for silence and got it. The chattering stopped, and the ten men in the crowded conference room turned to him and waited.

He had returned from Washington this afternoon with a mandate from the Director: Find Mohammed Asri, penetrate the Dallas operation, stop it cold. Period. No excuses. *Just stop it cold*. Very helpful, he thought on the shuttle back to New York. The Director's stern eyes, tight lips and firmly clasped fingers placed on the center of his desk were certainly inspiring, but he could have used something a little more practical, like a suggestion or two on precisely how he was supposed to accomplish this. Like, for example, where to start?

*Never mind*, he told himself. *You're the expert, aren't you?* The Director's job is to tell people to do things, and to get the money from Congress and the authority from the attorney general to allow them to do it. The agent's job is to know how to do it. There wasn't really any doubt about how to proceed at this point; the good thing about having no choice is that you don't waste time worrying about alternatives. They had to find Mohammed Asri, but they couldn't actually go out and look for him; he could be anywhere in the country.

They would do what they could to find him, of course. They would saturate the police offices of the country with his description and photograph, and if he robbed a 7-Eleven, shoplifted a skateboard from Toys 'R Us or maybe even drove twenty-five miles an hour in a school zone anywhere in Oregon, Texas, Florida or Maine, somebody might remember the circular asking about a five-foot-nine gentleman of Middle Eastern countenance, and maybe they would hold him long enough for an FBI agent to take a look. Maybe, but most likely not.

So Werther looked around the quiet room and said, "It's time to get to work."

The agents knew what to do as well as he; there was no need to spell it out for them. There was just one way to begin to track down something as nebulous as Dallas, and that was to begin to haul in the net that the Bureau kept spread wide at all times and see what little fish might be trapped there. Then the little fish might lead to bigger fish. "Talk to your marks," Werther said. "As discreetly as you like, but talk to them fast."

Every field agent had his own little band of informers. Between them and the undercover agents who penetrated every organized band of known subversives in the country they covered the underworld like a net. It was dangerous to use them recklessly, for often the information they provided could be traced back to them, and then they would disappear, perhaps turning up weeks later in a fresh landfill or a forest grave. Usually the FBI was content to accept hints and generalities from their marks in place of specific information about particular operations; they were more concerned with keeping the net in good repair and their sources anonymous than with actually pulling in a particular fish.

Werther reminded them of all this and then said, "But now it's time to play hardball. This guy Asri didn't disappear without organized help, and organization only comes from people. The more organization, the more people have to be in on it, and we'd better goddamn well know some of those people. If we can't turn up somebody who knows something about what's going on in an operation like this, then we've just been sitting around jerking each other off all these years. I don't want anything held back, I don't care who you have to jeopardize, I don't care who gets burned, I don't care if you lose every goddamn one of your marks. No holding someone back for a rainy day. Gentlemen, it's pouring out there right now!"

He looked around the room at each of them in turn, finishing with Melnik who sat in the rear. This would show the Israeli how the FBI could operate, he thought. "Any questions?" he asked.

After a moment's silence a dark man sitting near the front asked, "How much do we let out?"

It was a good point. The more you know, the more you learn; the more you tell, the better questions you can ask. But the basic tenet of all intelligence work is secrecy: the least said the better.

Secrecy could go too far, of course. Werther remembered a story from World War II about a low-level scientist at Oak Ridge who had come up with a novel way of separating uranium isotopes. But when he submitted his idea to the people in charge, the security chief had noticed that the scientist didn't have a clearance high enough to allow him to work on a project as secret as this would be, so the idea was taken away from him. The trouble was, nobody else then at Oak Ridge had the specific training to pursue the method further. So while the FBI was conducting a thorough security check on the scientist, trying to raise him to a Q clearance level, the idea stayed on a few pieces of paper in a maximum security safe in the security chief's office at Oak Ridge. The war was over before the scientist got his Q clearance, and he returned to his university in disgust.

There were a lot of horror stories like that. Still, security was the name of the game. In this operation they had two bits of information: they knew the name Dallas and they knew Mohammed Asri. From the way Asri had given them the slip it was a fair bet that the people they were after were either aware that they knew about him or were at least worried about it, but they probably had no idea that the name Dallas was out in the open.

Werther decided to compromise. "You can mention Asri," he said, "but not Dallas. I want a total lock on that name: it doesn't leave this room. Everybody got that straight?" He looked around the room. "Any other questions?"

There were none. He nodded abruptly. "Okay," he said quietly but with authority. "Get moving. Let's squeeze some testicles, gentlemen. Let's squeeze hard and see what pops out."

Melnik didn't know what to say. He remained seated in the rear corner as the agents filed out of the room, until finally he was left alone with Werther. "You seem to have everything well in hand," he said.

Werther shrugged. "You never know. Maybe. We'll turn up something eventually."

"Eventually can be a long time."

"That's the problem," Werther agreed. "I wish I knew how much time we had."

Again Melnik didn't know what to say. He didn't even know what he wanted to say. "I guess that's it, then," he said. It was time for him to go back to Israel. He felt a twinge of regret, but didn't recognize it. He never felt regret about leaving the women he found on his travels, so he thought that what he was feeling must be a sort of relief. It had been a mistake to start something with a fellow operative's wife; it had been not only wicked but stupid. Well, now it was over. He would leave the U.S. and the Werthers not a moment too soon. But he was confused in his thoughts. Surely relief was supposed to feel good, not sad? He wondered if he could manage to see Lori one more time before he left. . . . No. For God's sake, no, he thought. She was this man's wife. It happened once; okay, things happen, but to skulk around behind his back? No.

"Hope you don't mind," Werther said.

"Mind?"

"Waiting around. Might be a while."

"Wait around?" Melnik was confused. "Me? Wait for what?"

"For us to find Asri," Werther said, smiling apologetically. "It will be boring for you, but you're the only one who can put a positive make on him."

Okay, Werther told himself; I did it. He hadn't liked it, but he'd promised the Director he'd be polite, even ingratiating, and so he had done it. But he hadn't promised to like it. He didn't want the Israeli hanging around his operation, and he'd told the Director so. His reasons made sense, but the Director hadn't bought them—or rather he had his own reasons, which took precedence. The Director wanted Melnik around to identify Asri when and if they caught him. Werther had argued that he'd seen Asri at the airport himself and could make him, but the Director made the point that Werther had thought they'd surrounded him at the restaurant, and it had turned out to be Rasheed Amon. Since he had goofed, he couldn't argue the point.

Then the Director went on to say it was also a question of diplomacy. This was a Near East problem and it had been decided "at the highest levels" that Near East intelligence operations came within the Israeli sphere of influence. The Israelis had to be stroked. "You, Werther, are the assigned stroker," the Director said, "and Mr. Melnik is today's strokee." End of argument.

So now Werther stood facing Melnik, smiling apologetically and expressing his hope that they would work happily together. The only thing that made it bearable was the clear indication from the Israeli's manner that he didn't like it one bit better than Werther did.

*   *   *

Melnik's first reaction had been a surge of excitement. It wasn't right for him to stay because of Lori, but if he was ordered to . . . Even as he began to realize the implications another wave of resentment swept over him. He was being *ordered* to stay by the FBI? The day would never come when the Mossad took orders from the FBI! If there was a legitimate reason, perhaps he'd accommodate them, but to hang around and do nothing for days, weeks, probably even months while the Americans chased shadows in the night because they couldn't tell one Arab from another was ridiculous. He simply would not do it.

And Lori? If he stayed he couldn't help seeing her again, and he didn't want to make love to another man's wife behind his back.

Melnik nodded politely, then strode off to find a phone to call Tel Aviv.

"So, David," Julian Mazor said. "It's good to hear from you again. This is a very good connection. Where are you calling from?"

"New York. FBI headquarters. It's raining. The sun hasn't been out for two days."

"Lovely." Mazor sighed. It was night in Tel Aviv, and as he glanced out of his window he saw in the darkness tomorrow's inevitable bright sunshine. It was worth your life to walk out into that sun. "So what can I do for you, David?"

Melnik knew it was no good. As soon as Mazor called him by his first name he knew that his superior had been expecting the call—which meant that it had all been settled. Still, now that he was on the phone, he might as well go through with the farce. "They lost Asri," he said.

"Yes, I know," Mazor replied. "Their people have been in touch with ours."

"I've been asked to stay here," Melnik said, "while they look for him."

"Yes, I know. Don't worry, it's all been cleared here. Think of it as a vacation."

"I don't—"

"Nonsense, David. Who deserves a vacation better than you? Go ahead, enjoy yourself."

He had a sudden vision of Lori naked falling backward onto the bed. "I don't want to enjoy myself!"

Silence. He knew that he must sound like a petulant child. Lori naked, holding her arms out to him. . . . "I've got work to do. I can't just remain here for a month. It could take *longer* than a month. They don't know what to do or how to—"

"Help them, David. It's not their fault they aren't surrounded on all sides by fanatical murderers, not their fault they don't have our advantages. Teach them a thing or two. It's all been decided, you see. The Director has been fussing for better relations with the Americans ever since he took office, and this is the perfect opportunity. Do a good job, David; put them in our debt."

Melnik could feel himself sinking with nothing but the telephone line to save him. He tried once more. "The thing is," he began, and then paused, for there was really nothing to say.

"Yes, David?"

"It's just that I really don't like it here," he said weakly.

"Oh." This time the silence was longer. "Well, you see, David, the problem is that Golda is dead."

"Golda?"

"Yes. I'm sorry, but what can I do? If Golda were alive I could go to her and say, 'Mrs. Meir, David Melnik doesn't like it in America.' And Tante Golda would say 'Cluck, cluck,' or 'Tcch, tchh,' and she would bring you home and make you a nice hot bowl of chicken soup and matzoh balls. But if I were to go to Yitzhak Shamir and say that David doesn't like it there—well, I'm afraid Yitzhak wouldn't be terribly impressed."

"What you're trying to say, ever so delicately, is that I stay here."

"Yes, David," Mazor said softly. "You stay there. Enjoy."

28

Special Agent Robert Abrams worked out of the New York office under Charles Werther, but just as the FBI is mandated to work on regional and federal crimes rather than on local problems, so each agent has tentacles spreading out beyond the confines of his immediate vicinity. In the first few days after Werther's exhortation to squeeze testicles, Abrams had spent his time among his New York contacts. Developing nothing there, he had began to move farther afield. This morning he was meeting Alfredo San Medro for breakfast at the York Inn in Cheltenham, a wealthy suburb fifteen minutes' drive from Alfredo's neighborhood and two or three light-years distant. No one who knew San Medro was likely to be there.

Still, Abrams's informer wasn't happy. "Hey, man," he said as he slid into his seat at the table. San Medro never actually stood, sat down, walked or ran; he slid as if on a film of oil from one place to another. "I don't like this, you know?" He glanced uneasily around the room, though he had perused it carefully from the bar before Abrams had entered. "What's the big circumcision, anyhow?"

Abrams thought this over; San Medro sometimes got his slang a bit mixed up in his efforts to assimilate. "Nothing," he said. "I've just missed you. Friendships atrophy if contacts dwindle. Besides, you never write," he added, echoing his mother's lament.

San Medro gave an unamused laugh as he pulled out a cigarette, glanced once more around the room and hunched over the table. "Look, man, don't be cute, you know? I'm a busy man, I got responsibilities. There's ten places I gotta be right—"

"Wrong," Abrams said with a sudden hard edge to his voice. "There's just one place you ever have to be, and that's with me when I want you." He allowed a slight pause. "You got that?" He laid his hand on the table, palm open, facing upwards. "Your ass belongs right in there," he said, slowly closing his hand into a fist and turning it over. "And when I say 'Jump,' the only thing I want to hear you say is 'When can I come down?' "

A waiter materialized at their side. "How are you this morning?" he asked with a bright smile. "My name is Teddy, and I'll be taking care of you today. May I suggest our Belgian waffles with strawberries and mocha ice cream? Or would you prefer—"

"Beer," San Medro said. "I'll have a beer."

"Yes, sir. We have Michelob and Heineken on draft, or in bottles we have Dos Equis, Bass Ale—"

"Just bring me a goddamn beer, man!"

"One Heineken and one coffee," Abrams said, and Teddy moved away in a tiff. He had come to work here in the expectation of a certain class of clientele, but the boors were everywhere nowadays.

The relationship between Abrams and San Medro had begun with a routine cocaine-trafficking bust in which San Medro, turned in by a junkie, had in turn fingered his local distributor. In the several years since then he had managed to pass on enough information to satisfy Abrams, while not giving enough to betray his identification as a source among his own class.

Now Abrams had to probe gently but deeply, like a dentist working on a difficult abscess without anesthetic. He didn't have to remind San Medro each time he worked with him (or rather, *on* him) that he had enough knowledge of his activities to send him away, but if San Medro proved recalcitrant he did have to point out that perhaps he didn't know enough about what was happening in the community to be worth the bother of protecting him.

He waited until Teddy had brought the beer and coffee, and taken their breakfast order. "So what's happening?" he asked.

San Medro visibly relaxed, slumping a little in his chair as he drank off his beer. So this was to be just another fishing trip. He shrugged. "Just the usual shit, man," he said, wondering how few tidbits he could get away with passing on.

Abrams had rebelled against his parents. He didn't want to be a doctor, he had told them, because he didn't want to spend all his life talking to sick people; they depressed him. So look at him now. He sighed. Rebellion against parental authority is perhaps the most self-destructive of all our instincts. How did evolution ever come up with it? He sat staring at this disgusting bit of flotsam, wanting nothing so much as to get up and walk out. He didn't want to spend his morning talking to this scumbag. But if he got nothing out of him—as he probably would not—he would only have to spend the next day, and the next, with one after another of his marks, each more disgusting than the last. What, he wondered, had he ever thought depressing about a simple honest man with leprosy?

"I'm looking for something big," he said.

San Medro waited while Abrams looked at him, then began to squirm. "That's it?" he asked finally. "Something big?"

Abrams had nothing else to tell him. He managed to look judicious, as if he could say more but chose not to.

*Christ almighty*, San Medro thought as he took another swig of beer. *What kind of assholes am I dealing with?* "Like, you know, man," he said, invoking all his linguistic tools, "what the fuck am I supposed to say to that? You tell me what you want, I see what I can do. But something big? Everybody got something big going down, man. You listen to all the 'something big' talk in this town, you don't have time to screw your sister." As he talked his mind was racing. What did he know that he wasn't connected with? What could he give this son of a bitch to get him off his back without word getting out and his ending up with both knees broken?

Abrams lifted his napkin to his lips and glanced over San Medro's shoulder in an unmistakable signal. San Medro spun around in his chair, looking around. "Hey, what you doin', man? Christ, what's goin' on here?" He couldn't spot anybody.

"Do you know what the FBI was founded for?"

"Huh?"

"The FBI was started as a federal police force to combat the white slavery trade. Girls sold into prostitution and transported across state lines for immoral purposes, the law said. The Mann Act."

San Medro looked bewildered.

"The penalty is life imprisonment, and that's what I'm going to pull you in on. White slavery."

"You crazy, man? All my girls are spics! Every one, I swear!"

Abrams pushed his chair back from the table. "Those two men over there," he said as San Medro swiveled around to look at them, "will pick you up when I leave." He wiped his lips with his napkin again and dropped it conspicuously on the table. "It would be better if you didn't make a scene."

San Medro grabbed Abrams's wrist, looked around once more at the two men who seemed to be paying them no attention, and said, "Wait a minute, man. Let's deal."

"You don't have to worry. Any public defender worth his salt will make sure the jury finds out how you've cooperated with us in the past. The courts will be lenient."

"You crazy?" San Medro whispered violently, looking around the restaurant to be sure no one heard. "I be a dead man!"

Abrams nodded. "Sure, I understand. You'd want to stay silent about our past association. You have a reputation to defend. You'd rather go to jail. But your lawyer will also have *his* reputation to defend. He'll find a way of bringing it all out at the trial." He smiled at San Medro and freed his wrist, but waited.

San Medro licked his lips. This motherfucker was crazy. He had to give him something. If only he knew what he was looking for!

He thought of something. "I don't know how big this is," he said, "but the man said it was big. Very big, he said. But I don't know if it's what you want?"

Abrams inclined his head slightly. His face remained unconvinced. San Medro was the tenth mark he had talked to in the past week. Nothing had come from the others and he expected nothing from this one. But Werther was right; their best chance was to talk to all these scum, and perhaps someday something would come from one of them. But it wouldn't be this one, or the next one or the next; it would be someone else's mark, on another day, in another century, in another city, in another state. "Try me," he said. "What man?"

"I don't know him, so don't hold me to this, but he said his name was Dallas."

Abrams was a field agent; he was not one of the ten men who had met with Werther in his office where the decision had been made to keep the name Dallas secret. He had never heard the name and knew nothing about it. So he yawned. *Here we go again*, he thought, taking out his little green notebook. *Another bubba myseh.* But he was a good agent; he would write it all down. "Tell me," he said.

"Hey, man, give me a break," San Medro whined. "This is worth my life, you know."

"What's your life worth?" Abrams asked. He took out his wallet, extracted two twenty-dollar bills and laid them on the table.

San Medro sniffed. "Man, you working for the wrong people. I tip my doorman that to take the fucking dog for a walk."

"If I pick up that money again, I pick up my napkin too," Abrams said, glancing again at the two men behind San Medro.

"Hey, don't get nervous," San Medro said, reaching across the table and picking up the money. "What did I say? I only—"

"Tell me about Mr. Dallas."

"Sure. That's what I'm going to do. But I don't know what you're so nervous about. That's all I'm saying, you know? 'Cause this guy Dallas, he's one crazy hombre."

"What do you mean, crazy?"

"Well, either he's crazy or he's looking to start a war, is what I'm saying. Like he wants me to find him a goddamn armoly."

"A what?"

"A whole goddamn armoly, man!"

Abrams looked at him for a moment; then it suddenly dawned. "An armory?" he asked.

"That's what I'm telling you, man! All *kinds* a' crap. Like rifles and Uzis—okay, why not? But a bazooka, man! And grenades!"

Abrams started to write in his notebook. "Give me the whole list," he said. "What did you get for him?"

"Hey, man, not me! Where I gonna get stuff like that? I'm just telling you what he *asked* for, man." He smiled greasily. "Hey, you know me, all I got's like a couple of girls and a little grass, right?"

Abrams didn't bother to look up. "Just give me the list," he said, and reluctantly San Medro did. "And the man's name?"

"Dallas," San Medro said. "I already told you."

"Is that his real name?" Abrams asked.

San Medro gave him a look as if he should know better. "That's what he told me to call him, man, you know? Like I don't ask questions. Not like you, man. We're in different lines of work, you know?"

All of which was true, according to San Medro's concept of truth. In fact he did know that Dallas's real name was Gee Hardy, and that he had smuggled drugs for several years. When the word had been passed that a man named Dallas was looking for guns and heavy stuff, that he would pay well for finding them and that he could be trusted, San Medro's reaction had been reflexive: "Skip the bullshit, man. What's he offering and who the fuck is he?" And being a comer in the local crime structure, he had been told. He hadn't really cared what the man's true name was; he simply wanted to be sure that the people above him trusted the guy, and that the money would be worth his valuable time. So now he was acting in strict accordance with his concept of honesty when he reported only that he had been told to call the man Dallas.

Abrams was thinking about his own problem as he wrote this down. "Dallas, that's all? No first name?"

"Man, he wasn't looking to date my sister, you know? It's just a business deal. You hear what I'm telling you? Dallas, that's all I know. Now, if that helps you"—San Medro spread his hands wide to show his innocence—"you know I'm always glad to help any way I can. But if it don't help, well, I can't tell you no more if I don't *know* no more, can I?"

"How do you get in touch with this man Dallas?"

"Man, I don't get in touch with him, he got in touch with me."

"How did you tell him when you found the guns for him?"

"I just got finished telling you, man! I ain't *got* no guns! I tell him he gotta go find somebody else—"

"Yes, you told me all that."

"That's what I'm telling you, man! I *told* you! I *keep* telling you! I told you everything! That's all there is. There ain't no more!"

That was the problem. *Had* San Medro told him everything? Abrams had to make a judgment call. It was clear that San Medro wasn't going to say anything else at this time. He had played his cards and was sitting tight. Was he bluffing? If Abrams put on more pressure, would he crack? The only way to put on more pressure was to take him in, but once he did that he'd lose him. Because word would get out—word always got out—and if he released San Medro after questioning, his friends would never believe that he hadn't talked to regain his freedom; he would never again be trusted, and so he would be useless. Alternatively, if he was sent up for several years, he would obviously be lost for that time, and he in his turn would never trust Abrams again. Either way he would be gone forever. Was it worth it? Did he in fact have anything else to tell?

San Medro sat picking at his little fingernail. He knew what thoughts were racing around Abrams's head, and he couldn't lift his head to look him in the eye.

That meant nothing. It didn't mean that he was dishonest in this particular instance; it meant only that he had lived a lifetime of dishonesty and never believed anyone, so he couldn't believe that anyone would believe him. If people did, San Medro felt he had conned them, even if he'd told them the truth. He could look directly into the eyes of anyone he had power over, whether he was lying to them or not. He could swear to each of his girls that they were number one, could look straight into a junkie's eyes and call on heaven to witness that the crack supply hadn't come in this week and so the price for what he happened to have had to be doubled, and they knew he was lying and he knew they knew it and they knew that he knew it and didn't give a damn because they were *his*, man, their ass belonged to him. But even when he was telling the truth to anyone who owned *his* ass, he cowered and played with his fingernails, biting off little pieces, inspecting them and throwing them away. It wasn't truth and lies that counted; it was power and fear.

So Abrams knew that he couldn't get any clues from San Medro's overt behavior; yet he had to decide whether to go back to Werther with this or bring the punk in.

In the end, there was no real choice. A field agent's career depends on his marks more than on anything else. San Medro was one of his best. Abrams could destroy him on the chance that what he was saying was important and that he was lying about not knowing more, or he could take back to Werther what information he had. Twenty years from now no one would remember what information he had brought back today, he thought, but twenty years from now someone would be looking over his career record to decide if he should be moved up into high administrative levels or passed over, phased out or retired, and the thing that would make the most difference in his record would be the quality of his marks.

Abrams decided that the story San Medro was telling was not important enough to risk losing him, and was probably all he knew anyhow. He closed his green notebook, put it away, pushed back from the table and started to get up.

"Hey, man! What you doing?"

"I'm leaving," Abrams said. "Thanks a lot. We'll be in touch."

San Medro leaned across the table and whispered, "What about those two?" He gestured secretively across his chest, indicating the men behind him.

Abrams had forgotten. Glancing back now, he saw that the two men he didn't know had left some time before. He hadn't noticed them go. "They've gone," he said. "You've been a good boy. Nobody's going to bother you." He stood up, then leaned over the table again. "I'll be in touch, kid. Don't get lost."

"Hey, man, what you think? I'll be around. You know where to find me."

"Yes, Alfredo," Abrams said softly. "Don't you forget it. I know where to find you."

As Abrams drove back to New York, Lori Werther was opening the door to her apartment. David Melnik stood there, looking uncomfortable.

"Hello," she said. "Come in."

"Yes. Thank you," he answered formally and took two awkward steps across the threshold.

She closed the door. "Nice jacket," she said. Sunlight was streaming in through the open windows, and she realized it was the first time she had ever seen him in daylight.

"Thank you," he said again. "This is the one I got at the store you sent me to, remember?"

"Yes, of course I remember. Come in, won't you?" She led the way into the living room, tingling as she walked in front of him. My God, she couldn't believe it. She felt like a schoolgirl waiting for something wicked to happen. What *was* going to happen? He had called her this morning at her law office and asked if they could meet. He felt they should talk.

"Yes, of course," she replied. "Let's have lunch." Since she had to go down to the bank district to take a deposition later that morning, they might as well meet at her apartment. She'd have her secretary make a restaurant reservation somewhere close by. There was no need to hide their meeting, for it would be their last. She felt perfectly innocent. What had happened had happened—there was no denying *that*—but it would never happen again. He was Charlie's temporary business partner, a charming man, and she would be pleasant and friendly. Then the doorbell had rung, and as she walked to the door to answer it she felt a quick nervous thrill, almost like an electric shock. Then when she saw him the tingle permeated her whole body. As she walked in front of him down the hallway to the living room she was aware of him following close behind her, and at each step she wondered if his hands were going to descend on her shoulders and pull her backward into him, against his lean, hard, clean body. . . .

He couldn't just continue to ignore what had happened, Melnik had thought as he awoke that morning. It had been three days since he had visited her at the fencing *salle* and she had ended up in his shower, and he couldn't just forget about it. It had been wonderful, but it was terrible. He had to talk to her.

At first he had thought that he could afford to say nothing. He would leave America in a day or two and they could think of each other as figures in an erotic dream inhabiting other worlds. But now that he had to stay they would have to make their peace, to acknowledge with honesty what had happened and to make a mutual commitment not to allow it to happen again.

He had thought all this as he woke up, as he talked to her on the phone, as he walked to her apartment and as he climbed the steps. He thought all this as he knocked on her door, right up to the moment he felt a tremor of the flesh, and as she opened the floor it swept up from his ankles and left him weak as he stood staring at her.

"Hello," she said. "Come in."

As she turned and walked in front of him down the hallway to the living room, chattering away as casually as if he had come to clean the furniture, he felt a terrible longing to reach out, put his hands on her shoulders and pull her backward, to run his hands down the front of her dress and—

She stopped so suddenly that he nearly bumped into her. He fought to catch his balance, skipping sideways to avoid touching her. If he touched her, he knew he would be lost.

She said, "We could eat here."

She thought she might faint; she had to turn and look at him. "We could eat here," she said without thinking. They had to settle this, after all, and it would be awkward in a restaurant. She had to make him understand that this couldn't go on. "What would you like to eat?" she asked.

"You," he said, the word forcing itself out of his mouth, which was so dry that he could barely breathe. The word came out of his subconscious, ripping away the lining of his throat.

"You," he said, and the clotted huskiness of his voice crumbled the barriers she had held in place. She felt her clothing dissolve in the lust of his eyes, burning into her flesh. As she stepped forward he raised his arms and enfolded her, and slowly they fell together to the floor.

<br>

## 29

Charles Werther's late lunch consisted of a chicken sandwich on stale rye, sent up to his office from the Puerto Rican delicatessen down the block. He had spent the hour reading through reports of his agents' activities. Now, midway through the afternoon, he struck gold.

"Bingo!" He slapped his hand down on the desk. He couldn't believe his luck. He had been looking for the dragnet to turn up some clue to Asri's whereabouts, but he hadn't dared hope Dallas would surface instead. He pressed the buzzer on his desk. "Get Abrams and Melnik in here right away," he said when his secretary answered.

Abrams entered his office within the minute. "Who is this San Medro?" Werther asked without preamble.

"One of my marks," Abrams said. "A punk." He was surprised to be called into the boss's office within half an hour of submitting his report.

"Where is he now?"

Abrams was taken aback by the question. "Right this minute? I don't know."

"You didn't bring him in?"

"No sir, I didn't think—"

"You didn't think what?" Werther demanded.

"I didn't . . . I didn't think what he had to say . . . was anything terribly important—" Abrams stuttered.

Werther spun around in his chair, facing the rear wall for a second, then quickly got control of himself and turned back. It wasn't Abrams's fault. Maybe he should have let everyone know about the name Dallas. Still, this was better. If Abrams had known how important the name was, he might have given it away to this San Medro, and who knows how far up the line his reaction might have traveled? This way the Dallas group still didn't know that the name was known. He glanced down again at Abrams's report.

His buzzer sounded and his secretary said, "Mr. Melnik's still out to lunch."

Werther looked at his watch. It was nearly four o'clock. "Christ," he muttered, "do they take siestas in Israel? Well, have him see me as soon as he gets in." He turned back to Abrams. "You know where to find this San Medro? You know where he lives?"

"Yes, sir."

"I want a tap put on his phone, and a twenty-four-hour tail. I want photos of anyone who talks to him, who even *looks* at him. Can you handle that?"

"Yes, sir," Abrams said, but Werther saw the worried look in his eyes. It would take someone with clout to ram this through the Philadelphia office. Werther pressed the buzzer. "Alice," he said, "get me a car. Also, put in a call to Philly." He gave her instructions to relay on to the Philadephia office, then turned back to Abrams. "Let's go," he said.

The buzzer sounded again. "Mr. Melnik's just come in," Alice said.

Werther grunted. Taking his hat from the rack, he opened the door and strode out. The Israeli was standing there looking guilty. As well he should, taking four hours for lunch.

"Alice says you wanted to see me?" Melnik asked.

"Where the hell have you been?" Werther countered, and was mildly surprised to see the man so taken aback. He looked like a little kid caught sneaking off to the movies instead of doing his homework. Hell, he didn't have anything to do anyhow—not until they caught Asri—but the Director wanted him involved. "Never mind," he said. "Put your hat back on. We're going to Philadelphia."

San Medro had paid the bill at the restaurant and then waited another five minutes. He was in no hurry. He wanted to give Abrams plenty of time so that he would know exactly where he stood. Finally he pushed back his chair, walked out to his car and drove off.

From that moment he looked around a whole lot. He wanted to see if any other car pulled out of the restaurant parking lot after him. None did, but that proved nothing; maybe they just weren't stupid. There was too much traffic to be sure that no one had begun following him from a side street. He drove half a mile down Old York Road and then turned left. Three cars followed. He continued on for a few blocks, then turned left again. None of the three followed. Instead of continuing back to Old York Road he struck out cross-country, taking side streets, twice coming to dead ends, at which he had to back up and turn around.

When he was convinced that no one was following him, he pulled in at a gas station to use a pay phone.

"Office," a female voice said after the fourth ring.

"This Dallas Enterprises?" San Medro asked.

"The office is closed now; this is the answering service."

The office was always closed. "I wanna leave a message for Mr. Dallas," San Medro said. "Tell him to contact Alfredo."

## 30

"How did things go in California?" Freddy asked.

"On the button," Hardy said. "Nakaoka's perfect. Cold as a dolphin's tit, and a better shot than I am."

"Is that necessary?"

"Toss me another beer." Hardy finished off the first one, kicked off his shoes and leaned back on the couch, closing his eyes. It had been a long flight from San Francisco and he was tired. "Yes, it's necessary," he explained with quiet satisfaction. "He's got to be either piss-poor or precision-perfect. Anything in between is dangerous."

"Speaking of dangerous," Freddy said, "San Medro called."

Hardy opened his eyes. That couldn't be good news. "What did he want?"

"The FBI picked him up."

"How?"

"He thinks it was just a cold sweep. They didn't seem to know anything."

"They're not holding him?"

"No."

"Did he give them anything?"

"He says he had to. He told them you tried to buy some guns from him but that he turned you down."

"Nothing else?"

"He swears."

Hardy smiled. "That's the first good laugh I've had today. Did he swear on his mother or on his sister's virginity?"

"Both, and on his hope of eternal rest in heaven."

Hardy crossed himself and bowed his head. "Sweet Jesus, full of grace," he said, "do you think the little prick's telling the truth?"

Freddy nodded. "If he was setting us up he'd have overplayed it."

"Okay," Hardy said, trusting Freddy's judgment, "but let's get him out of town before they lean on him again."

"Already taken care of. I wired him ten thousand and told him to take a few weeks in Cancún or Yucatán."

Freddy watched Hardy sip his beer. He knew the signs. "What are you thinking?" he asked.

"If it was a blind bust, if they were just looking around to see what's going on, they didn't find anything. A man named Dallas is looking to buy a bunch of arms. Big deal. The only other thing they know is that a man named Dallas sneaked Mohammed Asri into the country. It might even be two different groups within the Bureau that know these things, and with their bureaucracy neither may know about the other."

"So they don't know anything," Freddy said.

Hardy swirled the beer around in the bottle and stared down into it. "Probably," he said.

The word had a somber ring to it. It wasn't a word you wanted to use often on an operation like this.

"What's done is done," Freddy said. "They've got all they're gonna get. The only other thing San Medro knows is that you actually got the guns, and he's out of town by now anyhow."

Hardy nodded. "Probably," he said. He looked up regretfully but with resolution.

"You want to have a little talk with him?" Freddy asked.

"I think I'd better."

Instead of calling San Medro and making an appointment, Hardy called the man who had originally put them together and got directions to where he lived. He flew into Philadelphia the next day, arriving at 2:00 P.M. He took the subway to the Logan stop in North Philadelphia, walked down Lindley Avenue to Ninth Street, turned south past a school and its basketball courts ringing with the multinational cries of multicolored students, crossed Ruscombe Street and walked down the 4900 block toward San Medro's flat.

Then he kept walking; there was a white van parked midway down the block. No reason why there shouldn't be a van among all the parked cars; lots of people in this country own vans. Probably that's all it was, just somebody's private van.

But there was that word again: probably. He turned east on Rockland up to Broad Street, and went to a movie.

After setting up the surveillance team the previous night, Melnik and Werther had taken a room at a motel a few miles from San Medro's neighborhood. For Melnik it was an awkward situation. As he came out of the shower, rubbing his head and face dry, Werther was already in bed and on the phone to Lori, telling her to pack some clothes for him; he would have an agent pick them up, together with some of Melnik's, and drive them down to Philly. He expected they'd be here for three or four days.

Melnik didn't want to listen. He went back into the bathroom and brushed his teeth with his finger and some cold water, but when he came out again Werther was still on the phone. There was nowhere else to go. He sat down on the bed, his back to Werther, and concentrated on drying himself. They were talking about a problem she was having with a current case. Nothing terribly important or interesting, just the kind of chat that husbands have with wives. It wasn't necessary for Werther to express an interest in her work; she knew he was interested—not in the work itself, but because it was *her* work. They had a good relationship, you could tell, more of a relationship than he had with her. With him it was only sex; they hadn't said a dozen words to each other. No, that wasn't true; it was an exaggeration. Still, he had no right to jeopardize a solid marriage for his simple lusts.

But she had lusts too. He couldn't help smiling at that. He sat on the bed, his back to Werther, smiling at the thought of Lori's naked lust. *What a bastard you are, Melnik*, he suddenly thought.

It wasn't funny. He stopped smiling.

They breakfasted early in the motel, had some sandwiches wrapped up for later and then drove back to San Medro's neighborhood. Driving down Ninth Street past the house, they didn't see anybody, but a white van was parked halfway down the block. They continued past it, pulled around the corner and parked. Werther picked up the walkie-talkie. "Good morning. Anybody there?"

There was no reply for a few seconds, then a burst of static and a vaudeville voice. "Who dat askin' if anybody be here? Dat you, Boss?"

"Werther here."

"Dat you, Boss! We be reading you loud and clear."

Werther glanced at Melnik and sighed. Every city seemed to have its own comedian in the Bureau, and today he'd got lumbered with Philadelphia's. "Okay, it's me," he said into the walkie-talkie. "Who are you?"

"Rasputin Velikovsky here, Boss, a.k.a. John Mortinson, reading you loud and clear."

"Are you in the van?"

"Yeah, that's us. Is it that obvious?"

"Only because I knew you were there. Is Abrams with you?"

"Sleeping like a baby, boss." Abrams was on twenty-four-hour duty with the surveillance crew, who had orders to wake him whenever anybody went in or out of the San Medro house; he was the only one who knew his mark by sight.

"Anything to report?" Werther asked.

"Nada." The van had a videotape running constantly, with a view of the whole street and everybody who passed by. "The tapes are running, but no action so far."

"Okay. We're around the corner. Hope you've got some good books in there to keep your mind busy."

"The collected plays of Noel Coward, volume two. And, oh, yes, *Playboy*."

"I won't worry about you, then. Is the alleyway covered?"

"Hey, Boss, what you think?" Mortinson reverted to his stage dialect. "You can relax, man. You be in good hands with Allstate."

"Fine. Just remember, if anything goes wrong I'll have your balls for breakfast. With ketchup."

"That's disgusting," Mortinson said with dignity. "Over and out."

Werther slid the walkie-talkie under the seat and scrunched around trying to get comfortable. He glanced at Melnik. It was going to be a long day.

It was several hours later that Hardy walked down the street, passing the van and turning at the corner so that on his way to the movies on Broad Street he went by the car in which Werther and Melnik were sitting.

At three-thirty that afternoon the walkie-talkie finally crackled. "He just came out, heading north on Ninth Street."

San Medro hadn't gone to Cancún or Yucatán with the money Freddy had wired him. Why should he? Blow town every time somebody he did business with got excited? He had too much to do here; he had his girls to look after and his coke deliveries to see to. Besides, he wasn't some little punk who took orders. He threw his shoulders back and swaggered easily as he started on his rounds.

"Right," Werther answered over the walkie-talkie. He and Melnik got out of the car and walked around the corner. They would take the first leg of the tail.

After the movie Hardy stopped in for dinner at a Chinese restaurant. It was nearly seven o'clock and just getting dark when he walked back down Ruscombe street. As he crossed Ninth he glanced up the block. A brown van was parked where the white one had been that afternoon. Instead of turning up Ninth to San Medro's place, he stayed on Ruscombe, working out the possibilities. Two different vans in the same spot was too much of a coincidence for him. He had to figure they had the punk under surveillance. Which meant they had connected the two Dallas stories, San Medro's and Rasheed Amon's. He would have liked to know if San Medro had actually skipped town as Freddy had told him to, but it wasn't worth trying to bust their surveillance to find out. At least he knew what they now knew, and he didn't think San Medro knew any more even if they found him. The best thing to do was get out of here. He walked down Fifth, caught a taxi and headed back to the airport.

\*       \*       \*

The next day Werther decided to call the operation off. A succession of vans had kept tabs on San Medro's flat while a squad of agents took turns tailing him wherever he went. The problem was, Werther began to realize, that he went to too many places and talked to too many people. They were taking long-range photos of everyone he spoke to, trying to check them out as quickly as possible, but the list kept getting bigger. Abrams had warned them about this; besides San Medro's stable of girls and the growing circle of pushers working for him, the punk had a wide range of working contacts. He was ambitious, and what he didn't already have his finger into he was trying to horn in on; he wanted to own the neighborhood and everything that went with it.

By five o'clock on the second day Werther acknowledged defeat. San Medro must have talked to fifty or sixty people, any one of whom could have been a contact for Dallas. He could have passed on a warning, received instructions, anything by now. The only thing to do was to haul him in, lean on him, and see what leaked out. They'd also have to start pulling in everyone he'd met with to see if they could get something out of them. He stared at the list he had been making notes on; it was already so big that it would strain all his resources. He hated to do it, but he had no choice.

He called in to the central command post in the van. "Tell them to bring in San Medro," he said.

"Uh," the voice began to answer him, then fell silent.

Werther felt a clammy premonition. "Did you hear me? I said to tell them—"

"Roger, loud and clear. The problem is . . ."

"What? What's the goddamn problem?"

"Johnson and Murdoch already called in. I was just going to buzz you. They lost him."

San Medro hadn't actually spotted anyone, but he had a nervous feeling that he didn't like. He had started doubling back on his tracks, stopping suddenly and looking around. He didn't see anyone, but he *felt* them. Or was it his goddamn imagination? Maybe the Dallas people were right; he ought to get out of town for a while, maybe just for the weekend. Things were slow anyway, and he was rolling in bread, what with the extra they'd wired him and all.

If he was going to do it, he might as well do it right. Suddenly he flagged down a taxi and took it to the North Philly train station. He walked quickly up the stairs to the men's room and without pausing went out through the window that had been broken for at least the past two years. This put him on a grass slope behind the station, leading to the suburban line. He crossed over to it and took the first train, getting off at the first station and doubling back to Lindley. By the time he got off the train he was sure he'd thrown off whoever might have been on him, and was in fact beginning to think it had all been nothing but his nerves.

Still, once he had begun thinking of a few days on a sunny Mexican beach it had begun to appeal to him. He might as well pack a few clothes and go.


The search and arrest warrants had been prepared the first day. Now Werther, Melnik, Abrams and two local officers banged on the door of San Medro's flat, and when there was no answer they broke in. They searched carefully but found nothing that might link him to Dallas or give them any indication where he might have fled to. Werther sat down heavily on the bed and tried not to notice Melnik's contemptuous expression. The Israeli wasn't saying anything, but what he was thinking was clear enough: the FBI had lost its quarry again.

Werther didn't know what to do. Maybe he should have picked up San Medro right away, but it didn't do any good to think about that now. He left the two local officers in the flat and was walking down the stairs with Melnik and Abrams when a key turned in the outside door. When it swung open a thin young Spanish man stood there looking up at them.

Abrams smiled.

"Oh, shit," San Medro said.

# IV
# Preparations

## 31

On the plane back to Kansas, Hardy leaned back in his seat, closed his eyes, and thought about the past twenty-four hours. All in all, he decided, it was working out. Now that he thought about it, he was even glad they had found San Medro. All the little punk could tell them was that he'd actually supplied the arms, and it would be good for them to know about that; it would scare the hell out of them. Yes, it was going well. He smiled. It really was a damned clever plan. At first, when he had accepted the job from the Libyans, he hadn't had any idea of how to proceed. He had worried over it for weeks before even the first glimmer had come to him.

Hardy's seat was facing the door, so he saw the middle-aged officer in Air Force blue enter and ask the maître d' a question. The man gestured in his direction, and Hardy pushed his chair back from the table and stood up. The officer came over and asked, "Major Emerson?"

Hardy extended his hand and said, "Just plain mister now. Call me Tom. Colonel Lindgren, I presume?"

"Robert," the Colonel said. "Glad to meet you." He had a firm handshake, of course. He was nearly as tall as Hardy, with short-cropped gray hair and what pilots like to think of as steely-blue eyes. He was running just a bit to fat, but still looked in good shape.

They shook hands and sat down, and Lindgren said, "So you're writing an article?"

The waiter came over, they ordered cocktails, and then Hardy answered. "That's right. I'm out of the Marines now, and to tell the truth I've been drifting for a while. Nearly a year. Don't like business—not smart enough, I guess. I thought I'd try my hand at writing. Aviation stuff, you know, to take advantage of my background."

Lindgren nodded. "You flew Phantoms in 'Nam?"

Hardy smiled. "For my sins," he said. "Not one of the favorite periods in my life." He paused while the waiter placed their drinks, then sipped his. "That's good. Nice and cold. Skoal." They lifted their glasses and drank. "Were you over there?"

The colonel nodded. "Look," he said, "before we go any further I ought to tell you that I can't tell you anything. I mean any of the operational details, anything that might be secret. We don't really like a lot of publicity, you know."

Hardy waved his objections away. "Of course, I understand that. I'm just interested in background. Everybody knows all they have to know about your job; I thought they might like to know a bit about *you*. After all, this isn't for *Time* or *Esquire*, right? I assumed you checked with *Aeroreview*?"

Lindgren nodded. Of course he would have. Hardy had called them and told them he was Tom Emerson, using the name of one of his mates in 'Nam, that he was trying to get started as an aviation writer, and would they consider an article on Colonel Robert Lee Lindgren? They knew who Lindgren was, and thought it might be a good idea, but of course they couldn't promise anything without seeing the piece first. That was good enough; all he wanted was that when Lindgren called them after he had written to request an interview, they'd confirm that Emerson wanted to write an article for them about him.

"So just tell me who you are," Hardy said now. "How'd they pick you? Were you top ace in 'Nam, or what?"

Lindgren laughed a little self-consciously. "Not exactly. Quite the opposite." He laughed again. "I don't think a jock would have quite the proper experience for this job."

Hardy smiled with him. "I guess not. So how'd you get it?"

The colonel smiled and toyed with his cocktail glass, swirling it around and looking at it. "It was all just an accident," he said. "That's why I knew what you meant when you said you've just been drifting since you got out of the service. I'm not really a military man at all, though I've spent more than twenty years wearing this uniform. I joined up after college just so I wouldn't be drafted into the infantry during the Korean War."

Hardy laughed. "A damn good reason."

Lindgren nodded. "I guess so. Jesus, I feel sorry for those grunts in the mud, don't you? I don't know how they do it." Hardy nodded, and he went on. "So I passed flight training and they put me in bombers, which was fine by me. I never could have tossed a Phantom around. Straight and level, that's the kind of flying I like to do."

An honest man, Hardy thought. There were just two kinds of multiengine pilots: one admitted he couldn't fly a fighter, and the other pretended that the big monsters were harder to fly and even more fun. He had a hard time being polite with the latter, so he was glad Lindgren was the former.

"I learned to fly a B-29," Lindgren continued, "but not in time to see action before the war was over. Which was also okay with me." He looked Hardy straight in the eye. "You fighter jocks take on a MiG one on one; it's like they say, a duel to the death, but what the hell, you're each paid to do your job and you know what it involves. But a bomber pilot cruises along way up high, opens the bays and drops tons of bombs out onto anyone living below—civilians, more'n likely. People trying to live, not trying to fight, not even wanting the goddamn war, for Christ's sake. They weren't all Commie soldiers down there in Korea, believe me. Not in the cities, not even in the war zones. Christ, a bomber pilot can't steer his bombs, you know what I mean? You hit everyone down there; you kill them all."

"I know what you're talking about," Hardy said. He shook his head briefly. He didn't want to talk about his own war; he was here to find out what he could. He didn't know exactly what he was after; he was just fishing, hoping to come up with something. The main thing was to keep the guy talking. "Did you all feel that way? Bomber pilots, I mean?"

Lindgren shook his head. "The 'real' bomber pilots weren't like me; nothing bothered them. I never felt at home with them; I was always sort of odd man out. Look, *Aeroreview*'s not going to want to hear this kind of stuff. They're going to want an old-fashioned blood-and-guts hero."

"Let me worry about that. Let's try the truth first. Maybe people ought to hear this, you know?"

Lindgren shrugged. "You're the writer," he said. "So, anyhow, I left the Air Force soon as I could when my tour was up, and then found

I didn't know what I wanted to do with my life. All I thought about in the service was getting out, you know? And then when I was out, I didn't have anything to do. So I wandered for a few years, and had just about decided to try for law school when they started the crap in 'Nam and I was recalled."

"That was rough."

"Not really. What could they do, anyhow? They had a war to fight. Some of the guys were called three times: the Second World War, Korea and 'Nam. Anyhow, I'm glad it happened." He stopped and tried to explain. "Christ, I don't mean I'm glad we went to war there, but I couldn't find myself out there in civvie street. I hadn't grown up yet, you know what I mean? The point is, I didn't object when they brought me back, especially when they said they needed cargo pilots more than bomber pilots. To tell you the truth, I was relieved. I didn't mind one bit the loss of 'glamour.' By the time they decided to bomb Charley back into the Stone Age and needed all the bomber pilots they could find, I was in solid as a C-124 commander, and they left me alone."

The waiter came to take their order, and Lindgren went on. "I found a niche there. I'm a damn good pilot—I don't want you to misunderstand that—and I'm proud of it. I just didn't like being told to kill people. I kept thinking about my wife and daughter, and other people's wives and daughters. I don't know if you can understand that, coming from where you do."

"No sweat," Hardy assured him. "Don't worry about it."

Lindgren nodded. "So, anyhow, without the pressure of trying to bomb anyone, I turned out all right. In fact, I was the best damn pilot in the wing. Then by the time 'Nam was settled I was too old for law school, and was finally doing something right and enjoying it, and with the years I already had in I figured I might as well stick it out. Which was a good thing, because right after reenlisting they offered me a transfer to the VIP Flight operating out of Washington."

"Was that good?"

Lindgren nodded. "Turned out good for me. I fit in there. It wasn't only the flying—all the pilots in that group are good—but it turned out that I had a knack for getting along with the big shots. You know, the glamorous, important and very difficult passengers the Flight handles.

It's easy to say yes to people, but it's not easy to say no without giving offense, especially to someone like a senator or secretary of state. I found I could tell a congressman he wasn't allowed on board, and I could even say it to his wife, which was a damn sight harder, believe me." He laughed. "Actually, it's a knack I put on and take off with the uniform. Any time I try to discipline my own teenaged daughter, her eyes fill with tears and I crumble. Still, it's a knack not everyone has. Anyway, when the vacancy opened they gave me the top job."

"Pilot of Air Force One," Hardy said. "The President's pilot."

Lindgren smiled modestly, shrugged and nodded.

The first Air Force One, a propeller-driven DC-4, rolled out of the California plant of the Douglas Aircraft Company in 1944. Over the years it was followed by five other prop-type carriers, until the first Boeing 707 jet presidential craft was delivered to Richard Nixon. Actually, none of the planes was ever called Air Force One; Roosevelt named the first one the *Sacred Cow*, and Truman called his DC-6 the *Independence*. Air Force One is the radio call sign that designates the president's Air Force plane, whichever one he happens to be on, whether it's a Piper Cub or a Phantom fighter. But ever since Kennedy neglected to give his plane a special name, Air Force One has been used to describe the president's private craft that has been fitted out as a flying White House, with communications that link it directly to Washington and to national defense command centers throughout the country.

All this is taken for granted today. It was not always so. In 1790 the young and freshly united states of the North American continent decided that the capital of these United States, as they called themselves, should be among the states but not in any of them. It was a decision born of the rivalry between New York and Philadelphia in particular, and the New England and Southern states in general. Each of these had reasons it should house the seat of government, and even stronger reasons why its rivals should not. In 1790 they compromised, establishing a new city in the new District of Columbia, centrally located among the states but not in any of them; by Act of Congress the new federal government would be housed in this city of Washington, and would "cease to be exercised elsewhere."

Clearly this meant only that no other city should rival Washington in providing offices for the federal government, that all such should be removed as soon as possible to the new city, and that all federal powers should be concentrated there henceforth. But when Woodrow Wilson left this country in 1919 to participate in the Paris peace conference at the end of World War I, many Americans were upset. Never before had there not been a sitting president in Washington, except for brief periods of travel about the country and one even briefer period when Teddy Roosevelt visited Panama, becoming the first president ever to leave the United States. (His advisers were so concerned about the public effect of this trip that he was actually absent from United States territorial waters for only a few hours, hurrying back before a palace revolution could develop.)

Woodrow Wilson, however, was gone for months in 1919, and the natives became restless. Illinois Senator Lawrence Y. Sherman introduced a resolution declaring that the presidency was vacant, since obviously no lawfully elected president was *in situ* in the city of Washington, where by the Act of 1790 all federal governmental powers must be exercised.

There was some justification for Sherman's anxiety, though it is hard to imagine today. Radio had just been invented, the first transmissions across the English Channel having been made barely twenty years previously. When the *Titanic* sank in 1912, the story of the brave wireless operator sending out signals for help, saving hundreds of lives by summoning rescue vessels and giving them the exact position of the ship, made a story as exciting as that of the tragedy itself. It wasn't until 1924, five years after Wilson's journey to France, that radio contact was first made from the ground to an airplane, and even then the contact was so fleeting and flimsy that the experiment was deemed a failure.

So when the President left Washington in 1919, he was *gone*. How could the government function when the Senate, whose duty was to advise and consent to presidential decisions, could not even communicate with him? The problem turned out to be a real one in fact as well as in theory. When Wilson returned exhausted but triumphant from France with his concept of a League of Nations fully established in the Versailles Peace Treaty, the Senate of the United States refused to accept and ratify it. Whether it was because the Senators were spiteful for having been excluded from the decision-making process or because Wilson failed to communicate his concerns and rationale to them upon his return, the lack of mutual communication during the decisive months of treaty-making took its toll; the United States remained outside the League, an abstention that contributed more than any other single factor to its downfall twenty years later and to the coming of the Second World War.

Today there is no such problem. Even when the president is in the air and Air Force One is only a speck in the vast wastes over the world's oceans, radio and air-to-ground telephones linked via satellites to communications nerve centers on the ground provide instant and continual communication not only with Washington but with the centers of military action, with the NORAD command post hidden under the Colorado mountains, with SAC bombers, Cruise missiles and nuclear-tipped intercontinental ballistic rockets that can be sent on their way in an instant, triggered by one message from the Flying White House.

There are other problems with presidential travel, of course, chief among these being security. No president has ever been personally attacked in the White House; security is complete there. But once he sets foot outside, he is vulnerable. If he can be killed in a theater only a few blocks from the White House, how much more easily could it not be done in Buffalo or Dallas? Operating through its Secret Service unit, the Treasury Department worries about this constantly. The Central Intelligence Agency continually monitors foreign governments and terrorist organizations, searching for any sign of an attempt on the president's life. The Federal Bureau of Investigation maintains similar surveillance within our borders. Yet with all this protection, there is anxiety every time the president steps beyond the comfortable confines of the White House.

Except during the few hours when he is actually aboard Air Force One, of course. The Flying White House is as secure as the one on Pennsylvania Avenue. Everyone knows that.

There is, in fact, good reason for this faith in the security of Air Force One. The reason is the lack of faith of the people responsible for the security, which includes everyone associated with the airplane and its operation. They trust no one and take nothing for granted.

This sense of unremitting vigilance takes other forms as well. The crew is determined that every flight will be perfection. Whenever they were not scheduled for other duties in the spring and summer of 1990 the crew took Air Force One on a private, unpublicized tour of the country. Their mission was simple and routine: to check out possible airports for the coming election campaign.

Although it was only a congressional election, the President would be as busy as any nominee, campaigning for his supporters, and it was Air Force One that would be carrying him from speech to speech, dinner to dinner, smile to smile, handshake to handshake, from Maine to California and from Washington to Florida. At every airport at which they would land, the crew would have been there before. They would have noted and recorded its personnel and equipment. When the welcoming crowds watched them land, they would see the majestic airplane turn off the runway at precisely the right point and taxi directly to the welcoming ramp; the doors would open and the President would emerge smiling and waving at precisely the right moment. None of the people watching would think about the details that have to fall into place precisely in order to stage this perfect entrance, but the crew of Air Force One was thinking about them for months ahead of time.

Colonel Robert Lee Lindgren was beginning to look forward to civilian life. With a new president there would be a new presidential crew for Air Force One, and it would be awkward for him to stay on in the VIP Flight, flying senators and congressmen and their wives around when he had once been the President's pilot. He had been promised just about any assignment he wanted, including a staff job in the Pentagon, but as he thought about it he realized he didn't want any of the assignments; he wanted to go home.

He had enjoyed the Air Force these past five years, the responsibilities as well as the perks; he was good at his job, which included everything that had anything to do with the airplane, from the clean-up crews to the weather, from the radome in the nose to the toilet paper in the rear john. One day over Minnesota he had received a call from the Secret Service informing him that there was a bomb on board the airplane. He hadn't even blinked; he took the Winston cigarette box out of his jacket pocket and told them that he had found it stuffed behind one of the passenger seats where the Secret Service agent had placed it before takeoff. They often tested him like that, and they had never yet succeeded in slipping anything on board that he or his crew hadn't caught.

He was proud of his crew, of his plane, of himself, of the job he had done, but it was enough. He would complete thirty years of service at almost the same time as the President's term was up, and he would leave the Air Force.

Until he did, of course, he was still the captain of Air Force One, and nobody was going to slip a cigarette box or a bomb or anything else on board; he would take his airplane and his president wherever in the world he wanted to go, and he would put him safely back on the ground at precisely the time and place called for.

"So?"

Hardy cocked his head on one side and thought about the question. "I don't know," he said finally.

"Nothing?" Mason insisted. "You didn't find out anything at *all* from Lindgren?"

Hardy took a beer out of the refrigerator. "I found out a few things, yes. After we rapped for a while, I finally got him down to the nitty-gritty. The point is, it's not going to be easy."

"Oh, I didn't know that," Mason said. "Not easy, huh? Imagine that."

Hardy smiled. "Want a beer?" He got another out of the fridge and threw it across the room. "Security is tight," he said.

"Well, we kind of thought it might be. Any ideas?"

"They don't trust anyone," Hardy said. "They take nothing for granted. For example, they buy the food from a different source for each flight. Sometimes they bring it in from the White House, sometimes from local shops. And always, no matter what its source, they inspect it and put it under secure storage afterwards."

"Got it down to a science," Mason commented.

"Hell, yes. They even unfold all the sheets and bedding when they come back from the cleaners to check for chemicals and be sure that nothing like a nerve gas has been sprayed on."

"I don't get it."

Hardy smiled. "The President comes in, lies down on his bed, and the heat of his body vaporizes the dried chemical. He never wakes up."

"Cute."

"Lovely. The point is, they've thought of everything. The fuel is taken from various storage tanks at random; samples are filtered and chemically analyzed for contaminants. Then they store it in tankers that are kept under armed guard until the fuel is pumped into the airplane."

"How about getting someone on board?"

Hardy shook his head. "No one is allowed on without escort, but escorts are not easily provided, the man says, and I believe him. Casual visitors, quote no matter how high their rank or political prestige unquote, find entry difficult or impossible. All luggage—in fact, everything that comes on board—is carefully screened by the Secret Service, the plane's own security guards or both. Wherever the airplane travels, four Air Force security guards go with it; whenever it's parked at a strange airport, local police or airport guards reinforce these men and establish tight security around the aircraft."

He looked at Mason, pursed his lips and took a long swig of beer. "Everybody is alert," he said. "Nobody takes a chance, because nobody wants to be responsible for losing a president." He paused, leaned forward on his chair and stared down into his beer. "On the other hand . . ." he said slowly.

Mason waited awhile, then prompted him. "On the other hand?"

"Did you ever see the Evansville Phantom?"

"The who?"

Hardy smiled. "When I was stationed at Da Nang he used to come through on USO tours. You never saw him? He was pretty funny. Lots of quick patter, but he really was a magician. Sleight of hand. He was damn good. You knew what he was doing, but you couldn't follow it. He'd wave his hands around with a silk scarf crumpled up in his fist, giving you a quick line of patter to distract you, and you'd be determined he wasn't going to fool you; then all of a sudden he'd do something with his other hand and you thought you'd missed it and would take a quick glance, and right at that instant when you weren't watching, the scarf would turn into a bunch of flowers."

Hardy looked up. "The point was," he said, "that the more you tried to follow him and the harder you tried to look at the right thing, the easier it was for him to make you look at the *wrong* thing at exactly the right moment. Then he had you."

"All he needed was the right moment."

"That's it. The harder they're looking, the easier it is to fool them. The trick is to make them know something's coming, but not to know what or when. Then, when they're running around looking at all the wrong things . . ."

Mason nodded and smiled. He lifted his bottle of beer in a toast. "To the Evansville Phantom."

Hardy lifted his bottle and clinked it against Mason's. "The Phantom strikes again." They burst out laughing.

32

That was the beginning, but as the days lengthened into weeks and months, they began to think that perhaps it wasn't a laughing matter after all. For days and weeks on end Hardy sat quiet and unmoving, trying to get a handle on the problem, looking not for a solution but just for a simple idea.

When it came, it came quietly, sneaking in through the fog on a rainy day, bobbing along on little cat feet. He sensed it coming. He got up that morning and afterward swore he could feel it; he knew that something was in the air. He waited like a hunter waiting for the ducks to come. He knew there was no hurrying it, but just as certainly he knew it was there. Then suddenly it flashed like a meteor and was gone.

He sat up and slammed his fist into the palm of his hand. He didn't have it all yet, but he knew now where he was going. He had begun to think that maybe it couldn't be done; maybe just for once the damned government knew what it was doing; maybe you couldn't get to the president. But now he had faith again: he could do it.

"What's up?" Freddy asked. "You look like you just swallowed the canary."

"I think I just swallowed Air Force One," Hardy said, grinning.

"So tell me."

"Lindgren's a Texan."

Freddy waited. "That's it? That's your insight? Lindgren's a god-damn Texan? So what?"

"I was trying to think. I *knew* there was something important when we talked, and that's it. He's got an accent you can cut with a knife."

Freddy looked baffled. "What do we do with it?" he asked.

"We get to work. Finally we get to work."

The next day Hardy took a six-month lease on a small office in a business complex across the highway from Andrews Air Force Base outside Washington, D.C. He put up a notice on a couple of community bulletin boards in nearby Mellwood, and by the time he'd found and bought the equipment he needed from a local electronics store he had hired a high school kid named Marvin who had two stereo sets, one in his car and another in his room. The one in his room had a double tape deck, and he was used to taping music from the radio as well as from borrowed albums. Using a similar cover story, that he was doing an article on Air Force jets operating out of Andrews, he arranged for Marvin to spend his afternoons in the office, wearing earphones so he could hear properly, listening to the transmissions from the other side of I-95.

Midway through the third day Marvin got what he had been sent for, although he didn't know it.

"Andrews Clearance Delivery, Air Force One standing by for clearance."

"Roger Air Force One. You are cleared as filed. Maintain three thousand until further advised. Squawk four four five six. Contact Andrews Departure Control one twenty-seven point five when airborne."

Following Hardy's directions, Marvin spun the dial around to 127.5, zeroing in on the next transmission.

"Andrews Departure, this is Air Force One, squawking four four five six."

"Roger, Air Force One. We have radar contact. Maintain heading and climb now to five thousand. Advise leaving three."

"Andrews Departure, Air Force One out of three for five."

"Roger, Air Force One. Turn left, heading two seven zero, maintain five thousand and contact Washington Center one nineteen point three five. Have a good trip."

"Roger. Good day."

Marvin took off the earphones, switched off his radio and turned the dials on the tape recorder, which began to spin backward. When it came to the end of the tape, he switched it to play.

"Andrews Clearance Delivery, Air Force One standing by for clearance."

"Roger, Air Force One. You are cleared as filed. Maintain three thousand until further advised. Squawk four four five six. Contact Andrews Departure Control one twenty-seven point five when airborne. . . ."

Marvin played the tape through to the end. Then, satisfied that it had all been recorded properly, he reset the recorder and leaned back for a smoke, waiting for the next transmission. It was a good enough temporary job, he thought, except that it was boring. But it was better than school, that was for sure, and a lot better than being nagged by his mother to clean up his room.

"Andrews Departure, this is Beechcraft Alpha seven five, clearing runway three. . . ."

With a small groan Marvin turned to his recorder and flipped the switch.

## 33

"I'm offering you nothing," the realtor said. He stopped and smiled. He was a fat man named Fred Robinson, and wore a flowered vest under his suit jacket. He was nearly bald, with a few thin wisps of unnaturally black hair drawn carefully across the dome and slicked down tightly. If he'd had a sense of humor he would have worn a gold tooth; instead he wore a Rolex. "Nothing at all," he repeated. "Just two things."

Hardy waited.

"Location and luxury," Robinson said. "That's all. If you don't want that, I'm wasting your time."

Hardy nodded and looked around the apartment. It was newly furnished and redecorated in a Spartan, modern Swedish style.

"Sit on the couch," Robinson said. "Just do me one favor and sit on that couch."

Hardy walked to the window and looked out as bells came clanging down Powell Street.

"What, the noise bothers you? That noise don't bother you. That's the cable car. Loveliest noise in God's greatest city. You don't like that noise, you don't want to live in San Francisco. Where are you from, you mind my asking?"

"Back East," Hardy said.

"Well, sure, back East, that's where everybody's from. I'm from Ohio, myself. To some people, that's out West, but here it's back East." He laughed. "Here *everything's* back East. Let me tell you about the cable cars, since you're not from San Francisco. I used to call it Frisco, you know? When I first came here? But people here don't like that. San Francisco, that's what they say. So I'm telling you, those cable cars are the heart of San Francisco. And Powell Street is the main artery. Anything happens in San Francisco, it happens right here on Powell Street. To your right "—he came up beside Hardy, leaned out the window and pointed—"you got your Fisherman's Wharf right over the hill. To your left "—he pointed again—"down there is your Union Square. Anything happens in this town—Thanksgiving Parade, Halloween festival, you name it—it comes right down Powell Street, right under your window."

Robinson stepped back into the room and beamed at Hardy. "You worried about the office buildings across the street? Is that what's bothering you? 'Cause if it is, I can understand that, I see where you're coming from, but let me tell you, you're wrong. Now, you want to live somewhere out in the country, I'm not telling you to take this place, and I've got nothing against the country. If that's what you want, let's shake hands and say good-bye and no hard feelings. But if you want to live in the city, this is exactly where you want to be. Take New York," he said. "You know New York?"

Hardy shook his head.

"You got people buying your town houses there up around Central Park and beyond. Now what's the point of that, I ask you? Anywhere you want to go, you got to take a taxi or, God forbid, the subway. No, in New York where you want to be is right down in the Village. Does it bother you there are office buildings right there on the street with your condo in the Village? No, of course not, why should it? That's the city. That's what life in the city is all about."

"I'll take it," Hardy said.

Mr. Robinson beamed. As soon as this man had walked into the office, he knew he had a sale. He could tell; it was a talent he had. But his sales pitch hadn't exactly hurt either. A man in this business had to know how to spot them and how to sell them; he had to know what to· say and when to say it. Maybe he'd go for broke now. "Have you considered taking it for two weeks?" he asked.

The apartment was a luxury high-rise time-share condominium at the base of Nob Hill. Each apartment cost nine thousand dollars for a week. This meant that the owner had its use for one week a year, and the builder could sell it fifty-two times.

"The way people are snapping these up, they're going fast. All I hear from people is how they wish they'd taken two weeks. I really think you should give some consideration to a two-week purchase."

"I'll take three months," Hardy said.

Robinson nearly fainted at the thought of the commission. "You're being very wise," he said quickly. "Come down to the office and we'll sign the papers on the spot. Congratulations."

Hardy nodded and followed him out the door. The President's cavalcade would have to come right under this window, and the setup was perfect. With weekly owners there was no problem of anyone noticing that the apartment would be empty for a while, and when a tenant did move in, nobody would pay any attention.

Later that afternoon he repeated the scene three blocks further down the street, at 937 Powell, with another agent. This one too wouldn't stop talking, and when he looked out the window she tried to distract him from the building across the street onto whose bleak rooftop the window looked. It was the location he wanted, especially because of that rooftop. She seemed a bit disappointed that he agreed to take it before she had finished her hard sell, but he'd heard enough real estate talk for one day.

Hardy spent that night in San Francisco, and early the next morning flew to Los Angeles. On Sunset Boulevard just below Highland is a narrow five-story building with a false stucco front and a double-glass doorway flanked by two potted palms. Most of the offices are accounting or legal firms, a couple are literary agencies and one is a casting agency specializing in commercials; with one exception, all have occupied their premises for three years or less.

In that one exception, an office at the end of the fifth-floor hallway, L. P. Peterson sat looking out the window, resting his chin on his hands and his elbows on his desk. He thought vaguely about opening the window and stepping out, but he was afraid of the terror he would feel during the five-floor drop. He sighed. He wasn't serious, he told himself; he just liked to dramatize things and there wasn't really anything in his life worth dramatizing. There was nothing terrible, nothing wonderful; there wasn't much of anything. He swiveled around and looked at the glass door that led out to the hallway. He could read backward through the glass the sign lettered on it: L. P. PETERSON, SPEECH AND DICTION CONSULTANTS. What could be duller—and less profitable? There were probably a thousand offices just like his in Los Angeles alone. He had given up dreaming that one day a beautiful young thing would walk through the door, that he would teach her how to speak, that she would become a great actress, and that . . . He had given up such dreams because they always degenerated into fantasies that left him more depressed than ever. Also because it had been too many years since he had opened this office, too few people had in fact walked through that door, and none of them had been beautiful young things capable of anything at all.

The glass door darkened now as a figure approached it, and as it opened he dreamed for a split second that it would be a beautiful young thing. . . .

It was not. It was a muscular middle-aged man. He sat down at Peterson's invitation and put a package on the desk. He said he was an actor named Frank Carver; he was up for a part on a television show back in New York, and wanted to brush up on his Texas accent. He wanted to talk like the voice on the tape, he said, gesturing toward the package he'd placed on the desk.

Peterson opened it, put the tape on his machine and listened. "Andrews Ground Control, this is Air Force One ready to taxi. . . ."

"The part is that of a pilot who's a Southerner. Do you think you could help me imitate that voice?"

Peterson shrugged and asked Carver to try an imitation, saying the same words that the voice on the tape had said. There shouldn't be much trouble, he thought, and when Carver suggested they begin at once, he outlined his terms and they got to work.

34

Mason met Hardy at the airport when he returned from L.A., but he seemed distracted, as if he had something on his mind. Hardy didn't ask; he knew Freddy would tell him soon enough. Then as they pulled off the highway into the farmyard he saw another car parked by the house. "What the hell is that?"

Freddy smiled sheepishly. "Surprise," he said.

"What are you talking about? Who the hell is it?"

"Alison."

Hardy was furious. "Freddy, we're not playing games now. We're not stealing from the five-and-dime. This is no time to have your kid sister hanging around."

"Christ, Gee, you know Alison. How could I stop her?"

"Easy to stop her, you goddamn idiot. All you had to do was not tell her where we are!"

Freddy shrugged apologetically. "She got it out of me," he said. "I have to call her once in a while, you know that, and she got it out of me."

"What else did she get out of you? Did you tell her what we're doing?"

"No! I swear. I just couldn't keep her from coming down, that's all."

"Shit," Hardy muttered as the car stopped next to hers. He got out, slammed the door, and walked into the house without waiting for

Freddy. He didn't even notice the smell of lamb roasting in the oven.

Alison watched from the window as he tramped through the dusty yard and up the steps. Now she said, "Hello, Gee." She paused. "Are you angry?"

He turned away from her, staring out the window.

"You're angry," she said.

They ate dinner in silence. Afterward Hardy and Freddy cleared away the dirty plates and Alison served coffee. "I know it's something big," she said finally.

Hardy turned on her. "How did you know?" He swiveled around to Mason. "I ought to break both your—"

"It's nothing to do with him," Alison said. "You told me."

"What? I never—"

"You didn't tell me what it is, but you certainly told me it's something big. Or do you think I can't translate actions like sneaking off, keeping your whereabouts secret, telling Freddy not to tell me anything, not—"

"You've got your own life to lead," Hardy said angrily. "You shouldn't be hanging around us all the time. You ought to be figuring out what you want to do with yourself without always thinking about Freddy. You always wanted to be a nurse, remember?" he said, suddenly recalling how she'd always been around to put bandages on their scraped knees and cut fingers when they'd been kids. "Go be a nurse, go back to school, do something with your life."

"I am," Alison said. "I'm doing very well, thanks. Going back to school, in fact, starting next semester."

"Good," Hardy said. He even smiled. "Going to be a nurse?"

She shook her head. "Emptying all those bedpans? I guess I'm not dedicated enough. I'm going to med school instead."

"You're going to be a doctor?" He laughed and shook his head. "That's great, Al. That really is. Congratulations. Now go to bed early and get the hell out of here first thing in the morning."

"Let's take a walk," she said.

"I was glad that you came for Freddy when you got back from Africa. He was about ready to give up. I was, too."

She paused. "I wasn't quite so happy when I found out you were smuggling marijuana, but I told myself it was like Prohibition. Grass really isn't as bad as alcohol. It isn't even as bad as nicotine. It's a bad law, I told myself; it deserves to be broken."

"Lots of laws are bad."

"That's the problem, Gee! You begin breaking one law, and pretty soon you're deciding for yourself which laws are good and which are bad."

"Isn't that what Gandhi said? Didn't we make that claim at the Nuremberg trials? Isn't it—"

"Goddamn it, Gee, Gandhi didn't break laws for personal profit! You're not doing it because of some great philosophy about personal freedom; you're just doing it for money!"

"You've got some prejudice against money?"

"I've got a prejudice against your killing yourself and Freddy."

"It's not that bad."

"Isn't it? Tell me."

"I can't. Just trust me for a little while."

They walked along aimlessly. "Promise?" she asked quietly.

He hesitated, then nodded. "Promise."

They stopped and looked back at the farmhouse. The sun was setting over the flat horizon, and the house stood out like a Wyeth portrait of loneliness, the lights shining out through the windows in emphasis.

Alison didn't look at him as she asked, "Haven't you missed me at all?"

"Yes," Hardy said. "Oh yes, I've missed you."

She turned to him then, and when he held out his arms she melted into them, lifting her face and softly opening her mouth.

Hardy gave Alison his bedroom and moved in with Freddy. As he sat on his bed, taking off his shoes and socks, he studied Freddy's face. Something else was bothering Freddy. "What is it?" Hardy asked.

"It can wait till morning."

"Come on, what's bothering you?"

"It's the goddamn Libyans again."

"What now?"

"Mahouri's coming in again. He called this morning. I don't like it,

Gee. Every time he comes here is one more time he might be followed and give us all away."

Hardy sighed heavily. "I know. When's he coming?"

"Friday."

Hardy had to think for a moment. Today was Tuesday. "I'll take care of it," he said. He would have to do something, but he had other things to think about first.

He finished undressing, turned out the light and lay in bed listening to Freddy's breathing. He didn't know if it was necessary; he just felt better waiting. It took nearly twenty minutes, but finally when the only sound was of long, deep breaths, Hardy drew back the sheet and got out of bed. He stood naked in the moonlight, then walked out of the room and down the hall to where Alison lay waiting.

Alison lay curled up next to Hardy, drifting in and out of sleep. She had always loved him, at first with a puppy love when he was a magnificent demigod bursting into her house to carry Freddy off to football games, dances, movies or simply to that mysterious place called "out."

"Where are you boys off to now?" her mother would call.

"Just out, Mrs. Mason," Gee would answer, and they'd go running off together, laughing.

She had resented the phrase "puppy love," and the indulgent smiles on her parents' faces, but by the time she was eighteen she recognized it for what it was, and waited for it to wear off. It never did, though. She went through college dating other boys and enjoying life in general, but always waiting for him in particular. Then in her senior year at college Gee had called to tell her he was getting married. The call itself was an admission of something neither had voiced: that they had a relationship different from that between brother's friend and brother's kid sister. But at the moment of recognizing that relationship, the call also destroyed it.

She had gone on with her life, as Hardy would have advised. She had become engaged and finished college as a biology major, gotten married, took a job as a lab technician and got herself unmarried again. Then had come the news that Gee and Freddy had both been shot down on the same day and were missing in action.

She didn't really know what she had done with herself in the following years. She had waited for the pain to fade, as she had once waited for her puppy love to vanish. Instead it was the months that had faded, peeling off into years and disappearing into a miasma of loneliness, until suddenly out of the dead past Freddy and Gee had come home again.

She didn't see Gee, but Freddy was a broken shell of a man whom she'd tried to put back together. She had just begun to admit to herself that it was hopeless when Gee had walked into their trailer in Virginia and taken Freddy off to smuggle drugs. She wouldn't have believed she could ever condone such a thing, but look what people had done during Prohibition, and look what they had done to Freddy—and to Gee too—in a war they now admitted was all wrong.

She didn't know anymore what was right or wrong. She only knew that Freddy had come back to life and that Gee had done it.

Early the next morning Alison left, and Hardy flew up to Seattle to meet with the Cubans.

## 35

The main Cuban was Xavier Guarez, who had flown transports in the Cuban Air Force but had defected nearly twenty years ago. He was delighted to have an opportunity to return to his country with a 707 full of military men and equipment, spearheading the counterrevolution. He had been born into a wealthy Cuban family that had prospered under Batista, but in his early twenties he had begun to see how wicked that dictatorship really was, and when Fidel Castro came down out of the mountains to free the country, he had joined a large group of fellow officers who deserted from the Air Force to embrace the revolution.

But as Castro followed an increasingly Marxist line, Guarez became disenchanted. His marriage had gone sour, and when his mother died he decided there was nothing to keep him in the land that had once been his own. He defected to the United States, bringing with him a cynical attitude about national borders and identities. To him the United States was not the land of the free; it was simply the closest place that hated Castro and offered a chance of earning a livelihood.

He flew for several charter operations out of Miami before landing a job with a small airline. Now he was retired, and with retirement had come a realization of how empty his life was. He was a strict Catholic who had never attempted any sort of meaningful liaison with another woman since he left his wife in Cuba. He had no communication with her, nor with his children. He realized now that all that mattered in life was his family. He didn't even know if he had any grandchildren. He began to dream of one day returning to Cuba. He moved back to Miami to at least be among his countrymen, and as word of his sympathies spread he was invited to work with first one group and then another who were determined to topple Castro. At first his enthusiasm had been ignited, but as the years went by he realized how ineffectual they all were.

So when this gringo, Captain Dallas, had approached him one day at his favorite restaurant on Calle Ocho in Miami, he'd thought he was just another one of those crazy dreamers. But this man not only had plans, but also had backing and money. Guarez had become a believer and had sworn to help him. Following Captain Dallas's instructions, he left Miami for Seattle. Together they had picked out a Boeing 707 in prime condition. Captain Dallas had signed a check, and they had taken a six months' lease on the machine.

Today, as he awaited the captain, Xavier Guarez was satisfied. He would show his leader what he had done in the last few weeks. He thought of the coming inspection with calm assurance that Captain Dallas would be pleased; he thought of the day soon to come when Xavier Guarez of the Cuban Air Force would no longer be an old has-been but captain of a Boeing 707 flying back to Cuba with a cargo of military men and supplies to begin the counterrevolution.

They shook hands, and Xavier Guarez introduced Captain Dallas to the crew he had recruited. Alfonso Martinez, the copilot, had been with Pan Am, but had walked away from his job the minute Guarez propositioned him. "The man is a firebrand," Guarez said proudly.

Hardy studied him. The man was a fool. He was one of those romantic, macho Cubans who would answer the call to arms sounded by any lunatic. Miami was full of them. Hardy wished Guarez had been more careful. Still, he'd probably do. He couldn't be kept on the string too long because he would grow impatient for action, shoot his mouth off and endanger the operation. But there was no need to keep him quiet for long; the summer was well on its way, and soon they would be too. He smiled and shook Martinez's hand.

"And this is our radioman navigator," Guarez said with a flourish. Hardy frowned; he had thought that the woman was Guarez's or Martinez's girlfriend. "Miss Gloria Carollo," Guarez said formally.

She was young, impossibly young, somewhere in her mid-twenties, with thick raven-black hair, a voluptuous body and full lips rouged ruby-red. Then Hardy noticed her eyes; they were tunnels, deep and dark. This woman was not someone to be judged too quickly.

Carollo spoke a heavily accented English. She had come to America only a few years before, Guarez explained, with the rash of *Marielitos* who had burst out of Castro's jails and asylums. But she was not one of them; she had simply sneaked into their midst, taking advantage of the mass exodus that confused the paperwork of the Cuban authorities. She too had been recruited in Miami, where she was already well known among the Cuban counterrevolutionary exiles. She had trained at the technical university in Havana, and was well versed in modern electronics and communications instruments. Hardy nodded. He would soon see.

They boarded the 707 and took off for a test flight. By the time they landed again he was satisfied. It was too early to tell much, but it was clear that they were as good as could be expected. With sufficient training there should be no problem. Actually, the only important one was the pilot. The duties of the other two would be routine, and he intended to train them arduously during the next week; they had to be competent, but the pilot had to be perfect, and in Guarez he had found a jewel, the kind of man who could fly anything. He was not, as in the movies, the pilot who looks a new plane over, takes her up, wrings her out and conquers her by instinct; the only real thing about such movies is that the pilots are always young and handsome, because pilots who fly by instinct alone never live long enough to get old and ugly. No, Guarez was the kind of pilot who reads the manual until he can see it on the back of his eyelids, who flies the bird in his mind until he can anticipate every situation, his fingers moving immediately to the hydraulic levers, flaps or throttles without thinking before he ever sits in the cockpit and hears the motors begin to roar.

Gloria turned out to be a jewel of another kind. At first she was cold and distant, obviously aware of her body and sex, afraid that she would be treated as a woman instead of a soldier. But by the third day she began to accept Hardy's attitude as real, and her own attitude changed. As soon as she realized that he was not interested in her as a woman, that she would not be treated as a plaything, she began to be interested in him as a man. By the end of the week her friendly smiles and casual touches became more insistent, until finally on his last night in Seattle he had to face it, and found that he could not. He had drilled them endlessly and from now on they could practice on their own. They would spend the next few weeks flying under all conditions, following the route again and again until they could do it in their sleep. There was nothing more for him to do, but she had asked him to come to her room because she wanted to talk to him. As soon as he entered she kicked off her shoes, came up to him and put her hands on his shoulders, sliding them around his neck, pulling his lips down to hers.

Hardy found he could not do it. He pulled away, disengaged her fingers and stepped back, looking down at her as gently as he could. "I'm sorry," he said.

"It's not me, is it?" she asked. She looked at him with understanding. "It's not my fault?"

"No," he said. "It's not you. It's me." It was easier to let her think that than to admit the truth.

"I'm sorry."

"So am I." He smiled sadly. "But it's not important."

"It's all there is," she said simply.

"I thought you were a counterrevolutionary. I thought *that* was all there is."

"No. Perhaps I thought so at one time. But the reason for the counterrevolution is to make our country once again our home, and the reason for that is to live in it. It is life that counts, and life is love. That is really all there is for any of us."

*Yes,* he thought. *Yes, when you come right down to it, that's all there really is.* Then he shook his head, erasing the thought. "Not for me," he said.

"I am sorry," she said again.

"Don't be," he answered. "Don't be sorry for me. I have other compensations."

She shook her head sadly. "I don't believe that. I don't even believe you do."

"Good-bye," he said, and turned and left the room.

He lay awake for nearly an hour, thinking about what Gloria had said. He tried hard to understand his own motivations, but couldn't pierce the barrier he had erected to protect himself from the world. Gloria Carollo had taken him by surprise, and a sudden vision of Alison had flashed before his eyes. He didn't like that. Of course he didn't want to sleep with Gloria, but it had nothing to do with Alison.

Or did it, he wondered? Lying in bed, staring at the ceiling, he tried to consider the situation. He knew now that he had once loved Alison, though he hadn't known it at the time. But that had been long ago; he had no time for such things now. Yet, lying here in the middle of the night, impaled on his own prickly uncertainties, he wondered if he still loved her and still didn't know it. Was he incapable of living in the present? Was he able to understand only the past, to understand only when it was too late to act? Did he in fact prefer it that way, so that he was relieved of any responsibility?

He took a deep breath, let it out in a long sigh and pulled the covers over him. It didn't matter. He couldn't have slept with Gloria Carollo anyway. It would have been like sleeping with a dead woman.

The next morning Hardy left, and the three Cubans spent the day inspecting the plane exhaustively and planning a practice flight to New Mexico. That evening Gloria walked from the hotel to a phone booth in an empty shopping mall and made a collect call to Miami. "No," she reported when the connection was made. "It didn't work. I think maybe he doesn't like women."

## 36

Everything was settling into place. The only problem was the damned Libyans. They were becoming a nuisance, always wanting to know the details of the plan, insisting on progress reports. In a way it was understandable, for they were like children. They wanted the President and were paying for the plan to kidnap him, but they couldn't tolerate the delay of gratification any more than an impatient child can wait months and months for Christmas.

But it was precisely because of their childish instincts that Hardy didn't trust them. The day that Mohammed Asri had arrived the Libyans had also sent Wahid Mahouri to see what was going on. Hardy hadn't told him anything, but now he was coming again. Mason had been right when he'd said that first evening, "I don't like him coming here. Every contact is an added risk."

On the way back from Seattle Hardy realized that he couldn't put it off any longer; it was time to face the problem.

Dr. Mahouri was a Libyan-born businessman who had lived in Egypt for over ten years and had taken out citizenship there. In the course of his international export business he traveled frequently to the United States, but Hardy was afraid that he wasn't fooling anyone. He was a Libyan mole, of course. It was possible that he hadn't yet been identified by the Egyptian secret service; it was also possible that they had. It was possible that even if they knew who he was, they hadn't informed the FBI; it was also possible that they had. There were no two ways about it: it was dangerous for Mahouri to visit them, and every visit only increased the danger.

When Hardy arrived at the farmhouse he found the Libyan waiting for him. "Good day," Mahouri said.

"Get your bags," Hardy said. "We're leaving."

Mahouri expressed no surprise, gave a slight bow and left the room.

"What's up?" Mason asked.

"We're getting rid of him. For good."

"Not . . .?"

"No, better than that." He smiled. "I'll wait for him in the car."

He sat in the car with the engine running and the trunk open. Mahouri came out, put his bags in the trunk, and got in beside him. In silence they drove to the airport. There Hardy parked and carried Mahouri's bags to the ticket counter. "My friend has a ticket," he told the girl, "but we've changed the reservation." He put out his hand to Mahouri, who raised his eyebrows but handed over his ticket.

After they had checked in, Hardy led the Libyan outside for a little walk. "I know you're dissatisfied," he said.

Mahouri politely declined to answer, merely tilting his head in acknowledgment.

"I understand your feelings," Hardy said, "and I'm sure you understand ours. Security is the first order of business in any clandestine operation. However, you have a right to know; I acknowledge that, and I am now prepared to reveal everything."

Mahouri lifted his eyebrows.

"All the details," Hardy said. "But not to you."

Mahour lowered his eyebrows and frowned.

"You know too much already," Hardy went on. "If you were caught coming into or leaving the country, the entire operation would be blown. Tell Ja'far to send me someone else—someone who knows nothing at all about what's involved. Absolutely nothing, do you understand? Except the code name, of course. That way, if your security is lax and he's picked up on his way in, they'll find out nothing. I will meet him in Los Angeles exactly two weeks from today in front of the Mark Taper Forum. I will then show him everything we're going to do, and send him back to you so that he can make a full report."

"And if he is picked up on his way back to us? Doesn't that destroy your security?"

"Of course," Hardy answered impatiently. "There's always some danger. But on the way in he's your responsibility; on the way out he's mine. I'll make sure no one finds out anything about him while he's here, so if he comes in safely there should be no problem about his leaving safely. But there's one more aspect we have to discuss."

"Which is?"

"I want you to send someone you can trust."

"Of course. That goes without saying."

"Well, *I'm* saying it, mister. Now listen up and hear me good. I don't want somebody you think you can trust because he's the second cousin of somebody's sister who once slapped an American for getting fresh. You hear what I'm saying? I want someone who's done some real work for you, someone you've tested and know is good. Send me someone like that two weeks from today, and I'll tell him what you want to know."

"The more work such a man has done for us," Mahouri objected, "the more likely he is to be known by your FBI and picked up or followed on his entry into the United States."

"I don't give a damn if he's picked up because he won't know anything. If that happens, just send me another one. I repeat: he's not to know *anything*. That's why I want to meet him in Los Angeles. You know that we're based here in Wichita, and if you're picked up I'm dead. That's why I get nervous when you come. But if he's followed to L.A., they still won't know anything. I'll make sure nobody's following him after we meet, and I'll take care of the security necessary to get him out of the country again." He glanced at his watch. "They must be boarding by now. You'd better get moving."

## 37

Moammar Qaddafi was a neurotic personality with paranoid tendencies toward what used to be called a Napoleon complex. He saw himself as the savior of his country, the leader of the world's Arabs, a new prophet of Mohammed sent to cleanse the world of its putrefying infidel nations. His family was Bedouin, and his inherited characteristics reflected that heritage: he was fiercely independent, religious and proud. These combined with his paranoia to produce a dangerous man.

Suleiman Akbar was a sociopath. The two men were meant for each other, and they found each other through Ayn Allah Ja'far. When Ja'far graduated from Cambridge and returned to Libya, he saw the country with new eyes. He had been brought up in a professional family, and had seen little of his country beyond the privileged sphere of his family and their friends.

He came back to Libya a grown man. Eyes that have seen a foreign civilization are eyes that have been taught to see, and what Ja'far saw in his home nation was poverty, a total lack of education, with 99 percent of the wealth and 100 percent of the power held by 1 percent of the population. The unfairness of the system did not bother him, but the fact that he was excluded from that 1 percent did.

He was not left totally out in the cold. He was admitted to the monetary sphere, and his education was useful to the ruling class. But the Arab rulers were strongly family-oriented, and Ja'far's family was not one of the ruling families. The only way open to him was to marry into the governmental circles, but he was unsuccessful.

Then in the later 1960s Ja'far saw another route: the young, charismatic, rebellious army officer, Colonel Moammar Qaddafi. He was dazzled by Qaddafi's brilliance. Napoleons often blind their cohorts with the brilliance of their visions; Ja'far was not blinded, but he saw that many others were, and that Qaddafi had a good chance of taking over the Libyan government. Because he perceived Qaddafi's neuroses correctly, he realized that the man could never turn Libya into a socialist heaven on earth, but he also saw that Qaddafi could take the reins of power, and that those who helped him take it would be the new ruling class of Libya. He became one of Qaddafi's earliest supporters, and when it became clear that violence would be necessary to bring the man to power, Ja'far was not unhappy about the prospect.

He was not a violent man himself. He had never pulled a trigger in his life, never wired together a bomb, never beaten a prisoner until the man's flesh parted from his bones. But he gathered around him a band of brothers who reveled in such brutality.

Such a brother was Suleiman Akbar. He was a small man, and a cruel one. He delighted in those aspects of life that make normal men sick. He was of a type not peculiar to any time or country; in Germany he would have become a Nazi, in Iran a SAVAK agent, in Italy a Black Shirt, in the United States a Klansman. He wore glasses, was balding and dressed conservatively; he looked the image of a Near Eastern businessman, even one that you might trust. But behind those black eyes was an even blacker soul.

Akbar was not unintelligent. He had already proved himself capable of carrying out specific tasks, if not quite clever enough to plan them himself. Given a map, a schedule and a team, he could infiltrate the Israeli border and place his group around the bend in the mountainous road that had been chosen, and when the targeted school bus appeared he would order the machine guns and bazooka rockets to open fire at the correct time. He would even remain calm enough in the aftermath to walk carefully through the bloody wreck of the bus, shooting with his own gun any children still alive.

Akbar was devoted to Ja'far for the opportunities to carry out such tasks. He was not ambitious for a seat in the tents of power; he was content to wait outside to be summoned and told to go to Israel to kill schoolchildren, to Athens to destroy an airliner, to Rome or Paris to place a bomb in a crowded synagogue. So when Mahouri came home and conveyed Hardy's request, Ja'far thought immediately of Akbar. He was perfect.

## 38

An airmail letter from Rome arrived at the farmhouse a week after Mahouri left, informing Hardy that the package he had requested would be sent out of London on August 28. The Pan Am London–Los Angeles flight landed at 4:24 P.M. that day, so Hardy arrived at the Forum at four o'clock. He watched to see if anyone took up a position there, reading a newspaper, waiting casually, killing time. When a cab pulled up at five-thirty and a small Middle Eastern man stepped out, put his suitcase down on the pavement and looked around expectantly, Hardy was sure that nobody had been planted there to wait for him.

Nevertheless, he took no immediate action. He waited another ten minutes, but still couldn't spot anyone taking an interest. Finally he walked up to the man and extended his hand.

"Mr. Dallas?" the man asked.

Hardy nodded, and they shook hands. "My name is Faldallah."

"Let's go."

They walked two blocks to a bus stop and took the first bus that came along. Once inside Hardy gave instructions, and at the next large cross street he got off; Faldallah was to stay on the bus to the end of the line, then take a cab.

Hardy stood on the street corner, making sure that no car that might have been trailing the bus came to a stop. After watching for five minutes, he took a cab to a house he had rented on a small street that curved up into the Hollywood hills from Sunset Boulevard. From the main bedroom of the house a sliding glass door let out to a balcony, and from there he could see down the curving road all the way to Sunset with a good pair of binoculars. Watching carefully, he saw Faldallah's cab turn off Sunset and begin the climb. It took a good five minutes, and during this time no other car followed.

The cab stopped out of his view in front of the house, and a few seconds later Hardy saw it descending toward Sunset. The doorbell rang, but he ignored it, still watching the cab. It reached Sunset, came nearly to a full stop, then inched out into the traffic and disappeared back toward the center of the city. None of the other cars parked on Sunset or the adjoining streets moved out to follow it.

Finally Hardy went down the stairs, opened the door and led Faldallah into the kitchen. Putting water on to boil, he said, "I asked Ja'far to send me someone who has done work for him in the past, someone he could trust."

"I believe I am that person."

"I'm not sure," Hardy said. "I've never heard of anyone named Faldallah. That bothers me."

Faldallah smiled with condescension. "That is the name on my passport. I am immodest enough to believe that my true name would attract the attention of your passport agency."

Hardy glanced over his shoulder as the water came to a boil. "Tea or coffee?" he asked.

"Tea, thank you," Faldallah replied. American coffee was a putrid brew; the tea could be no worse than innocuous.

"A small sandwich, perhaps? Some cheese?"

Faldallah nodded without interest; food was not one of his passions.

"And your real name is?" Hardy asked as he prepared a small platter.

"Suleiman Akbar," Faldallah said, and Hardy gave a small bow with his head, acknowledging his guest's fame. Placing the platter of food on the table, he brought over the tea and his own cup of coffee, and they sat down to eat and to talk.

Ten minutes later Faldallah-Akbar was unconscious. Hardy pulled him out of the kitchen chair and dragged him to the living room, where he laid him out on the couch. From a small black bag he took a hypodermic needle and a rubber-capped vial. He filled the hypodermic, injected the sleeping man with sodium pentothal and then sat down to wait.

It took another five minutes before Akbar began to stir and make moaning noises. "Good morning," Hardy said. "My name is Kartoxan. What is your name?"

"Suleiman Faldallah."

"What is your name?"

"Suleiman Faldallah."

"What is your name?"

Akbar began to sweat. He rolled back and forth and tried to turn over, but Hardy restrained him. "What is your name?"

"Suleiman," he began.

"Yes?"

"Suleiman . . ."

"*What is your name?*" Hardy hissed.

Akbar began to sing nonsense words, disconnected syllables interspersed with humming and whistling.

Hardy remained composed. He was used to this standard defense against the drug. He waited patiently until the sounds died away, then asked again, "What is your name?"

The game continued for another ten minutes, Hardy asking over and over, and Faldallah-Akbar growing more nervous and upset. Finally Hardy asked and got no answer as Faldallah-Akbar struggled with all his reserves against the drug. Again he asked, "What is your name?" quietly, softly and authoritatively.

Akbar couldn't answer. He was sweating profusely; his skin was hot and he was twitching.

Hardy said, "You are not Suleiman Faldallah. Your name is Suleiman Akbar."

As the name was spoken the unconscious, tortured body relaxed, and in another moment began to breathe deeply.

"Your name is Suleiman Akbar," Hardy said again quietly and authoritatively. The unconscious lips moved silently. "What did you say?"

"Yes," the voice said simply.

"What is your name?"

"Suleiman Akbar."

Hardy nodded. That wasn't difficult, he thought; some guys are hard, and some aren't.

"What are your orders?"

"I am to contact Mr. Dallas in Los Angeles. He will tell me details of the operation called Dallas. I will take this information back to Ayn Ja'far. I will speak to no one else."

"What is the operation called Dallas?"

"That is what I will be told."

"What do you know of it now?"

"Nothing," Akbar said without strain.

"What is the operation called Dallas?"

"I do not know."

"What is Operation Dallas?"

"I do not know."

"Who is Mr. Dallas?"

"He is in charge of Operation Dallas."

"What is his real name?"

"I do not know."

"What is the purpose of that operation?"

"I do not know."

After nearly half an hour Hardy was satisfied that Akbar was telling the truth. Ja'far had followed instructions. Good. He walked into the kitchen, put two lamb chops under the broiler, took out a beer and waited for Akbar to wake up.

## 39

It was a small office, but the agent pointed out that the owner had done a good job of renovating the whole building at 511 Hill Street in downtown Los Angeles. "What sort of business will you be using it for?" he asked, but Hardy didn't appear to hear him. He was walking around the empty space, looking it over.

"Mr. Ellison?" the sales agent asked. "What sort of business will you be wanting it for?"

Hardy stepped to the window and looked out. So far Faldallah had said not a word and continued to stand in the middle of the room. Mr. Anders now looked from one to the other, then decided to join Mr. Ellison at the window. It was always hard to tell exactly who the money man was in a situation like this; sometimes he guessed wrong, especially when foreign types stood there not saying a word. Goddamn inscrutable, they were. But you had to make up your mind sooner or later and go with your instincts. That was his motto, and he made a pretty decent living, after all, so how wrong could he be?

"Nice view," Anders said, coming up behind Mr. Ellison and stretching to look over his shoulder. "Not a better one anywhere in Los Angeles. The window opens, too. That sounds funny, doesn't it? But just go into these new office buildings they're putting up all over and you'll see what I mean. Central air conditioning sounds great, but to cut costs they put in these windows that don't open. So when you get a nice day, which we do get once in a while here . . ."

He was talking too much. He always did when he got these strong, silent types. He liked someone who could talk like a human being; he got along all right with people like that. But once in a while you got a cold fish, and that made him nervous and then he talked too much. "Excuse me," he said, leaning past Mr. Ellison, "let me just show you." He pulled on the window frame, but the damned thing wouldn't open. Well, the hell with it. You couldn't win them all. He decided to cut this interview short and get back to the office.

Mr. Ellison gently pushed him aside and yanked the window open without effort. A cool breeze wafted into the room, and Anders took heart again. "Look at that," he said, turning to the Middle Eastern gentleman. "Feel that breeze? You don't get that in a modern building."

Mr. Ellison leaned out of the window. "Nice view," he said.

Anders stuck his head out too. "You can see all the way down to the freeway." He pointed, one hand holding on to the window frame; he was afraid of heights.

"Take a look." Mr. Ellison turned to his companion, and the small gentleman walked across the room. He touched his spectacles, making sure they wouldn't fall off, and leaned out the window and admired the view.

"I'd like a six-month lease," Mr. Ellison said. "Occupancy within thirty days."

Anders beamed. This was the way he liked to do business.


40


That same morning, while Hardy and Akbar were renting the office on Hill Street, Matsuo Nakaoka was flying in from San Francisco. Traveling without luggage, he walked quickly through Los Angeles International and took a cab to Grauman's Chinese Theatre. During the long ride he sat turned around the entire time, looking through the rear window to make sure he was not being followed.

His real name was Hideki Nakagawa and he should never have been born because in 1945—five years before his birth—his father had been a kamikaze pilot learning to fly the Yokosuka MXY-7 Ohka, which was nothing more than a flying bomb carrying a pilot who would steer it directly to its target. In June, July and the first few days of August of 1945 he was practicing with the unpowered glider version, waiting for the next batch of operational planes to be shipped from the factory. His unit was to be the first line of defense against the Allied invasion force expected in early fall.

But on August 6, 1945, a lone B-29 sailed high over Hiroshima, and a week later the war was over. The projected invasion of Japan was never launched and Ichiro Nakagawa came home in disgrace to the bride he had married in 1942. The disgrace was absolute: he was kamikaze, and Japan had lost the war, and he was alive. But by 1950, when Hideki was born, most Japanese were beginning to wonder how they could ever have been so taken in by the stirring chords of bushido; they were glad they had not died for their emperor. It was better to live for their families.

Shizuko Nakagawa, Ichiro's wife, told the boy Hideki how lucky he was to be alive at all: his father had thought himself destined to die five years before the boy was given life. It was a story he heard throughout his childhood; it was repeated whenever he was bad, whenever he was sad, whenever he succeeded, whenever he failed. Life was all; that was the message his mother taught. Whatever happened, be happy simply to be alive.

He would glance at his father as she prattled on, and he saw in the man's eyes a different story. Later, when they left the house and walked alone in the woods, his father would tell him how he had trained to give his life to his emperor, and how that glory had been taken from him; he learned from his father what a worthless gift is life without glory.

When he was twelve years old his father died in a traffic accident in Tokyo. A meaningless death, just as his life had been rendered meaningless. Hideki realized that his father was right: a life without glory is empty, and an empty life is not worth the pain of living it.

He never spoke of this to his mother; he never argued with her. When she told her story again and again he listened politely, but in his heart he knew better.

At Grauman's Chinese Theatre Nakaoka waited for half an hour until a rental car pulled up and Hardy motioned for him to get in. The Arab Hardy had told him about was in the front seat, so he got in back. Hardy took four consecutive right turns while Nakaoka looked out the rear window to be sure that no other car did the same; then they headed down Sunset and up into the Santa Monica mountains.

Forty-five minutes later Hardy pulled off the road onto a dirt path that led down through the trees, emerging a couple of hundred yards away in a rough clearing. When they got out of the car Hardy introduced the two men, using their aliases, then from the trunk of the car took a suitcase, opened it and showed Akbar the rifle. He pointed across the clearing where three Coke bottles had been set up on a tree stump, and handed the rifle to Nakaoka.

It might have been more impressive if the Japanese had taken it, spun around and squeezed off three quick shots. But he was a professional assassin, not a showman. First he inspected the rifle carefully; then he threw a few leaves in the air and took his time watching them settle, gauging the wind. Finally he found a suitable tree to lean against, then took what seemed like an unconscionable length of time sighting on the target. Finally, without warning, he pulled the trigger three times in rapid succession, so that the sharp cracks merged into one explosion, and in the same instant the three Coke bottles shattered and disappeared.

Hardy put the rifle away again and they drove back into town.

"The parade will come up Hill Street," Hardy explained as they sat in the hotel parking lot. "Nakaoka will be in the office we rented today. He will spend two or three days a week there in these next few weeks, right up to the time of the President's visit, so that people in the building will be used to seeing him. If anyone asks, he'll be setting up an import-export business, dealing with Taiwanese curios. There are probably two dozen businesses in this city alone doing the same thing, so there won't be anything unusual in it. You saw yourself how the view from the office is unhindered the entire length of Hill Street. He can't possibly miss. It's basically the same plan that worked in Dallas, and it will work here. The only difficulty is getting away afterwards, and Nakaoka is willing to take that chance. Any questions?"

Akbar looked carefully at Nakaoka. "I assume you are being well paid for your efforts?" he asked.

Hardy interrupted angrily. "That's between him and me. I'm in charge of this operation and I hand out the paychecks. You're here to carry back a report on our progress. Do you have any questions?"

There were no questions. Without another word Akbar got out of the car and walked into the hotel. By then it was after seven, too late for him to catch the 6:05 Pan Am flight back to London, so he would have to take the next day's plane.

"From your conversation," Nakaoka observed as Hardy drove him back to the airport for the flight to San Francisco, "it would appear that Mr. Akbar is under the impression that the attempt will be made in Los Angeles."

Hardy nodded. "Akbar is a messenger for the people who are paying us. They want to know what's happening. That's reasonable, but I don't like to take chances, which is even more reasonable. So he can tell them the plan, but it doesn't really matter to them where the actual attack will take place. It does, however, matter to us if their security is lax. That's why I warned you not to say a word during this meeting. I didn't want you to give anything away."

Nakaoka nodded. He understood and approved of such precautions.

* * *

Since Akbar had been told nothing of Operation Dallas by Ja'far, he offered no objections when he was told the President was to be assassinated. Hardy was not worried that when Akbar reported back there would be anger and consternation; he did not intend that Akbar should ever see Ja'far again.

After dropping Nakaoka off at the airport he stopped at a pay phone in a gas station, from his pocket took out a handful of quarters, dialed a long-distance number and began to feed in the quarters in accordance with the recorded voice's instructions. When a switchboard operator answered he said, "I'm calling long distance and I don't have any more money, so don't try to transfer me. Just take down this information. A supposed businessman traveling in this country on a Lebanese passport in the name of Suleiman Faldallah is actually a Libyan terrorist named Suleiman Akbar. He is in Los Angeles at the Biltmore. Tomorrow evening he is flying Pan Am to London. He's setting up some kind of terrorist action here. Do you have all that?"

The operator read the message back to him, and then asked, "May I have your name, sir?"

Hardy hung up.

41

The message reached Greg Winter at just after 11:00 P.M., Eastern standard time. He read it and cursed silently, then read it again and cursed out loud. He hadn't been scheduled for the late shift tonight; he had switched because he was leaving on vacation tomorrow and wanted to get an early start. Ordinarily he would have been happy to pick up an unexpected tip, but the last thing he wanted on this particular night was to get involved in something that might carry over into tomorrow and interfere with his vacation. His wife would kill him. They had tickets to fly out tomorrow morning to Chicago and visit her parents for the first time in nearly a year. The tickets were nonrefundable. His mother-in-law would kill him too.

"Goddamn it," he said plaintively. He had been careful to get everything cleared up this week. His desk shone, with not a scrap of paper on it, and the in-tray was empty. Now this. For one brief second he thought of erasing the message from the computer. No, that wasn't a thought, it was a fantasy. He stared at it on the computer screen, stored it and typed in an inquiry to Records.

The reply came back at 1:57 A.M.; there was no record in the FBI files of either Suleiman Akbar or Suleiman Faldallah.

Winter smiled the smile of the righteous. He had done his duty and God had taken care of him. It had been just one more dirty Arab calling the FBI to try to get a legitimate business competitor in trouble. They never learned. In their country such a call would have meant fists banging on the poor guy's door in the middle of the night and hands dragging him off to a secret dungeon where he'd be beaten for two weeks before his innocence was established. *Well, we don't do things that way in this country, buddy. You'll have to find another way of getting ahead in business.*

As a matter of routine Winter pressed a key on his computer switchboard, sending the inquiry to CIA headquarters at Langley and to NSA at Fort Meade. There was always the possibility that this guy was indeed a terrorist but had never before operated within U.S. boundaries and so was not in the FBI files. The odds on this were maybe one in a thousand, but Greg Winter was not the kind of man to make a mistake as simple as ignoring this possibility. That was not the way to get ahead in the Federal Bureau of Investigation. Finally, his thoughts returning with relief to tomorrow's vacation, he hit the save button so that any reply would come directly to this terminal and would be readily identifiable to the agent taking his place in the morning.

Unfortunately, he hit the wrong button.

## 42

Melnik felt he was going crazy. He was in an impossible situation. Every day he would sit in the office assigned to him and stare at the walls. For variety he would turn around and stare out the window and try to think of something they could do. He had often come up against such blank walls; tracing Arab assassins was not easy. But there were so many of them that there was always *something* to do. When he lost the trail of one there was always a lead to follow on another. He was never stuck in one spot, on one case, after one person who had vanished like a phantom.

He had only one other thing to think about, and thinking about her didn't help. He had to see her again, but since their lunch together there hadn't been an opportunity. He wished he had never met her.

Every afternoon at two o'clock Werther called Melnik in for a brief meeting to exchange ideas, but aside from trying to break San Medro, neither of them knew what to do.

There was one other line of attack open to them, and it was being pursued diligently by several entry-grade agents. The videotape that had been taken continuously during surveillance of San Medro's house showed everyone who had passed by on the street. They were starting with those who had passed more than once, or who had seemed to have shown an interest in the house. Armed with prints of their faces made from the tape, the agents were canvassing the neighborhood and putting a name and a history to each face.

Or at least trying to. It wasn't easy, since many of the people in the neighborhood didn't want either their faces or their names known to the FBI. Even people with nothing to hide were usually protected by their neighbors, who didn't know what they might be guilty of. Better safe than sorry. It was a long, slow process.

They still had San Medro, of course. He was in custody, notwithstanding the advice of his lawyer to allow him to fix bail and get him out. San Medro knew that Abrams had enough on him to put him away for a long time, so a temporary release on bail wasn't much use. His only hope was to hold out against the constant questioning until he managed to convince them that he knew nothing more about Dallas than he had already told them. He knew they didn't really want him on the old drug and prostitution charges. They wanted information, and if he could convince them he didn't have any, eventually they would let him go.

Or if they could convince him that they knew for certain he did know more, then he could always talk in return for his freedom. It was like a chess match, each party making its moves and trying to confuse the other. At the moment it was stalemate.

\*     \*     \*

"Well, let's not get discouraged," Werther said, trying to convince himself that he wasn't discouraged. "We hit these nadirs in every case. We'll work our way out of it." He paused. "The Director's asked me to go down to Washington to see him first thing in the morning. He wants a report on our progress"—he laughed mirthlessly—"and I think he's taking some action to coordinate efforts with the Treasury people and the CIA. Maybe if we all look at the same data we'll come up with something. It certainly can't hurt."

No, it couldn't hurt, Melnik agreed. An idea had occurred to him as Werther was talking, and he nearly held his breath to keep it from appearing on his face. After he left the office he walked around the block, thinking it through. Everyone knew about the Director. The man worked around the clock; he never seemed to sleep. Werther had said he'd be seeing him "first thing in the morning." In the Director's language that must mean 8:00 A.M., or even 7:00 A.M.

He didn't dare ask around the office. Instead, when he returned he dialed a travel agent and asked about flight schedules to Washington. When he hung up he was grinning. The first shuttle flight in the morning couldn't possibly get Werther there in time. He left early, too excited to sit and stare at the wall.

"It's me, Melnik," he said, speaking into the mouthpiece.

"Come on up," Lori's metallic voice came out of the wall, and in the next instant the door began to buzz. He walked upstairs to her apartment, and as he reached the landing she was standing by the open door.

He had waited as long as he could. He had eaten at the small Italian restaurant around the corner, hoping that she might actually drop in. When he finished it wasn't even seven o'clock. Much too early. He went to a movie. When he came out it was only a little after nine. He walked around the Village for over an hour, but finally at ten-fifteen he couldn't wait any longer.

Now he walked down the hall and came toward her. "I was just passing by. I thought I'd talk to Charles about what he's going to say to the Director tomorrow."

"Oh, dear," Lori said. "I'm sorry to disappoint you. You're too late.

His appointment in Washington is at seven A.M. Evidently the Director never sleeps. Charlie took the shuttle flight in this evening; he'll be staying there overnight."

They stared at each other. Suddenly Melnik couldn't contain it any longer; he smiled sheepishly. "Actually, that possibility had occurred to me," he admitted.

She nodded. "I thought you might have figured it out. Aren't you a clever boy?"

She took him by the hand and led him into the apartment.

Lori lay awake, watching him sleep. She glanced at the clock on the night table; it read two-fifty-five. She turned onto her back and stared at the ceiling.

She hadn't intended this. She closed her eyes in despair. She *had* intended it, of course. She had hoped . . . Oh, God.

They hadn't seen each other since their lunch nearly a week ago. He hadn't called, and she hadn't wanted him to. It was best forgotten— Well, not forgotten, but it was best for it to be over. She had thought of calling him when Charlie told her he would be spending the night in Washington, and had been ashamed of the thought. At least she hadn't called. But when he showed up at her front door, she hadn't sent him away, had she? Far from it, she thought now, staring up at the ceiling.

Well, she supposed it was fate. She hadn't called him, she consoled herself. She never would have called him. She was a passive instrument; if he hadn't come this evening she would have stayed home alone and it would have been over. She looked up at the ceiling, bit her lip and wondered if she was lying.

It was 3:00 A.M. when Greg Winter's mistake was discovered. It was reported to the Director's overnight staff chief, who, knowing about the meeting tomorrow with Werther and about the Director's penchant for interrupted sleep, decided to wake him up. That was the main part of his job, deciding whether or not to wake the Director in the middle of the night. He had learned that to wake him unnecessarily was a minor mistake but that to let him sleep was a major one.

The staff chief's decision tonight was the right one, and he was told to find Werther right away. He called the New York office, where the operator gave him the name of Werther's Washington hotel. By 4:30 A.M. Werther, the Director and he were sitting around the huge oak table in the FBI's conference room on Pennsylvania Avenue.

The meeting was over at 5:23 A.M., and by five-thirty Werther was standing outside in the early morning chill. The sky was overcast and there was still no hint of the morning sun, but it would soon come. He thought of returning to his hotel and getting some sleep, but after that meeting he knew he could not. Christ, how had they let it happen? Allowing a known Libyan terrorist into this country was bad enough, but then, after being tipped off, letting him out again?

He shook his head angrily. He hated having to tell Melnik about the foul-up, but as he started to walk through the long dark streets he realized he would have to. He had known it, really, even while hearing the story. At this point, Melnik was the only one who could help. He would have given his right arm to find someone else to turn to. He liked Melnik, he really did, but there was that damned arrogance about him. He hated confessing to him what had happened, especially after the Asri debacle, and he hated even more having to ask him for the Mossad's help.

He never slept well in hotels anyway, Werther thought. There was no point in going back and trying to rest, particularly not the way he was feeling right now. Christ. It was the aggravation, and he shouldn't let it get to him, but what can you do?

Turn it to your advantage, that's what you can do. If he hustled he could be at the airport by six, catch the first shuttle of the day and be at La Guardia by seven. He could be home by eight and get an early start on the day.

He stopped at a phone booth and dialed Melnik's hotel in New York. It rang several times before a sleepy operator answered and he asked for David Melnik's room. It rang another dozen times before the operator came back on the line to tell him that no one was answering. Where could the damn Israeli be at 5:30 A.M.? He left a message for Melnik to meet him at home for a breakfast session at eight o'clock.

## 43

David awoke at seven feeling wonderful. He stretched, turned over and bumped into someone. At first he was startled; his eyes popped open and he stared at the mass of red hair spilling over the pillow. Then he remembered why he was feeling so good.

It was just beginning to get light. From the open window a dull gray morning glow seeped into the room, leaving the corners still in darkness. He could see the building across the street, a few of whose windows glowed with electric light. In Israel the light would have been blinding by now. He decided he liked the noises of the garbage collectors, the honking of cars and the gray comfortable light of morning. He stretched again and pulled the sheet down.

Lori stirred, came awake, turned over and looked at this naked man in her bed. She felt sad.

She felt incredible, he thought, as he traced his fingers over her exposed breast and trickled them down her flat, taut belly.

She would have to explain to him, she realized, that they couldn't meet again; she didn't know what had come over her. She giggled suddenly; she knew what had come *in* her, but—

My God, he thought, that must be the world's most lascivious giggle. He bent down, and as he covered her open lips with his, their tongues met.

It was just an accident that they met, she thought. If he hadn't come to the fencing *salle* they would never— Oh, God, thank God he had, she thought, as his hand swooped down and she raised her hand to his body.

He gasped as she touched him lightly, and as his mouth opened wider and he caught his breath, her body arched toward him. *Later*, she thought wildly. *I'll explain later. Oh* . . .

At 8:15 A.M. Lori was cooking breakfast while David finished showering. As he slipped into his shoes he realized he had been incommunicado since early last evening; that wasn't smart—he decided to call his hotel and check for messages.

They didn't eat bacon much anymore because of cholesterol, but this morning Lori decided to treat herself. She had just opened the package and dropped the first slice into the sizzling pan when she heard the key turn in the lock. The door was in the hallway, just outside the kitchen. Her mind refused to function, whirling uselessly in neutral. Charlie was in Washington. This must be a burglar. Stupefied, she stood with the bacon in her hands and watched the door open.

"Hi," Charlie said, half turning his back to pull the key out of the lock and closing the door behind him. Her body went hot and cold at the same time. She turned her head to the other end of the hallway: down there were the living room, bathrooms, bedrooms—and David.

"I couldn't sleep," Charles said, "so I came home early. Then the damn plane was a half hour late. Is Melnik here?"

The question stunned her. How did he know?

"What's wrong?" he asked. "You're as white as a ghost."

In the bedroom, David was hanging up the phone, trying to deal with the message the operator had given him, when he heard the door open and Charles call out his greeting. He moved more quickly than his thoughts. Leaving the bedroom untouched—somehow Lori would have to clean it up—he hurried to the bedroom door and sneaked a look around the doorframe just in time to see Werther move into the kitchen. "What's wrong?" he heard him ask as he disappeared from view. Without hesitation, as his thoughts began to catch up, he darted quietly down the hall into the bathroom and shut himself in. There he flushed the toilet, opened the door again and walked noisily down the hall to the kitchen.

"Are you all right?" Charles asked, putting his hand on Lori's shaking shoulders.

She nodded convulsively. "You startled me," she said. "I thought you were a burglar."

He laughed. "Sorry. I guess I should have knocked or something. I didn't think."

Her mind was still racing around his question: *Is Melnik here?* How did he know, and why was he acting so nice? And where the hell was David? He must be in the bedroom. Oh, God, did he hear Charles come in? Then she heard the toilet flush and David's footsteps coming down the hall. Simultaneously there was a flash of fire and a puff of smoke. "The bacon!" she called out, hoping to distract Charlie. For a moment it worked, he turned and grabbed the pan from the stove. It gave her an instant to save everything, but she stood there helplessly, not knowing what to do.

The next moment was the worst in her life. As if in slow motion she saw David appear in the kitchen doorway, and Charles put the pan down and turn inexorably around. She thought she might faint; she *hoped* she would faint.

"Hello, David," Charles said. Just that. Nothing more.

"Morning. Just in time for breakfast," David answered as if without a care in the world. "What happened to the bacon?"

"I scared Lori. She thought I was a burglar."

"Do you really worry about things like that in New York? It seems an awful way to live."

*What the hell is going on?* Lori thought. She couldn't understand this conversation. Why wasn't Charlie . . .? Why was David . . .?

"We've got a doorman," Charles was saying now, "but I guess women are always worried about break-ins. You hear a lot about them, even in places with security. Sorry I'm late. Just get here?"

David nodded, and smiled at Lori. "You're squeezing the bacon," he said.

She looked down and saw that her fingers were strangling the greasy strips. "Oh," she said, not knowing what the rules were. A stupid thought occurred to her and she was thankful for something to say. "You're Jewish. You don't eat bacon."

"I love it once in a while," David said, "but between the Old Testament and cholesterol, I don't have it often. Sorry I wasn't in when you called," he said to Charles. "I was out jogging." He turned back to Lori. "You still look shook up; Charles must have frightened you. Let me make the bacon." He took it out of her hands and she said, "Yes. Yes, thank you. I'll just wash the grease off my fingers," and left the kitchen. "Take some coffee," she called over her shoulder. "It ought to be ready." She heard the cups clattering as she reached the bedroom door and went in to straighten up, still not quite sure how she had been saved.

## 44

"So what's new in Washington?" Melnik asked, imposing an appearance of calm over his inner turmoil. He slid the burned bacon off the pan into the sink, put in fresh strips and placed the pan back on the fire. When he looked up, Werther was staring at him, and Melnik's stomach began to turn. He didn't like being in this situation; he was crazy to have let it happen.

"Life is a bitch," Werther said. "But it's our own fault."

Melnik glanced up, but Charles wasn't looking at him. "We have to take responsibility," he said. "Responsibility for our own actions."

Werther stopped, lost in thought. Melnik wondered what he was talking about; did he suspect them? He waited, but Werther was lost in contemplation. Finally he could take it no longer. "What do you mean?" he asked.

"It's all too complex." Werther looked at Melnik. "Our relationships." He shook his head with regret. "Our relationships are too goddamn complex."

Melnik didn't know what to say.

"We can't handle them properly," Werther went on. "I'm not excusing anybody, but I want you to understand. I'm not saying it's anybody's fault. It is, it certainly is, but there are reasons. The point is, they aren't good reasons."

"You're right," Melnik acknowledged. "I'm—"

"I don't know how it happened," Werther went on without listening. "It must have seemed a good idea at the time, but people don't foresee the future, so instead of one coordinated program we've got all these people out there looking after their own little territories."

Melnik stopped in mid-confession. What was the man talking about? He realized he still held the frying pan in his hand and flipped the bacon to the other side. "I guess that's true," he said cautiously. "Where are the eggs?"

Werther took half a dozen eggs out of the refrigerator and began to crack them. "We're supposed to take care of things inside the national borders, but not if it's all within the borders of any one of the states.

The Treasury Department has responsibility for anything that threatens the life of the president. Problems outside our national borders become the province of the CIA, except for NSA, which conducts intelligence surveillance with mostly technological resources. Now, even if you ignore military intelligence and the Foreign Service Intelligence Advisory Board, you can see it's too goddamn complex, can't you?"

Melnik nodded.

"We get in each other's way. We try to cooperate; we really do. We're not fighting for territory—well, I guess there're always going to be some people who are, but basically we try to cooperate. It's the bureaucracy that swamps us. I can't blame anybody, not really."

"Blame them for what?" Melnik asked.

Werther sighed. "FBI headquarters in Washington got an anonymous call three days ago saying that a Lebanese businessman visiting this country was really a Libyan traveling under a false passport. The call was from Los Angeles. The informant said the man was going to take Pan American flight 120 the following day at six-five P.M., nonstop to London. So we had nearly twenty-four hours to stop him."

"What happened?"

"The call gave both the name the man was traveling under and his supposed real name. Headquarters had no record of either name, so they checked with the CIA, and somehow they lost it."

"Lost what?"

"The inquiry. The original paperwork. The CIA checked it out and found the Libyan name on their list of suspected terrorists. When they replied to our headquarters, somebody had lost the initial entry, so when they got a message from CIA saying the name we'd requested information about was a suspected terrorist, the man receiving the message didn't know what to do with it. There was some input error in the computer, and it came in with a different number than the request for information had gone out with, so it got filed for a day or two."

"Long enough for the Lebanese to catch his flight the next day?"

"You got it."

"You checked the flight manifest? There really was a Lebanese with the name you were given?"

"He was on the flight, all right."

"So you're thinking that maybe the call was legitimate and he really is a Libyan terrorist, which means he might be connected with our problem."

"If the call was legitimate, he must be connected with us. How many Libyan problems can we have at one time?"

"Do you know his name?"

"His real name? Suleiman Akbar."

Melnik's eyes glistened.

"Do you know him?"

Melnik nodded. "He's one of Ja'far's men."

"Who?"

"Ayn Allah Ja'far. Head of the Kirballa, one of Qaddafi's in-house terrorist organizations. Very close to Moammar himself. Is Akbar still in London?"

"That's the good part. He's staying there, and is in contact with a known group of Libyans, presumably helping them get up to some mischief or other. Scotland Yard has had their eye on them, but they haven't done anything illegal yet. There's no reason to think they have anything to do with us."

"But the Yard knows where Akbar is?"

"What? Sorry, I was watching the bacon burn again."

Melnik snatched the pan off the fire and flipped the strips out of the pan. "Got the eggs ready?"

"Right here," Werther said, handing him the bowl. "Lori should be doing this. I wonder what's taking her so long."

Melnik poured the beaten eggs into the frying pan, added the bacon to them and they began to sizzle together. "It's got to be connected," he said.

"I think so. The Libyan connection is clear. Can't be coincidence. Well, it could be, of course, but—"

"There's no such thing as coincidence. Sigmund Freud said that. To all things there is a meaning."

"I believe you're mixing up your sources, but I agree with you."

"If Scotland Yard has their eye on Akbar, we're okay after all. You're sure they know where he is?"

Werther nodded.

"You'd better have them pick him up right away."

"Well, there's a bit of a problem with that," Werther said. "The

Yard keeps its eye on people like him, but they won't pick him up. He hasn't violated any law there, and they don't want to start an incident."

"False passport?"

Werther shook his head. "How do you prove it? The man says he's Suleiman Faldallah of Lebanon, and that's what his passport says. How do you prove differently? If you pick him up and try to grill him, the Lebanese embassy gets into the act, and before you know it you've got Arab students marching in the streets demanding an end to discrimination in the United Kingdom, and then you get skinhead morons coming out with car chains and rocks to bash the Arabs and— You get the picture? They don't need that kind of trouble, based on nothing more than a request from us that we can't back up with any hard information about any major crime. Besides, they haven't had the kind of relationship with the CIA that would make them trust everything they say, so they're not about to stir up a riot in London on our say-so."

"Could the CIA kidnap him?"

Werther shook his head again. "You must be kidding. After the Casey-North 'secret army' scandal? They don't dare even think about an illegal operation like that." He paused. Now comes the hard part, he thought; now I have to take my hat in my hands and ask for help.

Melnik nodded. "I understand. Okay, we'll take care of it."

Werther felt a surge of surprise and gratitude. Was it really going to be this easy? No scornful looks? No superior sighs?

Melnik was so relieved that all Werther wanted to talk about was business that he would have promised to kidnap Gorbachev if the FBI wanted him to. "You'll give me the details?" he asked. "The people he's seeing?"

"Of course," Werther said, "but I don't want to know what you're doing, understand?"

"Understand."

Werther wasn't sure how to say it, so finally he just said, "Thanks."

Melnik was embarrassed in turn. "We're in this together, aren't we?"

Werther nodded. He'd had this guy figured out all wrong. "How long?" he asked.

Melnik shrugged. "Twenty-four-hour delivery is our usual aim."
They looked at each other and smiled, then began to laugh.

Lori had tidied up the bedroom and was turning the corner into the
kitchen when she stopped in amazement. The two of them were
standing in front of the stove with a pan full of bacon and eggs all
mixed together and burning horribly, laughing together. *Laughing!*

## 45

"How did it happen?" Julian Mazor asked. "What's the weather like
there, anyway?" Of course in Israel the sun was still shining brightly.
He remembered as a child in Slovakia reading stories in Hebrew school
about the Promised Land and how the sun always shone there. He
used to think of it as a fairy tale, with bright yellow sunshine pouring
out of bright blue skies, the air clean and sharp, as he left the dirty little
building in which the cheder classes were held and walked through the
gloomy streets of the shtetl to his parents' small flat. He remembered
how happy he had been when Hitler had threatened invasion. He had
heard his parents shouting that the Germans were coming and they
would all have to flee to Palestine. His parents were crying, and he
didn't understand why: what could be better?

They left in August 1938 on a rainy day. He remembered the train
station, the clouds of smoke rising from under the wheels of the
locomotive, the rain streaming down the windows of the train as the
wet countryside passed away behind them, the tears running down his
mother's cheeks as he fell asleep dreaming of Jerusalem and the bright
sun.

He didn't realize till years later how lucky they had been—not only
to get out of Europe but to get into Palestine. Now he knew all too well
about the thousands of Jews who had been turned away at the borders
by British guards and sent back to horrible deaths. And now he was sick
of the eternally blazing sun. He loved Israel with a passion, but with
at least a small fraction of that passion he hated the sun.

"It's raining," David Melnik said. "It's been raining for two days."
*Bliss,* Julian Mazor thought. He pictured Melnik standing outside

while cool, fresh water fell down from heaven and washed over his face. He saw himself standing there, his arms outstretched, his face upraised, his mouth open to catch the nectar of the gods.

"It's cold and wet and clammy," Melnik went on, "and you can't open the windows or shut off the air conditioning in the FBI building. This whole country is run by computers, not human beings. When the calendar says winter is over, the computers turn off the heat no matter how cold it is, and when the calendar says it's summer, they turn on the air conditioning. I don't think the FBI has much faith in reality."

Mazor sighed. If God ever put a heaven on earth, he'd have to set up a complaint department. Perhaps that was why he had never bothered. "So what happened?" he asked again.

"You're sure this line is secure?" Melnik asked.

"What can I tell you?" Mazor answered. "You're calling from the Israeli embassy in Washington directly to Mossad headquarters on the most secure line we have." He paused. "Is it really important?"

"Yes."

"You'd better come home and tell me about it."

"I can catch a flight to London in two hours. Can you meet me there?"

Mazor's eyes lit up; it would probably be raining in London. But habits of economy cautioned him. "Why London? Why not come home?"

"Trust me."

He certainly wanted to. "You're sure this is important?" He would have to justify the trip to the administrative department. The new head of that department was a woman who didn't understand why anybody ever spent money on anything. "This isn't another one of your intuitive flashes of brilliance, is it?"

"It's important, Julian," Melnik said quietly. "Have I ever lied to you?"

The pub was dark, gloomy and cold. Mazor didn't own a pair of overshoes, and the light raincoat he wore wasn't hardy enough for the English rain; during the walk here it had soaked through, and now his jacket was wet and even his shirt was damp. His feet were squishing wet inside his dripping shoes; he felt like taking his socks off and wringing them dry. There was a mirage at the far end of the long room, a blazing fireplace, but every inch of space around it was jammed with chairs. Here at their table the warmth was nothing more than a feeble taunt.

"So what happened?" he asked, sipping his beer, the one thing in the room that wasn't cold. Never again would he complain about Israel.

Melnik pulled out a pack of cigarettes and offered him one. Mazor shook his head. "I've quit."

Melnik nodded without surprise. He'd heard this before. "How long has it been this time?" he asked.

Mazor looked at his watch. "Eighteen hours," he said. "Not counting the change in time zones."

"That includes last night, when you were asleep?"

"Never mind the humor," Mazor said. He would have to fill in fifteen forms to justify this trip, and he was cold and wet and miserable. "Let's get on with it. What happened? All you told me was that the FBI received a tip on a terrorist and let him get away. What went wrong?"

"FBI headquarters in Washington received an anonymous telephone tip that Suleiman Akbar was in the United States on a false passport."

"Akbar?" Mazor's eyes lit up. "In the United States? That's a first, isn't it?"

"Evidently. The FBI had no sheet on him, so they sent a routine request for information to the CIA. By the time the answer came back, the FBI had lost the original request and didn't know what it was all about."

Mazor shook his head in disbelief. "How did they explain it?"

"Simple: computer error. That's how the Americans explain everything that goes wrong. Nobody can argue with it; it's not their fault and nobody gets blamed. It's the deus ex machina of the twentieth century."

"You're becoming a bitter old man," Mazor said "When this is over, I'll have to arrange a little feminine companionship for you."

Suddenly Melnik blushed, and Mazor was taken aback; he had never expected such a reaction. *It's about time*, he thought. *Man*

210

*should not live by hand alone.* He opened his mouth to tease David, but then caught himself. Melnik looked really embarrassed, and Mazor decided he didn't want to know about it. "They did straighten it out finally?" he asked, reverting to their original subject.

Melnik nodded. "But by the time they did, Akbar had left the States on a Los Angeles–London flight. The FBI got in touch with Scotland Yard, and they promised to meet the flight at Heathrow and keep an eye on him."

"And you think this is related to al-Kuchir and Mohammed Asri? It's part of Dallas?"

"Has to be, doesn't it? Too much of a coincidence otherwise, don't you think?"

"At any rate, it would be nice to talk to Akbar."

"Exactly. It would be nice to talk to him."

46

"We've lost him. I'm terribly sorry," Detective Inspector Thwaite said. "As I'm sure you realize, it's almost impossible to maintain contact when an experienced man wants to lose you, and I'm afraid our underground railway system is made to order for such games."

Melnik glanced at the woman sitting next to him. Debora Stern had been assigned to him by Mazor before he left for home. Melnik had been surprised when Mazor returned to Israel immediately after their meeting; he was always telling everybody how much he loved London. Melnik had met Stern outside Scotland Yard, and they had discussed the situation before they went in. She told him that Mazor had instructed her to put herself and her group completely at his disposal for this operation, and she foresaw no difficulties.

But now this. Thwaite spoke again, but Melnik, lost for the moment in his own thoughts, missed what he said. He became aware of an awkward silence and looked up at Thwaite, who was evidently waiting for an answer. "I'm sorry," Melnik said. "Did you say something?"

"I said," Thwaite answered with just the trace of a satisfied smile, "that luckily we've had Akbar's friends under surveillance for quite some time."

Like most European states, England has a curious relationship with terrorists. Officially, and indeed within the deep recesses of their soul, the English abhor and condemn all terrorism. But souls are overlaid with a veneer of pragmatism. In the best of all possible worlds, terrorism would not exist. In the second best, civilized nations would have effective means of combating it. In this third-best world, one simply tries to make sure that what terrorism does exist finds somewhere else to happen.

Below the level of rigid law enforcement one comes to terms with things one cannot eliminate. When a bomb is exploded in a pub, Scotland Yard investigates with all its resources. If the perpetrators are apprehended, they are put on trial with no favor given. But all in all, both the authorities and the public would prefer that no bombs explode and no terrorists be apprehended. If this means shutting an occasional eye while persons suspected of terrorism elsewhere sojourn in the UK, then that eye must remain quietly shut.

The other eye is kept open, of course, to make sure that no laws are actually broken on British soil, and particularly to make sure that whatever crimes are being plotted are not directed against the British people. Charity and preservation begin at home, but they do not end there. So while officially the British authorities ignore Arabs of suspicious intent as long as they remain lawful within the boundaries of England, unofficially they are happy to cooperate with the security forces of other countries that might be worried about such activities.

The al-Ghaffouri are a terrorist group named for their martyred leader, Ahmed al-Ghaffour, who was kidnapped and assassinated by Al Fatah, Yassir Arafat's terrorist arm. As far as its members know, the al-Ghaffouri's basic aim is the liberation of Palestine. In actuality they have become a political extension of the Qaddafi regime. Their cell in London serves the same purpose as many normal embassies in Switzerland do: a home away from home for intelligence operatives, a safe place where information can be transferred, a secure base for organization and communication. They carry out no acts of terrorism in the United Kingdom, and the British police ignore their unwelcome presence, having enough problems of their own with terrorist groups active in the UK. Being fully aware of the nebulous armistice that exists between them and the British government so long as they remain peaceful in England, the al-Ghaffouri are careful to do so. They are aware that Scotland Yard knows of their existence, but they prefer to keep details of their actual day-to-day organization from British eyes. To this end they headquarter in a series of squatters' flats, moving continually to ensure their privacy. Nothing could be better designed to bring them to the attention of the British authorities, who, unlike governments in the Arab lands from which they come, are not prepared to accept as normal bands of homeless, out-of-work indigents taking over unoccupied but owned premises.

Therefore, when Suleiman Akbar had finished his half-day's criss-crossing through the London tube and bus systems, he had indeed successfully evaded the tail Scotland Yard had placed on him at Heathrow, but within twenty-four hours of his contacting the al-Ghaffouri cell in South Kensington, the Yard once again knew where he was.

The instructions Akbar received from the al-Ghaffouri could not have pleased him more. He was to make his report to its cell leader, who would in turn fly to Tripoli to report to Ja'far. No chances were being taken that Akbar might have been followed and could be perceived as a link between Los Angeles and Tripoli. He was to remain in London and await further instructions.

He took a room in a small hotel behind Victoria Station, careful not to express his pleasure at the order. Workers of the revolution are above such feelings as personal pleasure, personal comforts, personal lust. Nevertheless, London was one of his favorite cities in the world, ranking just behind Hamburg, because of the massage parlors in Soho.

If New York is a melting pot, London is a simmering stew of more than ten million people, including a variety of racial types and mixtures, many of them from the Near East. Once Akbar had made sure that he was clear of any tail set on him at Heathrow, he felt perfectly free and secure mingling among the populace. He left his hotel in the late morning and walked a mile and a half to al-Ghaffouri headquarters, which at the time was in one of a row of what had been in the previous century elegant town houses that were now being gutted prior to being remodeled as professional offices. This would take a good six months, one house after another lining the square being gutted before any of the rebuilding began. During this period bands of squatters moved from one abandoned house to the next in line, staying one step ahead of the demolition crews and enjoying semilegal status as "occupants" under the Borough of London Council rules.

After hearing that no instructions had yet come for him, and expressing the required disappointment at not being put to immediate use in confronting the enemies of the revolution, Akbar took a bus to Grosvenor Square and walked through St. James's Park before he finally entered a pub. Old habits of caution die hard, and he was careful not to spend much time in the vicinity of either his hotel or the cell headquarters. But his caution was born of habit only, not of any fear that he might actually be under surveillance, so it was a relaxed, incompetent sort of caution. Thus he never noticed the roly-poly little man in the derby hat who took the bus with him, the tall, lean gentleman wandering through the park, or the group of two young men and a woman who trailed even farther behind.

After a delicious pub lunch of Scotch egg, beans and chips, washed down with a pint of best brown ale—alcohol was forbidden by his religion, but he made an exception for English and German beer— Akbar wandered back into the park and fed the pigeons. When the sun went down he walked to Leicester Square and entered a porno theater on its northern rim. Two hours later he emerged in the proper mood, walked up Lisle Street and turned right into Wardour full of expectant enthusiasm.

It was the roly-poly little man, switching between close- and long-range contact with the others throughout the afternoon, who followed Akbar through the crowds into Wardour Street and watched him enter an establishment situated between two Chinese restaurants. Its wide windows were covered with deep red curtains, lined with photographs that showed smiling men covered in nothing but a towel being cheerfully massaged by bikini-bottomed women whose loosely dangling vests hid their bodies from the photographer but not from the smiling gentlemen on the tables.

Akbar's thoughts were totally on his forbidden pleasures. He talked to the receptionist, took out his wallet, paid his money and disappeared through the sequined doorway into the dark interior.

The roly-poly little man walked back to the corner of Lisle Street and gestured with his newspaper. The two young men and the woman came over to him and discussed the situation.

The girl in the massage parlor was sullen and tired. It was early in the evening, and all she could think of were the long hours ahead before she could return to her flat. When the man took off his clothes and said he wanted everything, she simply nodded.

Akbar felt a thrill in his groin. He had asked for someone Oriental and young—as young as you've got, he'd told the receptionist—and this one was perfect. She was even plump, which he had forgotten to specify. He was just lucky today. She also had hooded eyes. In the first porno film he had ever seen, the first time he had come to London, the girl had those same hooded eyes—eyes that never looked at you because she was ashamed of what she was thinking and of what she wanted to do to you.

She asked him if he wanted a towel, and he shook his head. She gestured to the table and he lay down on it. He kept looking at her hooded eyes, but she never raised them. Obviously she was ashamed of what she wanted to do to him.

She was bored out of her mind. One of the English girls in the parlor had taught her that expression: "bored out of your mind." She poured a little lotion on his chest and began to massage him. She could see nothing but long hours ahead of her, stretching into long years, and at the end there was nothing but a dull blankness.

As she leaned over him her vest fell open. She didn't even notice. He stared at her breasts as they swayed with her movements, the tips like a watch in a hypnotist's hands. He felt her hands moving down lower on his body. He felt himself rising, swelling, stiffening. His eyes swerved from her breasts to her face, but she wouldn't meet his gaze—she dared not; she was frightened of his power and strength.

She never noticed. She was aware of nothing except another body she manipulated the way a housewife washes dishes without thinking. She was bored, oh God, so bored.

\*    \*    \*

Debora Stern's field was "sociological intelligence." She could hardly be called a spy; rather, she was an expert-in-residence. Her brief was to evaluate the mood swings of the British people about events pertinent to the state of Israel. She relied on public sources and on impressions she picked up, an entirely proper function of an intelligence service in a friendly country. If that country should at some future time become unfriendly, then Debora Stern would have no hesitation about going undercover and functioning as a true spy; she had been thoroughly trained for this eventuality. She would never want England to take that course, but she did feel gratified to work for David Melnik and at last use some of the hard-core training she had received in Israel.

Stern was an attractive young woman, and when she took up station in an unoccupied doorway on Wardour Street across from the massage parlor, there was a steady stream of inquiries to keep her busy. There was no problem disposing of the pests; she simply set her price a few pounds above the market price and they moved on to more promising doorways. Though it had been a sunny day, her umbrella attracted no attention, the vagaries of English weather being known even to tourists. She'd had plenty of opportunity during the afternoon to study Akbar through the binoculars she carried in her purse, and now she had no problem recognizing him when the door to the massage parlor opened and he came out.

Akbar could have posed for an advertisement: the satisfied customer. Zipping up his short leather jacket, he smiled benevolently at everyone, then wandered up Wardour Street and across Shaftesbury.

Debora followed, pushing her way through the crowd. He was in no hurry, obviously walking with no destination in mind, strolling through a lovely spring evening in London. Now he turned down Oxford Street, where the shops were still open and the crowds thick. Slowly she gained on him.

As Akbar waited in a crowd for the light to change on Great Titchfield Street she caught up to him, and as the light turned green she pushed gently past an elderly couple and came up directly behind him, her umbrella swinging as she moved. On its forward arc it actually bumped against the rear of his leg just above the knee. She pushed it forward and pressed a recessed button on the handle.

Akbar gave a little jump as he felt the pinprick, but when he turned she was already moving past him on the other side, and he saw nothing but the elderly couple and an empty sea of faces moving with him across the street.

The prick he had felt was momentary and slight. He didn't give it another thought as he turned again and crossed the street with the crowd. He walked another half block before he began to feel dizzy. He nearly reached Oxford Circus before he stumbled, then fell against a woman carrying bundles of shopping. He almost knocked her down, but she gave him a disgusted glance and kept moving. He was on his knees when an arm grabbed him around the shoulder and supported him. People stopped to look. Someone asked, "What's wrong?"

"My friend's sick," he heard a voice say, and the strong arms propelled him through the crowd to an empty space at the curb. A cab pulled up. He couldn't see or talk. He could barely hear the voice at his side calling, "Cabbie! My friend's not feeling well. Victoria, please!"

His tongue was fuzzy. He felt himself being pushed forward, and then he fell into the dark interior of the cab. The last thing he heard was the door shutting behind him; then the cab whirled away down the street and he whirled away into oblivion.

## 47

"What do we do with him now?"

Akbar's eyes were open. He felt that he could move them if he really wanted to, but he couldn't summon up the energy to do it. He lay there staring at the ceiling, listening to them talk. He was at once afraid, hanging on every word, and yet removed from it all, in another universe, listening to strange sounds that had nothing to do with him.

"The obvious thing would be to dispose of him," a woman said. "He's told us all he knows."

"Yes, we could kill him, of course," the man agreed, "but I'm not sure it would be a good idea. It might be necessary, but there are problems."

Debora looked angry, and Melnik suppressed a smile. She was inexperienced, young and dedicated. She saw only a dirty savage, one of the enemy who wanted to kill her and all her family. She wanted only to kill such scum.

Melnik wanted more; he wanted to defeat them. He stood looking down at Akbar, thinking. He had been easy to crack. Debora was right: he had told them all he knew. But did he know all there was to know? Was Dallas really a plan to assassinate the President in Los Angeles? It seemed too simple for all the preparations they had uncovered.

If we release him, Melnik wondered, what will he do? He wanted to get into the Arab's mind. If he was a true revolutionary, he would have to tell his comrades that he had talked, even though he must know that they'd kill him for his betrayal. He would have to tell them, for it would be more important that they know their plans were blown than that he live. But if he was the kind of trash who served the terrorists only because he enjoyed the legitimacy of violence and killing—and looking down into his eyes now, Melnik was almost sure that he was—then nothing would be more important to him than staying alive. In which case he might be of use.

"A traffic accident," Debora suggested. "We take him tonight to Soho, hold him in the car on Dean or Greek Street, wait till nobody's paying attention, then release him. He staggers down the street and we drive after him and hit him. We disappear around the corner, and he's just another statistic."

Melnik nodded. She had the germ of a good agent in her. If they killed Akbar, it would have to be a convincing accident. But surely Ja'far would be suspicious that the man might have been taken and forced to talk before his death. Under such conditions, could even the most innocuous accident seem truly accidental? He considered it carefully. There was stale beer on the man's breath, but would his coreligionists believe he had been drinking? Did they know of his weakness, or would they suspect he had been doused with beer by force?

He could simply disappear. His body could be buried somewhere in the New Forest, where it wouldn't be found for generations. What would they think then? Certainly they would suspect, but would their suspicions be strong enough to make them change their plans?

He looked at Debora. She was staring at Akbar, and it was easy enough to read her face. Her hatred was ugly to see. He sighed. He too hated, but though he had learned to control his feelings, it was not pleasant to see what they must look like to God. He must be careful not to kill out of hate, nor spare out of weakness.

Akbar had never completely lost consciousness. Now that he was recovering from the drug, he still could not remember clearly. They had brought him here—but he didn't know where *here* was. He remembered being half carried out of the cab and up some steps. Then he was lying on this bed and there was a pain in his arm, like the one he had felt in his leg on Oxford Street, but deeper and longer lasting. They were injecting him with something.

There had been questions, and he had tried to answer them with lies. But the questions were repeated and he had been afraid. They knew his name; they knew he was lying. He had tried to pretend that it was a game and that he was truly a Lebanese businessman, but they kept hammering away. So he had told them. He remembered that now; he had told them everything. He was a dead man.

"You're a lucky man," the tall man in charge said. "We've decided to kill you."

Akbar didn't answer. He turned his head, toward the wall.

The man grasped his neck firmly in his fingers and turned him back again. "You should say thank you."

Akbar looked up at him, not answering. What was the point?

"You're a lucky man, because if we let you go, your friends will kill you. Won't they? For betraying them. And as you know, their way of killing is more painful than ours. A lot more painful."

Involuntarily Akbar closed his eyes, then cursed himself. He didn't want to show them that he was afraid. But he *was* afraid. He had seen what his friends would do to a traitor. He had done it himself once—and had enjoyed it.

"There is this one possibility," the tall man suggested. "We could simply release you, and you could say nothing to anybody."

Debora gasped in anger, which made Melnik smile. He went on. "That way they would never have to know that you talked to us. You could continue to lead a happy, useful life."

"Why should . . ." Akbar's voice croaked. They were the first words he had spoken since the drug wore off. Melnik handed him a glass of water, and he struggled to a sitting position and drank it off. It gave him a chance to think, and he began to see a ray of hope. "Why should you release me?"

Melnik continued to smile. "I said you could lead a happy, useful life. I didn't say useful to whom."

"To you, you mean," Akbar frowned, but his heart was beginning to lift.

"To both of us. If you die we lose nothing, but you lose everything. If you live, you gain everything. It's only fair that we should gain something also."

"What would you want to gain?"

"Let's not pretend to be stupid. You would continue with the al-Ghaffouri, but you would be our man."

Akbar closed his eyes, ostensibly to think, actually to hide his relief.

Melnik saw the relief clearly, but didn't know what it meant. Was he relieved to be given his life? In which case he would not forfeit it by revealing to his comrades what had happened. Or was he relieved to be given the opportunity to atone for his failure by telling them everything? In which case he would surely die a most unpleasant death. It boiled down to the original question. Was Akbar a true revolutionary patriot or trash? Then the man opened his eyes and Melnik saw the answer clearly.

48

The next day Hardy flew to San Francisco and met Matsuo Nakaoka. They drove out into the desert behind the hills, leaving the main highway system and not stopping until they found a deserted area. There Hardy stopped the car and unlocked the briefcase in the backseat. In it, strapped in place, was a disassembled rifle. He handed the briefcase to Nakaoka, who studied it, lightly touching each piece. Then he took out one piece at a time and quickly assembled the weapon. "No silencer," he noted.

"Not necessary," Hardy assured him. "There'll be so much yelling and cheering that even you won't hear the shot. Besides, silencers affect the bullet's flight and are hard to correct for."

Nakaoka nodded. It was a pleasure to talk to a man who knew his job well. It was good to deal with professionals, but in this business it was not always possible.

"You should be able to escape out the rear entrance afterwards," Hardy said. "You'll be outside before people on that side of the block know what's happened. You can lose yourself in the crowd and be gone. Though I'm not promising anything; you know that."

"I know." Nakaoka didn't dwell on the possibility of being caught; he would devote himself to the cause without thought of self. "Let us test it."

Hardy paced out two hundred yards and set up a series of stones on top of a rock. As he walked back Nakaoka was aligning the sight of the rifle, and as Hardy reached him he fired at the first stone. The bullet shattered against the large rock a few inches too low. He adjusted the sight, aimed again and fired. This time the bullet's impact was just a fraction to the right. Twice more he made slight changes and fired. Each time he clipped the next stone in line, but still he wasn't satisfied. Finally, after one more hairline adjustment, the next stone jumped into the air. He smiled, nodded, took quick aim and splintered the remaining stones.

"A good weapon," he said.

Hardy nodded. Nakaoka repacked the rifle himself and they drove back into town. At the hotel he got out of the car, then leaned back in through the window and looked at the suitcase resting on the rear seat. "When?" he asked.

"Soon," Hardy said.

Hardy drove back out through the hills to the same field. Again he walked to the large rock and put a series of stones on top of it. Then he returned, took out the suitcase and reassembled the rifle. Like Nakaoka, he stretched out in the sand, took aim and fired. The first stone jumped in the air. He adjusted the sight, aimed at the second stone and fired. He saw the splat of the impact three feet to the left. He inspected the sight. No good; it was too obviously out of line. He adjusted it again until he had it just right, until it looked good but fired

several inches wide, then he carefully packed the rifle in its briefcase
again.

## 49

Like all governments, Fidel Castro's Revolutionary People's Government of Cuba is paranoid: it thinks everyone hates it. It is right to be
paranoid, for, like all governments, many people do hate it. To protect
itself against these enemies of the state the Cuban government, again
like all governments everywhere, employs secret agents to keep it
informed of any plots being hatched against it. Many of these
agents—most of them, in fact—are sent to the United States, and most
of these operate out of Miami for obvious reasons.

Gloria Carollo, hired by Xavier Guarez to navigate the Boeing
707, was one of these agents. Trained at the University of Havana
and graduating with high grades, she had looked forward to a job in
the armed forces. However, her superiors quickly noticed her special
skills and passed on the word. At a subsequent interview she was told
that the government was interested in her mastery of English and
political theory, as well as the more technical subjects such as
mathematics and engineering. They did not tell her that they were
also interested in her body. They explained that good engineers were
hard to find on their isolated island, but that good political theorists
with a deep love for the revolution were even harder to find,
particularly those who spoke good English. Still harder to find,
though they did not mention it, were those with such qualifications
and also a good body.

Her superiors were masters of psychology. They saw that she was
young and idealistic; they asked if she was prepared to serve her state,
and of course she replied that she was. When they asked if she was
prepared to sacrifice *everything* to protect the revolution, her eyes lit
up.

So they trained her to be a special agent, to leave Cuba as a refugee
for Miami, there to live and to infiltrate the Calle Alpha organization of subversives who plotted to overthrow the lawful revolu-

tionary government of Cuba. She came to Miami along with the swarm of *Marielitos* in the last years of the Carter administration and quickly became extraordinarily effective, for the charms that had attracted attention in Cuba were just as enticing in Miami and gained her instant entrée into whatever organization of Cuban men she chose.

When Xavier Guarez came to Miami to recruit a crew for his mission, Gloria was not an obvious choice, but when no one with actual experience as a navigator turned up, he was easily persuaded to take her on. Her technical background and obvious intelligence indicated that she would be easy to train, and he never had reason to regret his choice—because, of course, he never found out who she was.

For her part, Gloria found that she could not worm the secret of their mission out of him. All he would tell her was that they were being provided with a Boeing 707 that would be filled with military supplies for the counterrevolution, in return for their help in preserving the life of the President of the United States. She reported back to Cuba that she could find out no more.

That was when they suggested she might find her body useful in persuading men to part with their secrets. But it had not worked with Guarez, and it did not work with Dallas. She still did not know what their mission was to be.

Do not despair, her masters said. Be patient.

The Calle Alpha group began on Calle Ocho, Miami's Eighth Street, the nerve center of the Cuban ghetto. Comprising Cuban patriots living in Miami only until they could free their homeland from the tyrant, it was both an instrument of convenience and an embarrassment to the U.S. government. Convenient whenever the federal authorities wanted to show the world that love of freedom never dies, for at a word the group would organize demonstrations and dancing in the streets to protest a poet's incarceration or the visit of a Communist official. Embarrassing always, for simmering continually over the domino tables on Calle Ocho were schemes for a replay of the Bay of Pigs invasion.

So the federal government tolerated the Alpha organization, supported it in secret and spied on it incessantly. In point of fact most of the members were daydreaming old men playing checkers and dominoes in the sun and drinking Cuban coffee; the few intense ones were mostly agents of the Cuban government like Gloria Carollo, or of the FBI.

Ferde Grossman was the Washington agent to whom the various undercover FBI operatives in Miami reported. Though each of them operated individually, there were actually three who had infiltrated the Alpha group; more than a dozen others were members of various other groups. When one of them told him that one of the Alpha members, Gloria Carollo, a recent refugee from Cuba, had been recruited to become part of a team operating a Boeing 707 jet airliner in a plan to spearhead the coming invasion of Cuba after first saving the President of the United States from an unknown group of assassins, details unknown, Grossman was merely amused. Over the years he had grown accustomed to the wild imaginations of Cubans and to the extravagant schemes they devised. There were enormous sums of money in the community, and they could afford to indulge their fantasies. Nothing ever came of their schemes except brave talk in the tropic nights.

He filed the information.

## 50

Hardy finished his beer and stared down into the bottle. The incident in the hotel room with Gloria Carollo had started him thinking about Alison. He couldn't have slept with the woman anyway, of course, but his instinctive reaction to her overtures had been negative solely because of thoughts of Alison. He hadn't realized she had become so important to him. How long had this been going on? And as he thought about the past, his thoughts led him inexorably to the future. Where was Alison in his future? He would never again be able to live in this country. Would she come with him? Could he ask her to?

He exhaled sharply. Such questions were unanswerable now. He would have to wait to see how things turned out. His thoughts swerved to more immediate concerns. He thought of the forces ranged against him, intent on preventing him from pulling off this operation. It would be a magnificent achievement to foil these forces; if he could do it, it would be a coup of truly spectacular proportions. Then why was he sitting here staring morosely into his beer?

Well, there are reasons, he thought—Gloria Carollo, for one. It was sad that she had to die.

Sad, but *necessary*; that was the word. What else was necessary? He leaned back in his chair and tried to review the plan.

He wondered if the FBI had managed to catch Akbar. He had given them all the information they needed, and if they caught the guy they shouldn't have any trouble cracking him. But there was no way he could find out for certain. Too bad. It would be nice to know for sure that they were waiting in Los Angeles for Dallas and weren't worrying about anything else.

He opened another beer and decided not to worry about it. You had to trust *somebody* in this business.


Flying back from London, David Melnik was worried about something else entirely. He was confident that he had discovered the secret of Dallas, and in addition had placed a possibly useful double agent in the Libyan camp. Forewarned, they should be competently forearmed. He had done his job well. The one thing that worried him was what to do about Lori Werther.

# V
## Dallas

## 51

When Akbar's report, passed on by the al-Ghaffouri, reached Ja'far and told him that Hardy's plan was for a Los Angeles assassination of President Bush, his skin turned cold with anger in the hot Sahara sun. That was not the bargain they had made. His eyes closed to malevolent slits, and his first thought was to send an assassin to kill Hardy, and never mind the money he had spent on him already.

His second thoughts were a little more temperate. They began with an excoriation of Hardy as a scheming infidel—and then he stopped. Yes, Hardy was a scheming infidel, a wicked barbarian with no regard for the truth, so of course he was lying.

But to whom? To Ja'far, when he had promised to kidnap the President? Or to Akbar, when he told him of a plan merely to kill the President? If the former, why? If he was going to renege on their agreement, why not simply disappear and do nothing? If the latter, again why? Yes, he knew that Hardy was secretive and hated to reveal his plans, but then why not simply refuse to do so, as he had up to now? Why pretend to tell, and then concoct something so outrageous that he knew Ja'far would not be satisfied? As soon as Ja'far phrased the question this way an insight presented itself. Was Hardy perhaps telling something not to Ja'far but to someone else?

The malevolent slits closed all the way as Ja'far leaned back against the heavy cushions on his settee and thought. Then they opened again. Akbar was in London, awaiting further instructions. "Bring me Akbar," he said.

On August 18 it was announced that President Bush would campaign in California early in September, beginning his tour with a full-scale gala reception in San Francisco on September 9.

"D-Day," Hardy said to Freddy Mason, pointing at the article in the daily paper.

"Tally-ho, sport," Freddy said, raising his morning glass of orange juice. They drank to the beginning of the end.

Three days later Hardy was in San Francisco, waiting in the condo he had leased at 971 Powell Street. There was a knock at the door and he opened it to admit Matsuo Nakaoka, who bowed slightly and entered.

"No trouble finding the place?" Hardy asked.

"None at all. Your directions were explicit."

"How do you like it?"

Nakaoka ignored the plush furnishings, walked straight to the open windows and leaned out. "Suitable," he said.

Hardy nodded. "Eminently suitable," he agreed.

At first Ja'far was puzzled by Akbar's fear, but then his puzzlement turned to pleasure. Akbar was right to be afraid, of course, but the fear was a bit too hidden. Akbar was trying to appear as if he had nothing to fear, which was not normal. It was the tremor around his eyelids, the way his fingertips pressed against one another. No one else would have noticed, but Ja'far prided himself on seeing such things.

Ja'far was a creature of extremes. In England he wore pin-striped suits and stayed in the most English of hotels; in Tripoli he was as Arabian as his leader. Aside from his office in the administration building, he had a tent in the compound similar to Qaddafi's. Which was where he was now, dressed in traditional Bedouin robes, confronting the curiously frightened Akbar.

"Tell me again," he said, and once again Akbar told him about his journey to the United States.

"You were not followed from the airport?"

"Of a certainty not," Akbar replied, and Ja'far was satisfied.

"You took the full precautions and followed instructions to the letter?" he asked, and again Akbar answered affirmatively. "Continue," Ja'far ordered.

Akbar told him about visiting the apartment and meeting the Japanese marksman, and that was all.

"Nothing more? Are you sure?"

It was at this moment that Ja'far's puzzlement began to slip over into pleasure. The flutter of Akbar's eyelids and the pressure of his fingertips against one another infinitesimally increased. Akbar told him of how he had spent the night in Los Angeles, flown back to London the next day and reported to the proper persons in that city.

Ja'far had him now. He wasn't sure exactly how, but he was sure. "All?" he asked. "That was all?"

Akbar nodded, but with the look in his eyes the last doubt left Ja'far. "Take off your clothes," he said.

". . . All your clothes," Melnik said as Lori hesitated with one hand on her bra strap. "Take them all off." God help him, he hadn't meant to say that. He hadn't felt like this since he'd been a hormone-soused teenager, bursting into puberty like a chick bursting out of its shell. He was actually helpless, he thought, frightened and proud, angry at his own incompetence and intoxicated with his power over her. Which was only magnified by her mockery as she stood there in his hotel room in her bra and panties and hesitated, her fingers touching the clasp of the bra, pretending to ponder the possibility of disobeying.

"Take everything off," he said, and was amazed at the huskiness in his voice; he was nearly croaking, the desire in his throat making it almost impossible to breathe. He hadn't intended this at all. On the jet flight back from London, he had decided that it was a stupid mistake on both their parts, and that it should just vanish like a lovely dream.

Now she slipped the clasp and the bra fell away from her shoulders and dangled from her nipples. When she shrugged, it fell to the floor. Then she slipped her fingers into the band of her panties and pushed them slowly down with infinite grace. . . .

Hardy brought the last carton up, deposited it with the others in the center of the living room, took a deep breath and stretched. It had been a heavy load, seven boxes totaling about five hundred pounds. He took a beer out of the refrigerator and sat down, planning how to arrange it all.

He was in one of the condominiums on Powell Street, and the neighbors who shared the building with him seemed like nice people. Two of them had offered to help when they saw him carrying the boxes up in the elevator, but he had refused politely. He wasn't going to take a chance on a box dropping and splitting open.

Now, safely in the apartment with the doors securely locked, he finished his beer, turned to the first box and ripped it open: twenty grenades, one bazooka and ten rocket shells. He looked around the apartment and decided to put this load in the bedroom.

The next case contained rifles and ammunition, and he began to stack it carefully on the floor beneath the window that overlooked Powell Street.

How to account for Akbar's nervousness? It must mean that in some way he had betrayed Ja'far. It was useless to speculate on why Hardy had corrupted him until he knew how he had done it. He knew Akbar well enough to decide that he could not be bought; his pleasures were simple enough to be cheaply satisfied, and he lacked the imagination to know what could be bought with larger sums of money. Also, he was a determined revolutionary, committed to the cause, who would not easily be persuaded to betray his comrades. He considered all this as Akbar took off his clothes and stood naked before him. He noticed that the man shivered slightly despite the warmth inside the tent. Something was definitely wrong.

Slowly and majestically Ja'far rose to his feet and stood in front of Akbar until he lowered his eyes. Then he walked slowly around him, studying him from all sides. Finally he asked Akbar to present his hands. Puzzled, Akbar hesitated, but Ja'far held out his own hands, waiting, and slowly Akbar lifted his. Taking them in his own, Ja'far studied the palms and fingernails. Nothing; flecks of black were lodged under the nails, and Ja'far wrinkled his nose in distaste, but there were no scars. He touched Akbar's nipples, feeling carefully, then the crotch. Still nothing. He told Akbar to turn around, bend over and spread his cheeks. Nothing.

It had been less than two weeks since Akbar had returned from Los Angeles, and the marks of torture could not have faded completely in so short a time. But there were no burns on the man's body, no scars, not even any simple abrasions. Was he wrong? Ja'far considered the question. It was certainly possible; yet, looking into Akbar's eyes, he saw there was something there he did not yet know. He could torture the man himself, and had no aversion to doing so, but he prided himself on being civilized; if necessary he would resort to it, but psychological torture gave him more pleasure.

He turned his back on Akbar, walked across the sandy floor of the tent to a small table laden with cheese and fruit and picked up a pear and a small, sharp knife. Slicing off a piece of the pear, he popped it into his mouth and stood chewing and staring at the naked Akbar, then tossed the knife to him. "Cut your wrist," he said.

Akbar stared back, uncomprehending, but Ja'far held his gaze. Finally Akbar touched the tip of the knife against the inside of his left wrist, hesitated, glancing up again to see Ja'far's indomitable stare, then pulled it down sharply across the vein.

" 'Not so deep as a well,' " Ja'far said, smiling. "You know the quotation, of course."

Akbar's eyes were uncomprehending.

"No? Well, it doesn't matter. ' 'Tis enough. 'Twill serve.' " He took back the knife, then picked up a small silver goblet and threw it to him. "I will have some of your blood."

Akbar held the goblet under the wound while his blood dribbled into it. Ja'far took it back, cut a strip of tablecloth and handed it to him. Gratefully Akbar bound up his wrist.

Ja'far tossed him another silver goblet. "Your saliva," he said.

Akbar simply stared at him, bewildered.

"Spit into the goblet."

Akbar raised the goblet to his lips and found that it had been easier to bleed than to spit; his mouth was totally dry. Ja'far smiled and poured a little water into the goblet. "Drink that," he said. "Swirl it around in your mouth and swallow. Keep your mouth closed and breathe deeply."

Akbar's eyes dropped. He sipped the water and swallowed. "Spit," Ja'far said.

Akbar managed only a few drops, but Ja'far was satisfied. It wouldn't matter, he was sure. He took the goblet and tossed him a third one. "Piss," he said.

Lori walked slowly back to her office, oblivious of the hurrying crowds who jostled her. What was she doing? she asked herself. She had run to David's hotel room like a randy cheerleader when he'd called from the airport. She'd been excited beyond all restraint by the excitement in his voice, had simply dropped the papers she'd been working on, and. . . .

It had to stop. She and Charles had a good marriage. They'd each had one affair during their ten years—though she suspected he'd had more than the one he'd told her about—but they had been nothing important, only an expression of personal freedom, a denial on both their parts of subjection to the artificial strictures of the world they lived in. That was all she had intended here. But now. . . .

"Where have you been?" Werther asked. "Your plane landed two hours ago."

Melnik hadn't been thinking—or rather, he had been thinking about the wrong things. "I didn't think you'd be at the office so early," was all he could say. "I stopped off at my place and showered."

"Well, sure," Werther agreed sarcastically. "Eight hours on an airplane, a man needs to freshen up. I didn't know Israelis were so fragile."

"Sorry. I just didn't think."

"You didn't think we'd be interested? I get a message in the middle of the night that says 'Bingo!' and you didn't think I'd be interested? Come on, Melnik, what happened over there? What did you find out?"

"It's an assassination."

"You're sure?"

Melnik told him what had happened in London. When he'd finished, Werther leaned back in his chair, put his feet up on his desk and chewed his lip. He wondered if he could trust Melnik. He also wondered how to voice his distrust without insulting him. He knew how touchy these Israelis were, but damn it, he couldn't worry about that. He wasn't a diplomat and had never pretended to be. "Those drugs are tricky," he said.

Melnik knew what was coming but just sat and waited.

"A good man can beat them," Werther said. "They're not fool-proof."

"And I'm not a fool," Melnik said. "I've used them before."

"Sometimes they don't work. You can't get the subject to say anything; he won't answer your questions. At least then you know where you are. But there are other reactions, too."

"I'm well aware of it," Melnik said. "The drug can be beaten. If the subject can convince himself that a lie is the truth, he can fool the interrogator. That's why you need an experienced interrogator." He paused. "I am an experienced interrogator."

"You're positive he wasn't lying?"

"I'm positive. *Dallas* was named after the city where they got Kennedy because it's the same type of operation. They probably thought the name might make us think that was where this one would take place as well. More likely, or maybe in addition, they picked it as a fillip to their morale, to remind them that it's been done successfully before."

Werther nodded thoughtfully. He didn't want to push the Israeli any further. "Los Angeles, eh? During the President's campaign visit." He nodded again, then smacked his hand against the table and gave a sharp laugh. "Goddamn! The CIA is going to spit nickels. They must have laughed themselves sick when they learned we lost Akbar's record and he got out of the country before we could grab him. But now we go after him and pick him up in England! That's the kind of stuff *they* love to do: covert operations crap." He leaned back and put his arms behind his head. "I'm looking forward to this, walking into Langley and telling those space cadets that we've done their job for them. An attempt on the President's life from an outside source and they don't know a goddamn thing about it until we tell them. Hot damn!"

"Not exactly *we*," Melnik reminded him.

"Don't worry," Werther said. "There's plenty of credit to go around. I'll be sure to tell them it was the Mossad that picked this guy up in London. They'll want to talk to you firsthand about it anyway. We'll also have to notify the Treasury Department. It's their Secret Service who'll set up the precautions in L.A."

"That's it, then?" Melnik asked. "The FBI is out of it from here on in?"

Werther pursed his lips. "The Treasury Department is responsible for guarding the President. The CIA will want to pick up on the Libyan connection; that's *their* job." He nodded cautiously. "I guess our job is done. I'll check with the Director, but you can probably go home now."

Akbar pissed into the silver goblet, filling it to the brim, and handed it to Ja'far, who placed it next to the two others on the table and smiled at Akbar. "These fluids from your body will be tested," he said. "Any trace of drugs will be immediately apparent."

"Drugs?" Akbar was surprised. "I don't use—"

"Of course not. No good Muslim uses drugs." Ja'far was smiling, but his eyes were terrifying. He waited a moment before continuing. "But if anyone has used drugs *on* you, we will know about it, and we will wonder why. Or perhaps we will *know* why," he added coldly.

For a long moment time seemed to stand still in the hot tent. Then suddenly Akbar threw himself on his knees, smacked his forehead against the sandy floor and began to cry, begging for mercy.

As Akbar cracked before his eyes the moment was almost orgasmic for Ja'far. He waited, savoring it, then walked over to the groveling figure. His face pressed against the sand, Akbar saw the boots of his master not two inches from his eyes. He choked down his cries and waited. Ja'far kicked him viciously in the face, knocking him over onto his back. "Talk," he said.

And talk Akbar did. It came blubbering out of him in a rush, the words spilling over themselves so fast it was hard to catch them all. He held nothing back, and when he was finished Ja'far made him tell it all again, and then once more. Finally satisfied that there was no more to be learned, Ja'far turned and snapped his fingers for his guards.

Akbar was sobbing as they pulled him away. He tried to turn back to Ja'far to beg for forgiveness, but the strong men supporting him held him tight. Only the bottom half of his body managed to turn, and as they pulled him away relentlessly his feet twisted, his legs collapsed and he fell. They dragged him out of the tent, his limp feet leaving a rippling trail on the sandy floor.

Ja'far smiled softly as his cries died away in the distance. He was tempted to watch while they interrogated him, but he had to think about what he had learned, he told himself.

The interrogation was almost certainly unnecessary. He had destroyed Akbar's will, he was almost sure. But one could never be positive, so it was best to take no chances. Akbar might have the intestinal fortitude to have held something back as one last bargaining point if he was tortured, so it was necessary to subject him to the actual ordeal in order to find out for certain.

While he waited Ja'far tried to focus his mind on the action he should take to counteract this security break, but he found his mind drifting as he imagined what was happening to Akbar. He would be moaning in terror now, as one of the men tied him down and the other . . . He refocused his mind. The real reason he wasn't watching was that he didn't like the actual physical torture; rather, he preferred to focus on the mind of the victim and on his pain. The thought of what caused the pain was ugly and unbearable, but the pain itself was exquisite. He concentrated on Akbar's face at this moment, on his mouth writhing and screaming, on the terror in his eyes as . . .

Ja'far's finger slipped from his lips and suddenly his teeth parted and snapped at it, catching the fleshy bit between them, biting it painfully. He closed his eyes, savoring the pain, envying Akbar.

Hardy flew Freddy in the DC-3 down to the little grass airfield in Florida that Mason had found several weeks before. It was a few miles outside the town of Glade City, a village on the edge of the Everglades west of Miami, halfway across the state toward Tampa. Glade City depended on stone crabs in the winter, frogs' legs in the summer and smuggling year round. It was lethargic, with that lack of hustle-bustle that so charms tourists and is probably due more to a contaminated water supply rich in lead derivatives than to conscious motivation. But there were always some people ready to pick up a few dollars for a few hours' work. Mason would have no trouble finding the few men he needed.

Now Hardy sat alone in a motel room in San Francisco, smoking one cigar after another, going over the plans again and again. He had left Mohammed Asri in Wichita; the Panther jet was ready, and so was Asri. In a few days he would move him to his final base. The Cubans were in Seattle with their 707, Mason was in Florida, Nakaoka was in one San Francisco condominium and the guns and ammunition were stacked and ready in the other. Well, not quite ready; he would take care of the final preparations at the last minute. He had covered all the possibilities; everything was under control; there was nothing to do now but wait.

Yet one inescapable thought kept nagging at him: there was entropy in this damned universe, and nothing is ever 100 percent under control. He had kept the plan as simple as possible, but it was necessarily complex. If any one element went wrong, what effect would it have? Could it be compensated for? Had he neglected anything?

He lit another cigar, and then another, trying to anticipate everything that might happen.

52

"So what's the bottom line? What do you recommend?"

Werther had thought about this carefully on the trip down to Washington and while he was waiting to see the Director. He was still thinking about it, but now it was time to talk.

"First of all," he said, "we turn over all the information to the Treasury Department, of course."

"Of course," the Director echoed.

"They'll stake out the apartment and put on extra guards."

The Director nodded. "They know their business," he agreed, waiting. "We can trust them to protect the President."

Werther nodded. "And we tell the CIA about Akbar."

The Director smiled. "Yes, they thought we missed the boat there, didn't they? It will be a distinct pleasure to tell them that we picked him up in London and, as they say in cheap romantic novels, had our way with him. We might even twist the knife just a little as we slip it to them," he said. "But then what? Should we drop it?"

"Well . . ."

The Director waited.

"I like working with the Mossad," Werther began. "I'd rather work with them than with the CIA. They're smart, they know their business and they're ruthless." He paused.

"But?" prompted the Director.

"But . . . Well, sir, they're arrogant as all hell. What I'm saying is they're not Superman. Hell, *nobody* is Superman, not even Captain Marvel."

"Meaning you're not one hundred percent sure they got the truth out of Akbar, is that it?"

"That's it in a nutshell, sir."

"What are your reasons? This guy Melnik doesn't look good to you?"

"No, sir, it's not that. There's something about him I don't quite trust, it's true, but I can't put my finger on it and I don't think it's important. I'm sure he's not lying to us, and he certainly seems to know his business. It's the background."

"Tell me."

"Well . . ." Werther waved his hands helplessly. "I'm floundering here; I know that. I'm searching for something and I don't know what. It's like a gut feeling, it just doesn't hang right. Look, sir, we've been hearing about Dallas for months now. We catch hints of a lot of money moving around, and it looks like something big."

"Killing the President isn't big?"

"No sir, it's not. That's the problem." Now that he had said it, he knew he was right. "Killing the President is too easy. It doesn't take that much money and it doesn't take all that much preparation. If they're not too stupid—like when they tried to bring a whole squad of killers into the country—it would be simple. The President is continually appearing in public, making speeches: that's his job. If they just hire a single hit man there's no way a repetition of the Kennedy assassination could be prevented, unless the assassin simply misses. What's-her-name, Squeaky Something, Frommer, shot at Ford and nobody stopped her. John Hinckley shot Reagan a few years ago, and there was no way he could have been stopped."

"Those were crazies—"

"But there are a lot of crazies out there. It can't be hard to find them, and all you have to do is give one of them a decent gun with a dumdum bullet or a mercury shell. That's the way to kill a President. This is too big, too well organized."

"You think the Akbar story is a diversion?"

Werther nodded. "Maybe *think* is too strong a word. I'm *wondering* if maybe that's what it is. I'm wondering if maybe we shouldn't stay on it and see what else we can dig up."

The Director looked at the calendar on his desk. "President Bush will be in Los Angeles next week. We'll know by then, one way or another, if you're right."

"Only it might be too late by then."

"What you're asking for is permission to stay on this until then? If you dig up nothing else and if the attempt is made the way Akbar says, that will be the end of it?"

"Agreed."

"How do you plan to attack the problem?"

Werther shrugged. "I don't know, sir."

The Director lifted his eyebrows and pursed his lips. He didn't like to hear that phrase from any of his men, certainly not from a chief agent on an important case. He looked as if he might press a button on his desk and cause a trapdoor to open under Werther's chair.

"I mean," Werther added quickly, "I don't know of anything *new* we can do. Our operation is going forward full speed on what we already have."

"Which is?"

"Well, of course we have Akbar's description of the man in charge. The man he knows as Dallas."

"But if Akbar's lying about the plan, presumably he's lying about this man too."

"Yes, sir. We also have San Medro and Rasheed Amon. They both know, at least by face, somebody in the Dallas organization."

"Do they know the same man? Is he the head of the group?"

Werther spread his hands. "We don't know that yet, sir. The description each of them gave us could be of the same man."

"What kind of pressure can you put on them?"

"We're holding off for a while, sir."

The Director frowned. "Why?"

Werther was beginning to sweat. "We've been able to pick up and talk to everyone San Medro met with during those two days we trailed him before we picked him up, but none of them are linked to Dallas in any way," he explained. "We also have the videotape of San Medro's flat when we had him under surveillance. What we're hoping is that maybe somebody from Dallas came to talk to him, but was scared off by our surveillance. If so, they might show up on the video, walking past the flat."

"How will you know?"

"We've been canvassing the neighborhood trying to identify everyone on the tape to see if there's anyone nobody knows, someone who's a stranger in the neighborhood. Someone like that, passing by the house at just that time, might reasonably be supposed to be part of the operation."

"Or maybe not."

"Yes, sir. That's right. Or maybe not. But if we can winnow out the faces on the tape to maybe half a dozen or so, then I can go to San Medro and Amon—separately, of course—and tell them we know who Dallas is and that we have his picture, and ask them to pick it out from a lineup of photos. If I give each of them the pictures of all the men on the tape, and if they both pick out the same man, then we have something."

The Director stopped frowning, but he didn't smile. "There are a lot of ifs in that sentence."

"Yes, sir."

"It will take forever. There must be a hundred faces on that tape."

"Actually," Werther had to admit, "there are two hundred and forty-seven. *But*," he went on quickly before the Director could erupt, "we were able to winnow them out quite a bit. We have their description of the man. It's not a very good description, so we've been conservative in order to make sure we don't eliminate the man we're looking for. But they both do describe him as a big, strong man, so we've been able to get rid of any little old men, and of course women—"

"But even if the tape does show a Dallas operative, it may not be the same man."

"Yes, sir. But since we're going to use the tape to have them identify the man we find, we're lost already if it's a different man. So we're going on the assumption that it might be the same man."

There was a pause. "How far along have you gotten?"

Werther had been afraid of this question. "We started with the multiple faces—people who showed up more than once on the tape. The idea was that they're people who have business walking up and down the street. They should fit into two categories: either they live there or are in business in the neighborhood. If we're lucky, there'll be a third group with just one person in it—Dallas."

"And?"

"And," Werther had to admit, "there turned out to be just the two categories. We've finished every single one of the multiple faces, and they've all been identified by somebody or other in the neighborhood."

"Which doesn't mean that one of them *isn't* Dallas."

"No, sir. But it doesn't mean that any of them *is*. As far as we know, anyone in the world could—"

The Director waved his hand impatiently, which was as close as he ever came to admitting that one of his ideas wasn't exactly state-of-the-art. "What else do you have?" he asked.

"We're starting now on the single exposures."

"Diminishing returns." The Director scowled. "Less likely."

"Yes, sir, but still a possibility. I don't see where else we can go. We'll also get a description of whoever rented that apartment in Los Angeles and see if we can find something that way." He paused.

The Director waited.

"There is one other thing," Werther began cautiously, and stopped. He didn't know much about interdepartment politics except that it was a morass that had trapped better men than he.

The Director waited. He wasn't going to prompt him. Werther was a big boy now, and if he had something tough to say, he ought simply to say it.

"The problem is that the responsibility is all split up," Werther said with a rush. "The CIA takes on the whole world out there and the Secret Service focuses on just the President and we try to cover everything in between, and there are just too many gaps. It's too fragmented; no one gets to see the whole story."

The Director frowned. "You know the rules of the game," he said. "Nobody likes it, but there are good reasons for it."

Werther knew that; he even approved of it. The reasons had been made obvious to everyone a few years ago in the Oliver North testimony before the joint committee, when he had revealed Bill Casey's plan to turn the CIA into a secret army, secret even from the Congress. The country had a fear of secret government organizations of any kind. So when the OSS had reluctantly been formed in World War II and had proved not only its usefulness but its necessity in that war and in the cold one that followed, Congress had dug in its heels and resisted any recommendations to merge it with the FBI and the Secret Service. They had created the CIA, but had specified that its responsibilities lie outside of the country. The FBI would handle internal espionage and federal crimes; the Secret Service would concentrate on the safety of the President and currency crimes; the CIA would handle external spying. There would be no overlap of responsibilities, to ensure that no one organization grew too big or too secret.

It was a good idea, but it spawned too much rivalry, which grew naturally into squabbling. The CIA and the FBI in particular were continually fighting for overall supremacy in the spy/antispy business. It had become a fact of life that both organizations and their employees had learned to live with.

"What are you suggesting?" the Director asked.

Werther took a deep breath and said, "I want to go through their files."

"Whose? What files?"

"The Secret Service's and the CIA's. I want to find out everything they know about stories or rumors or even hints of assassination attempts, everything they know about Libya and this man Ja'far that Melnik told us about."

"Everything they know, period?"

"Somebody has to do it, sir. Somebody has to know everything. Otherwise something important is likely to slip through the cracks. We're too fragmented to mount an effective defense against a well-organized attack, and that's the truth of the matter."

The Director was silent. Werther waited while he thought. It would not be easy to crack the tightly caulked barriers each department had built up around itself. These walls of secrecy were defended on grounds of national security, but everyone knew they were really based on turf, each agency staking out its own ground and defending itself not so much against the KGB as against its brother organizations, afraid not so much of international infiltration as of domestic competition.

But Werther was right, and the Director knew it. There were times when the walls had to crumble, when someone had to crawl through to see what was hidden inside. "I'll take care of it," he said. "Now, what about the Israeli?"

"Melnik? I don't see how he can help us anymore. We may as well send him home."

The Director thought a moment. "He was useful picking up Akbar in London. If something like that becomes necessary again—well, you said yourself you'd rather work with the Mossad than with the CIA. Less paperwork, easier to keep things to ourselves." He smiled. Here he was agreeing to insist to the attorney general that the CIA share its secrets, and he was still thinking like that. Old habits were hard to break. Still, there was no need to overdo it. "It's only another week; better keep him around."

"Yes, sir."

Lori became aware that someone was staring at her. She turned away from the window and saw her secretary in the open doorway. "What is it, Arthur?" He had a curious grin on his face.

"Oh, nothing, Mrs. Werther. I mean, your ten-thirty appointment is here. Mr. Cannister."

"Right. Send him in, then." She swiveled around to her desk, and noticed that Arthur was still lingering by the doorway with that silly grin. "What *is* it, Arthur?"

"Nothing, Mrs. Werther. It's just that . . . well, I wish I had a marriage like you do."

"What on earth are you talking about?"

"You didn't hear me when I knocked, so I opened the door, and you were staring out the window and—"

"I was thinking about Mr. Cannister's case," she said severely. "What's so strange about that?"

"Nothing," Arthur said, "but you were humming 'I've Grown Accustomed to His Face.' "

Peter Emmond had trouble with his lower back. An old football injury. Back in high school, playing on the junior varsity as defensive end, he'd hit the runner behind the line of scrimmage on a wide sweep and jarred the ball loose. It was his chance for glory. Even as he was still in the air, falling away from the tumbled runner, he saw the ball dropping and twisted around to gather it in, then fell on it. After which the other team fell on him. Someone's knee landed on a lower cervical vertebra, and something parted from something else, and now at the age of thirty-two Emmond's back hurt whenever he spent too much time on his feet.

Which was why he wasn't particularly happy with his current assignment. There were other reasons, of course. He had been in the Philadelphia bureau long enough to hope that stupid street-checking assignments like this one wouldn't be dumped on his shoulders. But this was a big one, and everyone not otherwise essentially employed was out on the streets.

*Spare me*, he thought wistfully, as he walked down Broad Street. It had been a nice neighborhood a long time ago. It wasn't particularly bad now, but it also wasn't particularly clean. Still, considering the normal state of American cities nowadays . . . *Nowadays*. He smiled to himself. He was getting old.

He came to the theater on the corner and identified himself to the cashier. It was midafternoon and there was no one waiting in line. He asked her if she'd mind taking a look at a bunch of photographs and seeing if she knew any of the faces.

Of course she wouldn't mind, she said; it was a bit of excitement. "What's it all about?" she asked.

"Just routine," Emmond said.

Twenty minutes later she had picked out half a dozen faces she knew, and Emmond meticulously noted them on his list. Among them was one face that she recognized only vaguely; she wasn't sure when she had seen him. She remembered him because so few adults go to afternoon movies, which are populated mostly by old people or by kids cutting school. Last week this man had come to a matinee, so she remembered his face.

Actually, that was all she knew about any of the pictures; she didn't know their names. That wasn't important, Emmond assured her, and walked away satisfied. He didn't care what their names were either; the ones she'd picked out were people who belonged in the neighborhood, and the FBI could cross them off their list of possible suspects.

"So what do you think?" the Director of the CIA asked. There were standing orders that any threat against the life of the President be brought to his personal attention.

"Well, you can't totally ignore anything like this; that goes without saying."

"But?"

"But I think it's a load of malarkey," William Albertson said. He had been an agent for nearly fifteen years, and he was used to—and getting bored by—the Libyan Connection, which kept cropping up in all assassination scares. "I don't think there's been a single six-month period in the past ten years that we haven't been told Qaddafi's going to assassinate the President or somebody else. Remember back in '81, when *Newsweek* announced we were trying to assassinate *him*? Everybody was sure he was going to hit Reagan then. You weren't DCI then, but—"

"I remember."

"Then when the two Tomcats shot down his jet fighters over Sidra? Our Ethiopian contact told us for absolutely goddamn sure that Qaddafi had given orders for an assassination. NSA even picked it up on satellite, remember? A microwave transmission supposedly giving the order? But nothing happened. Bill Casey used to panic with each report; he had guys running up and down the halls with guns in their hands—"

"A slight exaggeration."

"Only slight. You know how much time we wasted."

"How about the time they sent in a whole platoon of killers?"

"And we picked them up right at passport control, didn't we? The whole operation was so amateurish it was laughable. Look, a man who talks all the time about killing the President is a man getting his jollies from *talking*. Qaddafi's an egomaniac, a psychopath, a goddamn clown. Nothing serious has ever come out of his threats and nothing ever will."

There was a long pause while the DCI thought about it. "So we shouldn't waste our time and efforts running around in circles every time Qaddafi farts?"

"That's about it, sir. That's what I think."

Albertson was a good agent. But he wasn't the DCI. He was probably right, but *probably* wasn't good enough. If something *should* come out of it . . . The DCI sighed.

Albertson knew what a DCI sigh meant. "On the other hand," he said.

The DCI nodded. "On the other hand, we might as well keep our hand in."

"We'll maintain an open file and search for Akbar. If he shows up outside Libya again, we'll pick him up and have a little conversation of our own."

"Exactly." The DCI nodded with satisfaction, his hands folded on the desk. "Exactly."

San Medro was looking out the window when the door opened. "Hey, man," he said without turning around, "who's that?" He pointed out the window.

The guard came over to him and looked over his shoulder. "Who?" he asked.

"Right there, man. You blind? The statue on top a' that building."

"Are you kidding? That's William Penn."

"Yeah? Who's he?"

"Never mind. Stick out your hands."

"What for?" San Medro asked, but held them out, and the guard snapped a pair of handcuffs on him. "Hey, man, what's the idea?"

"Come with me."

"Where we going?" he asked, following along as they left the holding cell.

"Down to the courtyard."

"Yeah? How come?"

"Everybody's worried about you. They're afraid you're not getting any exercise."

"Hey, man, I never get any exercise."

"Sure, you do. You beat up your women, don't you?"

San Medro laughed. "You got some broads down there you want me to push around?"

"Afraid not. It's just a courtyard. You can walk around it for exercise."

"Fuck that. Take me back to my cell."

"The courtyard," the guard said, opening a door at the end of the corridor and gesturing San Medro through. "Walk."

"Is the light okay?" Werther asked.

"Fine."

"You can see him clearly?"

"Clear enough."

"They've got to be good shots."

"They will be."

They were looking out an open window on the first floor. The other man was kneeling, resting his camera on the ledge, snapping off photos as San Medro walked around and around the courtyard.

"Don't get the cuffs," Werther warned.

"We can crop them out later. Do you drive your wife crazy when you go shopping with her?"

"Sorry. Just make them good."

"They'll be good. Relax."

*Sure*, Werther thought. *Relax*. It was the first laugh he'd had today.

53

It hadn't taken long to finish off Akbar. The torturers reported nothing new, as Ja'far had been almost sure they would; his own method of breaking a man down with psychological pressures was superior to brutal torture. Still, the only way to be certain was to take the man to the brink of death, slowly and carefully, then watch as he slid over that brink as painfully as possible.

So what had happened? First, Akbar had entered the United States unseen; Hardy's care at their meeting had ensured that he had not been followed, and surely Hardy himself was not under surveillance. Yet Akbar had certainly been picked up in London. Possibly the cell there was under surveillance, and that was how they'd caught him. But the questions, as Akbar reported them, had concerned nothing but Dallas. Clearly the Dallas security net was broken, though it was not clear how.

Secondly, what was Hardy playing at? Did he really intend to murder the President instead of kidnapping him?

The pleasure of the torture faded quickly and was replaced with a sick feeling in his stomach as Ja'far realized that whatever the significance of Akbar's story, it certainly meant that something was wrong, and that he had made an awful mistake in trusting this American to carry out his orders. He had a sudden vision of Colonel

Qaddafi learning what had happened, and the churning in his belly turned to cold terror, tightening his gut and squeezing his sphincter in apprehension. His mind reeled at what awaited him in that eventuality, not the exquisite sensuality of pain but the terrible reality of it, and he was nearly physically sick.

There was no time to waste. He did not have the luxury of sending another messenger. He would have to go himself, and he would have to leave quickly, but most important of all his trip had to be secure. He didn't know where the break had come that had exposed Akbar, but wherever it was he would bypass it. He put in a call to Cairo.

Egypt and Libya are mortal enemies, facing each other with barely disguised distrust and hatred across their common border. Unfortunately Egypt has no choice but to dance when Libya calls the tune, because, like Libya, Syria and Iran, Egypt is competing for leadership of the entire Muslim world. The stakes are tremendous; if any one nation could gain the submission of the others, it could lead the Arab empire into world dominion, on a par with Russia and the United States. Given the fatalistic passions of their common religion, the promise of heaven in jihad, and the fact that they have three-quarters of the world's oil supplies, the Arab nations could easily rise to supremacy in the world order—if only one country could dominate the others.

Egypt's greatest strength in the Mideast comes from the security and peace that country enjoys, and its position as America's ally, but these factors are also its greatest weakness. Since Anwar Sadat made peace with Israel, Egypt has been able to sit within its national boundaries and build up its economy and military strength with American aid, but in the court of Arab world opinion it teeters on the brink of infidelity. Can an Arab nation really have peace with Israel without betraying its Palestinian brethren? Egypt is always open to this charge, and if it could be made to stick, her position as Arab leader would fall. Being so vulnerable, she is always careful to show her solidarity with Arab terrorists; she dares not turn her back on them. Though she is not an active sponsor to the extent that Libya is, Egypt never refuses to he'
when asked.

*     *     *

Kamel Salim sat at a table in a corner of the El-Shara nightclub in Cairo, looking at the belly dancer and the men watching her. At the beginning he used to tip the maître for a table close to the stage, but now he preferred to sit farther away to see the expressions of lust on the faces of the other men in the club. He lived for these Wednesday nights. Lately he had even begun to dream of a future when all nights would be Wednesdays.

He stayed for both performances, then went alone to his flat and prepared a small midnight supper for two.

Kamel Salim was an unimportant clerk in the Egyptian government's division of passport control. It was not likely that anything important would ever come through his hands, but everything of importance had to pass through many unimportant clerks' hands, so the Mossad reasoned that if they suborned enough unimportant people they would eventually learn about a lot of important developments. It was for this reason that the lovely young belly dancer spent Wednesday nights with Kamel.

The information she picked up on this particular night did not seem significant, but dutifully she passed it on. She didn't use the hidden radio transmitter she had for urgent messages, sending it instead through the twice-weekly diplomatic carrier pouch from Cairo to Jerusalem. The clerk who received the message in Israel also saw nothing urgent in it, and passed it on via routine channels. Thus it wasn't until Friday afternoon that the Mossad discovered that Ayn Allah Ja'far had requested an Egyptian passport from Cairo, to be made out in an assumed name.

Ja'far stood in front of the mirror staring at his face, wondering how hard it would be to say good-bye if things should come to such a pass. He glanced down at his open palm. Resting lightly in it was a small silver wedge. It was so light he could barely feel its weight, yet its impact could end his life in a flash. He wondered if he would ever ~~. But he comforted himself that he would almost certainly never make that decision. Still, it was well to be prepared. He took ~~dge in two fingers of his right hand and, holding his ~~de with his left, reached in and inserted it into the ~~ared cavity in a left rear molar. Now, if events ever reached the point of no return, he could pass easily from this life with a simple hard crunch of his teeth. He felt gingerly around the silvered vial of cyanide with his tongue. It gave him a little tremor of fear that was almost pleasant.

Werther was abstracted. Lori hadn't been herself lately, and they didn't seem to be on the same wavelength. He wondered . . .

He became aware of the silence and looked up to see the two men exchanging glances. "I'm sorry," he said. "You were saying?"

"If we're boring you," the short, heavyset man said, "we can forget all about it."

"I'm sorry. I just thought of something. Please go on."

They were obviously offended. Well, it's good for them, Werther thought. Goddamn CIA think they're gods. Think the world revolves around Langley. Suddenly he thought of the British saying: Sod 'em. He wondered what it meant. He caught himself beginning to wander again, and concentrated on what they were saying. Anyway, sod 'em.

"You know the NSA?" the short one asked rhetorically. "They've got these satellites circling all over the world. Incredible things. They say they can see when the guards at the Kremlin are sneaking off to the men's room for a smoke—even whether they're smoking Russian or American cigarettes." He nodded, lost in admiration of America's technological wonders, until Werther prompted him: "And?"

"And so yesterday they spotted a lone Arab walking across the Sahara from Tripoli to Cairo."

They stared at each other. "You don't believe me," the CIA man said.

"I don't believe you," Werther agreed.

"You don't believe we can do that? Spot an Arab crossing the desert?"

"I don't believe a single Arab could or would walk from Tripoli to Cairo."

The short man shrugged. "Metaphorically speaking."

Werther was beginning to lose his patience. "I certainly don't believe that your satellites can spot metaphorical Arabs. What exactly are we talking about?"

"It was a real Arab," the one with the mustache said, "but the walk was metaphorical. What the satellite actually picked up was a coded message from Tripoli to Cairo. We've got Egypt wired; we know everything they say as soon as they say it, did you know that?"

"Never gave it much thought," Werther said.

"Wasn't always that way," the short one went on. "Where were you in 1973? The Yom Kippur War, remember?"

Werther nodded. "I remember it, but it had nothing to do with us."

"Well, you probably don't know, then. What happened was the damned Egyptians told us they were mobilizing because they had information that the Israelis were planning to start a war. Now, we knew they weren't—the Israelis, I mean—so we knew the Egyptians were lying, but we figured they were mobilizing to provoke the Jews into starting something that would expose them to world opinion as aggressors. So we told their premier, Golda Meir, to play it cool and wait. But all the time the Egyptians were planning their invasion, together with the Syrians. They caught us flat-footed, the bastards."

"They caught *you* flat-footed?" Werther asked.

"The Jews too, I guess, probably because of what we told them. So anyway, we made damn sure it wouldn't happen again. We've got wires, bugs and satellites in, over and under every square inch of Egypt now. They don't fart without some NSA joker chokes, if you get my meaning."

Werther nodded. God, it took them a long time to get to the point. "So?" he prompted.

"So we called you in to let you know, because we have orders to cooperate with you on this business. I believe you know this guy. Name of"— he glanced down at the notes on his desk—"Ayn Allah Ja'far."

The CIA decided to kidnap Ja'far if he made a stopover between Tripoli and New York. Since he would be traveling under an assumed name on an Egyptian passport, no one would suspect that the United States might be interested in him, so they thought the risk worth taking. To that end the agency notified its operatives in Rome, Frankfurt, Amsterdam and London.

Ja'far left two days later from Cairo, on the afternoon nonstop British Airways flight to London, with a continuing ticket on the evening Concorde direct to New York.

The CIA notified the FBI that they wouldn't have a chance to intercept him because he wouldn't be leaving Heathrow. Werther decided that he couldn't take the chance of following him to discover his contacts in the United States; he was afraid they would lose him the way they had lost Mohammed Asri. He made arrangements to arrest Ja'far on entry at Kennedy, but he did not notify Melnik. Lately he had found himself getting upset at the Israeli without knowing why. There was something secretive and arrogant about the man's attitude. Typical Israeli, he thought. He still remembered the expression on Melnik's face when they had lost Asri. He would tell Melnik *after* they had Ja'far in custody.

Ja'far's plans to continue directly to New York did not satisfy the Mossad any more than they had the CIA. The difference was that the Mossad did something about it, and so when Ja'far landed at Heathrow he found that his connecting flight to New York had been delayed. A "mechanical problem," he was told. He waited with the other passengers in the lounge for one hour, then two.

Actually, British Airways had received a telephone call informing them, in a voice with an Irish accent, that a bomb had been planted on the Concorde. They began going through the airplane inch by inch, X-raying every bit of luggage. By the time they found the bomb, which was in a suitcase checked prior to boarding by a woman who had never bothered to show up, they had received another phone call with a correction. They were now told that there were two bombs on board.

They couldn't find the second bomb. But there *had* been a first bomb, so they began their search again. Finally they canceled the flight.

Together with the other passengers, Ja'far spent the night in London as a guest of British Airways. Ordinarily he would have taken advantage of the enforced delay to catch the RSC production at the Aldwych, but tonight his mind was on other matters. After dinner in the hotel he took a short walk through the adjoining park, intending to turn in early. Unfortunately, he was mugged in the park. The elderly couple who came upon him a few minutes later screamed and helped him to his feet, only to see him fall down again. Their screams brought a bobby on the run, and Ja'far was taken by ambulance to a hospital.

The London police are remarkably efficient in such cases. Unlike the New York police, they do not take muggings as an act of nature that city dwellers as well as visitors are not only subject to but in some way probably responsible for. By the time Ja'far woke up the next morning with seven stitches in his skull, the police had found his wallet and passport in a trash bin by Marble Arch, not far from the attack. Though all his money was missing, his traveler's checks and Egyptian passport were still there.

After nearly twenty-four hours of searching for a second bomb, the British authorities had gone over every inch of the Concorde, found nothing and at last had convinced themselves that it didn't exist. It had been the IRA's idea of a joke. Bloody bastards. These were trying times to live in. The New York flight was rescheduled for later that day.

Against the resident's advice Ja'far checked himself out of the hospital by noon, insisting that he was all right, and caught the delayed Concorde flight to Kennedy.

## 54

Hardy woke up choking. He was hanging upside down, his arms strapped painfully to his sides, his wrists crossed tightly in the small of his back, spinning slowly, swinging back and forth, blindfolded, gasping for breath, his blood pounding down into his head, building up pressure behind the eyes. Someone had grabbed him by the hair, stopping the spinning, holding him there, and now put a cloth over his nose and mouth. Then they dripped water onto the cloth. He tried to shout, but as he opened his mouth he sucked in the wet cloth and began to choke. The water was coming faster now, the cloth fully soaked, clinging to his nostrils and filling his mouth. All his blood was rushing to his head so that he thought it would pop his eyes out of their sockets. He couldn't *breathe!* He was drowning, hanging upside down, and now hands grabbed him and spun him around and around—
He fell out of bed.

The room stopped swirling and the blindfolded blackness faded into the quiet dark of a hotel room as he sprawled on the floor, holding tightly to the carpet, digging his nails in to stop the spinning, gasping deeply for breath, afraid it would all start again.

In his hotel room David Melnik received a phone call from the Israeli consulate. Arriving there half an hour later, he found a messenger who had just flown from Tel Aviv, via Rome, with an unusual-looking little transistor radio.

In London Debora Stern watched Ja'far with his bandaged head board the British Airways Concorde for New York. She was glad to see him turn up at the airport today; she'd been afraid they had killed him last night.

Their group had been waiting in the park across the way; a simple phone call from a "concerned mother" had established the name of the hotel at which the passengers would be put up. They had intended to break into his room in the middle of the night, and couldn't believe their luck when they saw him come out for a stroll in the park. This would be easier, and more believable too.

The mugging itself was as easy as muggings always are. It takes only a second for a hand to be raised and to come crashing down with a sand-weighted sock in it, and only a few more for the unconscious body to be dragged behind the bushes.

"My God, he's dead!" Debora gasped.

"I don't think so," somebody said.

"You don't *think* so?" Debora asked.

"No, feel: there's a pulse here."

"My God, you could have killed him."

"Well, I didn't. Where's his bloody wallet?"

"Here."

"And the passport?"

"Got it."

"Let's get the hell out of here, then."

As they walked quickly away Debora took the money out of Ja'far's wallet, stuffed it in her purse and handed the wallet to one of her men. He dropped it in a trash bin as they reached Park Lane. They waited for the light to change and crossed to the other side, where the light from the streetlamps was better. There they formed a little circle around her, watching as she bent over the dark green passport. In her right hand she held a small needle. Carefully she bent the passport open and inserted the needle in its spine. It slid in easily, disappearing as she pushed it until it was perfectly hidden in the fold.

She passed it around for inspection. They all nodded appreciatively, and then walked back across Park Lane to the park. Debora opened her purse, took out a small radio and turned it on. Immediately it began to beep, and the needle on its face spun around to point at the man holding the passport. She motioned with her head and he walked in a circle around her, the needle following him.

"Okay," she said. "It looks good."

He walked away with the passport and dropped it in the same trash bin as the wallet while Debora gauged his whereabouts by the movement of the needle and the beep-beep of the sound.

Hardy flew from San Francisco to Wichita, arriving just after noon. He took a cab to the Ryder truck rental agency in town and picked up the six-wheeler he had reserved. It probably wasn't necessary, he thought, but he worried that too many people now knew about Wichita. Better safe than sorry. It was just turning one o'clock when he arrived at the small airport where Mohammed Asri was waiting. Together they checked over the Panther. Everything looked good.

Hardy backed the truck up to the hangar entrance, opened the doors and lowered the ramp. Everything was moving like clockwork. This morning's nightmare was forgotten.

Melnik took the subway out to Kennedy. He wondered if he should have told Werther about Ja'far coming to the United States, and about the transmitter hidden in his passport. But the Americans had shown their incompetence with Akbar; they hadn't done any better with Asri, either, and if he told them about Ja'far they would probably screw that up too. He could have made good use of their manpower if Werther would simply let him run the operation, but he knew that was impossible, and he felt he'd do better alone than with their help.

*     *     *

Werther had no such doubts. He saw no reason to tell Melnik about Ja'far's impending visit; this was strictly an FBI operation. When the Concorde landed at Kennedy at ten past two, just a few minutes late, Werther had his men dispersed around the passport control exit, waiting to pick up Ja'far as soon as he passed through.

His walkie-talkie buzzed, and he pressed the button and answered. "He's coming through," was the message, and he motioned to his men to be ready.

The door was opening continuously as the passengers filed through passport control. A few seconds after the message the door opened again and this time a thin, swarthy Arab dressed impeccably in a gray pin-striped suit, his head bandaged, carrying his hat in one hand and a Burberry raincoat in the other, came through the door. Werther started to move forward when suddenly there was a loud shout from behind him: "Werther!" The Arab—and everybody else in the room—turned to look.

Melnik nearly fainted. He had spotted some FBI men whose faces he recognized waiting near the door, but the room was so large and crowded that he hadn't seen Werther—and obviously Werther hadn't seen him. It had never occurred to him that the FBI group was waiting for Ja'far, and he had ignored them. But now as he saw Ja'far come through the door and the FBI agents began to move toward him, and as Werther stepped out of the crowd, he realized that they were going to ruin everything.

As he shouted "Werther!" time stood still. He ran forward, pushing his way through the crowd, forcing a smile to his lips, and grabbed Werther around the shoulders like a long-lost friend. Hugging him to him, he whispered in his ear, "Call them off! Now!"

Werther stared at him while his agents stared at *him*. He had no time to make a decision, but the look in Melnik's eye made it for him. He glanced around at his men, and then as they saw him turn to Melnik they realized what he wanted and stepped back.

"David!" Werther said loudly. "You old son of a gun! What are you doing here?"

Ja'far glanced at them as he passed through, picked up his luggage and walked out. The FBI agents started to follow but Melnik shook his head sharply and Werther motioned them back.

Werther turned to Melnik. "What the hell are—?"

Melnik took out the small transistor radio he had received that morning and turned it on. They heard the beep and saw the needle pointing toward the door through which Ja'far had just left.

"You son of a bitch," Werther said softly. "Why didn't you tell me? How did you know he was coming?"

"Those questions work both ways, don't they?" Melnik answered. "I guess we have a lot to talk about, but right now we should get moving. This thing only has a range of about ten miles."

Werther thought for a moment, but only for a moment. With a radio transmitter planted somewhere on Ja'far and this receiver they had a good chance of following him to wherever he was going, which would be better than picking him up and trying to make him talk.

It took nearly an hour for Hardy and Asri to load the rockets and machine guns into the van and strap them down properly for the trip. Then they had to drag the winch up inside and attach it to the front wall and floor with inch-thick bolts. Ryder would be upset about the holes in their truck, but neither of them worried about that. It was after three o'clock when they were ready for the next step.

They followed the airport bus in Werther's car, staying half a mile behind, out of sight. When Ja'far changed to the subway, Werther slapped a flashing red light on the roof of the car and they raced through the Queens tunnel following the transmitted signal. As Ja'far switched around from one train to another in the subway system below they tracked him from above, the siren and red light clearing a path for them through city traffic. Melnik had a subway map, and with the radio beeping they traced him until he took the F train out to Queens and got off at Roosevelt Avenue.

They stopped the car. "He'll be taking the Q33 to La Guardia," Werther predicted. They waited several blocks from the station until the needle started to move again, proving him right. Taking a direct route, but still monitoring the transmitter, they arrived at La Guardia first and were waiting for him as he came through the sliding glass doors. From a distance they watched him walk over to the TWA counter and buy a ticket. They waited until he had disappeared into the crowd, then went up to the counter, where Werther identified himself and asked the girl what flight Ja'far had booked. It was the four-thirty to Kansas City, she said.

Melnik took off his black hair, paying no attention as the clerk gasped and people around him stared, and put on a light brown long-haired wig. "Give me a ticket on the same flight," he said to the girl, "but in a different section." He turned back to Werther. "I'll let you know what happens."

"What kind of airplane is it?" Werther asked.

"An Airbus," the girl said, glancing at her computer screen. "An A-300."

"That's big enough. Give me a ticket, too."

Melnik looked unhappy but said nothing.

Hardy and Asri attached the hook on the end of the steel cable to the nose of the Panther. As Hardy fired up the gas-driven generator Asri climbed into the cockpit and, with the jet's electrical system plugged into the hangar circuit, actuated the wing-folding mechanism. The Panther had been built for carriers where storage space is vital, and the wings were designed to fold up so that more planes could be stored belowdecks. Now, sitting in the cockpit, he pressed the button; slowly the wingtips rose and came together above him, as if the plane were praying. He remained in the cockpit to steer the nosewheel as the winch began to reel in the steel cable. As it tightened, the Panther gave a slight shudder, then slowly began to inch up the ramp into the van.

From La Guardia Werther had called ahead to Kansas City, and they were met there by three local FBI agents. Werther pointed out Ja'far, and he and Melnik moved out of sight while the new men trailed him through the terminal. Following him to the Eastern counter, they checked the new reservation he had made.

"The seven P.M. flight to Wichita," one reported back to Werther. "It's a Fairchild turboprop, a small plane. Do you want to take the same flight?"

Werther shook his head; they couldn't push their luck too far. "There must be a charter service here," he said.

They found a twin-engined plane that could fly them to Wichita immediately. "How long will it take?" Werther asked.

"An hour and a half."

"Can you beat the seven P.M. Eastern flight?"

"No way. They'll do it in fifty-five minutes." The pilot looked at his watch. "We could take off in ten, maybe fifteen, minutes, and beat him out of here by ten minutes, but even if we push it he'll be there twenty minutes ahead of us."

"Get the plane ready," Werther said. "I'll be right back."

He ran through the terminal to the control tower, presented his identification and explained the problem. When they refused he threatened to go up the chain of command. It did no good until he explained that a man on the flight was conspiring to assassinate the President, and that they had to follow him to catch the actual assassin. At that point the controller reluctantly agreed.

They were in the charter five minutes later, with the engines running, holding just short of the runway. When one of the agents in the airport called in on Werther's walkie-talkie that the Eastern flight had begun boarding and that Ja'far was on the plane, they took off.

"Ah, good evening, ladies and gentlemen. This is the captain speaking," came the voice over the loudspeaker system on Eastern Flight 795. "We're all set to go, but we've been advised by the tower that there's a slight traffic problem and that we'll have to hold here just short of the runway for a few minutes. I expect us to be at the terminal in Wichita about twenty minutes late. If any of you have problems with connecting flights, please ring the stewardess button and we'll try to have them held for you. Thanks for your cooperation and my apologies for the delay. Thank you for flying Eastern."

Melnik and Werther arrived in Wichita at the moment Hardy and Asri were driving away in the van from their small airfield forty miles away. There was no FBI office in Wichita, but the charter was met by a car full of police detectives. A few minutes later the Eastern flight landed, and Melnik and Werther used the transmitter to stay out of sight, trailing their quarry through the airport. When Ja'far went to the Hertz rental booth they walked outside and waited in the unmarked police car, taking advantage of the delay to arrange for two more cars to lie in wait down the road.

When Ja'far drove off in his Ford, they waited until he was out of sight, then followed. Along the way they picked up the other two cars, and the strung-out cavalcade drove around the countryside as Ja'far evidently looked for a tail. Since none of them ever were within his sight, he was finally convinced that he was alone. Suddenly his erratic meandering stopped, and he drove straight out on an isolated stretch of State Road 932. Inside the cars the atmosphere became more tense; clearly they were now going somewhere. Coming over a slight incline, they saw the road stretching out in front of them through flat fields, extending in an unbroken line to the horizon, beyond which Ja'far's car had already disappeared. Without hurrying, they followed.

As they passed a crossroads they never noticed a Ryder truck waiting at the stop sign for them to pass. Nor did the two men in the truck think anything unusual about the cars speeding by.

When the transmissions indicated that Ja'far had stopped, they continued on cautiously. As they came around a bend in the road they saw the farmhouse and the parked rental Ford. They went on without stopping, but as they passed by they saw him standing on the porch, knocking on the door.

Once out of sight they halted and conferred. Werther decided they should return, and Melnik agreed. When they came back, Ja'far was still pounding on the door. As they pulled into the drive he was peering in the kitchen window, shielding his eyes against the fading sunlight. As they pulled up behind him he became aware of the noise of their car engines over the howling of the wind across the plains and turned to look at them. They pulled into the dirt driveway, one car blocking Ja'far's Ford. The other two cars screeched right up to the porch, one on either side; then all the car doors opened and a dozen men jumped out with guns drawn.

Ja'far stood bewildered, staring at twelve guns pointed at his chest, wondering what had gone wrong.

## 55

Their feeling of euphoria quickly dissipated as they broke into the farmhouse and discovered that it was not only empty but deserted. Werther quickly pulled everyone out, sealing the house so that there would be no confusion about fingerprints. He had the police take Ja'far into town; he would talk to him later. Now he stood disconsolately in the empty yard. Melnik kicked an oilcan and sent it clattering across the pebbles, the noise accentuating the desolation as it echoed and died away.

"Too fucking late," Werther said.

"We still have Ja'far," Melnik said, but without conviction. The sight of the Libyan banging on the door was all too clear in his memory: Ja'far had obviously been surprised to find the place empty and clearly didn't know what was going on. "He *has* to know," he said dispiritedly. "He's the boss, damn it."

"We'll soon find out."

"Bloody damn right we will," Melnik said angrily.

Werther lifted his eyebrows. "No rough stuff," he said. "No drugs."

"What?" He still couldn't be sure when Americans were kidding. He tried to smile.

"I'm serious," Werther said.

Melnik held his tongue. It was too soon to argue. Werther wouldn't be able to hold such an untenable position for long. "Let's go talk to the man," he said.


Ja'far didn't know how they had caught him. He supposed they must have been staking out Hardy's house. But the American was gone. Had he left for Los Angeles and the stupid assassination, or had he been arrested? Either way, the situation looked bleak. He tried to consider what he could do to lessen the political repercussions for Libya. He thought of the cyanide capsule lodged in his teeth. If they didn't know who he was, his death might stop them from finding out. But they seemed to know so much already.

He decided his only hope was to be silent and see what happened. If that idiot Hardy killed Bush, there was no doubt they'd hang him as an accomplice. On the other hand, if Hardy really did kidnap the President, his own release would surely be one of Qaddafi's demands. His one hope was to tell them nothing.

He laughed bitterly. He had nothing to tell! He had no idea what Hardy planned to do. He knew nothing except what Mahouri had reported about the fighter plane. Was it really part of the plot? How did it fit in with the Los Angeles assassin Akbar had told him about? He was confused. He could only hope that Hardy knew what he was doing. *As for me,* he thought, *I will be as the melting snow: silence, silence, all is silence.*

The door opened, and the space was filled with the hulking figure of a huge man. Looking up from his cot, Ja'far saw the brute staring at him. A threatening smirk moved across the man's face, and Ja'far felt the terrible tingle of a delicious fear.

Some police and some criminals are not much different from each other. There are those who are called to the profession of law enforcement through principle, just as some criminals practice their trade precisely because of a lack of any such feeling; these are the two extremes. But many are drawn to the police or criminal professions because of power, the violence inherent in each field, and the opportunity to exercise authority.

Such a man was John Mollanto. He could have gone either way. With a different family background he might easily have become a mugger or a Mafia hit man; being born into a low-income, honest family, he had become a police officer. Did he like it? He never thought about it. The job paid well enough, he could throw his weight around and he carried a gun; he had never asked for more.

But now, as he waited for the arrival of the FBI men, he thought about the Arab in the next room under his guard, and about the few hours he had. Suddenly he stood up. His companion glanced up from his newspaper. Mollanto walked across the room, took the newspaper from his hands and began to roll it tightly into a cylinder. "I'm going to have a little talk with this guy," he said.

"We're not supposed to," the other man said. "They said to leave him alone in there."

Mollanto nodded. What other people said generally irritated him; *he* ought to be the one telling people what to do. "Just a little talk," he said, and opened the door to the cell.

The smile that came to Mollanto's face was not intentional; he was not even conscious of it. It was simply his normal reaction to the sight of a man totally in his power and aware of it. The fear in the Arab's eyes was evident, though it was accompanied by a glitter of something else that the policeman didn't understand. Never mind; all that mattered was that he had the Arab in his care until the FBI showed up, and when they came, they'd find a prisoner who had already spilled everything he knew. That would bring him to someone's attention, and he would no longer be lost in a bureaucracy where every face was nameless, every name faceless. After this, everyone would know who John Mollanto was.

"On your feet," the monster said. "Yeah, punk, you! You see anyone else in this room?"

When Ja'far stood up, the monster walked heavily across the cell toward him. "What's your name?"

Ja'far started to answer, but Mollanto didn't wait. He had a philosophy: punks always lie, so it doesn't matter what they say at first. The trick was to let them know you know they're lying, and the first thing to do is to get their attention. So just as the Arab was opening his mouth, Mollanto jabbed him in the stomach with the tightly rolled newspaper, wielding it like an ice pick. Ja'far bent over, his legs gave way, and he fell to the floor gasping for breath. Mollanto had his attention.

As Ja'far lay coiled up on the floor, his face resting on the cold concrete next to a heavy pair of shoes, he had a fleeting memory of a tent on the hot desert sands and another face on the floor beside another pair of shoes. Then he had been looking down from above; now he was looking up from below. He shivered with terror, but not with fear. There is a difference.

Now he felt the man's fingers grabbing him around the neck and lifting him painfully to his feet; again the tightly rolled newspaper jabbed into his stomach, and again he curled up around it as his breath was forced out of his body and his legs gave way.

Newspapers are wonderful things, John Mollanto thought as he speared it deftly at the man's kidneys, eliciting a howl of pain. The Arab rolled away, but Mollanto followed and stabbed the paper into his groin. Wonderful things, he thought. Rolled up and wielded like a sword, they were pliable enough not to break the skin or leave marks, but rigid enough to inflict pain when used properly. He reached down and dragged the Arab to his feet again.

The fool, Ja'far thought. This kind of pain was well within one's ability to bear and, being bearable, it was even pleasant in a way. Pain provides pleasure, he thought as he was pulled to his feet, if it stays within the realms of what is bearable. He looked up at his tormentor and smiled in anticipation of what was to come.

The smile at first confused Mollanto, then infuriated him. Dropping the newspaper and all pretense of restraint, he reached down and grabbed Ja'far by the testicles. As he squeezed and twisted, Ja'far screamed, clutching at Mollanto's fingers and bending over in agony. As his head jerked down Mollanto brought his knee up into the Arab's face, smashing his nose and mouth, crushing his teeth and the silvered vial of cyanide that was lodged in them.

When the cell door opened a few moments later, Mollanto and Ja'far were a tableau; the policeman was still standing in the same spot and the Arab was lying where he had fallen. Mollanto's eyes were open and staring; so were Ja'far's.

"What the—" Werther started to ask, but immediately saw what must have happened. This oaf had been told to keep an eye on the prisoner but had thought he could— Christ. He shouldered the policeman out of the way and bent down. What was wrong with Ja'far? He looked dead.

Melnik knelt beside him and took Ja'far's wrist between his thumb and two fingers. "No pulse," he said.

Werther leaned over and put his head on Ja'far's chest. No heartbeat, no movement of the lungs. Immediately he went into CPR, banging the dead chest with the heel of his hand, then opening his mouth and spreading his own lips wide over the Arab's to give him the kiss of life. Suddenly he drew back.

"What is it?" Melnik asked, but as soon as he saw Werther's reaction he leaned over, put his own face close to Ja'far's and smelled the sickly odor. He looked down at the irretrievably dead man, then up at the brutish policeman, and shook his head sadly. "Schmuck," he said.

## 56

Melnik's natural language was Hebrew. He didn't like Yiddish: he thought the alphabet was nearly a sacrilegious use of Hebrew, the language itself a travesty of German, Polish and ignorance. But occasionally it gave birth to a word uniquely useful, a word like *schmuck*.

He repeated it bitterly to himself. It described all Americans, but none better than this dumb cop trying to be a hero. *Schmuck*. It had never occurred to the idiot that he wasn't an expert in interrogation, that it is impossible to drag out by force a secret unless you already know at least part of the secret before you begin, that others could do the job better, or that Ja'far might have a poison capsule in his mouth.

He shrugged; *Che sarà, sarà.* Anyway, it was Werther's fault more than the cop's. You had to know the kind of men you were dealing with, your allies even more than your enemies. Werther should have known that a small-town American cop might be dangerously stupid.

But didn't that apply to *him*, too? This was what he was really bitter about, he realized. He was the one who was supposed to be the big-deal international terrorist expert; he should have suspected that Ja'far might have an escape pill; he should have sensed that a parochial cop of any nationality might not be able to handle the job; he should have begun the questioning right away instead of moping around the deserted farmhouse feeling sorry for himself.

*Schmuck.*

They were back to square one. Sitting in the plane heading back to New York, staring out the window at the checkered countryside beneath them, half dozing, Melnik had a vision of a game board with farm-sized squares extending out into the distance, squares over which he had to hop, and way out there in the distance on the farthest square, half hidden by clouds but patiently waiting, stood Lori Werther.

He blinked the vision away. It had no right to be there. He remembered the days following his father's death. He had come home from England as quickly as he could, but it had taken several days because of the war. When finally he walked into his parents' apartment it might as well have been only minutes after the news: his mother lay sprawled and shattered on the couch, attended by friends and neighbors. Never, before or since, had he seen such grief. Years later he would come across a poem by Poe and would remember his mother's eyes as she stared up at him, the tears streaming out uncontrolled. Two lines of the poem stayed with him as subliminal subtitles to that memory; he realized that she had loved his father "with a love that was more than love . . ." and that now "neither the angels in Heaven above/Nor the demons down under the sea/Can ever dissever [her] soul from the soul of . . ."

He blinked hard, forcing the memory away, shutting his eyes tightly and twisting around in his seat, breathing the pressurized air deeply, feeling his ears pop with the pressure. He could never love anyone like that, and no one would ever love him like that. In this world how could you give enough of yourself to another person, trust her, allow someone else to become a part of you? You had no control over what happened to other people, and so to love someone was to offer a hostage to fortune and render yourself vulnerable in a hostile world. A man had to protect himself, which was barely achievable in a world where all nations were dedicated to your annihilation; it was possible only if you were alert, vigilant and unencumbered. Never again did he want to return home to find someone dead, and there was no way to prevent that except to avoid loving and being loved.

He was afraid. He hated the word, but he was honest enough to use it. He was afraid not to be strong, and love was a weakness that terrified him. He held himself tightly until the fear faded away, then waited for the inevitable sadness to flood in and fill the void. It came relentlessly, for what is life without love?

Melnik fell into a doze, with the reverberation and muted roar of the jet engines soothing him. His body relaxed, his clenched fists uncurled and he wandered off into a cloud-filled world of possibilities. Through the swirling clouds he saw a face, a vision half glimpsed, racing along beside the airplane, a hand held out to him, withdrawn, then raised again. ". . . this maiden she lived with no other thought/Than to love and be loved by me." He smiled in his sleep. His eyes remained closed but he began to float slowly toward consciousness. It had started with nothing but sex, a terrible passion that overwhelmed them both. Even now he felt it clawing at him, even as he realized that the passion had become something more than passion. Could he actually be falling in love with Lori?

He opened his eyes now, coming back awake, and saw the man in the seat next to him looking at him curiously. Charles Werther.

Christ, what a rotten world.

## 57

"Hello? Anybody home?"

Lori came into the apartment, kicked off her shoes and hung up her jacket. She took a drink of apple juice from the bottle in the refrigerator, then played the messages on the answering machine. The third one was from Charlie. "I've had a day and a half, toots," his voice said. "You won't believe it, but I'm calling from Kansas. Don't ask. We'll be home late tonight. Ciao."

He sounded depressed. Poor Charlie, she thought. What could have taken him to Kansas?

He said *we*, she thought as she looked through the refrigerator; David must be with him. She moved aside a dish of leftover asparagus, looking for something to eat. The thought of oral stimulation conveyed a sudden image of David's naked body, and she nearly giggled at her audacity: it made her mouth water. She licked her lips and remembered how it felt to open her mouth on his and then to slide it down his body.

She closed the refrigerator door and leaned against it. What was happening to her? *Don't panic*, she told herself, *you love it*. She closed her eyes and breathed deeply; what could she do? She smiled and began to hum a little. Opening the refrigerator door again, she took out the asparagus, eggs and butter, and put the coffee on to reheat.

Oh, yes, she loved it. It frightened her that she loved it because she lost control. It had started with his exotically naked body and her bewildering curiosity and desire to touch it, but that had led to his touching hers, and when he did, it was different from such touching that had ever been before. Then her own body ignited, and then she was lost. Thinking about it, she began to tingle now.

It worried her because of Charles. She didn't believe that monogamy meant never sleeping with anyone but your husband; it only meant never *loving* anyone but her husband, and she didn't love this man Melnik, she told herself. But he *was* different, and so was this feeling for him that was growing in her.

She fried the asparagus tips in butter, cracked the eggs and swirled them in, put half a bagel in the toaster and poured the coffee. She didn't care if their affair frightened her; she wasn't about to call it off. They'd just have to wait and see what happened.

The phone rang, but the eggs were done, so she let the answering machine take the call, ready to lunge for the phone if it was Charlie again. But it was only a call for him. "This is Fred Basker, calling for Charles Werther. It's about the videotape search. Call me whenever you get in." He left his number at work and at home.

Oh, dear. She wrote down the name and phone numbers. She wasn't sure what a videotape search was, but she hoped it wasn't anything that Charlie would have to handle tonight. From the way his voice had sounded, he must have had a terrible day already. Poor Charlie.

## 58

Werther and Melnik reached La Guardia at 2:00 A.M., exhausted, dirty, but also hungry, and Charles invited David to come down to the apartment for something to eat. They hadn't eaten all day; at the Kansas City airport where they'd caught the red-eye flight back to New York the snack shops and restaurants were already closed. On the plane they had been offered drinks, but not even a peanut. "Come on up," Charles said. "There are always some leftovers."

Melnik was indecisive, torn by conflicting desires, the least of which was hunger. If he went up he might see Lori, and he both wanted to and didn't want to, not with Charles there. But Werther pulled him along and he went.

Werther put his fingers to his lips as he opened the door. "Lori will be asleep. Let's be quiet."

He motioned David in ahead of him, and felt a frisson of surprise as his guest walked directly to the closet, opened it and hung up his hat and jacket. *How many times has he been here?* He tried to remember.

David had the same thought at the same moment. He stiffened and bit his lip in anger at himself. He was tired and wasn't thinking clearly. He turned away from the closet and looked up and down the dark hallway. "The kitchen is . . . that way?" he asked.

Charles nodded, and Melnik turned down the hall, mentally kicking himself awake. Now he'd overdone it; there was no other direction the kitchen *could* have been. *Wake up and get the hell out of here,* he told himself.

Lori came into the kitchen in a robe as Werther was bent over rummaging through the refrigerator. "Hello, David," she said, then turned to kiss her husband as he straightened up. "Bad day, guys?"

"Sorry we woke you," Charles said. "Was I making a lot of noise? I can't find anything. Bad day? Did you ask if we had a bad day? Tell her, Melnik."

"We had a bad day."

"There's no food in here," Werther said.

"How about an asparagus omelette and coffee?" Lori asked. "I'll make it while you tell me all about your day."

"We picked up a guy coming in from Libya, the boss guy."

"Good," Lori said. "Oh, no," she murmured, looking into the refrigerator.

"What's wrong?"

"I used up all the asparagus. How about a broccoli omelette?"

There was a moment's silence. "You're kidding, right?" Werther asked.

"No, really," she assured him. "My mother used to make them all the time."

He smiled, but when she smiled back he realized that he couldn't tell whether she was lying, whether she'd ever eaten a broccoli omelette in her life. She didn't look as if she was lying, but how could he tell? He glanced over at Melnik and began to think uncomfortable thoughts.

"So what went wrong after you picked up the boss guy from Libya?"

"Well, we didn't pick him up right away. Melnik's boys had planted a radio transmitter on him, so we followed him all the way to Wichita. Of course nobody bothered to tell us about it in advance so that we could plan—"

"And did you tell me that you were going to arrest him at Kennedy? That you even knew anything about his visit?" David replied.

"Wichita? In Kansas?"

Charles turned back to her. "In nowhere," he said, "that's where. Yeah, Kansas. But when he finally reached his destination, nobody was home. Then, before we got a chance to question him, he popped a cyanide pill."

"Is he dead?"

Charles nodded. "That's what cyanide does to people." Melnik was standing in a corner of the kitchen, not saying a word, and Werther kept glancing over at him. Was he acting suspiciously? He wasn't even looking at Lori. Was he purposely *not* looking at Lori? Was that suspicious? She certainly seemed normal enough. Maybe Melnik was only guilty of lascivious thoughts; Charles couldn't blame him for that.

"Eggs are almost ready. Want to set the table?" Lori asked, and again Melnik reacted too quickly, without thinking, almost as if subconsciously he wanted to give Werther something to think about; he moved to the cabinet and took out two dinner plates, cups and saucers. With a little wrench in his gut Werther wondered how he knew where they were kept.

"How's the omelette?" Lori asked.

"Rather good," David said. As Charles stared at him, he grinned shyly and said, "Well, it's interesting."

"Your mother never made a broccoli omelette, did she?" Charles asked. "Nobody ever made a broccoli omelette."

"I thought it would be good," she said, admitting the lie with a small apologetic smile. "I'm sorry I ate all the asparagus."

Werther smiled at her, but he felt panicky, realizing he didn't know her at all. "It's fine," he said. "I was just wondering about your mother making it, that's all."

"I thought if I said that, you'd be predisposed to like it."

He nodded. It was easy to lie if you had a good reason.

"Oh, my God, I almost forgot!" Lori gasped.

"What?"

"You had a phone call from a man named—what was it? I wrote it down. Wait a minute." She rummaged through the newspaper, mail and assorted flyers. "Here." She brandished an old envelope at him, reading from it. "Fred Basker called about the videotape search. He said to call him whenever you got in. He gave his home number as well as his office."

Werther took the envelope, still chewing and swallowing the last of his egg, from which he'd managed to remove most of the broccoli. "Anytime, he said?"

"Whenever you got in. Could it be important?"

"Not likely, but possibly."

"CIA?" Melnik asked.

Werther shook his head. "Our man. He's the one in charge of identifying the faces on the San Medro videotape, remember?"

"Maybe he found something."

"Not likely," Charles said, shielding himself against any further disappointment today, and reached for the phone.

"You're not going to believe this," Fred Basker's voice sounded through the kitchen as Charles put the call on the speaker phone. He was mumbling as he struggled out of sleep. "You're not going to fucking believe this," he said again, coming awake at last.

Werther smiled. "What am I not going to believe?"

"You are not going to believe that we're finished. Done. *Finito.*"

Werther had to smile again. Basker was so young. Though he was well into his thirties, somehow he remained a kid full of enthusiasms. It was nice to have people like him around, but just now, at nearly three o'clock in the morning, it was a bit much. He wanted to say something congratulatory, but he simply couldn't. "Explain," he said.

"We've got the unidentified faces down to seven. Everybody else belongs in the neighborhood, or is familiar to somebody."

Werther was impressed. That was fast work; he hadn't expected Basker to call for another week. He began to feel less tired. Not only fast work, but good work. Even better than good, it was lucky: only seven faces. He began to feel positively exuberant. "Seven?" he asked, suddenly afraid that Basker had said seventeen or even seventy, and that he had misheard.

"Affirmative." He could nearly hear Basker glowing through the wires. "Only seven. That's well in the range of a lineup, isn't it?"

"Damn right," Werther said. He had been hoping they'd be able to knock it down to nine or ten; even a dozen wouldn't have been terrible, but seven! "That's great, Basker." He glanced at his watch. "I'll meet you at the office at six-thirty."

There was a moment's pause. He could imagine Basker glancing at his bedside clock and wondering if everyone at the Bureau ended up keeping hours like the Director. "Yes, sir."

Werther hung up and turned to Melnik. "Did you get that?"

Melnik nodded.

Their eyes locked, both of them trying to digest the news, all other thoughts discarded. They could get back to work first thing in the morning.

"Rasheed Amon," David said quietly, "your time has come."

Charles began to smile, mimicking Melnik's nodding head, and they sat quietly smiling and nodding, planning their next move as Lori looked musingly from one to the other.

59

Werther walked down the corridor to his office at 6:25 A.M. and found Basker waiting outside his office door. The kid was carrying a portfolio, and as soon as Werther unlocked the door he opened it, took out a sheaf of photographs and spread them on the desk. As Werther bent over to look at each of them, Basker took out another batch and placed them in a pile on the corner of the desk.

Werther looked at each of the seven pictures in turn. It would have been nice if he'd been able to put his finger on any one of them and say, "I know that man. Let's bring him in," but he couldn't.

The door opened and Melnik walked in. Werther couldn't help glancing at the clock. It was 6:37. "Glad you could make it," he said. "Want to take a look at these?"

Melnik looked at each picture in turn, then shook his head. He didn't recognize anyone.

"Right," Werther said. "Let's go have a talk with Mr. Rasheed Amon."

"What are those?" Melnik asked, pointing to the stack on the corner of the desk.

"Oh, yes," Basker said, "I wanted to ask you about these."

Werther stopped and waited.

"These have all been cleared," Basker said, "but I'm just not one hundred percent positive, and I thought I'd better ask you about them."

"What do you mean?"

"Well, for example," he said, taking out his notebook and referring to the top picture on the pile, "this guy here"—he glanced at his notebook—"was identified by a waitress in a diner on Broad Street, but all she could say was that the guy looked familiar. She couldn't really place him as a regular, say when she last saw him or anything like that."

Werther's heart began to sink.

"This next one," Basker went on, "was identified by a cashier at the movie theater. Again, all she could say was that he looked familiar."

Werther's voice was calm, but strangely deep. "What are you trying to tell me, Basker?"

"Well, sir, most of the people we were able to clear by several i.d.'s, like a waitress thinking they looked familiar and maybe somebody in a store or someone living in the neighborhood also knowing them, so we're sure they belong in the neighborhood. But this group here were just i.d.'d by one person who couldn't really identify them. I mean, no one actually knew who they are; the person would just say they looked familiar." He noticed the way Werther was staring at him and began to feel a little nervous. "That's all," he finished lamely.

"They're not really identified. Is that what you're telling me?" Werther asked.

"Well, like I say, in each case someone's said that they've seen them around," Basker answered. "But they don't know how often," he added weakly.

"So, for example," Werther asked, "any of those faces in that pile might have been in the neighborhood just on the day we picked up San Medro. Is that right?"

"Well, yes, sir," Basker admitted, "that thought occurred to me. That's why I thought I'd better ask you about them."

Werther looked at Melnik, whose face remained blank.

"How many of these extra pictures are there?" Werther asked.

"Twelve, sir."

"So if we include these we're up to nineteen unidentified."

Basker nodded. He wasn't feeling happy anymore. "But they *have* been identified," he said.

"They have each been noted by one person as looking familiar, is that what you mean?"

"Yes, sir."

Werther sat down heavily, still holding the original group of seven pictures in his right hand. He had only one card to play; if he played it and lost, he had lost Rasheed Amon forever. And the more faces, the weaker his card. He was strongly tempted to go only with the original seven, but he knew this was wrong; the others could not really be eliminated. He looked up at Melnik, hoping that he would urge him to go with the seven. Seven faces were perfect; nine or ten he could handle; nineteen was too many. It made his story seem funny. Melnik shook his head slowly. *The son of a bitch can read my thoughts*, Werther thought. *I wish to Christ I could read his.* Then he pushed it out of his mind; he didn't have time for that now. "You think we should use them all?"

Melnik nodded. He was right and Werther knew it. He thought for a moment that maybe it would be better to postpone seeing Amon and return to the neighborhood with these twelve half-identified faces and see if he couldn't winnow some of them out. But Basker was a thorough man; they weren't likely to turn up anything he had missed. Besides, Werther was only human. Tired as he was, he was too psyched up for this coming showdown. He simply couldn't postpone it.

"Right," he said, picking up the batch of twelve and adding them to the original seven.

Werther had called as soon as he talked to Basker several hours earlier and there had been no difficulty in obtaining an arrest warrant from the U.S. Magistrate's office. The probable cause might seem a bit weak for a normal case, but with the FBI invoking the security of the President no magistrate in the country could have hesitated.

At 7:30 A.M., without any sleep except for a couple of fitful hours between 4:00 and 6:00 A.M. but excited beyond fatigue, Werther and Melnik knocked on Rasheed Amon's apartment door. There was the answering babble of children's shrill voices, but nothing else. The apartment was on the second floor, at the top of a badly lit flight of stairs littered with toys and newspapers and smelling of urine. They waited a few seconds, then knocked again, louder and sharper.

Again the children's voices erupted, and this time footsteps shuffled toward the door. Again there was a pause, and then a woman's voice asked, "Who is it?"

"Federal Bureau of Investigation. Please open the door."

"What?"

"We are the federal police. Open the door or we'll be forced to break it down."

"Just a moment." The woman's voice was frightened.

"Open right away or we break the door down!"

"I can't. Rasheed!" she called. "It's police—"

Werther lifted his foot and kicked out with a piston motion directly against the door at the base of the knob. The doorknob stayed in place against the jamb, but the wood around it splintered and the door sprang open a few inches, held in place by the chain lock. When Melnik threw his weight directly against it, it too splintered and he fell forward into the room, followed by Werther, his gun drawn.

Three children stood terrified against the far wall. The woman threw herself in front of them, shielding them with her body. From a hallway Rasheed Amon came hurrying out, hopping as he pulled on his pants over his naked body. "Who are—" He stopped as he recognized them. "What is wrong?"

"We have reason to believe," Werther said in a purposely deep, resonant voice, "that you are involved in a plot to murder the President of the United States."

The woman shrieked and looked at Amon, who stood dumbfounded.

"No," he said. There was a moment's silence. He licked his lips and looked from Werther to Melnik, to his wife and children and back to Werther. "No," was all he could say.

"I have a warrant here for your arrest," Werther said, waving the paper.

Amon's wife began to wail in a continual rising and falling sound. The children clutched her and began to scream. Amon took a step toward them, then stopped as Werther moved in front of him. "Tell me right now," Werther said. "Right now."

"What—?" Amon began.

He looked like a scared kid himself, but Werther didn't feel a moment's pity. He had to break him immediately; it was their only real chance to find someone in the Dallas operation.

A kitchen table stood in the room, covered with bowls set for breakfast for the children. Werther turned and swept his arm across the table, knocking the dishes to the floor, consciously acting as brutally as possible, giving the impression of irresistible power in this pitiable apartment. He threw the pictures down on the table and spread them out. "Sit down," he said to Amon, who scuttled over obediently.

"I'm not going to waste my time," Werther said. "The man who paid you is trying to murder the President of the United States. Were you aware of that?"

"No! I swear!" Amon shook his head frantically, waving his hands in front of his face. "I thought—" He rose agitatedly to his feet.

Werther pushed him down again. "What? What did you think? Don't tell me any more crap about a movie!"

"No. No, I swear, I thought maybe drugs, but I never—"

"You never thought your ass was going to end up in trouble?"

"I thought—"

"I don't give a damn what you thought! You're a dead man."

The woman shrieked and the children wailed.

Rasheed Amon looked at his wife, then back at Werther. "Don't look at me," Werther commanded. "Look at these pictures."

Rasheed looked at them in bewilderment.

"I'm going to give you just one chance to help us."

"Yes, sir, anything you—"

"We've arrested the man who hired you to deceive us, and I want you to identify him."

"Yes, sir."

"But this is the United States of America," Werther went on. "We have to be sure that you can give a positive identification; otherwise it's worthless. We don't want you to identify an innocent man just because we tell you we want to hang him. You understand?"

"Oh, yes, sir!"

"This is what we call a lineup," Werther said, gesturing at the photographs. "We've mixed in the picture of Mr. Dallas with pictures of innocent men. You pick out Mr. Dallas for us."

*There are too many pictures,* Werther thought. *He's going to realize this is just a fishing expedition.*

"Yes, sir," Rasheed said eagerly. At this moment he would have believed anything and was pathetically eager to help. This was his one chance to extricate himself. He looked quickly at the pictures, one after another, while Werther and Melnik stood behind him, waiting. As he went through the group of seven without pausing, Werther's mood began to sink. He looked at the next picture, and the next— And then he stopped. "Oh, yes!" he exclaimed.

"What?"

"This is Mr. Dallas," Amon said, pointing to the picture that had looked familiar to the cashier at the movie theater.

## 60

So now they had a face. What next?

Someday there will be computers that can look at a face, compare it with millions of others in its files and pick out the name and history that go with the face. Someday. Not yet. Instead of a computer they had Alfredo San Medro.

They gave the videotape to Torgersen, the photographer, as soon as they returned from Amon's apartment. The tape showed the man Rasheed had identified walking down the street past San Medro's house. By 5:00 P.M. Torgersen was back in Werther's office with a stack of photographs. He handed them to Werther, who looked at each of them and smiled. "Very good," he said, handing them to Melnik. "What do you think?"

They were photos of the man and San Medro together. They were close-ups, showing only heads and shoulders, sometimes only faces. The background was blurred, but the unmistakable impression was of a series of meetings between the two men over a period of time—if you didn't notice that the clothes they wore were always the same. This wasn't obvious, since in some photos the clothing was blurred, while in others only their faces were seen. Someone looking at them in a hurry would not be likely to notice.

"Excellent," Melnik said.

"Right," Werther said. "Let's go for it."

"You little shit," Abrams said.

"Say what?"

Abrams stood in the doorway looking at him. "I don't know why I waste my time with a creep like you," he said finally.

"Whatta' you talking, man?" San Medro asked.

Abrams shook his head resignedly. "I did my best for you. I went way out on a limb for you. I told them you were my main man." He sighed. "You little shit."

"Hey, what'd I do?"

"It's out of my hands now," Abrams said. "I can't do anything for you. Your ass is in a sling, boy."

"Hey, for Chrissake—"

Abrams turned and left as abruptly as he had entered, the cell door slamming behind him. "He's all yours," he said to Werther and Melnik out in the hall.

"You did well," Werther said. "You might consider a career on the stage when you retire from the Bureau. Let's have a cup of coffee and give him some time to sweat a little."

San Medro jumped nervously when the door opened.

*Good*, Werther thought, *he's nervous.* He looked ready.

"Oh, it's you," San Medro said, and relaxed a bit, comforted by seeing someone he knew.

Werther disabused him immédiately. "You lying little half-assed turd," he spat out. "I'm going to have your ass in Leavenworth for fifty years."

"What for, man?" San Medro yelped. He was frightened now. First Abrams, then this honcho. "What'd I do? I told you—"

"You told me shit. You gave me a name and then went straight to Dallas and told him—"

"I never did! What'd I want to do that for? Tell him I squealed? You crazy, man?"

Werther threw a photograph on the floor in front of him. San Medro looked at him a moment, then bent down and picked it up. *Uh-oh*, he thought. *Oh, shit.* For an instant he wondered if he could pretend to wonder who the guy in the picture with him was, but the expression on Werther's face convinced him otherwise before he had a chance to open his mouth. "That's the guy," he shouted happily, outacting Abrams by half. "That's the son of a bitch who wanted the guns!"

Werther flung another photograph at him. San Medro tried to catch it in midair, but it glanced off his fingers and fell to the floor. He bent down to pick it up, and as he did so Werther threw another at him, then another and another. For a few seconds the air was filled with flying pictures. San Medro grabbed at one after the other, but soon gave up and stood there as they fell to the floor. "Look at them, you little fart!" Werther whispered coldly.

San Medro looked down at the photos, and his blood stopped running in his veins. He tried to think what to say. He saw himself and Hardy over and over again. Christ, there must be a hundred photos of them together! They must have had him followed, they must have known, they must—

"I ought to kick your balls right through the wall," Werther said. "We've had this guy followed for months, but we know him under another name, so these pictures didn't surface until we found out who he was. Then when his file is sent down to me, what the fuck do I find? There he is, buddy-buddy with you. You, my little smart-assed friend who told us 'everything'! You're going to rot in Leavenworth until your nails grow through your shoes! You're—"

"Wait a minute!" San Medro screamed. "What do you want from me? I'll tell you anything you want to know!"

"There's nothing you can tell us now, you little shit! We know everything you know, but it took us an extra week to find it out, and—" He paused for a moment as if reconsidering. "Where is the bastard now?" he asked.

"I don't know, man."

"That's it! Fuck off!" Werther yelled and turned to the door.

"Wait a minute, man! I *don't* know! All I got is the phone number where I call him—"

"We've already got that," Werther said with convincing disgust, but he paused again as if thinking it over. "What number do *you* have?" he asked, and when San Medro told him he nodded as if he already knew it. "Okay, at least you're telling the truth now."

"Hey, man, I was always telling the truth—" He stopped, wilting before Werther's gaze. "Well, okay," he gave a little laugh, "like maybe I didn't tell you everything before, but I never flat out *lied* to you. I'll tell you anything now. *Everything,* I swear it! Just ask me."

Werther stood looking at him for a long time. Then he asked, "What's his real name?"

"Hardy, man." San Medro answered so fast that at first Werther thought he had said "Hardiman." Then he said it again more slowly. "Gee Hardy, man. What else d'you want to know?"

61

So now they had not only a face, but also a name. They still didn't know who he was, but the name made all the difference. They checked it in everyone's memories. Word spread throughout New York headquarters, and Werther spent the evening on the phone to Washington, Chicago, St. Louis, San Francisco and Los Angeles. No one had heard of any G. Hardy. The name went into the computers and was checked against known terrorists, Communists, crackpots, Arab sympathizers, IRA sympathizers, Castro sympathizers, Sandinista sympathizers. Negative. It was checked against criminals, not only everyone convicted of a crime in the United States but even those who had been arrested and later released. Negative.

By the afternoon of the next day Werther was beginning to feel that San Medro had conned him. He called the phone number the little creep had given him and found, as he had expected, that it was an answering service listed as Dallas Enterprises. The billing address was a box number in Wichita.

None of this helped, but it indicated that San Medro was not lying after all. Werther and Melnik went over and over the tape from the concealed recorder he had worn in the cell. They decided that maybe "G" meant something else, and orders went down to the computer programmers to search for any Hardy in their lists of criminals. Two hundred and seven Hardys turned up, but the pictures that accompanied them were not of the man they were looking for.

As they were about to leave for lunch on the second day another batch of files and pictures were delivered to Werther's office. He had forgotten who made the suggestion, but acting on it he had directed the programmers to search all branches of the military, dating back to when the computer records first began being kept in the 1950s.

Werther was hungry; it had been a long morning. He dropped the thick envelope on his desk and grabbed his hat; then, as he was moving to the door, he turned back for one quick check. Ripping open the envelope, he skimmed through the contents and found the seriously posed full-face official photograph of Major Robert Hardy, United States Marine Corps, Retired.

At this moment Hardy was flying from Seattle to San Francisco. He'd had a busy three days since leaving Wichita with Mohammed Asri and the wing-folded Panther in the rental truck. They had driven four hours across the Kansas prairie, stopped for dinner, and then had pulled into a rest stop and slept crumpled up in the truck until 3:00 A.M. before driving to their destination. He had planned their arrival for this hour so that no neighbors would be watching.

Hardy backed the truck up to the garage/hangar and turned off the ignition. The small housing development was one of a kind that had promised to blossom throughout the country after the Second World War, when private aviation had been thought to be ready to take over the role of the automobile in the new world. The house was one of a dozen lining the runway. The development was called AirView; a hundred and fifty miles equidistant from Topeka, Kansas City and Wichita, it was built for people who commuted to these cities by flying their own planes. The three-thousand-foot runway was the focal point of the development, and each house had its own garage/hangar with enough space not only for a car but for a small airplane. The garages opened directly onto the runway, so that the residents could taxi out and take off with a minimum of fuss.

Hardy and Asri opened the hangar and truck doors, attached the airplane to the winch and rolled it slowly into the hangar. Then Hardy showed Asri around. "If any of the neighbors come around to say hello," he told him, "pretend that you don't speak enough English to make conversation. Indicate that your wife will be joining you next week, and she'll be glad to meet them then. That ought to keep them off your back." The previous owners had been happy to leave most of the furniture when Hardy bought the place, and he had stocked the refrigerator and freezer with enough food to last a week. "You won't have to poke your head out for anything," he said.

Then Hardy drove the truck back to Wichita, returned it to the rental agency the next day and flew to Seattle. He found the Cubans ready to go, explained to them what their part in the operation was, and then flew from Seattle to San Francisco, bringing the briefcase with the disassembled rifle to Matsuo Nakaoka. Hardy watched while he put it together and checked it carefully. There was no way he could detect the slight misalignment of the gunsight.

Gloria Carollo called her contact in Miami that evening. "The operation is set for Wednesday," she said, "but I still don't know what it is. He has explained our part, but it makes no sense. Guarez thinks he understands, but he's a fool. Hardy tells us there is a Castro plot to kill the President, but that's not true, is it? If it is, it would be better for me to know."

The voice on the other end of the line assured her that there was no such plan.

"Hardy says our part is to help the President escape and go into hiding, from where he will direct a massive retaliatory strike against Cuba. We have been hired because the President cannot trust his own FBI and CIA, which the fool Guarez believes because all these old Batista Cubans are used to treachery and corruption in the government."

Her Miami contact told her to continue to cooperate with Hardy, and to maintain contact with him. He wished her a good night, an that God might go with her.

Werther sat slumped in his office chair, staring out the window, the swiveled around to face the group of agents sitting in a semicircle Melnik sat in a corner beyond them, taking no part, watching an listening. "Okay, we're in pretty good shape," Werther said and turne to the first agent. "Jack, you've got photos of Hardy from his Marine Corps files, and you're liaising with the Treasury Department."

"Right. They've been warned to expect an attack on the President i Los Angeles, and they're beefing up their security forces. They're als distributing our pictures of Hardy up and down the line. There's n way he's going to get anywhere near the President."

"Don't forget he's not working alone," Werther said. "At this poin he's probably sitting holed up somewhere else, and some hired gu will do the work. But in any case I don't think we should count on th hit being made in L.A. We don't really know what's coming off here so let's not concentrate all our eggs in one basket."

"We're already taking care of that. The T-guys are sending Hardy' picture and description to every stop on the President's tour. They eve tried to get him to cancel the trip, but no dice."

Werther nodded. "Teddy, you're checking through the compute system for everything you can find about Hardy. Friends, relatives business associates, buddies from the Marines."

"Right. We're looking for anybody who knows Hardy and has an other kind of connection with smuggling, the mob, whatever. We're also looking for anybody who's seen Hardy recently, trying to at leas trace some of his recent movements. That's a much slower job, o course. We'll try to reach everyone by telephone, but first we're tryin to go through the computer data to zero in on the most likely peopl before we start calling. We should be on the telephone by thi afternoon."

"One other thing," Werther said. "Look for anyone tied to both Hardy and the President. Any old Marine buddies flying the President' helicopter, cooking his food or handling his press releases—anything a all."

"You got it."

"Okay. Bill, you're working the Asri link," he said, turning to another man. "The photo we have of him from Israel isn't very good, but if he's in Wichita he ought to stand out like a sore thumb."

Bill shook his head. "No way. It turns out that Wichita has the country's largest population of Middle Eastern students. They've got some kind of specialized program at Wichita State, the college there. Everybody we talk to knows ten people who look like the guy in the photo."

"You think maybe that's the reason they chose Wichita as a base?"

"Could be. Or maybe because it's centrally located, so it's a convenient starting point no matter where they decide to make their hit."

Werther nodded. "Okay, gentlemen," he said, "let's get on it. You'll all report directly to me. I want to know about any lead, or anything that looks like it might be a lead. Got it?"

They nodded and left the room.

Werther turned to Melnik. "What do you think? It looks like we're in reasonably good shape."

Melnik looked at him sourly. "Then why aren't we happy?" he asked.

Werther slumped forward over his desk, resting his forehead directly on his calendar pad. "Because we're not in such good shape," he admitted. He lifted his head and rested it on his folded arms. "On the surface it looks good. We've got a pretty good dossier on Hardy from the Marine Corps, with a dozen pictures. The ones from when he got out of the hospital after Vietnam aren't that old; he couldn't have changed much. The DEA has heard a few rumors about his smuggling grass into Florida and Louisiana, and we've got agents circulating his picture all over the coastline down there. He has to have left a trail, and we'll pick it up."

"Not likely. Anyone with his background must have several sets of identification in different names. He's not going to be going around renting cars and charging restaurant checks in his own name."

Werther bit his fingernail. "He can change his name, but not his face. We've got a lot of resources when we put our mind to it. We'll pick up a lead on him soon."

"But how soon is soon? The President visits Los Angeles in six days."

Werther inspected his fingernail. "I just wish we knew for sure we had even that long. I see two problems. One is Ja'far. If Hardy knows we had him, he won't know if he talked or not. Which means he might do anything; he could call it all off, he could hole up somewhere and postpone it for weeks or months, or he could accelerate and pull it off right away. Tomorrow, today, who knows?"

"The second problem is also Ja'far," Melnik said. "It certainly looked as if he was surprised to find nobody at the farmhouse. Which leads to the possibility that he didn't know what was happening. Which means that *anything* could be happening, something we don't even suspect."

Freddy Mason had modified the DC-3, tying the rudder controls in with the ailerons so that he could steer the airplane with the wheel alone and didn't need the rudder pedals he couldn't reach. With the addition of a hand-operated brake system he could handle it as well as anyone, and now he flew it down to the small airfield in the Everglades. Driving into Glades City, he made sure that the crew he had signed up were ready, then retired to the small wooden house at the airfield. There was a narrow creek behind the hangar, fed by the Everglades. He would do some fishing while he waited.

Hardy sat alone in a motel room, smoking a cigar and checking off all the details in his mind. By now the FBI would be expecting an assassination attempt in Los Angeles. If Ja'far was upset because his messenger had never returned, too bad. He'd be happy enough when Bush was delivered to him in Libya. In the meantime, if he tried to send someone else, the only contact he had for Hardy was the Wichita farm and airfield, both of them now deserted. Hardy grinned at the thought of Ja'far sending someone to bother him there and what they would think when they found him gone. Then he put Wichita behind him. That part was over. Check.

He had worked on the radio transmissions that Marvin had recorded from Andrews Air Force Base, and his diction coach had assured him that he had the intonation and accent down perfectly. He would certainly get the part of the Texas pilot in the play, L. B. Peterson had assured him. Check.

Marvin's schedule had been changed. He was now waiting in the office across from Andrews for tomorrow's departure. Check.

Nakaoka was in place in San Francisco. The Cubans were gassed up and ready to go in Seattle. Mohammed Asri was waiting with his Panther in AirView, Kansas. Check, check and double check.

Everything was in place, like a chess set waiting for the match to begin. There was nothing else to do except wait through the night for tomorrow. While the FBI was running around in circles, the Phantom would strike tomorrow.

# VI
# Assassins

## 62

The small dinner party at the White House broke up early that evening, and President Bush spent the next hour going over his itinerary for the California swing of the 1990 congressional campaign. The first item on the agenda was the Secret Service's report about the FBI warning that an assassination attempt was to be expected, and the previous request for cancellation of the trip was repeated. As before, it was denied without serious consideration. The President was determined that his tenure in office be seen by history as more effective than the Reagan years, and this required the cooperation of a Republican Congress. At the moment it was not at all clear that this would happen. Although his personal popularity still ran high, there were strong public doubts about the Republican congressional platform. It was entirely possible that the Democrats might retain their majority, or even increase it. Who knew what the damn voters were thinking? It was incumbent upon the President to spread his coattails and give Republican office seekers a better ride than they'd ever got from Reagan, and California had more congressmen up for election than any other state. He would fly to San Francisco tomorrow morning as scheduled.

Colonel Robert Lee Lindgren had spent the day checking on the President's airplane, crew and support personnel. He and Jeannie had tickets for a concert at the Kennedy Center that night, and had planned to have dinner first at a favorite Georgetown restaurant, but by four-thirty he realized he wouldn't be through in time. He asked his secretary, Staff Sergeant Karen Bright, to cancel the dinner reservation and inform his wife that he'd try to meet her at the concert.

There were no more delays or unexpected problems, and by six o'clock Lindgren had dismissed the crew and satisfied himself that all preflight preparations had been carried out satisfactorily. He sat in his office for another half hour reviewing everything. It wasn't simply a question of flying a jet airliner from Washington across the continent; it was a question of doing it perfectly. The plane had to be ready to go on time and to land on time. He had to be prepared for last-minute delays on the part of the President, and to be able to compensate for these without changing the flight plan. The day in San Francisco was orchestrated down to the minute, and although they would probably begin to run late as the day lengthened, he was determined that they would not start late because of anything he was responsible for.

There was a knock on the door. "You should be in time for the concert, sir," Sergeant Bright said. "Would you like a dinner reservation for afterwards?"

"Thanks, Karen. Make it the Harbor Light. Then go home. See you bright and early by the dawn's early light."

By six-thirty Lindgren had managed to convince himself that there was nothing left to do, and reluctantly left the office. In their quarters across Andrews Air Force Base where Jeannie was waiting he changed into civilian clothes. Then they set off, pulling into the Kennedy Center parking lot a few minutes before eight and settling into their seats while the last stragglers were still moving down the aisles. "You always hit your ETA on the button," she whispered as the lights began to dim. He smiled; it was true. When he retired he decided that he would be late purposely for everything, just for a change.

After the concert they walked to the restaurant in Georgetown, where Jeannie chose flounder stuffed with crabmeat and he ordered steak. Jeannie laughed. "You can't order steak here," she said.

"Oh, that's all right," said their waiter. "Lots of people have steak here. It's pretty good."

"No," she insisted. "We wouldn't have come here if we'd wanted steak. That's silly."

Her husband laughed and changed his order to the flounder stuffed with crabmeat.

In the rented house alongside the private airstrip in AirView, Kansas, Mohammed Asri was standing on a small stepladder in the garage/hangar beside the polished blue fuselage of the Panther jet fighter. He was holding a can of paint, and he looked at the fuselage as he stirred it with a small brush, visualizing the effect. Then, wiping the brush delicately against the can to remove all excess, he leaned against the fuselage to steady himself, and with a calm hand began to paint on the Panther the two-starred rounded military symbol of his native land.

The Panther was now a jet fighter of the Syrian Air Force.

"Just checking in," Ted Whittle said. "Hope I didn't wake you."

"No," Werther responded, shifting the telephone to his other hand. "Just reading in bed, going over some reports. You have something?"

"Maybe. Remember you mentioned we should look for something like an old Marine buddy flying the President's helicopter?"

Werther sat up straight in bed. "You didn't—"

"Not quite. But we did learn that when Hardy was shot down an old buddy who was a helicopter pilot tried to rescue him. There are indications that the two of them have been mixed up in drug smuggling since they got back from Vietnam. No arrests, but there are stories. We're trying to find the buddy, a guy named Fred Mason, but he's disappeared too. He's got a sister, though, living in Charlottesville, Virginia. We'll talk to her first thing in the morning."

"Right now," Werther commanded. "Go talk to her right now. People talk better in the middle of the night."

"Sorry, boss. I already checked. Nobody flies into Charlottesville late at night. No trains or buses, either, and if we drive all night we still won't get there any faster than the first plane in the morning. We could call the local police and have them talk to her, but—"

"No. Better do this yourself." All they needed was to start calling in local police and get the story in the papers. Goddamn it. Sometimes it seems like everybody conspires against you.

"First thing in the morning, then," he said. "Keep me informed."

At 6:00 A.M. the President was awakened. The kitchen staff was already on duty, waiting for his breakfast order.

Colonel Lindgren had slept well after the concert and dinner. He awoke at five-thirty without benefit of an alarm clock, and by six he was shaved and dressed. Leaning over the bed, he kissed his wife good-bye as she slept. He'd had a glass of orange juice and coffee, and would eat breakfast on the flight.

Jeannie was only vaguely aware of the touch of his lips on her cheek. She was dreaming that she was pregnant; something was stirring in her belly.

In the shack at the airfield in Florida, Freddy Mason slept like a baby. In California it was 3:00 A.M., and Hardy too was finally asleep.

## 63

At seven o'clock Jeannie Lindgren woke up suddenly, her pregnancy dream transformed into an upset stomach. She got up and went to the bathroom.

Colonel Lindgren was going over details with Pete Johnson, pilot of the backup aircraft. This was a duplicate Boeing 707, the understudy ready to substitute at a moment's notice if the first plane didn't check out right at the last minute. If everything was normal, as it always was, the backup would carry the overflow supporting staff accompanying the President, the reporters who couldn't fit on the primary aircraft, extra members of the President's staff, Secret Service men and State Department officials. To avoid confusion at San Francisco the backup would take off half an hour later, and land after the President had deplaned.

Now Lindgren and Johnson went over the flight plan together, then separated for the preflight check of their airplanes. Everything had already been taken care of by specialists, but the pilot had the ultimate responsibility, and neither of them was ever satisfied until he had gone over the list himself.

As Lindgren concentrated, intent on every detail, his mind focused only on the list, he was not even aware that his hand was moving to his stomach and rubbing it.

At 8:00 A.M. the presidential party came on board, the doors were closed and the engines started. Lindgren ran through the checklist with his crew, then clicked his radio button. "Andrews Clearance Delivery, Air Force One standing by for clearance."

"Roger, Air Force One, you are cleared as filed. Maintain three thousand until further advised. Squawk five-two six-two," the tower instructed, giving him his transponder settings for automatic radar identification during the flight. "Contact Andrews Departure Control one twenty-seven point five when airborne."

"Roger. Cleared as filed, maintain three, departure on one two seven five, squawk fifty-two sixty-two," Lindgren repeated.

At the rear of the airplane the stewards were preparing breakfast when the wheels began to roll so gently that no one on board noticed. The President was being briefed by his staff in the conference room amidships on the planned activities for the day.

"Andrews Tower," Lindgren called in, "Air Force One approaching runway three five, ready for takeoff."

"Roger, Air Force One, cleared into position, cleared for takeoff. Contact Andrews Departure one twenty-seven five when airborne."

Lindgren looked left down the runway, checking the skies automatically as his copilot did the same toward the right, then goosed the throttles a touch, pulling the aircraft out onto the runway and turning it so that its nose pointed straight down the center line. Giving one last look around, he pushed the throttles all the way forward. "Air Force One rolling," he radioed the tower, then switched frequencies. "Andrews Departure, Air Force One is with you one twenty seven five, squawking fifty-two sixty-two."

"Roger, Air Force One, we have radar contact," was the reply as the heavy airplane became weightless and lifted off the runway and into the air. "Maintain runway heading, climb now to five thousand, advise leaving three."

There were a few moments of radio silence as the crew concentrated on the dials and gauges monitoring their progress through the air. Takeoffs and landings are the most dangerous times of any flight—really the only times when a sudden equipment failure can mean disaster. Lumbering into the air at full power, barely gaining flying speed, or sailing down in a glide barely above stalling speed, planes are literally in the hands of their mechanics during these moments.

Then the moment was past and they were on their way. As the altimeter flipped past the three-thousand-foot mark Lindgren called in again: "Andrews Departure, Air Force One out of three for five."

"Roger, Air Force One. Turn left heading two seven zero, maintain five thousand and contact Washington Center one nineteen point three five. Have a good trip."

"Roger," Lindgren signed off. "Good day."

Across the highway from the base Marvin sat listening to the radio transmissions through his headphones. He'd had to skip school this morning, but Miss Worthing, his homeroom teacher, didn't take roll call every day as she was supposed to, so maybe he'd be lucky. He was being paid a whole week's wages for this one day, so he wasn't going to worry about school.

Today his instructions were different. Mr. Dallas wanted a complete record of a single day's radio traffic, including the exact times of transmission, so he sat taping them and carefully writing down the exact time of each one. At first it was less boring than just listening and taping, since he had to pay closer attention, but after the first couple of hours it was just as much of a drag. He drifted off into a fantasy: he was a spy, listening with one ear to the radio and with the other for the sound of footsteps along the corridor, tensing himself for the sudden knock on the door, the sound of a Luger spitting bullets at him—

He jumped when the telephone rang suddenly. Embarrassed, he reached for it, glad that no one had been there to see him. The big, brave spy. "Hello."

"Marvin? Hi, how goes it?"

"No problems."

"Not too much traffic for you?"

"Nah, not so far."

"Want to read off to me what you've got?"

Marvin turned his pad back and read off the identification and time of departure of every flight so far today. Hardy let him go through the whole list, although he lost interest and stopped listening as soon as Marvin reported that Air Force One had departed at 8:17 A.M. He thanked the kid and hung up. The call sign Air Force One meant that the President was on board. Six hours' flying time would bring them in at just about 11:15 A.M. The good old Air Force. Right on time.

The early morning shuttle flight to Washington also got in on time, and the connecting flight to Charlottesville was only a few minutes late.

"Miss Mason?" Ted Whittle smiled blandly, holding out his wallet opened to his identification card. "FBI. We'd like to ask you a few questions."

Alison's eyes opened wide. She had just finished dressing and was ready to sit down for a quick breakfast, but the shock took her breath away.

*Oh, boy,* Ted thought as she blanched. *This is one frightened lady.*

"Yes," she said, hoping she'd caught herself before giving anything away. She opened the door to let the two men in. "What could you possibly want to talk to me about?"

Hardy washed and dressed, but for once was too nervous to eat breakfast. He checked all the items in the small leather carryall, then zipped it up, slung it over his shoulder and set off for the airport.

As soon as he arrived he found an empty locker in the passenger terminal, put the carryall in it, dropped two quarters in the slot, closed the door and removed the key. Then he walked through the terminal and stopped in for a morning cup of coffee with his old Marine buddy, Bud Malcolm, the airport manager. "You picked a bad day, Gee," Malcolm said. "The President's on his way in."

"Yeah, I know. I saw in the papers he's starting a California tour today. Is that a big hassle for you?"

"You better believe it! You know how jammed we are here. All right, it's not like O'Hare or JFK, but it's bad enough. And you can't put Air Force One in a holding pattern for twenty minutes, can you? Hell, no. He comes right straight in, and I have to clear everyone else out of his way. We're gonna be jammed up all day trying to clear up the mess left behind. And you wouldn't believe the ground security," he added, shaking his head. "It's a goddamn headache, is what it is."

"But kind of fun, right?"

"Hell, yeah, I guess so." Malcolm laughed. "Anything to keep from being bored, right? So do you want to hang around and see the Big Man?"

"Could I?"

"Sure, why not? I can't get you on board the plane, or even up close—the security guys are practically paranoid. I mean, who'd want to kill a nice guy like Bush? He's harmless enough, not like Kennedy. But they're all afraid someone will piss on their turf."

"Can't blame them. There are a lot of crazies out there, you know."

"I guess. Anyway, you can watch from here if you like." Malcolm gestured at the large window facing the tarmac. "They'll be pulling up right over there. Worth seeing, I guess, if you've got nothing better to do."

"As a matter of fact, I don't," Hardy said. "I'm supposed to be meeting one of my boys in the plane later on today, but he just called to say he's going to be late, so I wouldn't mind hanging around to see where all my tax dollars are going."

"Be my guest," Malcolm said. "Shirley!" he called. "Fix Mr. Hardy up with a visitor's badge, will you? I gotta run now," he said to Hardy. "I'll be in and out all day, so we'll talk when and if, okay?"

"Don't worry about me. Enjoy your moment of glory—and thanks."

Hardy stopped at Shirley's desk, signed for the visitor's badge, clipped it to his belt and walked through the terminal to the FAA office, where he introduced himself and asked to see the national weather advisories.

The Federal Aviation Agency's weather services are open without charge to any private pilot, and the staff is always glad to help. They directed Hardy to a bulletin board in the corner where the last several hourly weather advisories were tacked up. There was no immediate problem; the weather across most of the states was clear. There was one mass of low-pressure dirty weather moving down from Canada into the Dakotas, but he didn't think it would hurt; in fact, if God cooperated on the timing, it might even help. It was too early to tell, though.

He wandered out and sat down in one of the main waiting rooms of the terminal. There was nothing for him to do now but wait. Across the corridor was a glass door leading into a shop, and as it opened and closed he could see his reflection swinging back and forth. He looked calm enough, but inside he was a ticking bomb. Nothing could stop him now. If the weather turned bad he'd have to deal with it, that was all. He felt tingly all over. It was like 'Nam, when he was getting ready to strap himself into the Phantom and become King of the Sky. He nearly laughed, catching himself just in time. He glanced around, but nobody was paying any attention. He was just one more passenger waiting for his flight.

After a few minutes he couldn't sit any longer. He got up and started walking rapidly through the terminal, not with any destination in mind but just to keep in motion.

The plan was dangerous, he knew. There are no sure things in love and war, but the danger only made it more exciting. He'd have to be lucky, but he *felt* lucky. He'd have to be good, but he *was* good. Good and lucky, he thought: you can do anything if you're good and lucky.

He focused for a moment on the fifty million dollars, and again felt like laughing. The money was the prize, but like most prizes it was more an excuse than a reason for the attempt. It was the winning of the prize that was important, not the prize itself. It was a symbol, at once the most important and the least important aspect of the whole affair. For the first time since coming home from 'Nam he felt in charge. If he could pull this off against all the odds, if he could do something that nobody thought could be done, he'd be back where he belonged: on top of the world. Beyond the world! Beyond the stupid laws and restrictions and entanglements. He would have proved—to himself more than anyone—that he was what he had always thought he was, what he'd always had to be: someone special, someone beyond everyone else. That was why he had become a pilot, though he hadn't realized it at the time. That was one thing the Cong had done for him: they had taught him to look inside himself, to push the world away and see what was inside. He looked inside himself now and saw only that he had to be different from all the others. He had done that once by learning to fly, by soaring above all their heads, alone and free in the stratosphere. He would do it once again by reaching into their deepest vault and taking away their richest prize.

The magnitude of the prize, the amount of the money to be paid, simply meant that it was a one-time operation. If he pulled it off he'd never have to do anything ever again. Right now he had to concentrate all his energies, all his thoughts and all his luck on this one point in time and space. Just do this, make it work, and he'd never have to worry again. He had made the operation as tight as it could be, so there was no room for error in anything he'd planned, but he knew that there was always plenty of room for error in the factors beyond his control.

That was all right. It was like tipping the Phantom over and diving down into a bombing run. Your nerves were alert and ready to react at the first appearance of the electronic blip signaling a SAM; you had scanned all the skies and were sure there were no MiGs waiting to pounce; you had preflighted the plane and knew that everything was as perfect as it could be. But when you tipped that nose over and rode down the slide onto the target you also knew that every gook in Asia was pointing his peashooter up into the sky and throwing a hail of small-caliber bullets into the air, bullets that you couldn't see or dodge, that you simply had to fly through. If one of them hit a cooling valve or opened a leak in the fuel supply, you were going to go down, and that's all there was to it.

Some pilots worried themselves into sick bay over this, but Hardy never had. You worried about things you had control over until you were sure you had them right; then you stopped. You didn't worry about things beyond your control. Because you knew you were lucky. If you weren't, life wasn't worth living, was it? So either way there was nothing to worry about.

## 64

Werther and Melnik were each trying to look busy, as if they were doing something important, but neither of them could think of anything to do. The net was being spread wide by the FBI's supporting staff. The Treasury Department's Secret Service was taking care to erect impenetrable barriers around the President in California, and the two of them were left sitting in Werther's office trying to think of some action to take.

Werther had just stood up and walked over to the window when the telephone rang. Sitting next to his desk, Melnik looked at him; he nodded, and Melnik picked up the phone. "Werther's office," he said. He listened for a moment, then held the phone out. "It's Ted Whittle."

Werther walked over and pressed the button that put the call on the speaker phone. "Werther," he said. "What is it, Whittle? Where are you?"

"Charlottesville, boss, and I think we've got something here. We went to see the Fred Mason sister. Name is Alison. Lives alone in Charlottesville, planning to start med school here next semester. A bit old for school, early thirties. Nice-looking broad. Pleasant."

"And?"

"Just giving you the background. Knocked on the door, said we were FBI, and she damn near fainted. Guilt all over her face."

"Did you come down hard?" Werther asked. There were two ways to handle a situation like this. One was to go in saying it was just routine, ma'am, nothing wrong, just checking background, get them relaxed, even gossiping, and find out what they know without their suspecting it. The other way was to come down hard, scare the hell out of them, see if they panic. Picking the right approach wasn't easy, but if she was scared by a visit from—

"Came down on her like a ton of bricks," Whittle said, "as soon as we saw her reaction. Told her that her brother was involved with Robert Hardy in a plot to murder the President of the United States."

"And?"

"Clammed up like a shell. She turned white, and we thought she was going to faint, but she wouldn't say a word beyond 'Oh, no! Absolutely not! Impossible!' Her brother's a good boy; so is Hardy. They'd been shot down in Vietnam, tortured by the gooks, abandoned by our government, couldn't we leave them alone? You know the line."

"What do you think?"

"They're bad ones and she knows it. Probably knows about their smuggling drugs, that's why she was so scared when we showed up, but I don't think she knows what's going on now. She knows *something*, I'd bet on that, but she doesn't know what it is."

"What did you do?"

"Asked her where her brother is now. She started to answer, then caught herself. Transparent as glass. I said, 'No, he isn't,' taking a chance, but it worked. I told her she thought he was in Wichita, but he and Hardy had left there. She turned white. Said again she didn't know anything about it. 'About what?' I asked her. She just shook her head."

"Then what?"

"Left it at that, as if we believed her, but that we still wanted to talk to her brother and she should call us if she heard from him or Hardy."

"And?"

"Waited outside down the street. She came tear-assing out in two minutes, looking around to be sure we were gone. Followed her to the airport—"

"She try to shake you?"

"Sure, what do you think? Like all amateurs. Why do they bother? She didn't pick us up, but she must have thought that if we were somewhere behind her some fancy turns would throw us off. Pitiful."

"Never mind. You wouldn't look so competent as a brain surgeon. So what happened?"

"She booked onto the next flight to Washington, connecting to Miami."

"Florida? Not California?" That was odd. So far her behavior was textbook perfect: evidently she knew something was going down but hadn't ever suspected it was as big as murdering the President, so she panicked and ran to find her brother. If she wasn't experienced, she'd be easy to follow. But Florida? What was Freddy Mason doing in Florida? Maybe she was cleverer than she appeared to be.

"What time's her flight due in Washington?" Werther asked.

"Leaving here in five minutes. Half an hour into National. Transferring to Eastern flight 173."

"I'll have someone at the airport to make sure she actually gets on that Miami flight. Description?"

"Five three, weighs one hundred pounds, maybe one oh five, good tits, light brown hair worn straight to the shoulder, brown eyes, dressed in a green suit, brown shoes, low-heel open toe, no makeup, just a light lipstick, carrying a shoulder traveling bag."

"Okay, Ted, it sounds good. We'll take it from here. You did well."

"Thanks, boss."

Werther hung up and cocked his head at Melnik.

"Interesting."

Werther nodded. "But Florida? You think she's trying to fake us out?"

"Didn't sound like it, not if your man Whittle knows what he's talking about."

"Good man, Whittle. I'd trust his judgment." As he got up and walked over to the window, the telephone rang again. "Werther here."

It was Fred Basker, his voice full of excitement. "We've got something!" he shouted. He tried to control his excitement and failed. 'We've been doing a computer search of all Hardy's friends and contacts from his Marine days and we've come up with something real."

"What is it?"

"A guy named Bud Malcolm. Major, U.S. Marines. Flew Phantoms in Vietnam, same squadron as Hardy. Now he's manager of the airport in San Francisco, where Air Force One is scheduled to land today."

Werther looked at the clock on the wall. For a moment he couldn't figure clearly. He put Florida out of his mind. "When is the President scheduled to land in Frisco?" he asked Melnik.

Melnik thought for a moment, looking up at the clock. It was 10:35 A.M.; that meant 7:35 in California. "About three and a half hours from now," he said.

"Do you have anything else?" Werther asked Basker, purposely keeping his voice calm. "Have they been in contact since they left the Marines?"

"I haven't followed up yet, except to check on Malcolm's reputation. He's totally clean; no hint of any funny business anywhere. I haven't called him to see if he's heard from Hardy; I called you instead."

"Right. I'll get hold of this guy. What's his name? Bud Malcolm? I'll get hold of him right away. See what else you can dig up." He started to hang up, then spoke again into the phone. "That's great work, Basker. Really great."

He put the receiver down and buzzed his secretary. "Get me Bud Malcolm, the manager of the San Francisco airport, on the telephone right away."

It was the combination that counted; luck combined with quick thinking and fast action was the key. When it happened a few moments later, Hardy was as much surprised by his reflexes as he was by the event itself. The only thing that didn't surprise him was his good luck. He was on a roll. He couldn't lose.

He had stopped in to see Bud Malcolm again, not for anything special, just trying to kill the last half hour until Air Force One was due. Shirley told him he'd just missed him; Mr. Malcolm had just stepped out, but he could wait in his office if he wanted.

Just then the phone rang. She answered it as Hardy started to walk into Malcolm's office, and he noticed her suddenly sitting up a bit straighter. "Yes, sir," she said, "this is his secretary. I'm sorry, but Mr. Malcolm's not in his office right now."

Walking through the entrance to the inner office, Hardy saw Malcolm outside the window, talking to a group of mechanics on the tarmac. "I'm sure he'll be right back, but I don't know exactly where he is right now," Shirley was saying. Hardy stopped, listening, and she turned to him, put her hand over the telephone and whispered excitedly, "It's the FBI. It must be about the President."

Without consciously thinking it out, Hardy said immediately, "Bud's out there," pointing out the window of his office. "Maybe you'd better go get him."

She nodded her thanks and said into the telephone, "I see him right outside the office. If you'll hold for a moment I'll run out and get him, but it may take two or three minutes."

As soon as Shirley put the phone down and hurried out of the office. Hardy went inside and picked up the one on Malcolm's desk. "Hello? Bud Malcolm speaking."

"Mr. Malcolm, will you hold one moment for Special Agent Charles Werther of the Federal Bureau of Investigation? Thank you."

"Mr. Malcolm?" Werther asked.

"Speaking," Hardy said.

"This is Special Agent Charles Werther. I'll come right to the point, since I know how busy you are right now. We're investigating a possible attempt on the President's life during his California visit. Do you know a man named Robert Hardy?"

Hardy felt a cold chill pass through him. "Hardy?" he repeated. "Gee Hardy? I flew with him in Vietnam. Is that the man you mean?"

"That's him, sir. Robert Gee Hardy. Have you been in contact with him recently?"

"What . . . what's this got to do with the President?"

"We believe there may be a connection. Have you been in contact with him recently?"

"No." He was trying to think fast. How did they get his name? And how had they connected him with Malcolm? They must know something, but what? "Well, a few months ago he dropped in."

"Mr. Malcolm," Werther said, "a few days ago you and airport managers all over California received a letter from the Treasury Department that included a picture of Robert Hardy and a circular asking you to be on the lookout for him. Why didn't you report this contact?"

Hardy was stunned. "I don't know what you're talking about," he said. Malcolm couldn't have received any such letter; he wouldn't have acted as he had. Then he noticed the pile of unopened mail sitting on the table next to the desk, and reached over and began riffling through it. There it was, a large envelope with a federal-metered stamp and a Treasury Department return address.

"You were sent a—" Werther began again.

"Oh, I see what you mean," Hardy said. "Look, this place has been a madhouse the past week; we've been getting ready for the President's visit. I've got a pile of mail sitting here I haven't had a chance to look at yet. I never figured it was anything important. After all, if the FBI is worried about the President I'd have thought you'd do something more than just—"

Outside the window he saw the secretary run up to Malcolm and speak to him. He nodded and started walking back with her.

"Anyhow, what do you want me to do?" Hardy asked. "Keep an eye out for Hardy?"

"I'd like to impress on you the seriousness of the situation, Mr. Malcolm. We have reason to believe that Robert Hardy is involved in a plot against the President, and that action will be taken during this coming tour."

"I'll get on it right away," Hardy said. "I'll duplicate this picture and circulate it through the airport. If he shows his face anywhere around here today we'll pick him up. But I have to say I think you've got the wrong man."

"Thank you, Mr. Malcolm." Werther gave his name and telephone number in case Hardy was sighted.

Hardy slipped the Treasury envelope inside his jacket a few seconds before the door opened. Malcolm looked at the telephone. "Shirley said there was a call for me," he said.

"I picked up the phone to tell them you were on the way when I saw you coming," Hardy said. He gestured out the window. "It was some guy at the FBI. He said it was just a routine call; he was calling all the airports and people along the President's route urging you to be careful. I said I'd tell you."

Malcolm turned to look at Shirley, who gave an embarrassed laugh. "When I heard it was the FBI, I thought it must be important," she said.

Hardy laughed with her. "You know the FBI," he said to Malcolm, one old Marine to another.

"I'm too busy for this goddamn foolishness today," Malcolm growled, and hurried out again.

"Alice!" Werther bellowed, hanging up the phone.

His secretary hurried in.

"Those circulars the Treasury people sent out with Hardy's picture, how did they go?"

"How?"

"How did they go? How did you send them?"

"Well, I didn't send them. I don't know how they sent them. How should they have sent them?"

He looked at her sourly. "Evidently they went out by normal mail."

"I guess so. How else should they have gone?"

"Express mail? Overnight delivery? Jesus!" On December 6, 1941, he remembered reading in history class, the Japanese code had been broken and an attack in the Pacific was indicated. The War Office in Washington had sent a message to Pearl Harbor, but it had gone by ordinary telegram. It was Sunday in Hawaii, and the Western Union office was closed. The telegram had been delivered the next day, the day after the attack.

"Call up everyone on that list," he told Alice now. "You do it personally. Call them up and make sure they've seen the picture and read the circular, and tell them to distribute it to everyone they work with. I don't want Hardy to get within fifteen miles of the President." *Christ*, he thought. *Do I have to do everything myself?*

## 65

Somewhere over Nebraska the pain surfaced. Jeremy Robin, the navigator, noticed it first as he was leaning over Lindgren's shoulder, talking about their final flight path. "Are you okay?" he asked. "You're white as a sheet."

Murchison, the copilot, glanced over. Lindgren was not only white but sweating. "How do you feel?" Murchison asked.

"Cold."

"Cold?"

"Shivering. I guess I don't feel so good."

"Let me take the wheel. You better go lie down."

Lindgren shook his head. "I'll be okay," he said. He didn't want to be sick while the plane was under his care. He *couldn't* be sick when the President was—

Suddenly something rumbled in his stomach and tried to force its way up his throat, making him gag as he choked it back down. "I guess you're right," he muttered, forcing himself up out of the seat. "I'll lie down for a minute."

"Want the Doc to see you?"

"No. I'm okay. I'll just lie down for a minute."

As he was passing the lavatory his stomach rumbled again and something shot up again into his throat. He pulled the lavatory door open and lunged toward the toilet bowl.

Hardy got into his car at the airport parking lot and then reached inside his jacket, pulled out the manila envelope that had been sent to Malcolm, and shook out the two photographs. In one he was a smiling, cocky twenty-two-year-old kid, a Marine jet fighter pilot. In the other he was gaunt and hollow-eyed, a returned MIA and hospital inmate, who looked a hundred and ten years old. He stared at them for a moment. Christ, had he ever really looked like either of those people?

He stuffed the pictures back into the envelope and threw it on the backseat. He sure as hell didn't look like either of them now. He started the car and drove around the perimeter road to the cluster of office buildings that formed an industrial park. Pulling into the parking lot of a city-wide messenger service, he got out, opened the trunk of his car and took out a briefcase similar to the one he had earlier delivered to Nakaoka at 971 Powell Street. Inside the briefcase was a disassembled rifle like the one Nakaoka would soon use. Its sights had never been aligned or misaligned, but that didn't matter. He carried the briefcase into the messenger service office and asked that it be delivered to Mr. Arnold Mizel in room 804 of 1117 Market Street between one and one-thirty that afternoon.

"We can't guarantee a particular time," the boy behind the desk said. "The President's in town today and the traffic's all screwed up, but we'll get it to him as soon as we can."

"Not good enough," Hardy said. "Mr. Mizel's only going to be there at that time, and he's got to get this package."

The kid started to shake his head, but at the same instant Hardy began to reach into his pocket and he decided to wait and see. Hardy pulled out his wallet and started taking out bills. "This is for the delivery," he said, laying the payment on the counter. Then he laid another five twenty-dollar bills next to the first payment. "This is for you," he said. "Between one and one-thirty."

"You got it," the kid said, reaching out to sweep up the money.

Hardy put his big hand out and covered the boy's, pinning it to the counter on top of the money. "Just think for a minute," he said. "You want the money?"

"Yeah," the kid said. "Sure. Why not?"

"If you take it, the package gets delivered between one and one-thirty this afternoon. Guaranteed. No mistakes."

"Okay. Don't worry about it."

"I won't worry about it," Hardy said in a quiet voice, "because you've guaranteed it. If it's not delivered at that time I'll come back and break both your knees. You got that?"

It worked; he got the kid's attention. He stared at Hardy, nodded and said, "I'll take care of it. Honest."

Hardy nodded. "Between one and one-thirty. This afternoon."

The call came in from National Airport at 11:30 A.M. "You're sure?" Werther asked.

"No question about it. She looked just like the description, and she was the only one getting off the Charlottesville flight that resembled it. We followed her directly to the Eastern counter, where she checked in for the Miami flight. She was obviously distressed, and wasn't checking to see if she was being followed. We checked with the counter clerk; her name is Alison Mason, seat 17D on flight 173. We watched her board the flight, and stayed until it took off. She's on her way to Miami right now."

"Okay. Thanks." Werther hung up. "I don't get it."

"Unless she really doesn't know anything and thinks her brother is in Florida," Melnik suggested. "Or maybe he is, and doesn't have anything to do with this business."

"Maybe."

"Still?"

"Oh, yes," Werther agreed. "You never know." He picked up the phone and called Miami headquarters.

Air Force One touched down on runway 14 at 11:16 A.M. Pacific time, just one minute late, with copilot Tim Murchison at the controls. It taxied to its preassigned spot, where it was met by the President's limousine and official entourage. President Bush emerged, smiling and waving at the television cameras, walked jauntily down the steps into the limousine and it pulled away across the tarmac, heading for the crowd waiting for the welcoming ceremony beyond the gates.

When the entourage had left and the television cameras had followed them, a small golf cart trundled across the airport and pulled up beside Air Force One. Lindgren came out of the airplane, leaning heavily on his copilot and navigator, and they helped him down the steps and into the cart. They were driven around the terminal to the exit, where they all got into a taxi and headed for Baptist Hospital.

Hardy drove from the messenger service to the condominium at 1371 Powell Street, took a small package from the trunk of the car and went up to the apartment. Kneeling by the ammunition that had been stacked carefully by the window, he opened the package and took out the small electronic radio receiver and control charge. He unscrewed the back of the receiver, exposing a pair of disconnected wires, attached them to the wires dangling from the charge and sealed them with black tape. Then he placed the contraption carefully in the space he'd left for it in the middle of the ammunition. The last thing he did before leaving the apartment was to turn on the receiver and check the frequency it was tuned to.

Back in his car, he glanced into the glove compartment, making sure the microtransmitter was there and that its transmit switch was sealed down tightly with tape, then drove toward the corner of Powell and Market. He wasn't able to get closer than three blocks because of the crowd, but that was good enough. He pulled into a filled parking lot, and when the attendant tried to wave him away he got out of the car and flashed his airport identification. "I'm with NBC at the airport, covering the President's visit," he said. "How would you like to pick up a quick hundred bucks?"

The attendant's eyes jerked from Hardy's ID to the hundred-dollar bill he had taken out of his wallet. Everybody knew how the networks threw money around, but most people never got a chance to benefit from it. "We've got to have the parade route timed right," Hardy explained, "and the goddamn thing always runs late. For a hundred bucks, all you have to do is let me know when it turns the corner up there from Market into Powell."

"You can't see it from here," the attendant began, but Hardy interrupted. "You don't have to. You'll hear the crowd on Powell roaring when they turn in." He held out the hundred-dollar bill.

"Sure," the kid said. "What's your phone number?"

Hardy smiled. "The lines will be busy." He reached back into his car, took the transmitter out of the glove compartment and showed it to the kid. "This switch, under the tape, is how you transmit. When you hear the crowd begin to roar, pull off the tape and turn the switch on. Then you just speak into the microphone and tell me what's happening, okay?"

The kid grinned. This was right out of *Miami Vice*.

"Keep the tape on till you're ready to use it. I'm gonna be getting messages from all over town, and they'll interfere with each other if you transmit when you're not supposed to. Okay? You got that?"

"Sure. No problem."

"Great. You can even keep the transmitter as a bonus."

"Hey, all *right!*" the kid said. He pocketed the money and held the transmitter gingerly as Hardy drove away.

Back at the airport Hardy went directly to Malcolm's office. He wasn't there but his secretary smiled at him. She was standing by the window in the manager's inner office, looking out at the President being welcomed to San Francisco by the mayor and a cheering crowd.

Hardy paid more attention to Air Force One, which stood half a mile away. The four Air Force guards were setting up the stanchion-supported cords around it and were preparing to take up their positions on each side. They would remain there throughout the day, awaiting the President's return, and no one would cross that barrier without proper identification.

The ground crew came out, presented their identification and began to swarm over the plane, refueling it and checking all the systems. Inside, the stewards were cleaning and straightening up.

At 2:30 P.M. in New York the intercom buzzer sounded and Alice said, "I have a call for you on line two from an agent in Miami."

Werther picked up the phone. "Werther speaking," he said. He listened for a moment, and then his eyes began to bulge. "What?" he shouted. He listened again, then said, "That's not possible! You must have missed her!"

Evidently there was a long explanation. Melnik sat watching Werther's face turn red, wondering what was happening, until finally he slammed the phone down in anger.

"What's wrong?"

"She's not there."

"Who's not there?" He knew whom Werther must be referring to; he just couldn't believe it. The FBI couldn't have lost *another* one.

"Alison Mason isn't in Miami," Werther said slowly. "Flight 173 just landed, and she wasn't on it." He slumped down in his seat. "It's not possible," he said weakly.

66

Ted Whittle had been right: Alison had panicked.

"We have reason to believe that your brother is involved with one Robert Hardy in an attempt to assassinate the President of the United States."

"Oh, no! Absolutely not! That's impossible!"

She couldn't believe it. But they *were* doing something different, something 'big.' Gee had admitted that. But they wouldn't kill the President— Not Gee, not Freddy.

The room began to spin. "Freddy wouldn't do anything really bad. He's a good—"

"And Hardy?"

She couldn't think. Gee was deeper, she knew; he went so deep that she couldn't fathom what was down there. But surely nothing like killing the—

"Where are they now?"

"What?"

"Where is your brother now?"

She started to answer, then caught herself. But it didn't matter. They already knew more than she did. "You're wrong. You were going to say he's in Wichita, but they've left the farmhouse there. They're on the run, trying to kill the—"

"No!"

The house spun down to a quiet stillness while they stood watching her. "Do you know where your brother is now?"

She shook her head.

"If you hear from him, please notify the Federal Bureau of Investigation. Here's my card."

She took it. Then they left, and once again she was alone in the house. Where were Freddy and Gee? What were they doing? It couldn't be . . . But whatever it was, they were in trouble and she had to find them. But if they had left Wichita, how could she . . .

She thought of Florida. Oh, God, she should have stopped them right at the beginning, right when they began smuggling. She couldn't elieve she had known and had let them. . . . But Freddy had been ying alive before her eyes. She knew where the airfields they had used n Florida were. Maybe that's where they'd gone.

She ran upstairs, threw a change of clothes into her traveling bag nd hurried out to her car. It took her long seconds to fit the key in the gnition before she could race to the airport.

astern Airlines Flight 173 left the gate right on time, and Whittle valked away to report in to Werther back in New York that Fred Mason's sister was on board and on her way to Miami.

The plane taxied out to the flight line, where it joined a long queue waiting clearance. Ten minutes into the wait a red light began to blink in the cockpit. "Oh, shit," Captain McCulloch muttered.

Fifteen minutes later they had edged their way nine planes closer to akeoff but the red light was still on. Meanwhile the flight engineer had checked all the instruments and was sure the problem was only a malfunction in the warning system, since all other indicators were normal. But three weeks before, a similar indicator had been ignored on a flight from Atlanta to Houston, and over New Orleans the port engine had fallen off. The plane had made an emergency landing and no one had been killed, but McCulloch was not about to take a chance. He turned the wheel and began to edge out of the waiting line as his copilot called ground control for clearance back to the gate. He himself picked up the in-ship microphone and pressed the switch. 'Ah, good morning, ladies and gentlemen, this is Captain McCulloch speaking. We have an indication of some trouble up here in the cockpit, and we'll be returning to the gate for a quick checkup. We're sorry for the inconvenience, and we hope to be on our way to Miami just as soon as possible. Thank you for flying Eastern."

When they returned to the gate, Whittle had already left the airport. They sat there while mechanics swarmed over the plane. Half an hour later the chief stewardess announced, "Ladies and gentlemen, Captain McCulloch has asked me to inform you that it looks as if we may be delayed indefinitely. You may return to the terminal if you wish, but please take your boarding pass with you and do not leave the immediate area. We will be taking off as soon as the trouble is located and fixed."

There was a wild rush for the doors. Once inside the terminal everybody stood around asking questions. Nobody from the airline could tell them anything, the flight crew had disappeared, and the stewardess could only keep repeating that they would take off "soon." A mechanic wandering by told someone that they might have to fly in another engine from Atlanta.

Alison thought she would go mad. Lugging her carryon bag she ran back to the ticket counters and found a flight leaving for Tampa in twenty minutes. Tampa or Miami, it didn't matter; she just had to reach south Florida as quickly as possible. Transferring her ticket, she boarded the new flight minutes before it took off.

"She gave us the slip," Melnik said.

Werther glanced up at him. He hadn't missed the slight intonation on the word *us*; was he being polite or maliciously subtle? It didn't matter. Either way, she was gone.

"Excuse me," Alice said.

Werther swiveled around to see her at the door.

"I couldn't help overhearing the conversation on the phone." Werther waited. "I called Eastern, and Flight 173 was delayed on the flight line because of mechanical problems. It returned to the gate and the passengers got off." Werther sat up straight. "They finally tracked the fault to a warning indicator light and took off again, but meanwhile some of the passengers had transferred to other flights."

"She left the airplane there!"

Alice nodded. "She must have."

Werther thought for a moment. "She couldn't have known there was going to be a problem with the plane. She must have panicked at the delay and looked for another flight. Get down to the computer boys, Alice, and see if she bought another ticket on Eastern or any other airline for a flight to Miami."

It took a half hour before Alice called back. "She didn't buy another ticket to Miami," she said.

"She must—" Werther began.

"She didn't, so I had the computer check all other flights out of National."

She paused, and Werther raised his eyes to the ceiling. "Alice—" he
arned.

"She had her ticket transferred to Flight 189 going to Tampa."

"What's the schedule?"

"It landed in Tampa forty-five minutes ago."


## 67


t one o'clock in California the welcoming ceremonies were com-
leted right on time. Then the President got into his limousine and the
rge car pulled slowly away from the crowd and around the terminal
uildings. Ahead and behind, a fleet of cars drew into place, and like
giant caterpillar the procession wound its way toward the city.

The crowds lining the streets and hanging out the windows of the
ll buildings began to exude a roar of sound that seemed to blanket the
ntire city. Barricades had gone up hours before, barring all vehicular
affic from the route, and the streets were so lined with people that the
essenger carrying the briefcase Hardy had left for delivery had to
rce his way through to reach 1117 Market. He'd had to leave his
otor scooter three blocks away. Finally he reached the building,
ushing the door open at 1:10 P.M. Inside, a guard post was set up,
ith monitoring equipment for everyone who entered. This had been
one by the Secret Service on every public building along the route,
nd would be duplicated in every city on the President's California trip
s a result of the information provided by the FBI. The cost was
rohibitive, but the alternative was unthinkable.

As the messenger passed through the monitor, bells rang and he was
sked to open his package. "We're not allowed to do that," he said.

The guard repeated the request.

"You don't understand," the messenger said. "We're just a delivery
ervice and the package don't belong to us. It's not ours; we can't open
."

The guard reached out and took it.

"Hey," the messenger said. He didn't know what to do. Nothing like
his had ever happened before. Maybe he should just take the package

and leave. But by then it was too late; he no longer had a choice. Th‍ briefcase was made of plastic, but it set the metal detector ringing. Th‍ guard looked at the kid, who shrugged.

The briefcase was locked. The guard took out his revolver an‍ hammered the lock with it.

"Hey," the kid objected. He was thinking of his hundred dollars an‍ the man who'd threatened to break both his knees.

The guard ignored him, and after a minute the briefcase spran‍ open. Inside was a dismantled rifle with a telescopic sight. Immediatel‍ the guard flipped off the safety switch on his revolver and leveled it a‍ the messenger. "Up against the wall, boy," he said, while his partne‍ called in on a walkie-talkie to his superior.

The messenger couldn't believe what was happening, and when si‍ cops burst into the lobby with guns drawn he nearly fainted. H‍ quickly told them everything he knew, and stood shivering with fea‍ and excitement as they disappeared into the elevator and the dial spu‍ up to the eighth floor.

It seemed an eternity before they came down again, herding a small‍ noisy crowd with them. He heard the chief speak into his radio‍ reporting everything that had happened. "There's no one in that room‍ who admits to being Arnold Mizel, or who knows anything about th‍ delivery," he reported. "Yeah, we're taking them all downtown now.‍ Then he clicked the radio off and motioned to his men, who began t‍ herd the protesting people into a waiting van. As the messenge‍ watched he became aware of the chief standing behind him and turne‍ to him.

"What are you waiting for, kid? Let's go."

"Me? I'm just a messenger."

"You, kid. You most of all."

There were four Secret Service agents in the car behind the President'‍ in the parade. Jeremy Weinstein sat in the front seat beside the driver‍ his eyes, like those of the others, never resting for a moment. The‍ scanned the crowds, the windows of the buildings, everything. Th‍ walkie-talkie radio on his lap crackled; he raised the receiver to his ea‍ and listened. The next instant he had shoved open the door of the ca‍ and hit the sidewalk running. The cavalcade was moving so slowly tha‍

he could easily catch up to the next car, where the President was smiling and waving to the crowd from the rear seat of the open limousine.

Weinstein trotted beside the car. Bush didn't stop smiling, but he leaned his head toward him. "We've arrested a man with a rifle a few blocks ahead," Weinstein shouted above the noise. "I suggest we turn off the route and cancel the rest of the parade."

"You've arrested him?"

"That's affirmative, but there might be others."

"There always might be others." Bush smiled, still waving at the crowd. "That's show biz."

At two o'clock the parade rolled past 1117 Market Street, where the messenger with the rifle had been apprehended. The President's car was now surrounded by Secret Service men on foot, loping along beside it. Without incident the procession passed the building, and the agents relaxed a bit. Just a very little bit. There were many buildings still in front of them, with hundreds of windows in each of them that could hide an assassin. The street was lined with thousands of people, any one of whom might be clutching a revolver in a brown paper bag, and their eyes shifted continuously from building to building, from window to window, from person to person, as the cavalcade rolled on.

At two-twenty-five it turned the corner from Market into Powell Street, and the rumble of the waiting crowd swelled into a roar. In the parking-lot office the radio transmitter lay on the desk, the attendant sitting next to it, his legs braced against the wall, happily lost in a sexy conversation with his girlfriend.

The United States is surrounded by a radar curtain through which no foreign plane or missile can fly undetected. The Ballistic Missile Early Warning System, consisting of stations in Alaska, Greenland and England, covers the northern border. The Pave Paws system, in California, Cape Cod, Georgia and Texas, each transmitter of which resembles a gigantic truncated pyramid whose walls are lined with thousands of eight-inch antennas, looks out across the Atlantic and Pacific and sweeps south across Mexico, the Gulf and the Caribbean. There is no chink in this armor. In effect the United States is covered by a semispherical electromagnetic dome reaching from ground height up into space.

Inside this dome, however, security is not nearly so perfect. Complete radar surveillance is, in fact, prohibited by international arms-limitation agreements. The Federal Aviation Authority operates a system of interlocking radar grids that keep an eye on commercial flights, but the only thing that makes this workable is the fact that it is voluntary; commercial flights want to be seen by radar and are not trying to escape it.

All these flights, as well as all private airplanes operating within certain airspaces along the routes of commercial airports, must carry transponders. These are the refinement of an idea developed originally by the Royal Air Force and called IFF: Identification-Friend-or-Foe. During the Battle of Britain it was necessary to distinguish radar echoes made by German Heinkel bombers from those of the British Spitfires, so each fighter was provided with an instrument that would be turned on by an impacting radar beam; when radar bounced off the plane, the IFF would flash a response indicating that it was a friendly.

Today's transponders are a good deal more sophisticated; when triggered by radar surveillance, they respond automatically with the airplane's identification and altitude. When Air Force One was instructed by the tower at Andrew to "squawk fifty-two sixty-two," Lindgren was being told to set his transponder to respond with that signal. During the flight to California, as the Boeing 707 passed from one radar controller to another, its blip on the screen was automatically accompanied by a small tag, so that the controller knew without asking that this blip was Air Force One traveling at its assigned altitude.

The system is excellent, awesome in its complexity and performance, and it never fails. But it is voluntary. For various reasons many flights do not comply with the requirements. Charter flights operating below FAA maintenance requirements and not wanting to come to the FAA's attention may fly without filing flight plans or turning on their transponders. Private pilots, irritated by restrictions on their freedom, often ignore the radar surveillance. The primary reason for this radar watch is to protect commercial jet airliners and keep them at safe distances from each other during takeoff, landing and in the air. In order not to clutter up radar screens with every little Piper Cub taking off from grass airfields over which, thirty thousand feet higher, commercial jets are flying, the FAA has imposed a ceiling of eighteen thousand feet. Planes that fly below this limit on VFR—visual flight rules—rather than depending on instruments, and that stay outside restricted airport airspace are not required to file flight plans or to have active transponders. Though they are picked up by radar they are not automatically tagged with identification and altitude, and with a simple flip of a switch the FAA radar operator can erase them so that his screen shows only tagged aircraft. Since his job is to keep track of those, this is the standard operation mode; aircraft without active transponders are ignored unless a special situation arises.

At 2:30 P.M. Xavier Guarez and his two-man crew lifted their 707 off the runway at Seattle. Flying VFR, they had filed no flight plan. As soon as they left the restricted airspace around the Seattle airport they turned off their transponder. Staying below eighteen thousand feet, their plane was registered, but not identified on FAA radar, as one of a number of meaningless blips cruising the western skies. In essence the plane was invisible once it left the airfield flying space. It headed southwest until it reached open space over Utah. There it began to circle lazily, hanging in the sky, waiting like a carrion crow.

At 2:15 P.M., just before takeoff, Gloria Carollo had telephoned her Miami contact. By 2:37 the Miami section chief of Castro's secret intelligence service in Havana received her report that the operation was beginning. He had no idea what it was all about. She had been able to report only what she had been told, which was that her 707 was taking off to rendezvous with the President of the United States in order to protect him from a threat to his life engineered by Fidel Castro. But as the section chief knew, no such threat existed. He had filed Carollo's previous reports, to be analyzed later, and now he filed this one.

At FBI headquarters in Washington Ferde Grossman received a similar report from his agent in the Calle Alpha group from which Carollo had been recruited. His reaction was the same as his Cuban counterpart's. That group was always imagining Castroist schemes and inventing ways to save the world from Communism. He too filed the report.

68

Hardy walked briskly across the tarmac. He worried briefly that he might be recognized; surely the FBI had sent to the Air Force One ground crew the same pictures they had mailed to Malcolm. Then he banished the thought. He didn't look like either of those photos; he wasn't the same man he had been in the hospital, and he sure as hell wasn't the kid who had joined the Marine Corps twenty years ago. Clipped to his shirt pocket was the official visitor's permit that Malcolm had issued him. In his wallet he carried an even more official-looking press card that identified him as Tom Emerson, the name he had used when interviewing Lindgren. He presented this document to the sergeant standing guard at the stanchions surrounding the Boeing 707. "Is Colonel Lindgren around?" he asked. "I'm writing an article about Air Force One. We're doing a series of interviews," he added as the sergeant studied his identification carefully.

"I'm sorry, sir," the sergeant answered, handing the card back. "Colonel Lindgren has left the plane and I don't know where he is."

Sergeant Mario Delia was in charge of the four Air Force guards responsible for ground security while the plane was on the tarmac. He had been with the VIP Flight for four years, with Air Force One for a year and a half, and he liked the duty. It was clean, simple and prestigious; he got to see the world and never had to work up a sweat. Best of all, when he was on duty he took orders from no one: *he* was the boss. Well, in theory he took orders from the President, the Colonel and the other crew officers, but in practice they knew he knew his job and left him alone. He took orders from no one else—not from generals or admirals or congressmen or movie stars.

"Colonel Lindgren was going to show me through the plane," Hardy said.

"I'm sorry, sir," Sergeant Delia said, handing him back his identification. "I can't allow you on board without authority."

"Sure, I understand," Hardy answered. "I'm Marine Corps myself. I'll dig Lindgren up."

"I'm afraid Colonel Lindgren has left the airport, sir."

"Ah," Hardy said. "I guess he forgot our appointment. Well, he's a busy man." He took out a pad and pen. "Would you mind giving me your name, Sergeant? I assume you're in charge here?"

"Yes, sir. Sergeant Mario Delia, sir. I have full responsibility for ground security during the President's travels."

"That's an interesting slant," Hardy mused as he made notes. "Might make a good starting point for my article. Tough job? It must be interesting."

"Well, I guess it is, sir—tough, but interesting."

As Delia talked Hardy kept writing in his pad. He knew how to stroke a man as well as anyone. Watching Hardy writing down every word, the sergeant began to think about what it would be like to have his name in the newspapers. Maybe there'd even be a picture.

Ten minutes later, when Hardy mentioned again that he had just wanted to take a look around the inside of the plane for his article, Delia didn't hesitate; he called over a corporal to take his place and led Hardy on board. They walked down the length of the plane, entering just forward of the President's office and walking aft through the sitting room, lounge, conference room, staff room, and through the aft lounge and security compartment to the rear passenger area. Hardy scribbled notes furiously, examined the walk-in galley and bathrooms, and then they walked back forward again. He had been hoping that somehow he could get on board without being seen, or that once inside Delia might leave him alone and forget about him, but he had always known this was a remote possibility, and now he saw that it was impossible. Delia didn't leave more than six inches of space between them as they moved through the plane, and his eyes didn't leave him for a moment. The sergeant may have been suckered by the glamour of the press into allowing him on board, but that was as far as it went. Whenever Hardy reached out to touch anything—anything at all— Sergeant Delia's eyes were as tight as a cobra's on him.

Still, it was useful to see the inside of the plane and to establish himself as a legitimate visitor. As they walked back toward the entrance again, just after passing the President's office, at a point where the aisle curved from the left-hand side of the aircraft back to the center, he noticed that the carpeting—which all through the plane was tacked down from side to side—was here laid down in a separate panel. He stopped, turned and looked down the aisle, as if giving it one last look. Actually, he was feeling the deck under the panel with his foot. Talking to the sergeant about the in-flight facilities and the problems of maintaining security with so many people wandering around, he felt cautiously back and forth with the toe of his right foot. Then he found it.

Hardy had spent a lot of time in libraries since first talking with the Libyans, finding out everything he could about Air Force One. There had been books written about it, both factual and fictional, as well as countless newspaper and magazine articles, but he had stumbled on the vital bit of information while browsing through a biography of Henry Kissinger. That intellectual powerhouse never stopped working for a minute. On Air Force One he continued his habits, which meant that an enormous quantity of books, pamphlets and papers had to accompany him. There were so many of them that they took up too much room in his on-board office and had to be stored below. But he needed access to them during his long transoceanic flights, and so a special door had been cut in the floor of the aisle, leading to the storage compartment below. This was what Hardy had been searching for, and as he stood talking with the sergeant he felt with his foot its outlines under the carpeting.

No other source had mentioned the access door in the floor of Air Force One; it was of no interest to anyone. But Hardy felt a surge of relief as his toe traced its outlines; for the first time he knew that it really was there and not simply a figment of some writer's imagination.

As the procession moved up Powell Street the roar of the crowd finally caught the parking-lot attendant's attention. "Oh, hey," he shouted into the phone, "they're coming!" He had been telling his girl about his hundred-dollar windfall and how they were going to spend it on a classy hotel room with dirty movies on the television and breakfast in bed. Now he picked up the transmitter. "You want to hear me radio in to NBC?" He pulled the tape off and flipped the transmit switch on, then spoke into the microphone. "Uh," he said, "uh, this is Mike in the parking lot. Off of Powell? Uh, over?"

He waited, grinning, but there was no reply. "Hello? Hey, is anybody there?"

\*    \*    \*

In the apartment a few blocks away at 1371 Powell Street, one block
in front of the President's slowly moving car, the control charge blew
up the moment the transmit switch was flipped, exploding the
ammunition stacked around it. The window above it shattered and
blew out into the street below, followed by a puff of billowing black
smoke.

For a moment the crowd was stunned, but the Secret Service men
reacted instantaneously. In one moment the presidential car was
covered with men as the escorting agents threw themselves on it,
attempting to shield the President with their bodies. Jeremy Weinstein
was the first, and now lay crumpled on the floor of the backseat
spread-eagled over the President of the United States, crushing him
and being crushed in turn by the weight of a half dozen others on top
of him. Weinstein tried to push himself up and form a protective
canopy over the President, but the weight of the other agents was too
much. He was afraid the President might be suffocated. As he twisted
around he came face-to-face with the President. He tried to pull back,
but couldn't move more than a few inches from Bush's face.

"You fellows sure are enthusiastic," the President gasped. "You're
going to save my life if it kills me."

"I'm sorry, Mr. President," Jeremy said. "Are you all right? Can you
breathe?"

"I'm fine," the President said. "It only hurts when I laugh, and right
now I'm not laughing too much."

Leaning on his horn, the driver jammed his foot on the accelerator
as hard as he could and the car jumped forward, only to halt again as
it came up behind the preceding car. Pulling out and around, the
convertible jerked forward again, its horn blaring against the crowd
that had surged into the street to see what was happening. Bucking and
swerving, covered with frantic bodies, it pushed through the shrieking,
churning mass.

Weinstein fell forward again, pinning the President to the floor. As
he struggled to give him some breathing space his hand pushed against
his walkie-talkie. Pressing the button, he called in to headquarters,
while at 1371 Powell Street the police were already pounding up the
steps to the burning apartment.

*     *     *

Matsuo Nakaoka had not left the condominium apartment for three days. He had slept comfortably each night, and had spent the days in meditation, in the psychic presence of his father, thinking of the lives of his ancestors, and of the purpose for which all of them had been born. None of this was clear to him verbally or in concrete visual images; yet on another level it was all clear, logical and valid. There is a truth to which we all aspire, a truth that lies far above the petty events of our transitory existence. As human beings our problem is that we cannot find it; even worse, we cannot know if we have found it. However, some of us have hints, intimations, glimpses; some even convince themselves of certainty. These people are either psychotics or religious zealots; we others have no way of knowing whether the terms are synonymous or, if not, into which category these people fall.

Matsuo Nakaoka had found his certainty. It was not a vision of heaven or hell, nor of right and wrong, but a vision of oneness with his ancestry, a linkage of his genetic pool transcending time that brought him together with those from whom he had begun his ascent into life, and with whom he would continue his progression into whatever life exists beyond the brief encounter we have with our transient world. He was content, with a calm that begged the questions of happiness, righteousness or fear.

He awoke at dawn and spent the morning sitting by the large window overlooking Powell Street, watching the preparations for the coming parade. At noon he ate a sandwich at the window, then took the briefcase out of the closet and assembled the gun.

For several hours now he had been watching the street below fill with people. He had seen the sawhorses being set up to close off the sidewalks from the street, and the people beginning to stand behind them. As the hours passed the crowd grew, until the sidewalks were so crowded that it was impossible to walk along them. Now he looked out the window and saw a federal agent armed with an automatic rifle take up his position on the rooftop opposite. Up and down the street there were several such agents, agitated like wasps around a disturbed nest; it was bad luck that this one happened to be exactly opposite Nakaoka's room. It was more than bad luck; it was a catastrophe that had to be

ealt with. As soon as he poked his rifle out the window, he would be
potted.

Far down the street he saw the presidential procession swing into
°owell Street, and simultaneously the sound of the crowd swelled into
roar that drowned out everything. Then suddenly the presidential car
ped up and began racing toward him. It was approaching rapidly, and
ie had to make an immediate decision. The only solution was to kill
he agent first, then the President. Staying deep inside the room so that
he man could not see him, he lifted his rifle and aimed at the agent
n the rooftop across the street.

As the rifle cracked Nakaoka darted forward to the window and
eaned out, shifting his vision to the street below, not waiting to see
vhether or not he had hit the agent; he never missed. The shot
everberated throughout the street, and all heads spun around. As he
eaned forward, resting the rifle on the windowsill, he noticed out of
he corner of his eye that the agent he had aimed at was still there
acing him, surely seeing him clearly. He had missed him! His mind
vhirled; there must be something wrong with the rifle, but what?
;hould he shoot again? No, because he couldn't have missed him at
hat range unless there was something wrong with the rifle, so he
vould miss again. He didn't know how the rifle was misaligned, and
f he missed again he wouldn't see the path of the bullet, so he would
;ain nothing. But then how could he possibly hit the President? His
only chance was to aim at him and see where the bullet struck below,
hen correct his aim.

All these thoughts took only a fraction of a second, and with them
:ame the action. He leaned forward on the windowsill, hanging over
he edge, his rifle protruding out into the air as the presidential car
oared down the street. He fastened the long-range sight on the rear
;eat, and through it saw a confusing jumble of bodies like dolls tossed
n a heap by an angry child. He didn't understand what was
iappening, but surely somewhere under that pile of sprawled bodies
ay the President, and the penetrating power of the bullet would be
;reat enough to reach him. Fixing the cross hairs of the long-range
ight firmly on the center of the pile, he pulled the trigger. The crowd,
vhich had already begun shouting and looking around, now erupted
nto confusion as Nakaoka saw the bullet strike the right rear fender of

the car, opening a flowerlike hole. He switched his aim to compensate moving the cross hairs diagonally to the left so that the correction would speed the second bullet into the floundering mass of bodies

At that instant the agent on the opposite rooftop spotted him and opened fire. The automatic rifle pumped out six bullets, two of which hit the side of the building, one splintered the window a few inche above Nakaoka's head, and three thumped into his body. His finger lost their grip on the rifle and he spun backward as if kicked by an enraged horse. He was dead before he hit the floor, the rifle falling from his hands into the shrieking crowd five floors below.

Buried beneath the pile of Secret Service agents the President was the one person on Powell Street who didn't know what was happening Spurred on by this new attack, the chauffeur yanked the wheel and drove the car straight at the crowd, scattering them before him and pulling off Powell into Sacramento Street. Ignoring the one-way signs leaning on the horn, he accelerated and roared away. Instructions were shouted over the noise, and he headed back toward the airport, away from what was obviously an orchestrated conspiracy, racing back to the safety of Air Force One.

The airport erupted in confusion. There was no public announcement but the news spread as quickly as if there had been. Agents accompanying the procession radioed back to prepare for immediate takeoff and as word somehow reverberated everywhere, the whole area resembled an anthill that had suddenly been kicked.

Colonel Lindgren's beeper went off, but he never heard it. He was in the emergency room of Baptist Hospital, where a series of blood test had established that he was suffering from food poisoning. The doctor had quickly zeroed in on the crabmeat stuffing he'd eaten last night with his baked flounder, and just as quickly had pumped out his stomach. Now he was lying semiconscious in a hospital bed, tranquilized by injections after the ordeal. The chain of command established long since had brought in Lieutenant Colonel Peter Johnson, the pilot of the backup plane, as copilot of Air Force One, and Terry Murchison, Lindgren's copilot, would take over as chief pilot for the flight home. Now, together with the rest of the air crew summoned by their beepers, they hurried back to the airport from nearby golf courses restaurants and, in one case, from a porno theater.

Master Sergeant Mario Delia and his contingent of Air Force security guards had never left their post, of course. Now they dashed around hurrying the ground crew to finish preparing the bird for flight. The steward in charge of loading food supplies was frantic; suddenly he had minutes instead of hours for his job, and he ran up and down the aisle, in and out of the plane, shouting for help from everyone he saw.

The gasoline tanks had been topped off as soon as the plane had landed to avoid moisture condensing from air in the empty space. Now the ground crew attended to the million and one little details that mustn't go wrong, while Delia and his crew of four tried to keep from being overwhelmed by the chaos and confusion.

Hardy stopped at a telephone in the terminal and put through a collect call to Kansas. Mohammed Asri answered on the first ring and accepted the charges; when he was told to take off in fifteen minutes he said only, "Good," and hung up.

Hardy stood in the booth for a moment, going over the calculations once more. Asri had little less than half the distance to fly. It would take at least fifteen minutes, probably more, before the President arrived back at the airport and the big jet was able to taxi into position and actually take off. So Asri would be there first, and he had enough fuel to circle for more than an hour. Perfect.

He went to his locker and took out the leather carryall, then hurried across the concrete apron to Air Force One, the pass clipped to his shirt getting him past the guards at the airport doors. At the plane he found the guards trying to control the confusion, and he grabbed Sergeant Delia as he turned away from one mechanic and before he could speak to another.

"I'm Tom Emerson, remember me?" he asked, flashing his identification and pass.

"I'm sorry, sir," Delia said politely but forcefully, "we have no time for reporters now."

"I'm not here as a reporter," Hardy answered quickly. "Bud Malcolm, the airport manager, sent me over to help. I'm a military jet pilot and know my way around these things. Is there anything I can do?"

"No, sir. Now you'll have to excuse me, I'm busy," Delia said, turning away.

Hardy nodded and looked around. One of the guards was helping a mechanic carry a fuel hose up the ladder to the wingtop, and he stepped over and took hold of the hose. "I'll help him with that," he said to the guard. "Delia says you've got other things to do."

"Thanks," the guard said, and hurried off.

After that job was finished, Hardy moved from the tail to the nose and back again, looking up at the fuselage and down at the wheels, keeping out of Delia's way, establishing himself as part of the scene, hurrying people to do their job faster and more efficiently, directing them here and there. For a moment he stopped under the towering nose, standing beside the nosewheel, feeling the tire, wiping off the hydraulic strut and testing it for leaks. As he did so he looked around. No one was watching him; this was the crucial moment when he had to take a chance. Despite all his planning and forethought, it all came down to this. He had to take a chance and if someone saw him now, it was all over. He glanced around again, then took a deep breath, reached up, grabbed hold of the bar in the nosewheel opening and pulled himself up; in the same second he lifted his legs, twisted and slid up out of sight. There was no door he could pull shut after him, but that didn't matter. He was deep in the cavernous opening, and no one could see him from the ground—that is, if no one had seen him during that critical second when he'd pulled himself up and in. He waited for the cry that would surely follow if anyone had been looking, but none came. The hustle and bustle flowed on beneath him, and he was left alone.

After waiting a few moments to be sure there was no outcry, and to allow his heart to calm down a bit, he crawled up through the nosewheel cavity to the bulkhead. Taking out his flashlight, he found the partition that led into the electronics communication section, and from there into the lower baggage compartment. In a niche in a tight corner he curled up and waited.

It seemed both long hours and short minutes until suddenly there were screeching tires, roaring car engines, hurrying footsteps, slamming doors and shouted instructions. Then there was an interminable moment of silence, followed finally by the beautiful whine of the jet engines starting up.

In New York it was just after 6:00 P.M. The September evening was still lit by the dying rays of a sun that had dropped below the tall buildings but had not yet set. Charles and Lori were walking down West

Forty-sixth Street. After weeks of chasing Hardy and Operation Dallas, Werther had finally decided he could take an evening off. There was nothing else to be done tonight. His men had checked the car-rental agencies in the Tampa airport and learned that Alison had rented a Ford Escort, license AIP 58F. Since she was making no attempt to cover her tracks, she was obviously not involved but was worried about her brother. She probably thought she knew where he was, but Werther wasn't sure that she did. Still, they'd track her down. Her description and that of her car and license plate had been circulated to the Florida State Police, as well as local police and all motels between Tampa and Miami. When she was sighted, the FBI was to be notified and she was to be followed discreetly.

In the meantime they had tickets to the new Alan Ayckbourn play that night, and now were trying to decide on a restaurant. Tomorrow the President would be going to Los Angeles, and he would be working day and night until Operation Dallas was over.

As they walked down the steps into La Vieille Maison a small crowd was waiting to be seated. Just as Lori handed her jacket to the checkroom attendant, Werther's beeper went off. At first she didn't connect the faint sound to Charlie, but as she turned away from the checkroom he smiled apologetically at her, said, "Excuse me," to the people in back of them and pushed through them to the telephone.

"I don't believe this," Lori said out loud as he moved off through the crowd. "I do not believe this," she said to everyone and to no one in particular. "The first time he takes an evening off in nearly a month!"

"Didn't your mother tell you never to marry a doctor, dear?" a heavyset blond woman asked as the maître d' gestured her and her husband into the dining room. "At least not for keeps."

69

The open limousine roared across the airport and pulled up with screeching brakes next to the steps leading up into Air Force One, and the President was pulled, pushed and nearly carried out of the car. The radio report from 1371 Powell Street had told of a whole cache of explosives—bazookas, grenades, Uzis and enough ammo for an army depot.

Several other cars from the parade managed to follow close behind the President's car, and some members of the entourage clambered aboard before the door was slammed shut. The rest would have to return to Washington on the backup airplane; they weren't waiting for anybody. In the cockpit Peter Johnson nodded to Terry Murchison, who flipped the starter switch. The starboard engines had already been idling, waiting for the President, and now the port turbines began to whine.

The President was escorted down the aisle to his sitting room, where he reclined on the couch, still trying to catch his breath, while his physician wrapped a sphygmomanometer band around his arm to measure his blood pressure, simultaneously taking his pulse.

"How'm I doing?" President Bush asked.

"I'll know in a moment, Mr. President," the doctor answered. "I can tell you this," he said, glancing up, "you're white as a sheet."

Bush chuckled. "Nothing strange about that. I know what a sheet feels like now. One of Jack Kennedy's after half a dozen strange women have been bouncing around on it."

"San Francisco Clearance Delivery, Air Force One requesting immediate clearance direct to Andrews Air Force Base. We have an emergency situation here."

"Roger, Air Force One. We will clear you direct to Andrews. There's some dirty Canadian weather extending over Colorado, but it tops out at angels twenty-five so we'll keep you above it. Squawk three six four two and contact Departure Control when airborne."

Ground control kept all the other traffic in their places as the giant jet moved slowly away from its parked position and out across the tarmac. As it turned directly onto the runway Johnson pushed the throttles full forward and it began to roar and gain momentum. When they lifted off the ground and the wheels were tucked away, everyone on board breathed a sigh of relief. On the ground the Secret Service agents, airport guards, police and everyone else watching echoed that sigh of relief. They stood on the tarmac staring into the sunlit sky, watching the glinting metal surface of the Boeing 707 disappear into the distance. They had returned the President to Air Force One. He was safe now.

The President put through an air-to-ground telephone call to his wife in Washington, assuring her that any television accounts of his death were greatly exaggerated. He was perfectly all right and was on his way home. After he hung up he gave a deep sigh and leaned back in his armchair. He was tired. His physician knew this was a reaction to the assassination attempt, but it was a healthy one. After a few more necessary phone calls had been put through, the doctor forbade any others, or anyone else talking to him. Now the President lay in his compartment breathing quietly, trying to compose himself, finally and blessedly falling asleep.

In the aft compartments the feeling was similar. It had been a time of great stress and of unimaginable excitement. The second attempt had been particularly frightening, indicating an organized conspiracy; they hadn't even known whether they would find Air Force One waiting when they arrived. But its starboard engines had already been turning over, freed from the ground energy supply system and ready to go, and when they felt the ground drop away beneath them they made the necessary calls to assure everyone that the President was safe and on his way home. Now they could relax.

"Are you sure he's okay?"

"That's affirmative. No question about it. They made it to the plane with no further shots being fired. They're on their way back here, so it's all over."

Werther looked across the crowded room at Melnik, asking him with his eyes if he believed that. Melnik shrugged; what could he say? If this was the Dallas operation, it looked as if it had failed. The first report said that the dead gunman was Oriental; could it be a police misidentification of Mohammed Asri? Certainly Melnik wanted to believe it was over.

Werther pulled him into a corner. "Is this it?" he asked. "Is this *all* of it?"

Melnik looked down at his shoes. When he looked up he said, "No."

Werther nodded. "It might be a part of it, right? But it's not enough.

Not with all the money we've traced and all the trouble they've gone to, then ending up with nothing but some klutz who blows up his stockpile and runs away, and an assassin who can't shoot straight. It might even have nothing to do with Dallas. Just a couple of screwballs operating on their lonesome. Am I right?"

There was a long silence. "I'll feel better when Air Force One arrives," Melnik said finally.

*That's it*, Werther thought. He looked at Melnik and the two of them stared into each other's eyes. Werther found it irritating that somehow this damned Israeli had the same thoughts as he did at the same time—and found it comforting that he was not thinking such ridiculous thoughts alone. Everyone else in the room assumed that it was all over and that the President was safe now that he was on Air Force One. Suddenly he remembered that Hardy was a friend of the San Francisco airport manager. Was it a coincidence that the assassination attempt had taken place in San Francisco instead of Los Angeles? He didn't see what possible connection there could be, but . . .

"There are too many possibilities," Melnik said.

"Hardy?"

Melnik nodded. "We know he has a connection at the Frisco airport. Hardy would have known that if there was an unsuccessful attempt they'd take Bush back there, and—"

"Alice!" Werther called. "Get me that sonofabitch airport manager on the phone again! The one in San Francisco—what's-his-name, Malcolm or something."

Hardy was impatient to start, but he made himself stick to the timetable. Finally, when fifteen minutes had passed, he got to his feet and began. By this time the plane had climbed to altitude, was on course, the pilot would have cleared his route with the FAA, the President would have been in contact with Washington, and everyone would know that he was safe and on his way home. Now the next step had to be taken quickly.

It was dark in the baggage compartment and he had to fumble a bit to open his carryall and find the flashlight. When he turned it on he saw a white mouse poking its head inquisitively out of the bag. Christ, he'd forgotten about it; it might have jumped out and he would never have found it again. Stupid, stupid. He gently pushed it back inside, then took out a gas mask, two plastic vials, a syringe and a small Haverhills portable welding torch. The oxygen-gas supply to the torch would last fifteen minutes, and it had taken only three to do the job when he had practiced on the leased 707. But the leased plane was a different model, with a few unimportant internal changes. One of these seemed to be that the air-conditioning line was situated differently. He crawled around on his hands and knees behind the stacked piles of goods, shining his light into the darkness and cursing quietly, searching for it.

Bud Malcolm was running from one end of the airport to the other, trying to get takeoffs back on schedule. By now the backup had left, loaded with all the people who had missed the frenzied departure of Air Force One. The local security agents and police had also departed, and the airport was back to normal—except that every plane was now clamoring to get back on line without delay.

He was in the north terminal baggage area, trying to settle a dispute over who would get dibs on the equipment shared by two local airlines, when he heard his name on the paging system. Glad of the excuse, he left the combatants and walked down the hall to the in-house telephone. "Shirley?" he said. "What's up?"

"The FBI is on the line for you, long distance from Washington. They're holding."

"I don't have time now, Shirley. Tell them the President left here and that we don't know anything more."

"I told them that. I guess they want to hear it from you."

"Tell them I'll call back when I get a chance. I really don't have time now."

"I told them that too, and that I didn't know where you were."

"Good girl."

"They say they'll hold until I find you. They sound like they really mean it."

"Goddamn it, I don't have time! Tell them to send me an official government form in triplicate and I'll put them on our goddamn mailing list!"

"Mr. Malcolm—"

"Oh, shit. Okay, Shirley, I know they're on your back. Okay, I'll go to Wizen's office, here in baggage. You know the number?"

"Yes, sir, I'll transfer the call there."

"Thanks a lot, Shirley," he said sarcastically and hung up.

Like the Cubans, Mohammed Asri had filed no flight plan with the FAA. Taking off from the private airstrip in front of the rented house, his departure was unremarked except by the startled housewives and children of the development whose houses were shaken by the sudden roar of the jet engine as the hangar doors slid open and the Panther suddenly appeared, rolled down the runway and sped off into the sky.

Staying high enough not to attract attention from the ground, low enough not to attract radar attention from the FAA, Asri cruised west–northwest across the empty plains of Kansas. Soon he would cross into the southwestern corner of Nebraska, then into the northeastern corner of Colorado, staying over sparsely populated areas, skirting the military-commercial airspace of Denver. Below him thick white clouds with black centers rumbled slowly in from the north, covering the ground, making him invisible to anyone who might bother to look up.

To the northeast the Cubans still circled over the vast area bounded by the two Eurekas: Eureka, Utah, in the east and Eureka, Nevada, two hundred empty miles to the west. Neither Asri nor the Cubans were aware of the other.

"Malcolm speaking."

"One moment, please. Special Agent Werther of the FBI is calling."

Malcolm grimaced. He'd hated formality in the Marines, and he hated it even more as a civilian. He didn't need these people; they weren't his bosses; he owed them nothing. He considered hanging up.

"Mr. Werther, I have Mr. Malcolm on the line now," Alice called.

"Right. Hello, Mr. Malcolm, this is Charles Werther, with the FBI in New York."

"This is Bud Malcolm. What can I do for you?" He knew what he could do. The FBI wanted his personal assurance that the President had left the airport all right. He'd be getting a dozen phone calls in the

ext hour from ten different FBI offices, from the CIA, from the Secret
ervice, from every agency that wanted to protect its ass.

"I just want to check with you again about Robert Hardy—"

"What?"

"I said I wanted to ask you about Robert Hardy—"

"Jesus Christ!" Malcolm exploded. "Don't you sons of bitches listen
the radio? Don't you at least watch television? Don't you know
hat's going on? The President was almost killed today! This goddamn
irport's in a fucking uproar, it's falling down around my ears, and you
ant to ask me about Gee Hardy? I don't have time for a security check
ow, goddamn it! Call me next month!" He slammed down the phone
nd walked away.

Melnik had been listening on the speaker phone. "He sounded a little
pset," he said. "I guess you can understand that."

Staring at the phone, Werther slowly lifted his hand and pushed the
utton. "He also sounded different," he said slowly, "and I *don't*
nderstand that."

"Different from what?"

"Different from earlier today."

"How different? More upset?"

"No," Werther said, not quite sure what he meant, talking to
imself as much as to Melnik. "Just different." He paused, then
dded, "Like a different voice." As he said it out loud he realized the
mplications. "Alice!" he shouted. "Get me Malcolm on the phone
gain!"


70


n Washington the scene was one of official calm and actual chaos.
Yes, the assistant presidential press secretary admitted to a room full of
houting reporters, microphones and cameras, there had been an
bortive attempt on the President's life. No, the President wasn't
armed. He was safe aboard Air Force One and on his way back to
Washington at this very minute.

Is it true that the FBI had advance warning of this attack and faile to stop it?

No, that's totally false, the press secretary replied flatly. (How in th hell did they find out, he wondered? God damn them all.)

Is it true that the assassination was plotted by a foreign governmen

No, that is not true; there's no evidence of anything other than single individual action.

Isn't it true that there were two attempts?

Yes, all right; *two* single individual actions.

Doesn't that mean a conspiracy?

No, not unless it can be shown that they are related, and as yet the is no such evidence.

Don't two attempts in a ten-minute span seem too much of coincidence for a noncausal relationship?

What? I don't follow your question.

Was one of the gunmen Oriental?

Yes, that is our information at this time, but you can understan that so little is known at this time—

Was he North Korean?

No more questions at this time.

Deafening clamor.

The assistant press secretary held up his hands and shoute "Gentlemen! As you can understand, we are trying to preserve a atmosphere of calm until we find out more about what happened. Th bottom line is that the President is unharmed and on his way home Please help us keep this situation under control. *Please*."

All incoming and outgoing traffic had been halted to allow th President's limousine to race across the airport tarmac direct to A Force One, and then to let the 707 take off immediately. The dela imposed by these actions had stacked up both commercial and privat airplanes in the airport's flying space; now that the President was safel on his way the control tower began to bring them in to land in never-ending stream, interspersing each landing with a similarl delayed takeoff. As each commercial flight landed it taxied into i space at the loading and unloading gates, and obviously these space couldn't be used by a later flight until the first ones got out of the way Hence it was imperative that the ground cleaning staff work fast to g

he planes back into the air again. But now it was time for their coffee
break. It wasn't so much the coffee as the principle. If they were to be
hassled every time there was a flap, management would begin taking
advantage. So they left the jets sitting in their spots, the passengers
waiting in the lounges, and took their coffee break.

Malcolm was bargaining with them, threatening them, begging
them, when Shirley found him. "Later," he said. "I'll talk to them
later. Next month sometime."

"He says it's important," Shirley said, pulling on his arm as he tried
to turn back to the attendants. "A one hundred percent emergency
about the President. He says that it's not a security check, and that he
doesn't have time to waste talking to a secretary just because a
mule-headed airport administrator doesn't have the sense to know
what's going on. He says for me to get your ass on the phone." She
smiled apologetically. "That's what he said."

He had to smile. "Okay, I'll talk to him. Get him on the phone and
I'll be back in the office as soon as I can." He turned away from her
again.

She pulled his arm again. "He's on the phone right now," she said.
"He's waiting. I can have the call transferred down here in just a
second."

"Shirley, I—" he began to protest.

"No problem," she interrupted, picking up the phone at a nearby
desk and dialing. "This is Shirley. Will you transfer that call to 9869,
please?" After a short pause she said, "Mr. Werther? I have Mr.
Malcolm on the line now."

She stood holding the phone out with extended arm, until Malcolm
grimaced, shook his head in defeat and walked over. "Malcolm here,"
he said.

"Mr. Malcolm, this is Charles Werther of the FBI in New York—"

Malcolm sighed. This was going to take a goddamn half hour.

"—and I want to ask you more about Robert Hardy. Do you
remember talking to me this morning?"

"Right. What do you want to know?"

"*Did* you talk to me this morning?"

"Well, I hung up on you, is what I did. I guess I talked a little before
that."

"No, sir. Mr. Malcolm, I'm talking about this *morning*. Not just a

few minutes ago, but earlier this morning. I called your office to ask
you had seen Robert Hardy anytime within the past several month
and to ask you to call me if he should turn up."

"What?"

"I said—"

"I heard what you said. I mean, what are you talking about? Yo
never called me this morning. Just that one call ten minutes ago.

"I spoke to your secretary this morning—"

"Oh, wait a minute, that's right. I wasn't in, right?"

"You were out of the office, that's correct—"

"So I never spoke to you, right?"

"She went and got you, and we spoke—"

"No. By the time I got back to the office you had already hung u
I got the message that you were just calling to bug me about security.

"But I spoke to someone who said he was you!"

"Well, I guess he was just trying to save me some time. He gave m
the message that you were worried about the President's security—

"I was worried about Robert Hardy! I wanted to know if you'd see
or heard from him in the past few months! He didn't tell you anythin
about that?"

Malcolm paused, his mind racing. "No," he admitted. "He didn't.

"Who was it? Who told me he was you? Who the hell was I talkir
to?"

Malcolm swallowed thickly. "Robert Hardy," he said.


"He was there!" Werther said as he clicked off the speaker phone.

"He was more than just there," Melnik answered, having hear
every word. "He talked to you, he lied, and now he's disappeared.

They both were silent, thinking it over. What was Hardy doing a
the airport? What had happened out there in San Francisco? Someho
it was tied in to—

"Oh, my God," Werther gasped. "Alice!" he shouted. "Find ou
how we can contact Air Force One!"


"Shirley!" Malcolm was shouting at the same moment. "Get m
airport security!"

He strode up and down the room, trying to work out what it al neant. The FBI thought old Gee was the one trying to kill the President. That was bullshit, but then what was Hardy doing here today, and why in the name of Christ had he told the FBI he was Malcolm and then never reported what they'd really said?

"I have Berner on the line," Shirley said.

"Berner? Malcolm here. I want you to find someone for me. Yes, here in the airport, right now. I don't know if he's here or not, but if he is, find him! Name's Robert Hardy. He's a big bastard, about six one or two, maybe one ninety pounds, black hair. . . ."

"Ah, sorry, Oakland Center, that's negative," Pete Johnson radioed back in reply. Replying to the telephoned FBI message, the FAA controller back in Oakland had just requested that Air Force One divert and land at the Sacramento airport. "The President has ordered us to return to Washington, and his physician has asked us not to disturb him along the way. Is this request officially necessary? Over."

"Air Force One, Oakland Center. Negative. You are cleared on to Washington."

"Roger, Oakland." Johnson snapped the mike off. "Wonder what that was all about?" he asked.

Terry Murchison, his copilot, shrugged.

Werther's message to the FAA had asked them to call Air Force One and without saying why request that it land as soon as possible. The reason was simple enough. Hardy could have used the airport simply as a center from which to guide the assassination attempts, but the airport wasn't a likely spot to have been chosen. More probably he was there because of the President's airplane. In the confusion following the shootings he might have tried to plant a bomb on board. He might even have sneaked on board himself. He might . . . Werther's imagination could devise a score of possibilities, none of them likely, all of them possible. Whatever, it was best to get the airplane back on the ground as soon as possible. But just as important—even more important, considering the unlikelihood of any of the on-board scenarios—was the necessity of imposing an air of calmness on the situation, to reassure the country and its overseas allies that nothing was seriously wrong; that the attempt was merely a case of a couple of isolated crazies; that there was no serious attempt in motion to overthrow the government of the United States. It was even more important to convey the message to the enemies of the United States that things were back to normal and it was business as usual; that the President was in full control; and that anyone attempting to take advantage of a disruptive situation by attacking the United States in one of its far-flung posts would find the defense establishment as ready to reply on a moment's notice as it had always been.

All radio and telephone communications to Air Force One are open. When the FAA called the airplane on a standard radio frequency, anyone else could listen in, for there is no privacy in radio waves. Hence, with no more to go on than that Robert Hardy had been at the San Francisco airport and was undoubtedly involved in the attempt, the FBI message had instructed the FAA not to even hint at further trouble, but simply to suggest that they land at Sacramento, the closest airport to its present position.

There was just one secure communications link to Air Force One, a scrambled radio-telephone line in the President's on-board office. As soon as he received Air Force One's reply to the FAA request, Werther was on the line to FBI headquarters in Washington, trying to get through to the Director in order to use that line to warn the President. Unfortunately, the bureaucratic procedures were difficult to hurry along.

Finally Hardy found the air-conditioning pipe leading up to the passenger and crew space, and set to work. He must have been nervous, for it took four minutes to burn the hole instead of the three it had taken on the Cubans' jet. Now he picked up one of the small vials he had taken from his bag, inserted the syringe needle into it and pulled back the plunger, sucking up the fluid inside. Then he inserted the needle into the hole in the pipe and slowly squeezed the plunger forward. As the fluid dripped off the tip of the needle the swirling air-conditioner air picked it up and vaporized it, carrying it upward. After putting on his gas mask, he repeated the operation with the other vial, then sat down again and waited.

*   *   *

Herbert Morrison, an assistant speech writer on his first presidential trip, was feeling pleased with himself. He was just about the least important member of the President's traveling staff, and yet he had managed to run fast enough to get on board the plane, when others more important had been left behind to catch a ride on the backup. It just went to show you: eventually all those mornings of jogging paid off. Everything you did paid off, he thought, if only you waited long enough. The thought of all the bigwigs left behind amused him.

Actually, everything was beginning to amuse him. For example, from where he was sitting in the last row of the aft passenger compartment he could see the top of everyone's head, and all the passengers were leaning back as if they wanted to be alone with their own thoughts. No one was talking. Then he began to realize, as if from a great distance, that something more was going on: everyone seemed to be falling asleep. Suddenly it wasn't funny at all. Something was wrong. . . . It was his last conscious thought.

The press secretary was on the backup airplane, which was also on its way to Andrews, half an hour and several hundred miles behind Air Force One. In Washington the assistant press secretary was running back and forth from the White House communications room to the crowd of reporters and cameras outside the west portico. His job was more or less impossible, but he was trying hard. He had to take an almost total lack of information and somehow convince the waiting mob that he knew what was happening and that it was nothing, nothing at all. Everything was under control. Just one more crazy nut trying to take a potshot at the President. Nobody had been hurt. Everybody was calm and relaxed.

Sure, they were.

At least on Air Force One everyone was indeed calm and relaxed. From the nonessential personnel, such as Herbert Morrison and the few reporters who had managed to scramble aboard and were now in the aft compartment, to the more important staff clustered in the security compartment and staff room, to the President in his lounge and the pilots in the cockpit, everyone was sound asleep. The only person awake on the plane was Hardy in the baggage compartment.

At this moment the scrambled telephone line to the presidenti
communications center amidships rang. Nobody answered it.

From his tests on the other 707 Hardy knew that five minutes w
enough, but it was still a tense moment when he climbed up to th
hatch and prepared to open it. He checked again to be sure that his g
mask was properly adjusted—it hadn't really been necessary till nov
with the gases being sucked up into the air conditioning ver
efficiently—and made sure that his feet were securely planted on th
small ladder leading to the hatch overhead. There was a stror
temptation to turn the handle slowly, lift the hatch an inch or two an
peek out. But that was stupid. If the gas hadn't worked, someone woul
see him; he had to burst out quickly, hope to catch one of the guare
by surprise, take his gun and . . . No, that was hopeless; his on
chance was that the gas had worked.

He shook his head. There really wasn't any doubt. He had tested
again and again and it had always worked. There were certain laws of
chemistry and physiology in this universe, and they had to be obeyed
He was just getting old. He would retire after this; he would never hav
to put his life on the line again; he would stretch out on a beach; h
would . . . He would open the damn hatch.

He twisted the handle, pushed the hatch open and clambered up
pausing for a moment on his hands and knees, looking around. Ther
was no sound but the dull rumble of the engines. Standing up, h
walked across the aisle and looked into the presidential office. Empty
He walked through it and opened the door into the sitting room. Th
President was sprawled there, unconscious.

He walked down the length of the airplane, looking into the loung
and conference room, staff room, aft lounge, security compartmen
and aft passenger compartment. Everyone was unconscious. On th
flight deck the crew were asleep. They would remain that way for eigh
to ten hours, long enough. Standing behind the two unconsciou
pilots, he checked the controls to be sure they were on autopilot as h
had figured they would be at this stage of the flight. Then he checke
the radios to see if anyone was trying to communicate with the plan
at this moment. As he scanned the instruments he pulled the pilot ou
of his seat with his left hand, paying him no more attention than if h

were a sack of potatoes, sliding him heavily into the passageway and slipping into the seat himself, not bothering to look at his face; he was too busy making sure that the plane was in good shape.

Hardy looked at his watch. The air was probably swept clean of chemicals by now. Jet airliners aren't like submarines, with an internal air supply isolated from the air and water outside. Instead the air inside the plane is constantly being changed by outside air being funneled in, which is then pressurized and heated or cooled the desired amount. All the air inside the plane is exchanged with fresh air every three or four minutes, the used air being expended through three outflow valves. It had gone through three complete cycles now, and should be safe to breathe, but he wasn't about to take any chances. He went back down into the baggage area, took the white mouse out of his valise and, cradling her in his hands, brought her up into the cabin. She remained conscious, and after a few moments he set her down and watched her sniff the rug, then move cautiously off to investigate her new habitat. Not until then did he take off his gas mask and breathe the air.

"Air Force One, this is Salt Lake City Center on one twenty seven two five, do you read me?" the radio crackled.

Hardy licked his lips nervously. "Show time," he whispered to himself, then sat down in the pilot's seat and flipped the mike switch. "Roger, Salt Lake," he said in his best Texas voice, admiring it as it flowed past his lips. L. P. Peterson, the Los Angeles speech coach, would have been proud. "This is Air Force One, reading you loud and clear."

The United States is crisscrossed with a network of invisible highways in the sky marked by automatic radio transmitters, each of which gives off a characteristic pattern at a set frequency. By homing onto these in succession, jet airliners and small private airplanes can find their way around the country as easily as a motorist cruising down the interstate highway system.

Air Force One had been routed along the J-84 jet route, which took it out of San Francisco under the control of the FAA center at Oakland. As it traveled east-northeast it would pass on to successive FAA control centers at Salt Lake City, then Denver, and so on. In each of these centers the plane, together with all others within the radius of the center's control area, would be automatically plotted on radar. Each controller had two modes of radar observation. One would simply show a picture of each airplane crossing his area. This mode was not usually used because there were so many aircraft that it would be nearly impossible to keep track of them all. By flipping a switch the controller could change to the more usual mode, in which only planes with active transponders would be shown on the screen. Next to each would be a small box indicating its identity and altitude, supplied automatically by the transponder in response to the radar beam impinging on it.

Air Force One had passed out of the Oakland control area into Salt Lake City. "Air Force One, Salt Lake City Center. We have a request from the White House to verify that your scrambler direct-telephone connection is in working order."

Someone must be calling the President, Hardy realized, and not getting a response. "Air Force One," he replied. "Ah, roger. We're just a tad busy here in the cockpit at the moment, but I'll send someone back in a minute to check on that."

"Salt Lake City Center, roger."

Hardy glanced at his watch. He ought to be able to stall them long enough. He switched the radio to a frequency channel not in normal use by the FAA, and called "Victor? Are you there? This is Charley."

Immediately the reply came back in a Spanish accent. "Victor here."

Hardy read his position off the inertial guidance system, taking the precaution to add the digit five before each coordinate in case anyone happened to be listening. He added the precise time, direction, altitude and air speed, and the four numbers showing on the transponder. If anyone *was* listening, the simple code of adding the number five would be enough to prevent them from plotting the data and realizing that this was Air Force One talking. It was probably an unnecessary precaution, since the odds that anyone with a knowledge of Air Force One's position might be monitoring an unused wavelength were high, and to anyone casually listening in the information would be meaningless, but he wasn't taking any chances.

Aboard the other 707 the Cubans were listening. Gloria Carollo plugged the numbers into the onboard computer and modified their heading to put them on a collision course at the prearranged spot. At the same time they began climbing from their current altitude of fifteen thousand feet to Hardy's altitude of twenty-eight thousand. As they crossed eighteen thousand feet they passed automatically into controlled airspace: above this altitude they were supposed to be flashing their transponder, and to have filed an IFR flight plan. But the radar coverage of the continental United States is nowhere near total, and so they were not noticed. Sooner or later, of course, they would be.

Hardy switched to another previously chosen wavelength and repeated the same information, this time omitting the transponder number. Several hundred miles away Mohammed Asri was circling in the Panther over the dark clouds and under the FAA center's height ceiling just west of Denver. According to his understanding, Hardy was transmitting from a spotter plane, giving him the coordinates that Air Force One was flying. He had to figure out the best heading for an interception without the aid of a computer, but his calculations did not have to be precise. There were only two jet routes out of San Francisco to Washington, D.C. The more usual, because of generally favorable jet streams, was J-32, connecting to J-94, and he was now circling astride it. Instead, Hardy's transmitted information indicated that Air Force One was flying along J-84, and so Asri gently banked his plane and drifted southward a hundred miles. There he once again circled slowly, like a sleek hawk in the sky, waiting for his prey.

71

"The President's airplane has passed the California border and is about a hundred miles into Nevada," Alice reported. "They've been contacted by the Salt Lake City FAA Control Center, and everything seems normal."

"Then why doesn't the President answer his direct phone line?" Werther asked.

"The pilot's checking on that now. He'll get back to Salt Lake, and they'll call us."

Werther frowned. "Who's the Air Force One pilot?" he asked.

"I don't know," Alice said. "I'll call Andrews and find out."

After she left the room Werther sat frowning. "What do you think?"

"The same as you, probably," Melnik answered. "I don't like it, but I don't know what to do. Scramble the Air Force?"

Werther shook his head. "What would be the point? All I can figure is that everything's okay, or that there's a bomb on board, or that Hardy's on board. Can you think of any other possibilities?"

Melnik shook his head.

"Well, if everything's okay, there's nothing for us to do. If there's a bomb on board, what can the Air Force do? The same if Hardy's on board; what can they do, fly alongside and pick him off with a long-range rifle?"

"There are security guards on board, aren't there?"

Werther nodded. "They should have the situation under control if Hardy shows up. He couldn't have gotten a whole group of assassins on board."

"Maybe you should warn the guards through the FAA radio?"

Werther shook his head. "We can't let word of any further attempt get out; we've got to keep this under control. Unless there's some real reason to think that Hardy's on board, of course. We can't throw the whole country into a panic just on a hunch."

Melnik didn't reply. He never defended his hunches publicly; he just liked to act on them.

"When we get the secure line cleared, we can warn them about Hardy. On the other hand, if there's a bomb on board," Werther continued, "at least we probably have some time. He couldn't have known exactly when the plane would take off, and since it's a six-hour flight he would have set the bomb at least two or three hours ahead to make sure it didn't go off before the President got on board."

Melnik nodded. "Be thankful for small favors."

"Either way, our next step is to find out why the secure phone system isn't working."

"What bothers me," Melnik said, "is that the secure phone must be redundant. There has to be a backup system, doesn't there? That line's too important to ever take a chance of its not working—and yet it isn't."

Werther didn't know what to say. Melnik was right. But the pilot had reported that everything was normal. Suddenly he had a sickening idea. "Alice!" he shouted. "Get on the phone to the FAA at Salt Lake City and find out if anyone there is familiar with the pilot's voice!"

"You think—" Melnik started. It was clear enough what Werther was imagining and he was right. Hardy was a Marine jet pilot, and he had already fooled them once today by answering for someone else.

They sat staring at each other for several minutes until Alice put her head in and said, "I've got the FAA on the line. Nobody at Salt Lake is familiar with Colonel Lindgren's voice."

"Who?"

"Colonel Robert Lee Lindgren. Andrews Air Force Base says he's the President's pilot."

Werther was on his feet and coming around the side of the desk. "I'm on my way down to Communications," he said. "Treat this as an emergency, and get them to provide a direct radio linkup to Air Force One. Next, get back to Andrews and find out whatever you can about Lindgren—particularly if he has any kind of accent or voice characteristic." Then he was gone, with Melnik on his heels.

When Werther burst through the door into Communications, he found Ed Beggle, the chief himself, with headphones over his ears, fiddling with the dials. "Do you have contact yet?" Werther asked.

"Hold your horses, sonny," Beggle answered, lifting the headphones off his ears to talk to him but still looking at his dials. "We can't reach California with this setup."

"It's flying over Nevada now."

"Nevada, California, it doesn't matter; they're both beyond the curve of the earth, and radio waves move in straight lines. Remember your university courses?"

"Are you saying we can't reach him from here?"

"Listen to me and you'll hear what I'm saying. We can't reach him by normal means, so I'm trying for a satellite hookup." He turned to face Werther. "This is not routine, boy. I hope you know what the hell you're doing."

"Trust me," Werther said. Beggle smiled sourly and said, "Trusting people when they ask you to break routine is not the best boost for your future career in the FBI." But he slid the headphones back down over his ears and turned again to the switches. In another minute he said, "Here they are." He took off the headphones and flipped the switch, filling the room with the crackle of the radio. "Air Force One," he spoke into the microphone in his hand, "this is FBI headquarters in New York. Over," then handed the mike to Werther.

Twenty-nine thousand feet over the Nevada deserts Hardy clicked on the microphone switch. "New York, this is Air Force One," he drawled. "What can I do for you?"

"Just a routine check," Werther said. "What's happening with the secure telephone line?"

"Doesn't seem to be much of a problem, they tell me. Should be back on line in another ten minutes or so. Any message you'd like me to pass back to anyone?"

"Negative. How's the flight going?"

"A-OK on this end. You fellows got any more ground problems?"

Werther grimaced. "No problems. Happy flight."

"Thank you. Air Force One, signing off."

Melnik looked at Werther, who shook his head. "It's not the same voice as this morning," he said just as Alice came running in.

"I got through to Andrews again," she said. "Lindgren is a Texan, with an accent so thick they all make fun of it."

Werther looked at Melnik and shrugged. "I guess that was him, all right." He glanced at his watch. "We'll wait until the secure line is cleared, then ask him to land at Salt Lake City or Denver, whichever is closest." He tapped his fingers nervously on the desktop. "I just wish we could get him down right away."

"Another ten minutes shouldn't matter," Melnik said.

"Air Force One," the radio suddenly crackled. "This is Salt Lake City Center Control. You are now passing out of our area. Contact Denver Center one thirty two five."

"Ah, roger, Salt Lake. Denver Control on one thirty two five. Thank you and good day."

He switched the radio frequency dial and spoke again. "Denver Center, Air Force One maintaining two nine oh."

"Roger, Air Force One," Denver replied. "We have radar contact. Maintain two nine oh."

Then silence as the minutes ticked slowly by. By now Hardy was visualizing two scenes. One showed the Cubans in their 707 closing in on him from the northeast, their course aimed at the same point in space and time as the plane he was now flying. He kept looking out the side window for them, although he knew that his first indication of their approach would be a warning call from Denver Center.

The other scene was FBI headquarters in New York. He'd never been there, but he could visualize what must be happening as clearly as if he were watching it on a television screen. Werther, the agent he had talked to this morning and probably the same man he had just talked to on the radio, would be pacing up and down, back and forth, waiting for the secure line to the President's on-board office to be cleared. He would wait ten minutes, perhaps fifteen, then would call back, and this time he would be harder to put off. Of course there was nothing Werther or anyone could do to save the President now if Hardy wanted to kill him. But that was not what he had in mind, and in order for him to carry out his plan successfully, Werther and all the others had to believe what Hardy wanted them to believe. Which meant that he had to put them off without arousing their suspicions.

As at all busy control centers, the controllers at the Denver FAA Center spent most of their time looking at the screen in the squawker mode. That is, only blips identified by transponder were shown on the screen, all other traffic being blocked out in order to reduce the blips to a number assimilable by a human being trying to maintain control over traffic. But every once in a while, in order to get the overall picture, they would switch to the total mode and then all radar contacts would appear on the screen.

"Murphy, you want to take a look at this?" one of the controllers called, and the section chief walked over to see what was happening. Bill Andler, one of the newly certified controllers, had just switched to total mode, and he pointed to one blip in particular out of several hundred on the screen. "Just look at it for a few seconds," he said.

They stared in silence; then Murphy said, "The son of a bitch is really moving, isn't he?"

Andler nodded. "I estimate him to be making five hundred knots."

They looked at the screen for another few seconds in silence. The other unmarked blips, the planes without transponders, were all private or light commercial flights, one or two prop engines at best. Most of them were cruising at under two hundred knots, none at more than three hundred. This one was moving through them like a bee through a flock of balloons.

"The other thing is—" Andler said, and he pointed at another blip, this one marked with a transponder code identifying it as Air Force One.

As they watched, the Air Force One blip moved steadily to the right, horizontally across the screen, corresponding to a west–east flight; the fast one descended at a slight angle to the vertical, corresponding to a northeast–southwest direction. Now, as they extrapolated the direction of each blip's flight, they saw that it looked as if they would intercept each other.

"This guy," Murphy said, pointing to the unmarked blip, "has to be a jet. An airliner, I'd say from the size of the echo. Flying without a transponder, he has to be below controlled airspace, and Air Force One is at twenty-nine thousand, so the indicated collision can't be real."

Andler nodded. There was no danger. The two planes were probably fifteen thousand feet apart in altitude and wouldn't come within three miles of each other.

Probably. But *probably* wasn't good enough. Murphy picked up the microphone. "Air Force One, this is Denver Center."

Hardy jumped at the sound. Which would it be, he wondered, the FBI or the Cubans? "Air Force One," he answered in his Lindgren voice.

"Air Force, Denver Center. We have indication on our radar of unidentified traffic approaching you at vector 160, on your eight o'clock at twenty miles."

"Denver Center, Air Force One," Hardy responded. "Verify unidentified aircraft?"

"That is a roger, Air Force One. The bogey is not squawking."

Imagine that, Hardy thought. He smiled, looking out his left-hand window for the contrails he would soon see, then took the plane off autopilot, assuming full control. Reflexively his fingers reached down to the transponder switch as he twisted around in the seat, looking backward and to his left. The view to his eight o'clock was blocked by

he wings and the engine nacelles, but he couldn't help looking. It
lidn't matter yet, anyway; Denver had reported it as twenty miles
away, and he couldn't possibly see it further than ten miles. But at a
closing speed of roughly three hundred knots they would cover the
lifference in less than two minutes. He glanced at his watch and
waited while the digital seconds flipped by. Two minutes later he
lipped his left wing and looked out, and suddenly the sky that had
been blue, clear, transparent and empty now had a speck in it that was
closing fast.

"Denver Center, this is Air Force One," Hardy called in. "I have a
visual on that intersecting traffic. He's a four-engined jet, about fifteen
thousand feet beneath me."

At about the same time Xavier Guarez saw Air Force One. His
computer had put him on an accurate heading, and he had only to
nudge the nose a bit to the left for what seemed like a perfect collision.
Martinez was in the copilot's seat; his main job would be the
transponder, and his fingers dangled over the buttons.

As they came closer they saw that their height was perfect; they were
flying at exactly the same altitude as Air Force One.

Without a radar transponder transmitting from the unidentified
airplane, the FAA control center did not have an estimate of its
altitude. On their screens it looked as if the two planes were about to
collide, but since Air Force One had reported visual contact and a
large difference in altitude, they weren't worried as they watched the
two blips approach each other.

The timing here had to be perfect. They hadn't been able to practice
with two planes, but Hardy had flown the mission with Guarez and
Martinez in the other 707 a dozen times, until he was satisfied that
they had it down pat. Then they had done it another dozen times.

Still, he was tense as the two planes approached each other, each of
them flying at nearly six hundred miles an hour. He maintained his
heading of 75 degrees, staring over his shoulder as the 707 sped toward
him. The seconds were compressed now, they were speeding toward
each other, he could see Guarez and Martinez in the cockpit. . . .
Now!

* * *

At the FAA Air Route Traffic Center in Denver Andler and Murphy watched the screen as the two blips merged into one, while twenty-nine thousand feet in the air over the empty Colorado plains Hardy yanked the wheel sharply to the right, at the same time reaching down with his right hand and turning his transponder off. At the same instant Guarez pulled his wheel all the way to the left, staring intently at the gyroscopic compass, while Martinez flipped the transponder on to Air Force One's call numbers. Hardy held the sharp right turn until the gyroscope approached 160 degrees, then quickly reversed the controls and straightened out sharply on the new course, while Guarez leveled his own wings on a heading of 75 degrees. The transformation was complete.

At Denver Center they watched their radar screen with apprehension until the single blip separated into two again, continuing on their previous courses: one heading southwest at 160 degrees, while Air Force One, identified by its transponder, continued on toward Washington at a heading of 75 degrees.

As Hardy watched the other 707 recede he breathed a sigh of relief. He was no longer Air Force One on anyone's radar screen; he had the President and his plane now, and no one knew it. Easing back on the throttles, he trimmed the plane slightly nose downward. In another few minutes he would sink below eighteen thousand and disappear from radar surveillance. Now, if Mohammed would only act quickly . . .

72

Melnik couldn't help thinking that maybe it was all over. If President Bush called through on the secure line and was warned about a possible bomb, and if Air Force One landed safely at Denver, it would be finished. They knew whom they were looking for now, and the Marine Corps had a complete dossier on Hardy. The FBI ought to be able to find him, or at least to close down his operation.

And then what? Simple. Back to Israel. Get on with his life. And Lori? What about Lori?

*     *     *

Verther couldn't help looking at his watch. He looked at it so often that he thought it was broken. It showed ten minutes to six; then he would stop looking at it for ten or fifteen minutes, and when he looked at it again it was still ten minutes to six. He stared at it; the second hand was moving. "What time is it?" he asked.

"What?" Melnik asked, startled out of his fantasy.

"What's the time?"

"Ten till six."

"Christ. How long's it been?"

"Since Lindgren said ten minutes or so? Nine minutes on the button."

"Think we ought to call him again?"

"I'd give him another minute or two."

"Let's call him again." He nodded to Ed Beggle, who flipped the switch and began the incantation: "Air Force One, this is FBI Headquarters in New York."

"Air Force One," Hardy replied, cursing under his breath. Where the hell was Asri? Looking out his port window, staring in the direction that the Cubans had taken on Air Force One's original flight path, he saw nothing. He wouldn't expect to see anything, of course; in only a few minutes they had flown out of sight of each other. His only indication would come over the radio, and the message he was hoping to hear was not the one he was getting. Asri had to act before the goddamn FBI got suspicious.

"Have you found the trouble with the secure line system yet?" the voice on the radio asked.

"Air Force One," he drawled. "Negative. I don't know what they're up to back there. You want me to ask for a progress report?"

"Please do, Air Force One."

"Roger. Is there any kind of emergency down there?"

"Negative. Just the usual urgent business."

"Roger, FBI. I'll try to find out what their problem is and get right back to you." He flipped the switch off. Damn it, where was Asri?

Mohammed Asri was zeroing in on the coordinates Hardy had transmitted to him; now that the two 707s had switched, he was aiming for the Cubans' plane, although he thought he was still tracking the

President and Air Force One. He was on a nearly reciprocal course, cruising at sixteen thousand feet to stay beneath radar surveillance, and had calculated the precise time at which his path should lead under the 707. He began to sweat when the digital numbers on his clock raced past that time, but just fifteen seconds later he saw the speck in the sky 13,000 feet above him, growing rapidly into the familiar swept-back wing shape. He held course while it passed over his head, then reached down, flipped on his transponder and pulled the stick back into his belly, while with his left hand he pushed the throttle to the wall and flipped on the rocket assists. Immediately he was shoved back into his seat as the accelerometer needle swung up, the Panther's nose pointed into the blue emptiness above and the altimeter whirled around as if a spring had burst within it. He leveled out of his half-loop at thirty-one thousand feet, above and behind the 707.

"What the hell is that?"

The FAA radar operator stared in bewilderment at the sudden appearance of the new blip on his screen. Two other operators came over to see what the fuss was. "Where'd he come from?" one asked.

"I swear to Christ I don't know. There was nothing there a second ago."

"It's tracking Air Force One. Better get on the horn and let him know."

The radio in Air Force One crackled again, and in the split second before the first buzz of static and the sound of the voice transmission Hardy wondered who it would be, the goddamn FBI or at last the first news of Asri.

"Air Force One, this is Denver Center. We have an unidentified blip showing up suddenly on your six o'clock at three one oh, same direction."

*God is good.* Hardy almost laughed out loud. "Air Force One," he acknowledged in his Texan drawl. "I'll keep an eye out."

On board the other 707, the Cubans who were monitoring the FAA frequency looked at one another and frowned. They knew that on the FAA radar this plane now appeared to be Air Force One. That was the whole plan: everyone in the United States thought the President was speeding toward Washington when in fact Hardy was taking him out of the country. It would not be for another four hours, when they landed in Washington, that anyone would know the truth, and by then Air Force One would have been off radar for all that time and could be anywhere at all. No one would ever find it.

Guarez was actually looking forward to the coming announcement at Andrews Air Force Base, although the arrest and treatment were likely to be harsh. But when the whole story came out about the Communist conspiracy to murder the President, and how he and Hardy had saved him, they would all be heroes. And then back to Cuba!

But what was this transmission about another jet? He didn't know what it meant. At any rate, there was nothing he could do about it. Hardy would have to answer as Air Force One. Gloria Carollo was operating their second radio, keeping it fixed on the unattended frequency they had picked for their air-to-air communications, and now she heard Hardy's voice: "Victor, this is Charley. Make a ninety-degree left and right turn."

She passed the message on to Guarez, and a moment later the big jet banked sharply to the left and held it for a few seconds. Guarez took the opportunity to look over his shoulder for the mysterious jet and saw it, glinting high up in the sun. It was a military plane, a fighter. He didn't understand. He banked sharply back to the right, and they were on course again.

Keeping the microphone open to the same frequency, Carollo clicked the switch twice to indicate that the instructions had been carried out.

Hearing the double click, Hardy knew that the double turn would have been seen on the FAA radar, indicating that Air Force One had turned left, banking its wings out of the way so that the pilot could look behind him, and had then returned to its original course. He flipped the mike switch. "Denver Center, Air Force One. I have your bogey in sight. It seems to be a military jet. He's a few thousand feet above me on a tracking course."

Guarez heard Hardy's voice in his earphones. Dallas seemed to know all about the fighter and was evidently expecting it, so everything must be all right.

* * *

"Get me the goddamn Air Force," the chief controller said angri\
"Find out who the hell that is."

One controller got on the horn to regional Air Force headquart\
while another tried to contact the jet. There was a minute of silen\
and then both turned around at the same time.

"He doesn't answer," the first one said. "I can't pick him up."

"The Air Force doesn't have any jet fighters in the vicinity," t\
second one said. "They don't know who he is."

"Shit!" the chief controller exploded. "Ask them to scramble sor\
fighters," he said to the second man. "Tell them somebody's up the\
tracking Air Force One."

In the Panther, Asri, who was monitoring the FAA transmissions a\
responses, smiled as he jockeyed into position. He wanted them\
know about him now; it was why he had turned on his transponder. H\
wanted them to see exactly what was happening, and to find him eas\
afterward. This was not a sneak assassination; it was war.

He held the flight pattern for another minute, maintaining positi\
above and behind the big 707, flying formation, waiting as the tw\
planes moved forward across the map of the United States, saili\
toward the towering peaks of the Rocky Mountains. Now that h\
rocket assists had burned out, he could maintain the same speed a\
altitude as the 707 only by holding his fighter at full throttle, and h\
couldn't keep that up much longer without overheating. But Hardy\
instructions had been explicit, and so as the temperature needle cre\
up toward the red line he held the power on high another minute, an\
another, until finally he saw the aiming point come into view f\
below. Then he dipped the nose and swept down toward the tail of th\
707.

"Air Force One, Denver Center," the voice broke over the loudspeak\
in agitation. "The bogey is accelerating. He is closing on you."

Gloria Carollo wondered what this meant. Who was out the\
trailing them? Was the plan going wrong?

"Denver Center, Air Force One," she heard Hardy reply as if h\
were the one being trailed. "What's going on? Should I evade?"

*     *     *

rdy was sailing serenely on his own path, miles away and out of
t of the action. He wished he could see what was happening; it was
d to play his part just by listening, but it all sounded right.

hammed had the 707 squarely in his sights now, and pressed the
ton on top of the joystick. With a *whoosh* and a bright spurt of
nge fire the air-to-air missile sped out of its bracket, its infrared
sor guiding it straight toward the jet exhaust of the 707.

hrist! What's that?" The FAA radar scope showed the sudden
earance of a third object between the two closing blips. From its
ed it had to be a rocket, but they couldn't believe it, though they
 it close with the 707.

"Air Force One, are you all right?"

om their tone, Hardy realized what had happened. He didn't reply.
"Air Force One, do you read me? Come in, please!"
He reached down and turned off his radio.

oria Carollo felt the plane lurch suddenly. Xavier Guarez felt the
ne lurch, and then watched in amazement as the wheel went limp
his hands. He moved it forward and backward, but there was no
ponse from the plane. Then he smelled the smoke.
Gloria screamed as the airplane slid off to one side and began to turn
er and fall out of the sky. She screamed as the smoke billowed
rough the cabin and the world began to spin crazily.
The FAA continued to call in to Air Force One as they watched the
p trail way down their scope. They couldn't believe what they were
eing.
Mohammed could, and he exulted in everything he saw: the rocket
erving away from the Panther, locking in on the 707 exhaust, riding
ht up into the tailpipe and exploding; the 707 flying on for another
oment, then sprouting a small but rapidly growing fire, then sliding
leward, dropping one wing, slipping off into a spin out of control,
wn, down, down.
He dropped his own wing and followed it down, spiraling around it.

He actually felt his heart jump when it smashed into the mountains
a great eruption of fire. He circled around as the pieces cascade
flaming and blackened, down the slope of the mountains, black a
red against the white snow, coming to rest piece by separate piece
crevices of canyons. He wondered why Dallas had been so insist
that he make the hit at this particular place; no one could have liv
through it no matter where it came to earth. *But perhaps Dallas is
his way just as thorough as I am in mine,* he thought, as he wheel
the Panther over in a steep chandelle and dived down to machine-g
the smoking pieces of wreckage.

# VII
# Disappearance

## 73

It would soon be over, Melnik decided. It had to be. What other choice did he have? Sitting in the crowded communications room at FBI headquarters in New York, waiting with the others to hear from Air Force One that the secure line had been fixed, he was a million miles away at an airport in Casablanca, waiting on the ramp with Lori and Charles, while in the mist behind them an old-fashioned propeller-driven airliner coughed its twin engines into life. Lori was looking at him with tears in her eyes, Charles was bewildered, and he was saying, *Good-bye. It's all over.*

She didn't answer. All her desires were in her glistening eyes, begging him.

*Someday you'll thank me,* he said. *Because you and I both know it isn't right. That's really all there is to it, it just isn't right. . . .*

*Casablanca.* His favorite movie. Lori. The one woman he had ever loved. He knew that now. But how could he ever live the rest of his life with her if in gaining her he was unfaithful to honor and trust? And how could he live with her anyhow? Take her back to Israel? A New York lawyer adjusting to life on a kibbutz or in Jerusalem? Or could he leave Israel and settle here?

He sighed. Operation Dallas was all over, and he would have to return home. The movie was over. He would have to tell her.

It was just about finished, Werther was thinking, but there was a residual doubt in his mind. He pushed it away. It *was* nearly over. But why was it taking so long to fix that damned secure line?

"Try contacting them again," he said to Ed Beggle.

Having Melnik as a partner had worked well and he would be sorry to see him leave, after all. He was an irritating man, to be sure, but was only because of his mannerisms, and you could sympathize with the reason for them. He was an Israeli, born and bred in a tiny

strip of desert on the edge of the world, surrounded all his life ▌
Arabs who wanted to kill him and everyone he knew and loved. It w▌
a tough life, and it made for a tough people. Aside from that, thoug▌
Melnik was his kind of person. Of all the people he had worked wi▌
on this project, it had turned out that this kinky Israeli was the o▌
person who understood things the same way he did. It had taken ▌
while to get to know him because they were so different in superfici▌
ways, but deep down they were the same. They were like brother▌
Werther thought, in a funny kind of way. He was going to mi▌
David.

"I want Lori," Melnik said from behind him.

"What?" Werther replied, turning around, not understanding wh▌
he was talking about.

"I want to marry your wife," Melnik said.

Melnik hadn't known he was going to say that; he hadn't known ▌
was going to say *anything*. He should have shut up and walked aw▌
into the mist like Bogart. But now the words were out. They hung ▌
the air and couldn't be taken back.

"Let's go outside and talk," Werther said.

They stepped out into the long, straight hall lit by neon ligh▌
recessed into the ceiling, cold, clean and as antiseptic as a hospita▌
People were hurrying by, but they seemed to be miles away, intent ▌
their own business. They were alone.

"What did you say?" Werther asked, but in the cold dark recesses ▌
his mind he knew. He had always known. From that first evenin▌
when he had taken this son of a bitch home because he felt sorry f▌
him, he'd seen something light up in Lori's eyes. Now he recalled ho▌
familiar the prick had been with his apartment, how he had know▌
where the dishes were. . . . He swallowed hard. He would kill the s▌
of a bitch! He would kill Lori! "What did you say?" he asked agai▌
ominously polite.

Melnik kept trying to swallow, but his mouth was so dry that h▌
couldn't make a sound. *This is ridiculous*, he thought. He hadn▌
meant to say anything; he had been determined to keep his silence an▌
his honor. Yet he had spoken—and now he *couldn't* speak! He wa▌
acting like a teenaged pimply kid caught trying to feel someone's sister▌
breast. Christ, that's what he felt like.

Werther grabbed him by his jacket. "What?" he demanded.
"What—did—you—say!"

"I want . . ." His voice squeaked, and he caught and brought it
under control. "I want to marry Lori," he said, and a great load
dropped off his shoulders. There, it was out. He had repeated it; there
could be no mistake. Werther could punch him now or pull out a gun
and shoot him; it was out of his hands. He had done it all now.

"Does Lori want to marry you?" Werther asked.

Melnik blinked. He hadn't got that far. But of course she did. What
they meant to each other, what they had done. . . . He nodded.

Everything erupted inside Charles Werther. Everything he had
known but had kept hidden, seen but refused to look at, now came
swirling up in front of his eyes. The world spun away and there was
nothing but this *bastard* standing in front of him. He raised his right
hand, clenched his fist, pulled it back and—

"Werther! Get in here fast!"

It was the look on Melnik's face as much as the startling shout that
stopped him. Melnik was staring over his shoulder in surprise, and
when Werther turned he saw Ed Beggle standing in the open door of
the communications room shouting at him.

The room was absolutely still. It was full of people, but no one was
moving. Everyone was stupefied, staring at the large speaker system in
the center of one wall. From the speaker came sounds of desperation
and hysteria that none of them were quite able to believe.

"Air Force One, can you read me? Over. Can you read me? Air
Force One, please come in. This is Denver Center Control. Air Force
One, Denver Control. This is Denver Control, calling Air Force One,
come in Air Force One. . . ."

Werther felt a cold shiver start at the base of his skull and run
quickly down his spine. Goddamn it, he'd known something was
wrong!

The first details were sparse, but they were enough to destroy all hope.
A small fast jet had suddenly appeared on the FAA radar, tracking Air
Force One and attacking it with a rocket. Then Air Force One had
tumbled off the radar screen. Air Force jets were on their way to the
site and would reach it in minutes, but it was already growing dark

there, with a heavy snowstorm moving down across the Rockies fro
Canada. FAA communicators were warning all commercial a
private air traffic to avoid the area. The jet that had carried out tl
attack was broadcasting its transponder, and they had it on radar. It w
making no effort to escape, and would soon be within sight of the A
Force F-16s. There was no radio or telephone contact with Air For
One.

By now Hardy was hundreds of miles away, heading southeast
fifteen thousand feet, below radar coverage. To people on the groun
he was just another airliner passing overhead. To the FAA he w
forgotten, a plane that had crossed Air Force One's route but, by dire
radio testimony from the pilot, had been a good fifteen thousand fe
below it. To the military and to Werther he had never even bee
mentioned.

In Florida it was raining. Freddy Mason wheeled his chair to the do
of the motel room he'd rented for the evening, and stared out at tl
rain falling on the grass patio. It might complicate things. Well, it w
unfortunate but unavoidable. The same applied to the timing. Th
707 wasn't due in Florida until 1:00 A.M., and he knew it was going
be hard to keep his four-man crew sober through the long evening
they waited in the motel. But the timing was dictated by th
circumstances, and he was determined that there would be no slip-u
at his end.

"Hey, look at that," someone in the room shouted, and Maso
wheeled around. Teddy and Mario were playing gin, Michael w
staring out the window at the rain, and Bill was watching television
"Look at that," Bill said again, gesturing at the set.

It was nothing much to look at, just a man talking into
microphone in front of the White House, but what he was saying wa
interesting enough.

"They shot down the fucking President," Bill said.

"Whattaya talkin'?" Teddy asked without looking up from his cards

"It's true. Somebody shot down the son of a bitch's goddam
airplane."

"What, are we at war again or somethin'?"

"I don't know. Listen."

The report was sparse. Details were lacking. After the unsuccessful assassination attempt in San Francisco today the President had been flying back to Washington when his airplane, Air Force One, was attacked and shot down over the Rockies west of Denver by an unidentified jet fighter. Nothing more was known at the present time. The condition of the President and others aboard Air Force One was not known. Further updates would be forthcoming.

"How about that?" Bill asked, laughing. "Is that something, or what? Crazy sons of bitches in this world!"

Teddy was having a tough time deciding whether he wanted Mario's discard or not. He kept reaching for it, hesitating, then taking his hand away again.

"You want it or not?"

"I don't know. Yes," he said, reaching for it. He stopped. "No."

"So draw already."

"Shut up."

It would have been easier for Mason if he could have told the group what the job was all about, but he never doubted for an instant Hardy's premise that all operations should be based on need-to-know security. What they *had* been told was that Hardy was hijacking a plane, and that he and Mason were to hold the passengers for ransom.

The four of them were not really included, which was fine with them. They were being hired for ten thousand dollars apiece only to help hide the plane, and that would be the end of their involvement with it. Considering the payoff expected from the cover story of hijacking an airliner, it wasn't much of a payoff for them, but there was no risk involved and they were satisfied. Mason had picked them for their brawn and tight mouths. Not that they were more conscientious or security-minded than others; it was simply that they had no interests except beer, cards, women and game shows on television. The news that the President of the United States had been shot down was not as interesting to them as the next beer commercial, which they liked better than the programs, or as important as whether or not the jack of clubs might still be in the pile waiting to be plucked.

Michael still stared out the window, occasionally turning to look at Mason. Freddy knew he was thinking he'd like to run out and get some

beer, and was wondering how Freddy would stop him. It was li
staring down a Doberman—simple, if you weren't afraid of him. A?
a while Michael turned back to the window.

Bill laughed whenever the laugh track told him to. Teddy and Ma
exchanged loud cries of "Gin!" or triumphant whispers of "Knock wi
two," and the long evening passed slowly by.

## 74

Mohammed Asri had time for just one strafing pass at the wrecka
before the clouds moved in, but it was more than enough. As he pull
out low over the mountain ravines he didn't find enough wreckage
any one place worth training his guns on. The giant jet had broken (
impact and scattered down the jagged slope—an engine here, a brok(
wing there, a dozen pieces of charred fuselage here, there an
everywhere among the trees and boulders. No one could possibly ha
survived. Nevertheless he pressed the gun button out of she
exuberance, spraying the whole area with .50 caliber bullets as I
whizzed down, then up again over the encroaching clouds, back in
the clear sky brilliant with the glare of the setting sun.

Below him the winds swirled over the wreckage, dispersing the bla
smoke as the dirty weather from Canada rolled in. He was alone in tl
sky. He didn't try to escape; that had never been part of the pla
Instead he climbed back up to altitude, where they could find hi
more easily on their radars, and circled there waiting. A minu
passed, and another, and nearly one more. Then in the empty sl
there appeared two little specks that grew into four and sprouted ta
of vapor. Suddenly they were on top of him, racing past at su(
incredible speed that they wouldn't even have seen him if it had
been for their radars.

As they chandelled up and over him, trying to slow down to h
speed, he saw that they were Air Force F-16s. He wondered ho
disciplined they were: would they shoot him down or escort him i
For himself he didn't care—he would have been happy to die at th
climax of his life—but it would be better if he could make h

atement. So he watched as they circled around behind and came up
n his tail. He twisted around in his seat and watched through the
ubble canopy, making no effort to escape, waiting to see the little puff
f smoke from under their wings that would be his first indication of
missile being fired.

They came closer, and finally settled into formation around him.
is radio was crackling with all sorts of messages, but they only
istracted him. Anyway, he wanted to make his statement in person,
ot anonymously over the radio, so he shut it off.

The leader waggled his wings, and Asri waggled his in return. Then
e F-16s banked left, and Asri followed them, as domesticated and
ubservient as a dog, as triumphant as Caesar entering Rome.

n New York the FBI was trying to reach people by radio and
elephone, but they weren't able to get through to anyone who knew
nything. They found out more by watching television. "We interrupt
his program for another news update," the set said. Melnik beckoned
Werther, who hung up the phone, where he had been put on hold,
nd came across the room.

"We have been told," the announcer said, "that the fighter plane
hat shot down the President was intercepted by the Air Force and has
een brought back to Lowry Air Force Base in Denver. The pilot
laims to be an officer in the Syrian Air Force, and has announced
hat his act is a declaration of war between Syria and the United
States."

"Asri!" Werther muttered. "Goddamn it, that's Mohammed Asri."

"As of this point in time we have no confirmation from the Syrian
government, but we are informed that all military forces have been put
on full alert. I have just received a report that the Israeli government
s mobilizing its forces. . . ."

"Oh, Christ," Melnik whispered. "Here we go again." His heart was
olling around somewhere below his ankles. It was an effort to look
nyone in the face. He had failed, he had missed all the signs, he had
messed up. What had happened to his famous intuition? Now Israel was
bout to be invaded again because of him. He should have realized
vhat it was all about, but he had been thinking of nothing but a woman,
vhile all around him the world had been slipping into the chasm.

"We take you now to the Pentagon for the latest report," television announcer said.

When Freddy Mason clicked the set off, Bill protested, but not much as he would have done if Vanna White had been on came Freddy ignored him. "Time to go," he said.

"Just a minute, I've got this sucker down for a schneider," Tec said.

Freddy wheeled over to the bed where they were playing a scattered the cards to the floor. "Fuck you," Teddy said.

"Let's go," Freddy said, and reluctantly they followed him out door.

It was still early, but Freddy knew it would be easier to get them there now. For the past hour they had been getting edgy, and couldn't blame them. Cooped up in a motel room with nothing to but watch the rain or the television or play cards, anyone would edgy, and since they had nothing to think about except women a beer, pretty soon they'd start to think they could kill the time bet with a bit of each. Also, he didn't want them watching the televisi anymore. They didn't think about anything they saw, but he did want to take any chances on their beginning to wonder what h happened to the President. He doubted that they had the brains make a connection between that and what they were hired to do, h why take chances? He had seen enough to be sure that the plan w operating on schedule, and that was enough. Once in the swar they'd think more about the mosquitoes and less about women, be and the President.

They drove down to the muddy area on the edge of the Everglac where they had stored their machinery. Mason was helped onto t airboat by two of the men, and the other two climbed into the Du with the hoisting rig. The engines blasted a noisy roar into the nigl but there was nobody to hear them as they rumbled off into t swampy waters. Motoring to an area they had staked out th afternoon, they fastened flashlights pointing upward to each stake. the front of the outlined rectangular area they found the steel pipe th had set into the swampy ground. To the top of it they now fastened small box that looked like a rural mailbox except for the front pan

ade of glass. Mason carefully aligned it toward the west-northwest,
nd checked the electrical connections to a car battery that they set
eside it. They didn't turn on the flashlights or the mailbox apparatus
et, but sat swatting mosquitoes in the darkness and looking at the
luminated dials of their watches.

The Syrian ambassador in Washington has denied any knowledge of
he pilot who shot down the President today," the television an-
ounced. "We have not yet received any statement from the govern-
ent in Syria— Just a moment. We have just received word that an
fficial statement will shortly be coming from Syria. The preliminary
nnouncement is that the episode has been engineered by Zionist
lements in Palestine, and is a trick designed to launch a new Mideast
ar. We'll get back to you on that. In the meantime, there is no
urther word on the President's fate."

Melnik and Werther couldn't understand what had happened. No,
at wasn't right; they could *understand* it, all right. They realized that
e lunatic they had been chasing all these weeks had evaded them,
ad caught the President thirty thousand feet over the Rocky Moun-
ins, and had shot him down and almost certainly killed him. What
ey couldn't understand was *how it* had happened.

When Melnik and the Mossad had caught and drugged Akbar in
ondon, he had told them about a gunman and an assassination
ttempt to be made in Los Angeles. Werther could understand that
Hardy might have found out what had happened to Akbar, and so had
hanged the locale to San Francisco. But he couldn't have arranged for
he jet fighter and the in-air interception in such a short time.
Moreover, Asri had been brought in long ago, so it all must have been
lanned then. If so, why hadn't Akbar known about it? Never mind.
Vhy had he trusted Akbar's information? That was the real question.
Vhy hadn't he seen that it was incomplete? Had he lost his touch?

Glancing up from the fingernail he was biting, he noticed Melnik
taring out the window—after this was over he would settle with that
on of a bitch.

Melnik's mind was racing through the same questions, together with
a different set that didn't concern Werther. What would happen now

on the other side of the world? Was there really a Syrian declaration of war? If so, he wasn't worried about the United States, but what would happen to Israel? Syria wasn't about to invade New Jersey, but what was happening now on the Golan Heights? Were the Syrian armored divisions rolling into position? Were Iraqi bombers fueling up right now? Could Egypt be trusted if the whole weight of the Arab nations fell on Israel?

One little flicker of Melnik's mind reached out and told him that Lori Werther still existed, but he gave an impatient shrug of his head. He didn't have time to worry about her now.

Alison was tired, hungry and dispirited. It had been a long day; she had done a lot of driving since landing in Tampa and so far she had found nothing. She would keep trying but she'd have to rest soon.

She was driving southeast on route 82, above the big bend heading into the town of Immokalee. Just beyond the bend a state trooper sat parked in his car, motor running but lights off, waiting for a speeder, a drunk driver, or for one of the cars that had been reported stolen or were wanted for one reason or another. Alison's Ford Escort, license plate AIP 585, was on the list.

As she approached the bend her responses were a little slow, and she began to drift off into the left lane. She was brought sharply back to life by a loud honking, and as she swerved back into her lane she was startled by a black shape whizzing past her with only inches to spare. *He must be doing ninety, the son of a bitch,* she thought, shaking from the scare as his rear lights swerved around the bend and disappeared. Actually he was doing eighty-seven as he roared past the parked state trooper, who turned on his lights and flashers and took off after him.

*Good,* Alison thought righteously as she came around the bend and saw the trooper pulling the speeding car over up ahead. *Serves him right.* As she drove past the trooper was just walking up to the black car to ask for the driver's license. He never noticed the little Ford Escort driving sedately past at a legal speed.

Werther was sure there was something they still didn't understand; he couldn't believe that what had *seemed* to happen had actually occurred. Everyone told him he felt that way because he couldn't accept the enormity of the situation. "That's what the code name meant: Operation Dallas," one agent said. "They tried to pick him off by rifle like Kennedy, but they were even better prepared. They were waiting for him to get away by air. Hell, who knows, maybe the Kennedy assassins had something else waiting in the wings in case Oswald missed."

The room was full of people offering variations of this scenario. They had to accept what had happened and go on from here. The Vice President had already taken control in Washington; the military was assuring everyone it was ready for any eventuality; and though no one was happy with the thought of Quayle as president, the country would survive. Now that they had Asri, the only task left was to get Hardy.

Werther couldn't argue with them all, or with what seemed to be the facts. Slowly he began to lose his conviction; he had nothing to base it on, after all. Perhaps they were right and he was only refusing to accept the fact that the President had been killed by a man they had known about but had failed to stop.

Then Melnik turned away from the window, and across the room the two men stared at each other silently while the others in the room gabbled on without noticing.

Slowly Melnik shook his head. No, he was thinking, that was not what had happened. He didn't know why, but his intuition had simply risen up overwhelmingly and told him that something was wrong here.

Werther walked across the room and sat down next to Melnik. "You don't buy it," he said.

"No."

"I don't, either. But why not?"

"I'm not sure. It doesn't *smell* right." He glanced at Werther to see if he would laugh, but the American nodded quietly. He understood, but he wanted more.

"What don't you like about it? Where does it start to unravel?"

"I don't know. Akbar?"

Werther shook his head. "A plant to throw us off the track, and we fell for it." He paused. "How about the name?" He nodded at the others. "They think it's perfect because it shows the link to the Kennedy killing."

"No. That's part of what's wrong." Melnik struggled to find the right words. "This was such a precisely and intelligently planned operation that the person who conceived it wouldn't possibly have made the elementary mistake of using a name that might give it away. Instead," he went on as several others began to gather around, "he chose that name to make us think exactly what we're thinking now. But something else happened instead."

"Something else? You mean Air Force One wasn't shot down?" someone asked sarcastically. "The President isn't dead? Everybody out there is lying? Come off it, Melnik."

The knot of people broke up again into small groups, each intent on trying to track down Hardy. Melnik and Werther sat there without moving.

They had forgotten about Lori.

The interrogation of Mohammed Asri convinced the officers at Lowry Air Force Base that he was telling the truth. Asri gave details that matched what the FAA had seen, adding that when he had strafed the wreckage he had seen no survivors. He volunteered precise details of where the crash had occurred. But there was still no declaration of war from Syria. In the next half hour a spokesman for that nation declared no knowledge of the attack and denied any responsibility.

Following Asri's instructions and searching with infrared detectors, Air Force planes located the wreckage by 6:15 P.M. that evening. It had crashed in the Pike National Forest, falling into one of the deep valleys between Gary's and Byer's Peaks. By then the sun had set behind the mountains so the site was in near-total darkness. Also, the snowstorm from Canada was moving inexorably over the site, its dark clouds bringing swirling gusts of snow. Floodlight-equipped helicopters joined the search planes, but the choppers couldn't descend because of the fierce winds rushing through the valley. They were preparing to land on one of the calmer peaks above and climb down to the wreck.

Asri was charged with murder and taken to jail, protesting that he should be treated as a prisoner of war. He did not believe that war had not been declared.

## 75

Within minutes after the first assassination attempt the beepers attached to the belts of all the Air Force One personnel had gone off, summoning them all back to the airport to prepare for immediate takeoff. Lindgren hadn't heard his; he was lying unconscious in the hospital after having had his stomach pumped out. But as soon as he woke up he heard the hospital staff talking about what had happened, and over their heated objections he put on his uniform and rushed to the airport.

He was too late; Air Force One had already left. He found a spot aboard the backup plane, though he was still too weak to fly. He was half asleep in the passenger lounge, in that state of wondering whether he was living a nightmare or dreaming a reality, when the announcement came over the intercom that Air Force One had been shot down with the President on board.

The backup plane was diverted to Denver, and Lindgren attempted to join the rescue operations, but there was no place for him. The air-rescue group was a team of professionals who had worked together for years and would have nothing to do with an enthusiastic amateur. They estimated it would take five to ten hours to reach the wreckage. Under intense pressure from headquarters to fly directly in, they pointed out that the darkness, weather and treacherous mountain winds made landing a helicopter at the site impossible. Lindgren bounced around the airport from one group to another, trying to find some place where he could help, but it was useless, and he soon recognized this.

At the base operations office he found a sergeant who gave him a copy of the Denver regional FAA map. On it he located a small private airport on the road to Boulder just north of Denver. He rented a car and drove out to it, not really knowing what he was going to do. Maybe something would turn up. He had a vague thought of somehow getting in there and . . . There must be something better to do than sitting around the airport watching everybody else do nothing. As he pulled off the main highway onto the road leading to the grass airfield he saw

a mirage. There were still a few of them in this country, scattered
around rural airfields like this one: a 1940s-vintage Piper Cub, painted
yellow with a black bolt of lightning down its fabric-covered fuselage.

There were two people in the office adjoining the single hangar.
They had tried to fly one of their own twin-engined airplanes into the
crash region, but had been warned off by the military, and now they
were sitting by a shortwave radio, drinking coffee and listening to the
aborted rescue attempts.

Lindgren rented the Piper Cub, elated to find that it had been fitted
out with a two-way radio, the one essential modern convenience. He
told the two men nothing, just rented the plane, borrowed a flashlight
and took off, not even mentioning the crash. Once in the air he
headed straight for the scene and called in by radio: "Charley Control,
this is Colonel Lindgren in a civilian Piper. I'm heading for the scene
of the crash to see if I can get in there. Over and out."

"Lindgren, this is Charley Control. Negative. Repeat, negative.
Area is closed to all civilian aircraft, and that includes you. Please
return to base."

He had expected this, of course. "Charley Control, this is Lindgren
in a civilian Piper Cub. Do you read me? Over."

"Reading you loud and clear, Lindgren. Return to base. That is an
order. Charley Control, over."

The weather had been clear around the little airport as he left, but
now it was rapidly worsening. If he went up above it he'd never be able
to come down through it, with mountain peaks lurking unseen inside
the clouds, so he stayed just over treetop height, flitting like a
dragonfly, following his progress on the map he held on his knees. He
transmitted again. "Charley Control, this is Lindgren. There must be
something wrong with my radio; I am not receiving you. Request
permission to see if I can get into the crash-site area. Please reply only
if negative; I will take silence for assent. Over."

"Lindgren, this is Charley Control. Get the hell out of there right
away! Your ass is on the line, boy. Do you read me?"

"Charley Control, this is Lindgren. I have received no answer, so
I'm going to try to find my way in. Will transmit again if I can land
there. Thanks for permission to try. Over and out."

The Piper Cub is the greatest little plane ever designed. With a top speed of only ninety-five miles an hour, it's slower than a BMW and a lot less comfortable because its flimsy body shakes with the vibrations of its lawnmower-type engine. But it can turn on a dime, fly as slowly as thirty-five miles an hour without stalling and land practically anywhere big enough for a man to stretch out his hands. It couldn't take off from the site of the crash again, of course, but Lindgren was thinking that he could do a lot of good simply by getting in. With the radio he could direct the rescue teams right to the spot if he survived.

He didn't blame Air-Rescue for not trying to fly in this muck. There wasn't much chance of getting in alive, let alone out again, and there was even less chance of anyone down there being alive, so there was really no hurry. But he belonged there with them. He should have been flying that plane, it was his men and his president lying down there, and one way or another he was going to join them.

The winds came roaring down the valley, bouncing off the sides of the mountains, buffeting the Cub with gusts every swirling second. The low dark clouds hung precariously over the mountains, settling down over the peaks and hugging the valley walls. He sailed in under them, skidding down the valley sides as a blast of wind suddenly propelled him sideways, nearly turning him tail-first and topsy-turvy.

Popping up over one crest, he saw a blank mountain wall rushing at him. He pulled the stick hard over and banked onto his side, spinning down again into the valley. An updraft caught him and pulled him up toward that ceiling of impenetrable snow clouds; once in it without instruments he would be lost, without any sense of direction, of up and down or forward and backward. He would be blinded in there, and would either spin out of control into the ground or fly into a hidden mountainside. With all his might he slipped and banked in an effort to get out of the updraft. He saw the wings of the Cub bending like those of a paper airplane, waited for the inevitable crack, and then suddenly the updraft released him and he was on his side fifty feet above the upward-sloping ground, spiraling down into it. He straightened out, pulled back on the stick and stalled just as the ground ahead of him fell away into a new valley.

He released the stick, letting the nose of the Cub dip to pick up flying speed again, and followed the terrain down. Somehow he still had a good sense of where he was, and as he gained speed he pulled the nose up and turned right, slipping the little Cub up over the next crest and sailing it down into the valley beyond, where Asri had told them Air Force One had gone down. He felt his way halfway down it, flitting over the tops of pine trees, at one point even scooting between two tall pines as a downdraft flung him nearly into the ground. Twisting around between the trees and popping up again to continue skidding, flying down the nearly sheer face of the valley walls, he was hit suddenly by a starboard wind. To fight it he heeled the Cub over on its side and then another gust hit from port, smashing him down into the line of trees.

Suddenly it was very quiet. The crash came so suddenly, after the long fight to stay airborne, that it was over before he realized it had happened. He seemed to have jumped without intermission from bouncing around in the air with the buzzing sawmill of the engine two feet in front of his face to the deep, dark quiet of a winter's night, alone in the forest. At first he heard nothing; then he became aware of the wind's moaning above him and the slow ticking of the cooling engine. Beyond that there was nothing at all.

He was lucky he had flown down the mountain low enough to find trees; otherwise he would have been blown straight into the rock face and killed. As it was, his face had been smashed open on the instrument panel, and he must have been unconscious for a few seconds. Now, as he listened to the wind and the engine ticking, he realized that his face was wet with blood, and that it was dripping down at a funny angle. He looked outside, but it was pitch-black; then the clouds parted for a second, the moon appeared, and he saw that he was hanging on his side, nearly upside down, dangling from his straps in the cockpit with high-octane gasoline dripping down on him from the wing tanks overhead. But he was alive, and there was no fire—yet.

He released himself and half climbed, half fell out of the Cub to the ground. In the cold he huddled against a rock trying to escape the wind until the engine cooled down and there was no danger of fire, then crawled back into the cockpit and tried the radio. "Charley Control, this is Lindgren. I'm on the ground about halfway down the slope. No wreckage in sight."

Control called back asking him to give a continuous transmission so that they could get a fix on his position, and he was about to reply when he remembered he wasn't supposed to be able to hear them. It didn't matter anyway; there was no way anyone was going to be able to get to him before this storm lifted. He thought he might as well try to straggle downhill and see if he could find anything.

The clouds had covered the mountain again and he was in total darkness. Rummaging around inside the cockpit, he found the flashlight, and turned away from the Cub. The next step was the hardest. In the swirling wind and darkness there was only emptiness and fear; the only solid thing he had to cling to was this wrecked Piper Cub, and he felt an overwhelming urge to climb back into the cockpit and huddle there until morning.

But he couldn't do that. He took a deep breath and pushed off. Slipping and sliding a few yards at a time, crashing into trees and boulders in the darkness, he worked his way down the valley. He used the flashlight sparingly; he didn't want to run out of light when he might need it most, he told himself, not wanting to admit that he simply did not want to be alone in the darkness.

So he very nearly passed it by. He didn't see it at first, and wouldn't have seen it at all if he hadn't stumbled. In the darkness he fell against something that felt different, and when he steadied himself against the dipping ground he turned on the flashlight and saw that he had fallen against a piece of bright metal. He shone the flashlight around in a wide arc, and saw on the other side of a clump of boulders the torn-off tail of a Boeing 707.

76

The FBI agents in San Francisco were interviewing Bud Malcolm about Hardy. Their first report, telephoned through to Werther, revealed that Hardy had been cultivating Malcolm for months. They had not been able to turn up any such preparations in Los Angeles, which didn't necessarily rule out that city at this stage, but it was beginning to look as if San Francisco had been the focal point the whole time.

Which meant that either Akbar had been lying or had been lied to.

Either way it was clear that they could not accept his story of the assassin as even a major component of Operation Dallas. Clearly the shooting down of Air Force One had been the primary objective all along. Unless . . .

Neither Werther, Melnik nor anybody else could substantiate the "unless" theory. Now that the deed was done the focus was on apprehending Hardy. All planes leaving San Francisco airport were searched, despite the chaos and confusion this imposed on the city. FBI agents armed with reproductions of Hardy's Marine Corps photos were carefully inspecting each passenger before allowing him or her to board. A similar barricade had been put up around railway and bus stations, and all rental-car agencies were being checked, though the highway system was too complex to make it practical to stop every car leaving the city.

There had been a significant but limited number of flights out of San Francisco between the time Hardy had been last seen in the airport prior to the assassination attempt and the moment the blockade was imposed. In all cities that were destinations of these flights FBI agents were hurrying to airports to meet the flights and examine each passenger alighting. In those cities where FBI personnel were not available local police were being pressed into service to do the job.

The organization and response time of the Bureau was impressive. There were some things that they could do well, Melnik had to admit. But there were other things they could not do well. Organization and efficiency were everything; originality of thought or intuition was not highly prized or prevalent. So if there was something beyond the ordinary, how would they ever unravel it? Werther and he were the only ones looking for a different drummer, Melnik thought, and they didn't know the tune.

He wanted time to think, but there was none; reports were coming back to headquarters faster than they could be digested. The stack of papers on Werther's desk was growing at an alarming rate. Melnik sat beside it, going through them with Werther, helping him look for the one needle in that paper haystack that might prick their consciousness into thinking of something useful.

He sat staring at one particular piece of paper for several minutes, then got up and crossed the room to a telephone on another desk.

When he came back he tossed the paper on top of the one that Werther was trying to read. At first Werther brushed it aside in annoyance, then looked up at Melnik, picked up the paper and read it. It was the official manifest listing the passengers and crew of Air Force One when it had taken off hastily from San Francisco. "There was a lot of confusion at the airport," Melnik said. "It's possible that they missed somebody who got on board at the last second, or they might even have got a name or two wrong."

"But not the pilot's name," Werther said, spotting Melnik's point immediately. The manifest listed Terry Murchison as pilot and Pete Johnson as copilot.

"Do you have the outgoing crew list?" Werther asked.

"I just checked it," Melnik said. "Colonel Robert Lee Lindgren was the pilot when it left Andrews Air Force Base this morning."

Werther looked up at him. "So what happened?"

"It seems Lindgren got sick during the outgoing flight. Stomach poisoning. He was in a local hospital having his stomach pumped when the President was rushed back to the airport, so they brought in the pilot of the backup plane and took off without him."

"Food poisoning. It could be a coincidence."

"But I don't like coincidences," Melnik said. "They bother me."

"On the other hand," Werther said, "what would have been the point? Get rid of Lindgren so somebody else would fly Air Force One? We've already checked out every member of the crew and the backup airplane. There's nothing suspicious in any of their backgrounds, and no connection to Hardy."

"That's not what bothers me," Melnik said. "You talked to Lindgren on the radio, remember? I mean, you thought it was Lindgren. You commented on his Texan accent."

Werther's eyes snapped back down to the crew manifest in front of him. "Where is this guy Murchison from?" he asked.

"I checked on that, too," Melnik said. "He comes from Portland, Maine. I'm not familiar with American regional accents, but I imagine it's different there?"

As the last light faded from the face of the earth Hardy sat alone and unmoving in the cockpit of Air Force One, suspended between heaven and earth, floating alone with a plane full of unconscious bodies. With the land lost in darkness there was no sense of motion, no sense of time or reality, and nothing for him to do but relax. He had slowed the plane from its normal cruising speed of five hundred knots down to three hundred so that any more-than-casual inspection of the FAA radar picture would not pick up a blip without transponder traveling at jet speeds. At three hundred knots he'd look like any one of innumerable small multiengine prop planes cluttering the airways, or at least he wouldn't appear different enough to attract attention. In principle all these planes should have filed flight plans and be squawking their transponders to let the controllers know who and where they were, but Americans in general and pilots in particular are reluctant to submit to regulations, so the skies below jet altitudes remain free in practice, though regulated in theory.

Now Hardy had time to think, and as he did so a slow smile creased his lips. Taken all in all, it couldn't be going better. He looked around the cockpit; this would be a good time to clear the bodies out of his way. He lifted the copilot from where he lay slumped in his seat, carried him out of the flight deck, stepping over the supine body of the pilot who lay in the aisle, and dumped him in one of the first passenger seats, strapping him in with a seat belt. He would have to check all the passengers and make sure they were strapped in properly, particularly the President. It was going to be a rough landing, and there was no sense in having them hurt. Then he would have to tie them up with the rolls of heavy tape he had brought along in his valise. They were going to be on board this plane a long time, and he wanted them secure.

He returned to the flight deck to pick up Lindgren, and as he bent over him he took a closer look. People look different when they're unconscious. The facial muscles are slack, the skin droops a bit, the expression is changed. But as he looked down at this pilot he realized that he wasn't Lindgren. He hadn't noticed when he'd shoved him out of his seat and taken over the airplane; he'd had other things on his mind. Now he stared down at the unconscious body and thought about it. He had talked to people as Lindgren, using his accent; would anybody think about this now? Well, there wasn't anything to be done about it. Anyway, he was nearly finished talking over the radio. Air

Force One had already crashed for the first time, soon it would be time for the second, and then would come the final crash.

"So what are you thinking?" Werther asked.

"The same thing you're thinking," Melnik said. "Was that Hardy in Air Force One, faking an accent to fool us?"

"If it was," Werther answered, "the clever son of a bitch managed to get himself shot down and killed."

They looked at each other. "Curiouser and curiouser," Melnik said.

Lindgren fell twice trying to cross over the boulders. The first time he hit his face against a sharp rock, reopening the split in his forehead suffered when he crashed. The second time was worse; he caught his foot in a rock crevice as he fell, twisting his ankle. But finally he pulled himself up to the crumpled tail section. Even as he realized that the airplane was so smashed that no one could have lived—it must have come down straight into the mountainside, totally out of control—he was looking around for the fore part of the fuselage, where the President would have been.

He shone the flashlight beam into the darkness, searching among the broken trees and immovable boulders for the rest of Air Force One, but found not one piece large enough to hold a whole human body, dead or alive. The only part of the airplane that had survived sufficiently to be even recognized was the jutting tail structure. He held it now pinioned in the flashlight beam, staring at it, not understanding. The night was dark, but the beam was bright and he could see the tail clearly.

Something was wrong. He moved closer, stumbling over the uneven ground, tripping on rocks, stepping carefully with his injured ankle over the smaller boulders, feeling his way in between the larger ones, until he could almost touch the tail. There was no American flag painted on the tail, and the identification numbers were wrong.

He was exhausted from the crash, his physical exertions and the cold, numbed with hypothermia, and at first he couldn't believe what it meant. But slowly it sank in: this wasn't Air Force One.

He shone the beam around the scorched and broken ground. Certainly this was the airplane that had just crashed. He didn't understand, but he knew he had to get back to the wrecked Cub and radio in the news.

It had taken him an hour to come this far, and it had been all downhill. Now he had to go back up, and he didn't see how he could. His ankle had begun to swell, and when he put his weight on it he fell. He was exhausted and terribly cold. He wanted overwhelmingly to climb under the tail, find some protection from the fierce wind and go to sleep. Even knowing that it would mean he'd freeze to death, he wanted with all his heart to do it. It was only the realization that this was not Air Force One that pushed him forward on his knees up the terrible slope.

At twelve minutes past ten, Mountain time, he was still crawling up the side of the mountain, grateful that the wind had died down but wondering if he was on the right course, fearful that he might already have passed the broken Cub in the darkness. His mind was working on two different levels. One part was directing his progress, peering a few inches ahead of his scrabbling fingers to find a better hold and more level terrain. This part was working automatically, the directions going from his sensory cells directly to the muscles without involving conscious thought. The other part of his brain, the conscious part, was laboring to keep up, not quite managing it, struggling along a few seconds behind in real time. So by the time he realized that he was beginning to see spots in front of him, the skin of his face was already wet with them. He stopped for a second to understand. It was beginning to drizzle.

It was twelve minutes past midnight, Eastern time, and Alison was pulling into a motel parking lot on route 29 just north of Jerome. She didn't want to stop, but since nightfall she had been getting lost. The airfields Freddy and Gee had used were not exactly major ones, and there were no signs to them or double-laned access highways. They were nothing more than reasonably level grass fields hidden in the swamps, hard enough to find by daylight. She had found two this afternoon, both deserted. She would have to give up for the night, and in the morning continue to work her way east toward Miami.

She parked the car and found she was too tired to get out. She sat for a few moments resting, then forced her body out of the car and across the lot to the dimly lit office. A bell rang as she entered, and in a few moments a woman appeared behind the counter. Alison filled out the registration form and waited, shifting her weight from one foot to the other, while the woman laboriously read it. "Car license?" the woman asked. "You forgot to fill it in."

Alison hadn't forgotten, nor had she purposely been evasive. She didn't realize that throughout the state of Florida police and troopers were keeping an eye out for the car she had rented with the license plate AIP 585. She simply didn't know the damned license number, and she didn't want to walk back to the car to learn it. She hadn't thought the woman would notice. What did it matter anyway? It was just aggravating bureaucracy, even out here in the sticks. "One three seven eight nine," she answered, picking the numbers at random.

"Florida plate?"

Alison nodded. The woman wrote it down carefully, and gave her a room key.

There was a television set in the room, but Alison didn't turn it on. All day long in the car she hadn't played the radio. She was too concerned with her own problems to have the patience to listen. After a quick shower she lay down on the bed and was immediately asleep.

Hardy was back in the pilot's seat fifteen thousand feet over Texas, approaching the Gulf coast, with the radio switched on once again. It was time for the Phantom's final flourish, just in case anyone had begun to think about the 707 that had crossed Air Force One's path and was looking for him. He increased his airspeed to a more normal five hundred knots. "Hobby Tower," he called in, "this is Boeing 707 alpha seven six, VFR from Seattle. My transponder is out and the radio navicom doesn't seem to be working. I should be northwest of you at thirty miles, angels fifteen. Over."

A few seconds went by and then he heard, "Boeing alpha seven six, Hobby Tower. We do not have radar contact. Can you see Houston on your twelve o'clock?"

"Hobby Tower, alpha seven six. Negative on Houston. I don't see anything ahead of me."

"Alpha seven six, Hobby Tower. We're scanning our radar field of view."

Again a few minutes went by and then he heard, "Alpha seven six, Hobby Tower. I think we have you southwest of us. Turn left and then right. . . . Good, that is you. You are nearing the Gulf coast southwest of Houston. Turn right to three oh five at seven. . . ."

He didn't respond, didn't answer.

"Alpha seven six, this is Hobby Tower, do you read me? Over. . . ."

He let the message sink into the dark night.

"Alpha seven six, you are southwest of Houston and heading out over the Gulf. Vector three oh five and come down to seven—"

Again Hardy didn't respond. Ahead he saw the black line of the Gulf waters creeping beneath the nose, replacing the duller darkness of the land, and he throttled back the jet engines and pushed the wheel hard forward. The big Boeing tilted on its nose and headed down toward the black water, the steepness of the dive overpowering the loss of engine thrust so that the speed built up over five hundred knots, over six hundred. . . .

He held the dive while the altimeter unwound, until he could see the thin white crests of breaking waves ahead of him, until he had dived down below the altitude at which the watching radar could possibly see him, until his reflected echo would merge with the ground scatter and be lost in it. Then he eased back on the stick, pulling her out of the dive and skimming the tips of the wet blackness. He held her there, flitting over the waves at less than two hundred feet, and let the speed bleed off before he brought the throttles forward again to maintain five hundred knots.

In the control tower at Hobby Airport in Houston there was sudden panic as the radar blip disappeared from the screen.

Hardy held his course out over the Gulf, peering through the windscreen to hold his altitude steady, with only the dimly breaking waves as his guide. If he went too low, he would dip into them and crash for real; too high, and the Houston radar would pick him up.

"Alpha seven six, this is Hobby Tower. Do you read me?" the radio called out in the dark cockpit, the disembodied voice rising into concern. "Alpha seven six, over, please. . . ."

He could picture the scene in the tower, all the controllers gathering around the one screen, searching for the lost blip that would never appear again, listening to the call for a reply that would not come.

"Alpha seven six, this is Hobby Tower. Do you read me? Alpha
even six, come in, please . . ."

He held his course steady at one hundred and fifty feet over the Gulf
waters toward Florida.

Lori Werther lay steaming in a hot bath, lost in fantasy. She had come
nome after her aborted dinner with Charles, and now everything
dissolved in the hazy steam. She lay with eyelids half closed, and
through the shimmering waves of heat rising from the tub she saw in
the distance a vision made of white suds, rising layer on layer. The
soapsuds shifted as she wiggled her toes, and became vast dunes of sand
drifting in a hot wind; the heat of the hot water became the heat of the
sun as in her fantasy she moved forward over desert dunes, her skin
glistening with sweat, reveling in the heat, and over the distant dunes
in the shimmering waves of heat she saw reflected the golden rooftops
of Tel Aviv.

At 1:00 A.M., Eastern time, Mason and his men started the airboat and
Duck engine and carefully chugged up to each of the stakes they had
planted in the Everglades. The stakes had been laid out in two parallel
rows fifteen yards apart, and now Mason, Michael and Bill in the
airboat took the left-hand row. Coming up to each stake in turn, one
man leaned carefully over the side of the boat and switched on the
flashlight tightly taped to it. Each flashlight had been fitted with new
alkaline batteries. No expense is spared, Freddy thought with a smile;
we aim to satisfy. When they finished he looked back to see two long
parallel series of lights shining vertically upward into the dark night.

He pulled the airboat up to the center and front of the shining rows,
where the mailboxlike apparatus they had screwed onto the top of the
metal pipe stood. Reaching out, he turned it on; it glowed brightly in
the darkness, its glass face revealed now in three colors: red, amber and
green. It was a portable Visual Approach Slope Indicator; a pilot
coming in to land would see only the amber light if his approach was
too high, the red light if he was coming in too low, and the green light
if he was dead on.

The Duck and the airboat pulled off to the downwind end of the
lights and waited, swatting mosquitoes and cursing quietly.

\* \* \*

At twenty minutes past one o'clock in the morning, Eastern time, by the light of the moon above scattered clouds, Hardy sighted land. He had left the Texas coast an hour and ten minutes ago, heading out into the Gulf of Mexico. The dirty weather was behind him; over the Gulf the skies were clear and the moon bright, but as he approached the Florida coast he saw towering clouds building up over the shore, glistening in the reflected moonlight.

As he crossed the coast he flew into the lowering rain, skimming the tallest trees as he flew inland just south of Marco, Cape Romano and the Ten Thousand Islands, where the only eyes to see him were those of a few alligators and the Miccosukee Indians who hunt them. Here the Everglades stretch from coast to coast. He held the huge airplane to within a hundred feet of the ground and raced across the swamp at just over five hundred miles an hour.

Now he began to throttle back and lower his speed, maintaining altitude by trimming the nose high. The inertial guidance navigation system worked perfectly, and by the time his speed was down to two hundred knots he saw nearly in front of him the long series of parallel flashlight beams pointing up into the sky, and directly in front of them a solitary amber light. He throttled back just a bit and corrected his direction to port, saw the light change from amber to green to red, inched the throttles forward until it shone green again, and then he flew right down the beam, coming in over the first flashlights at just over stalling speed. He cut the engines completely and the 707 settled lower in the wet air, riding on the wind-ground effect for a few seconds, nose high and tail low. He held it in this attitude until the wings finally lost lift and the tail slipped down and clipped the murky waters.

As soon as it did the nose came splashing down hard. The underslung engines caught the water, and the effect was like running into a concrete wall. But he had tightened his straps to the point of hurt, and now they held him without injury as his head snapped forward to within inches of the instrument panel. In the next moment the plane stopped and began to settle; everything was quiet and dark, and in the silence he could hear the soft rattle of the rain on the metal roof.

\*   \*   \*

The Everglades is a great saw-grass morass fringed by broad cypress swamps and savanna, intermingled with saltwater intrusive meadows and mangrove thickets, extending from the southwestern side of Lake Okeechobee in the north to the southern tip of the Florida peninsula below. It is fifty miles wide and a hundred miles long, covering five thousand square miles, but its water is only a foot deep, and the mud another two feet, so that now the fuselage sat embedded in the ooze but resting firmly on the coral bottom.

Together with Michael and Bill, Mason spurted ahead in the airboat and bounced up against the partially buried beast. Hardy released the emergency-door hatches, and they pulled them open. The murky water flowed in over the bottom, but was nowhere deep enough to threaten a flood.

Meanwhile Mario and Teddy brought the Duck alongside, lifted the previously prepared mangrove tree on the hoisting rig, lumbered it up against the high tail of the 707 and fastened it there with steel cables, so that when dawn came nothing but the tree would be seen. Hardy, Michael and Bill were busy covering the exposed top of the fuselage with a steel mat threaded through with grass, and soon the 707 was nearly completely hidden.

Finally Mason's men looked at Hardy, who nodded his approval. They boarded the airboat and sped away without a word, free now to find their women and beer; their job was done.

Sitting with Mason on the open deck of the Duck, the wet soft rain plastering his black hair and dripping unnoticed down the neck of his shirt, Hardy waited till the sound of their airboat faded. Then Freddy backed the lumbering Duck up to the doorway of the 707 and he went back into the plane. He walked down the aisle to the President's compartment, finding the unconscious Bush where he had left him, and stood for a moment looking at him, thinking about his dead son.

From the moment they had begun this operation, from the first moment he had listened to the Libyans and had begun to think about it, he had imagined this final moment of triumph when he would look down at a helpless President of the United States. He had even rehearsed a speech: "Welcome to the real world, Mr. President. How do you like it?" He waited for the reward of a triumphant feeling of vengeance, but nothing came. Finally he simply picked him up, slung him over his back and carried him out. Mason was holding the Duck steady against the fuselage, and he stepped onto it.

"Everybody tied up good and proper?" Freddy asked.

"A-OK. It will take them a couple of days to get loose."

"You put the radio out of commission?"

Hardy smiled. Freddy was in his little-old-mother mood. "I took care of it."

"Let's go, then."

They pulled a few feet away, then stopped and looked back. Hardy wiped the rain out of his eyes and took in the scene. It looked good. Mason gunned the engine and the Duck waddled away across the saw-grassed water, its wake quickly dispersing among the mangrove thickets. For a moment the clouds splintered and were blown away, leaving a clear sky and a bright moon illuminating the Everglades. There was nothing to be seen but swamps, grass, murky water and mangrove trees. Then the clouds closed and the rain came softly down again.

# VIII

# Excelsior

he drizzle had turned to rain, which had begun to freeze in the cold ountain winds. The flashlight was gone. Trying to save the batteries, indgren had used it sparingly, shining it ahead to light a path and en pushing on in the darkness until he came up against a dark bstruction, then shining it again to find his way around it. Somewhere had fallen from his frozen fingers unnoticed. When he tried to shine again, and realized after several moments of staring into the darkness at it was not in his hand, he had started to turn around to search for , but then realized he could never find it without the light it gave. 'ith an enormous effort of will he turned ahead again and continued p the slope, stumbling, crawling, pulling himself along, searching for e Cub, which lay crumpled on its side somewhere above, useless as 1 airplane now but invaluable for its radio.

As he pulled himself onward his body temperature began to drop, is metabolism no longer able to combat the onslaught of wind and old, and with it his consciousness began also to droop. He went on earching, not realizing that without the flashlight he couldn't find the ub unless he bumped up against it. He didn't realize anything; he ung only to the notion that he must keep crawling forward. . . .

Now he lay unmoving, freezing in the blowing wind, his blood ongealing in his veins while he dreamed of a land far away.

Suddenly a glaring light shone on his eyes and burned its way through the brain inside. The dream lit up first; the flowering fields seemed be dazzled by an atomic blast, and then his eyelids cracked open espite the icy drops of water lying on them as heavily as boulders. It was ae moon. The clouds had fled, and now its pale light seemed as bright s fire, where before there had been only the darkness.

He recognized the moon, but didn't know where he was. The wind as blowing, and he reached up his hand to close the window. He ouldn't find it, couldn't stop the wind. The moon seemed as bright as

a flame in the sky, piercing his eyes. . . . Without thought he foun
he was awake, and pulled himself to his knees to force himself up th
slope again, scrabbling like a broken crab slowly and painfully up th
side of the mountain.

A hundred yards below him and off to the right the Cub lay on i
side, half hidden in the rain and the black night.

Mason sipped champagne in the dark glow of an oil lamp burnin
from the roofed patio in front of the shack near the hangar, an
watched Hardy pacing along the grass airstrip from which their DC-
would take off. He strode along, impatiently watching his heels sin
into the soft grass at each step. It was no good, he reported when h
came back. Mason nodded agreement. If they tried to take off now, th
wheels would sink into the muddy grass and they'd be stuck for goo
"Lucky they crashed in the mountains," Freddy said. "It will take a da
or two to get to them, so nobody will be looking for us till then."

Hardy nodded. He was lucky because he made his own luck; it wa
paying attention to details that counted.

"They'll be waking up in Air Force One pretty soon," Mason sai
"They're secure. Don't worry."

"Even with the radio broken, they can signal pretty easily. The
could haul some of the seats on top of the fuselage, start a fire, and—

"I said don't worry. We'll be long gone before anyone gets loose i
there." He lifted his face to the sky and felt the soft small raindrop
"Might as well get some sleep," he said. "It's been a long day."

It's been one hell of a day, Werther thought. One real bitch of a day
He sat sprawled in his chair behind his desk, staring at the wall an
seeing Air Force One splattered on a mountainside, with charred an
broken bodies scattered like beans from a dropped bag of groceries. Th
vision sickened him.

The thought of Melnik and Lori made him sicker. He squeezed h
eyes shut for a moment, trying to banish them from his thought
When he opened his eyes again, he saw his desk cluttered with piles o
paper, notes and memos, charts and diagrams, all related to th
President's assassination. Staring at the mess of papers, he realized h
had not one single idea of what to do with any of them.

It was time to call it a day. There was nothing else to do. The President s dead and Hardy was gone. The dragnet was in motion, but Werther sn't optimistic. If Hardy remained active, eventually they'd pick him ; the word would be out that the FBI wanted him badly, and the FBI s known to pay well, so sooner or later they'd be tipped and he'd be ped. But if he went underground, left the country or stayed quietly led up somewhere, they'd never find him. He must have cleared a ndle with this hit. He'd have known there'd be so much heat he'd have retire; he would have demanded and certainly commanded a fee big ough to live on for the rest of his life. There were countries in this cked world proud and honored to shield a fugitive from American tice. Getting there would be difficult but not impossible; all he had do was wait. They couldn't maintain their present effort of looking at ry passenger out of San Francisco for long.

No, Werther decided at the miserable end of this long, terrible day, y'd never find him. He would certainly have organized a hole in ich to wait them out, a well-stocked hiding place with plenty of d, drink, feminine company, videotapes, compact discs and books, d someday next year he'd slip out of the country and never be heard m again—or at least not for several years, when some American blisher would pay him a million dollars for his memoirs.

He pushed his chair back from the desk and stood up. His knees hed. He tried to remember how long he had been sitting there. He etched, then slipped into his jacket, patting his shoulder holster tomatically to be sure his gun was still there, and walked out the door. He found Melnik leaning against the coffee machine, sipping rancid ffee out of a plastic cup. "There's nothing else for us to do here ight," Werther said. "Let's you and me go home. It's time we talked."

They could have gone to Melnik's hotel room, but it was 2:00 A.M., ri would be asleep, and Werther wanted to be on his own turf. He ught about this as they walked up Christopher Street in the quiet ght air, immediately pushed the thought away, then allowed it to ft back almost into focus. Not quite. He didn't want to see the ught; he didn't want to be made to realize why he wanted to talk at me. Unconsciously his hand reached up and patted his left ulder, touching the holster again. He would probably shoot Melnik ight. He didn't quite think about it. He kept it dangling out of

focus, but he kept it. Without consciously thinking about it, he kne
he would probably shoot the son of a bitch, so it would be better to
at home, where he could relax and wait for the police without a bun
of strangers banging on a hotel door, screaming and shouting. H
didn't want any more noise. It had been a long, hard day.

He didn't mind Melnik sleeping with Lori, he told himself, an
immediately began to grow hot. He could feel the sudden flush of he
at the base of his neck, the itchy tingling in his fingers, and he slapp
them together as they walked in silence. He didn't mind that, h
insisted to himself; what bothered him was the fact that the son of
bitch wanted to take her away from him.

What bothered him even more was the fact that she wanted to g
No, be honest. What was eating him up was simply the fact that sh
had slept with . . . But had she? He didn't really know, did he? H
knew only what Melnik had said. He had to talk to Lori. No, he didn
want to talk to her. He pushed the thought out of his head. This w
between Melnik and him, no one else. Lori was *his*, and this son of
bitch was trying to take her away from him.

Part of his mind was listening and couldn't believe what it w
hearing. Lori was *his*? As if she were a bag of groceries, a wristwatc
a fancy car? She didn't have a mind of her own? *All right*, he thoug
*Maybe I'll kill her too.*

Lindgren was still climbing, beyond exhaustion, beyond cold, beyon
conscious thought. He was an animal, a bird flying south, a be
searching for a hole, an elephant looking for a place to die. His han
reached forward for something to cling to, scrabbled around until th
found it, and then the fingers tightened in a prehensile grasp, his to
dug into the ground and he pulled himself another few inches forwar
The rain was intermittent now, the moon sneaking out and illum
nating the landscape, but it made no difference to him. His eyes wer
open but they focused only on the ground a few inches below his fac
Then the ground gave way beneath him; as he stumbled forward th
wet boulder he was leaning on fell away into a crevice, tumbling an
bouncing, and only his reflexes kept him from falling with it. As h
hands slipped he fell backward instead of forward, down the mounta
slope, helplessly tumbling head over feet. Powerless to stop his fall, h

e in to it, bouncing and sliding till he finally jolted to a halt against
ingiving tree. As he caught his breath, in majestic slow motion the
on came out again, and by its light he saw fifty yards in front of him
dark shape of the smashed Piper Cub. Too tired to be grateful, too
nbed to think, he crawled toward it and its radio.

·y sat in the kitchen, illuminated only by the hall light streaming
Werther didn't want to wake Lori, and somehow he thought it
ıld be quieter without lights.

Ie kept his jacket on to hide the shoulder holster. Melnik didn't
w the reason, of course; he was uncomfortably warm, but taking his
from Werther he decided the occasion demanded a certain
nality, so he kept his jacket on too.

hey sat at the kitchen table. "Coffee?" Werther asked.

Melnik had been drinking coffee all night and was sick of the taste.
shook his head. "No, thanks."

Werther went to the refrigerator, took out two bottles of beer,
ned them and put one down on the table in front of Melnik, who
itely took a sip. He wondered whether Americans realized how bad
ır beer was; did they drink it as a sort of national penitence in some
gotten streak of Puritanism? But what was he doing sitting here
iking about beer at a time like this? He had just told this man that
was in love with his wife. Werther must know what this meant,
st know that they had been sleeping together. He squeezed his eyes
itly, trying to concentrate. What had got into him? What had made
ı say that? *I want Lori. I want to marry your wife.* Did he want to
rry Lori? He was no longer sure.

"Thank you," he said, lifting the bottle to Werther in a small toast,
l took another sip. He had never intended to say anything to
rther. He must be crazy. He didn't know what he wanted. He
hed he could go to sleep and wake up in Tel Aviv.

"You want to marry Lori?" Werther asked.

"Yes." There, he had done it again! He *was* crazy. But with that
ught a great exultation came over him. He *would* marry Lori.
:ause she was crazy too. He would take her away to Israel and—
Take Lori to Israel? His exultation vanished. He hadn't thought
:ad. *I love her,* he thought, *and she loves me.* Surely this was all that

mattered. But as he thought it, he realized it *wasn't* all that matter
and he wasn't sure of anything anymore.

Werther's right hand strayed upward across his body, and his fing
tapped the gun under his armpit. It was comforting to know it w
there, and that in a few minutes he would shoot this son of a bit

Suddenly there was a blaze of light, blinding them momentari
Werther's hand flew instinctively to his holster, then stopped. Standi
in the doorway, her hand on the switch, was Lori, wearing pajamas a
a sleepy look. "Why are you sitting in the dark?" she asked. She look
from one to the other; as they stared back at her, slowly through h
sleep-shattered mind she began to realize that something was wror

He couldn't move the switch. His fingers were frozen and he could
feel what they were touching.

The moon was playing with the clouds, flickering on and off as
swerved in and out behind them, and by its intermittent light he h
found the radio in the crumpled cockpit. It would still be working,
thought; even when a Cub crashes, it crashes gently. He hadn't be
seriously hurt, so surely the radio was still working. It was just that
couldn't feel the switch and turn it on.

He put his fingers in his mouth. At first they didn't feel any warm
then slowly they began to tingle, then to burn, then simply to hurt.
he licked and sucked them they hurt more and more, and then he to
them out and before they could freeze again against the cold metal
flipped the switch on. As a reassuring buzz of static flowed through t
earphones he nearly cried.

"Charley Control, this is Lindgren at the crash site. Over."
Silence.
Oh, God. It *is* working, isn't it?
"Charley Control, this is Lindgren at the crash site. Come i
please. . . ."

"I understand congratulations are in order," Werther said.
"What?" Lori asked.
"Melnik tells me you two want to get married."

"Charley Control, this is Lindgren at the crash site. Over. . . . Con
in, please, Charley Control—"

.indgren, Charley Control." The sudden voice was deafening in
silent night, battering his ears. "Over."

Charley Control, this is Lindgren. I am on the ground with an
.erative aircraft. I have located the wreck."

.indgren, Charley Control. Confirm that you have located the
:k."

That is affirmative."

What is the condition? Are there survivors?"

Negative on survivors. But—"

Confirm, please. Negative on survivors?"

Right! No goddamn survivors! Will you listen to me? This is not
Force One down here!"

   long silence. Then, "Lindgren, Charley Control. Confirm,
se? It is *not* Air Force One. . . ?"


   legs felt weak. When she took a step toward them her knees
kled and she nearly fell down. As they both jumped toward her she
ght their outstretched hands and regained her balance. She pulled
a chair, sat down and looked up at their faces. This was the most
rible moment of her life.

Charles said something, and she answered. She didn't know what he
, so how could she know what she answered?

he turned to David, who looked at her. Something seemed to have
pened to time. She knew she had to say something to each of them,
she didn't know what.

he phone rang. No one answered it. They looked at each other. It
 nearly 3:00 A.M.

Do you want to marry him?" Charles asked. "Do you?"

David answered the phone.

he put her hands over her ears and shut her eyes. There were
ses, scurrying sounds, muffled shouts, but she kept her eyes
inched tightly shut and her hands pressed over her ears.

Then it was quiet. She took her hands away from her ears and
ned her eyes. They were gone. She was alone. She thought that
haps she had imagined it all, but there on the kitchen table stood
 open bottles of beer.

## 78

The operations room that Werther had set up at the FBI's Manha[t]
headquarters was a jumbled confusion of voices and bodies. "All ri[g]
everybody," he called out, skimming his hat at the rack in the cor[
and clapping his hands for attention. He waited a moment for the[m]
calm down and give him their attention. "Okay now," he beg[
"Does anybody here know what's going on?"

"Colonel Robert Lindgren is the pilot of Air Force One," b[e]
Barry Morton, the senior agent Werther had left in charge overni[g]

"I know who Lindgren is," Werther snapped.

Morton paused. "I don't know exactly what you do know and d[
know," he said, "and since—"

"Right," Werther said. "I'm sorry. Start wherever you feel
beginning is, only give it to me short and quick."

"Okay. Lindgren is the Air Force One pilot, but he got sick on
outbound flight and missed the takeoff from San Francisco. He was
the backup plane, which was diverted to Denver when the Presid[
was shot down. He tried to join the rescue operation there, but was t[
to get lost. Evidently he's a gung ho type, and it isn't entirely clear, [
from what I gather he went off to a private airfield nearby, rente[
small airplane and flew into the mountains to look for the crash.[

"Isn't the rescue party on the scene?" Werther asked.

"Negative. The weather's too bad to bring the choppers in y[
They're waiting for morning. In the meantime they've got a c[
climbing in on foot."

"But Lindgren went in?"

"He went in, but he didn't come out. He crashed somewhere in [
vicinity and they lost contact with him. Then, half an hour ago,
radioed in and said he'd crashed but was all right, that he'd located [
wreck and that it was *not* Air Force One." Morton shrugged. "I cal[
you as soon as we heard."

Werther stared at him, then shook his head in bewilderment. "[
does anybody understand what's going on? If the wreck isn't Air Fo[r]
One, what in God's name is it?"

"He says it's a 707 and is smashed to pieces."

"How can he tell it's not Air Force One if it's all smashed to pieces?"

"Every airplane has individual identification numbers," Melnik said from the corner. "Also, Air Force One must have had some kind of special insignia on it. It wouldn't take much for a pilot to—"

"All right," Werther said. "So what happened?" He looked around the room. "Air Force One takes off from San Francisco airport and crashes an hour later, only now it's not Air Force One anymore. Is that possible?" Several people opened their mouths at once and he quickly raised his hands in protest. "Don't tell me!" he said. "It happened. Okay, I know it happened. What I'm asking is, is it *possible*? If so, *how* is it possible?"

This time no one wanted to answer. Then Morton said, "I called the FAA as soon as I talked to you, and they sent over this gentleman here—"

A shortish young man with dark frizzled hair around a balding head stood up and extended his hand. "Tom Besvink," he said. "Pleased to meet you. They thought I could tell you exactly what happened from our point of—"

"Let me do that," Melnik said, pushing his way forward from the corner near the door.

"What do you know about it?" Werther asked.

"I'm a pilot, remember? I can look at it from his point of view and also from ours." He turned to Besvink. "Tell me if I go wrong," he said, then turned back to Werther. "Air Force One would have called the San Francisco tower for emergency clearance. Under the circumstances there would be no delay. By the time they were airborne they would have been assigned a jet route straight back to Washington. Is that correct?" he asked Besvink.

He nodded. "J-32 up to Reno, then J-94 all the way in."

"Thank you," Melnik said. "As soon as they were in the air they'd be picked up on radar, and this would have followed them all the way. They'd be squawking their transponder—"

"What's that?" Werther asked.

"It's an instrument that responds to a radar beam," Melnik explained. "Normally an airplane hit with radar sends back an echo. If they have a transponder, it's triggered by the radar beam to send out its own signal in synchronization with the echo, identifying the airplane according to a prearranged code and also giving the altitude, which is difficult for the radar operators to determine from the echo alone. Therefore when the FAA looks at their screens, they don't see just a blip heading from Frisco to—"

"It shows up on the screen with a little box attached, labeling it Air Force One and giving its altitude," Besvink explained.

Werther nodded. "Okay. Go on."

"So the FAA radar controllers would have seen Air Force One take off from San Francisco. There wouldn't have been anyone else taking off at that time because the tower would have closed the airfield completely, and they'd follow it all the way from takeoff nearly to Denver—"

"When suddenly it's shot down," Werther interrupted. "Did they see that too?"

Besvink nodded violently. "They saw the jet fighter appear suddenly on the—"

"How could that happen?" Werther demanded. "How could he appear suddenly? Where the hell did he come from?"

"He must have been down low with his transponder shut off," Besvink said. "Below radar coverage. Then he zoomed up to altitude and turned on his transponder at the same time. The effect would be that he'd show up on the screen suddenly, a new blip with an unidentified transponder. He came right up behind Air Force One's tail and shot it out of the sky. They could even see the missile on the radar scope."

"But when Air Force One crashes, it's no longer Air Force One," Werther complained. "Is that what you're telling me?"

"That's what Colonel Lindgren is telling us," Besvink said. "I don't see how we can disbelieve him; he's right there on the site."

"Right," Werther said. "So this airplane takes off as Air Force One and crashes as another airplane. I want to know how it happened." He looked around the room. No one had an answer. He put his head in his hands. "Do we know anything else?" he asked. "Anything at all?"

"He would have been in radio contact with the tower as he took off," Melnik said, "and from there as he passed in and out of FAA control center areas he would check in and out by radio with each of them."

"Is that right?" Werther asked Besvink.

Besvink nodded.

"Okay. So he takes off in full view of everyone around, and from the moment he's in the air he's under full radar surveillance and in continuous radio contact."

"Not exactly," Melnik said. "Not continuous radio contact. He wouldn't be on the radio continually; he'd just check in and out as he passed into and out of every control center's area. But the radar surveillance would be continuous."

"In effect he disappears right in front of our eyes."

Melnik nodded. "He changes to somebody else. Same thing."

"Great. Just great." Werther rubbed his eyes, then opened them and looked at Melnik. "When I was a little kid," he said, "I used to believe in magic. Blackstone, Houdini, Merlin, whoever. I really believed in it." He paused again. "I don't anymore. There's a whole lot of pretty things I used to believe in that I don't anymore, and magic is one of them." He looked around the room. "What else do we know? There has to be something."

"One more thing," Melnik said. "You talked to him too. Remember?"

"Yes," Werther said slowly. "And something seemed wrong."

"Right. He was talking with a Texas accent—"

"Because that's how Lindgren would have been speaking. Only it wasn't Lindgren." He turned to Besvink. "Get me the names of the 'risco tower operators and all the FAA personnel who talked to Air Force One on its flight. No, wait a minute; better yet, get them on the phone yourself. Talk to them right away. I don't care what time it is wherever they are. Find out from each of them if the pilot spoke with a Texas accent."

Besvink got up and left the room. Werther sat quietly on his desk, waiting for someone to speak, but no one had any suggestions. "Somehow," he said, looking around, "somebody switched airplanes on us."

"Which means the President isn't dead," someone said hopefully.

Werther nodded slowly. "Which means they've got the President," he said, "which is worse."

When the meeting broke up at 4:00 A.M. and the agents had disappeared down the hallways, Charles Weston hung back. He walked halfway down the hall toward his little cubicle, then stopped, turned and walked back. But at the last minute, as he approached Werther's door, he changed his mind and kept walking. Then once again he stopped.

Weston was a young man who had just completed his first year with the Bureau. He had graduated near the bottom of his law school class, but he was a lawyer, and on graduation he had felt, along with his parents, that he would settle down into corporate or tax or insurance law and quietly make a bundle. Instead, to the consternation of his parents, he had joined the Federal Bureau of Investigation because he wanted adventure. As a kid he had actually wanted to join the police instead of going to college. Then after graduating with his bachelor's he had thought of joining the army; again he hadn't. But last year he had finally burst the bonds; he had taken the FBI entrance examination without telling his parents, and when he was accepted he had stepped with one bound into a world of mystery, intrigue and adventure.

Or so he had thought as he lay awake all that night. Instead he found that one bound does not change a life. He was still the same person he'd always been, and the Bureau was an organization different from what he'd expected. He found himself doing the same sort of paperwork he would have done as a newly entered worker in a large law firm; he just did it for less pay.

At the meeting he had almost spoken out, but Mr. Werther was in such a tense mood that he'd decided to wait until the meeting was over and then have a quiet word with him. When the meeting did finally break up, he shuffled around quietly, putting his papers in order, waiting for everyone to leave. But one person, the Israeli, hadn't left. Finally, to avoid being conspicuous, he picked up his papers and walked out with the last of the other agents. Anyway, Mr. Werther probably knew already. It was presumptuous to imagine that he didn't read all the reports forwarded to his desk.

But there were so *many* reports. Could any one man keep track of them all? He stopped. Surely it was the duty of subordinates to keep superiors informed. . . . No, he'd just be making a nuisance of himself. Again he began to walk away. A man could ruin his career in the FBI by getting a reputation for bothering his superiors unnecessarily. Unnecessarily? There was the rub, wasn't it? He had to make a decision whether it was necessary or not. He couldn't ignore it; it was his moment of truth.

He spun around on his heel, walked back to Mr. Werther's door, knocked sharply and went in. "It's the Calle Alpha group in Miami," he blurted out.

Werther looked at him quizzically, and Weston realized that the name was not familiar to him. "I'd better start at the beginning," he said.

"Yes," Werther said. "Do that, please." He glanced at his watch. He had the feeling that he was wasting time, but he couldn't think of anything else to do. A couple of hours ago he had been thinking of shooting Melnik. He laughed.

Weston flushed and swallowed. He knew he shouldn't have come in. He could still leave, could turn and . . . No, he couldn't, not unless he wanted to keep walking right out of the FBI. Anyhow, what did he care if Mr. Werther laughed at him? He had something to say and he would say it. "Remember you set up with the Director in Washington a group to collect reports on everything related to presidential assassinations or attacks?"

Werther stared at the young man, trying to concentrate on his words. He was not an easy person to understand. Maybe he was nervous. Werther tried to be gentle. "Yes," he said. "I remember." *Get on with it*, he thought.

"Well, I was assigned as the New York coordinator for the project. I collect the data as they come in from Washington, collate and coordinate them, and . . . Well, there's this Calle Alpha group in Miami. Cubans."

"Our Cubans or their Cubans?"

"Oh, *ours*," Weston said. "That is, not Castro's. Very anti-Communist. They want to take Cuba back, you know."

"Yes, Weston, I understand."

"Well, we have an agent in their group. Several of them, actually. Anyhow, we have a report from one of them that one of the Alpha members, a woman named Gloria Carollo, was hired by somebody to be part of a crew of a Boeing 707 to provide sanctuary for the President in case he was ever attacked. I figured it was just the usual craziness these Cubans get up to, but I thought that since . . . Well, they *are* 707s we're talking about, and—"

"*What* are 707s we're talking about?"

"Air Force One. The President's plane that's disappeared, and the plane Colonel Lindgren found, the one that was shot down."

Werther turned to Melnik. "Is Air Force One a 707?"

"Yes." Melnik thought everybody knew that.

"She's been up in Seattle, practicing with the crew," Weston said. "And I thought that somehow—I don't know how—it's probably nothing, but—"

"Do you have the details of the Cuban 707? Identification number, company name or anything like that?"

"Yes, sir," Weston said, digging down into his briefcase.

"Get hold of that guy from the FAA," Werther said to Melnik. "Find out where this plane is located, where it's stationed or registered or whatever, and where it is right now. I mean right this *minute*! Also where it was all day today." He glanced out at the dawn beyond the window. "I mean yesterday."

"It's down."

"What?"

"Down. Crashed. Gone."

"Where? How?"

"Into the Gulf. No one knows how. They haven't found it yet."

"*They haven't found it?*"

Melnik nodded. "There's more."

"More? *More?*"

"Let's go back to your office."

He had found Werther by the coffee machine on the second floor. They climbed the stairs, both of them tired but too excited to wait for the elevator, went into Werther's office and closed the door behind them. Werther sat down at his desk, Melnik in front of it. "Now," Werther said. He knew from Melnik's manner as well as his words that he had something. "What happened?"

"I don't quite know yet, but I think we've got a slant on it. The 707 Gloria Carollo is crewing on, FAA number alpha seven six ought niner delta, is registered to a Mr. Xavier Guarez of Miami, though it's based in Seattle. Mr. Guarez has been a member of several anti-Castro groups in Miami. He has had alpha seven six for nearly six months and has set up a charter carrier company, but I couldn't find any record of any business he's ever done."

Melnik paused, gathering his thoughts. "Alpha seven six took off from

eattle this morning without filing a flight plan. Neither the Seattle
wer nor the local FAA control center has heard from them again."

Werther was confused. "That doesn't mean they've—"

"No one in Seattle has heard from them, but at twelve minutes past
idnight the control tower at Hobby airport in Houston got a Mayday
om them. The pilot was lost; some instruments were malfunctioning.
obby picked them up on radar going out over the Gulf, and a
oment later alpha seven six crashed. The Coast Guard has been
arching for them, but has found no trace."

"But—"

"Yes, of course. *But.*" Melnik smiled. "I don't think it crashed, and
don't think it was the same airplane that took off from Seattle."

Werther opened his desk drawer, took out a crumpled pack of
garettes nearly four months old, picked out one cigarette and held it
p in front of Melnik's face. "Do you see this?" he asked. "Do you
now what I'm going to do with it? I'm going to shove it right up your
ss if you don't stop screwing around and tell me what's happening."

Melnik smiled and leaned forward. "I'll tell you what I *think* is
appening. No, first I'll tell you what I *know.* I know that alpha seven
x was crewed by three Cubans, and that it left Seattle yesterday
orning and disappeared past Houston last night. What intrigues me
 that somewhere in between it had to cross the path taken by Air
orce One on its way from San Francisco to Washington."

"But—"

"I know more than that," Melnik went on. "I sat down with Besvink
nd talked by phone to everyone who had contact with Air Force One
n its flight. They *saw* it cross."

"What do you mean?"

Melnik hesitated. He got up and walked around the room. "Ac-
ually, to be absolutely honest," he said, "I'm not quite sure what I
nean. Again we're getting into what I *think* . . ."—he gestured with
is fingers, wiggling them around in front of him—"what I'm grasping
t. The Sacramento controllers saw on radar an airplane crossing Air
orce One's path. They warned the pilot, who said he saw it and that
t was thousands of feet below him. The paths crossed, and both
irplanes continued on their way."

Again he paused. "So?" Werther prompted.

"So that crossing airplane could have been alpha seven six."

"So? They never even came close, you said. They were thousand of feet apart."

"No," Melnik said. "I didn't say that. The FAA controller a Sacramento says that the pilot of Air Force One said that, and—"

Werther began to understand. Not really, but he felt something wriggling underfoot. "And," he said, not quite formulating the thought until the words spilled out, "*somebody phony was flying Ai Force One.*"

"Exactly."

"Hardy!"

"Or somebody working for him."

"Son of a bitch!"

"Right. He *said* the other plane was thousands of feet below him but—"

"But what?" Werther's sudden elation disappeared. "So what if i wasn't? I still don't get it."

"I'm not sure," Melnik said. "But the FAA would have seen the tw blips come together and merge on the screen. Normally it would loo like a collision, but they weren't worried because they were in radi contact with Air Force One and its pilot said the other plane wasn't close But"—he groped in the air, trying to work it out—"if it was all planned and if Air Force One turned off his transponder and the Cubans turne theirs on and they both changed courses at the same time, they coul have switched! Right then, in front of everybody's eyes!"

*That was it*, Melnik thought as the words spilled out. He was sur of it now.

Werther still didn't understand exactly, but he caught the gist. " was the Cubans that were shot down?"

"Right."

"And Air Force One continued on to Houston and crashed? No That's another fake, right?"

"Of course. That one's easy. All he had to do was call in with a fak distress signal, then push the nose down and dive right off the rada screen."

"Oh, shit," Werther said. "Then he's free and clear. He flies awa with Air Force One and the goddamn President. . . . A map. Let' find a goddamn map!"

In the second-floor conference room they found a wall-size map of oth American continents.

"They came across here," Melnik said, pointing with his finger and ndicating a track roughly from Denver to the Gulf coast southwest of Houston. "He must have headed south over the Gulf, down under adar."

"He could have gone anywhere," Werther said. "Cuba, South America or anywhere in the goddamn world!" He held up his arms. "Let's calm down a minute," he said. "Let's think."

They sat down at the long conference table. "First of all," Werther aid, "let's assume you're right. Hardy switched planes right under our oses and made off with the President. We'll work out exactly how fter it's all over. So Operation Dallas is kidnapping the President, not illing him. That makes more sense."

Melnik nodded.

"Okay, who's paying for this? Qaddafi, right? So they have to deliver im to Libya. Could they just fly Air Force One to Libya?"

"No," Melnik said. "They wouldn't have the fuel."

"That's what I thought. So how far *could* they go?"

They turned around and studied the map. "I'll have to check with our Air Force," Melnik said, "but after taking off from San Francisco, lying up to Denver and then crossing the coast just under Houston, I lon't see them going any further than either Mexico or Cuba."

"It couldn't be Mexico," Werther said, "because where would they and? You can't put a big jetliner down in a cow pasture, can you? All he airports there large enough to land a plane that big are under supervision, aren't they?"

"I should think so. We'll check, of course, but Mexico doesn't make sense from their flying pattern, either," Melnik said, pointing to the map. "If they were headed there, they'd have flown due south from the switch point and crossed the border somewhere between Nogales and El Paso. It has to be Cuba."

Werther smiled. "We have routine satellite coverage of Cuba. If a 707 landed anywhere on that godforsaken island tonight, it's in our satellite file right now." He stopped. "Which Hardy must know," he went on slowly. "So he wouldn't have gone there."

Melnik nodded. "He seems to have known quite a lot," he admitted. "And Castro must know it, too."

"About our satellite surveillance? Sure, he does. So he wouldn't let them land if they asked, would he? So Hardy's somewhere else, isn't he?"

They looked at each other, then simultaneously turned back to the map. It was obvious: there was Florida, extending from the bottom of the country as if gesturing to them. Of course. It was the only place that made sense. Land somewhere in Florida, transfer the President to another plane or a boat, and then leave at leisure while everyone thinks Bush is lying splattered all over the Rockies. Somewhere in Florida, but where?

It hit them both at the same time.

"Son of a bitch," Werther said.

"Alison," Melnik said.

Werther nodded his head. "Freddy's kid sister. On her way to Miami or Tampa or. . . ." He spoke softly, asking the question for both of them. "Where the hell is Alison Mason?"

## 79

She was waking up in the motel on route 29 just north of Jerome, Florida. She had purposely left the window curtains open; the first light of day streamed in as hot and bright as a blinding searchlight, and she awoke in confusion. She'd had a succession of dreams all night long, each seeming to make sense, but each totally different, belonging to different universes. As she came awake their collective memory distorted the world so that she didn't know who she was, let alone where she was, and then as she tried to focus on them they rushed away and left her awake, bewildered and alone in a strange motel bed.

Then she remembered, and quickly dressed. As she checked out she saw that the motel served free coffee in the lobby, and thankfully took a cup. She wouldn't have time for breakfast. She had to get on the road again.

It had to be Florida, Werther thought, and Melnik agreed. Why else would Alison have hurried down there? Hardy and her brother and the resident must be somewhere between Tampa and Miami, or in that eneral area. Now, if they could only find her . . .

They could be wrong, of course. Hardy could have landed in Cuba, nd to check this possibility the NSA was already scanning all satellite ecords of the pertinent time interval. Or he could have doubled back Mexico, but where could he land there unseen? Giant 707 jet irliners don't wander into airports unannounced and unobserved, and plane as huge as a 707 needs a large commercial airport's long and inforced runway to land on. But this argument applied to Florida as ell. So where was the son of a bitch?

Werther suggested he might have crash-landed the plane anywhere. Melnik shook his head. "You can't put a 707 down like a Piper Cub. 's not built for it. It would almost certainly catch fire and explode. utting it down without wheels on an unpaved runway is dangerous; nywhere else would be suicide."

"Then where—?" Werther began, and stopped in midsentence. He alked over to the wall map of Florida and pointed. "The Everglades," e said. "Thousands of square miles of swamp. It wouldn't catch fire he put it down there."

"It wouldn't be easy."

"But possible?"

Melnik considered, then nodded slowly. "Possible," he conceded.

"We have to go with it," Werther decided. "Florida makes the only ense from Hardy's viewpoint too. Look, the shooting down of the econd 707, the Cubans' plane, was necessary only to convince us that e knew where Air Force One was. It crashed in the Rocky Mountains, and so there was no point searching for it anywhere lse."

This would give Hardy time, he went on, time that would not be ecessary if he'd already flown the President out of the country. But me that *would* be necessary if he'd landed Air Force One somewhere Florida and was planning to transfer his captive to a less ostentatious node of transportation: a small plane or boat to take him to any one f America's enemies in Central or South America, from where he ould easily be flown to Libya.

As a result of a lengthy phone conversation with the Director in Vashington, a news blackout on the identity of the crashed 707 was

imposed. There would be no hint that anyone suspected the Presiden
had not been shot down and killed in Colorado.

As the sun rose in a clear autumnal sky Werther and Melnik wer
in a fast Air Force jet on their way to Homestead Air Force base ju
south of Miami.

Aboard Air Force One the crew and passengers awoke to fin
themselves strapped into their seats, bound and gagged, unable t
move. Their feet were wet, they noticed. The floor of the airplane wa
awash with water, and the air reeked with a musty, tropical smell, bu
the airplane was not sinking, was not even moving. Neither were the
They moved their heads around and saw everyone else in the sam
predicament, silently struggling against their bonds. Nobody knew
where he was or what was happening.

The President too awoke to find himself alone and bound. He wa
lying on a bed on his back. He looked around. It was dark and hard t
see, but in the gloom he could make out bare walls and a singl
window that looked out on a gray predawn. He tried to stretch his leg
and found they were tied to the sides of the bed. His hands were als
bound, taped at the wrists. He scratched at the tape but couldn
dislodge it. He called out once, twice; the second call dissolved into
fit of coughing, and he lay gasping for breath. Finally he gave up
exhausted from the ordeal and the struggle, wondering what ha
happened and where he was.

As the sun rose and lumbered slowly across a clearing sky, Hardy sti
slept. Mason was awake, watching the grass strip dry in the morning
heat, going over in his mind yesterday's operation and the remainin
details. None of the men who had helped them camouflage Air Forc
One last night after the Everglades landing knew where he and Hard
were now. They had no reason to connect the stories about the Presi
dent's assassination that would be in the newspapers today with what the
had done last night. They would begin to wonder why the hijacking the
thought they had participated in wasn't being reported, and eventuall
the story would come out that the President had been kidnapped rathe
than killed, and by then they would begin to put two and two together
At that point they would probably think they hadn't been paid enough

t there would be nothing they could do about it. They weren't stupid
ough to voluntarily indict themselves. They were too stupid to keep
m bragging, of course, but it would take weeks before their talk got
t and they were tracked down. By then it would be too late; he, Hardy
d the President would be long gone.

At least that's what he told himself as he let Hardy sleep. He wanted
get going as soon as possible, but there was nothing to be done until
e muddy strip dried out.

ison was feeling no better by the time she finished the motel coffee
the car. She was cursing herself for a fool. She should have stopped
em years ago, when they first contemplated smuggling. She should
ve . . . what? What could she have done?

She shook her head as she drove. She had done what she could. If she
d fought them too hard about the smuggling, she would have lost
em. This way they'd had someone to talk to. They'd even taken her
see the airfields where they brought the stuff into Florida to show her
w safe and easy it was, how no one but the federal agencies really
red, how it was accepted locally just as moonshining had been during
ohibition. Well, at least now she knew where their old airfields were.
they weren't in Kansas, they must be down here. God, she hoped they
dn't have some place new, and that she could find them and bring
em to their senses before they did anything really bad.

It was too much to think about. She turned off the air conditioning,
ened the windows, letting the moist morning air blow through her
ir, hoping it would wash out her thoughts, then turned on the radio
d learned that the President had been assassinated yesterday after-
on, his airplane shot down over Colorado. She had to pull over to
e side of the road. Her hands were trembling so hard that she nearly
ove into the roadside ditch. She sat and listened to the news. She
uldn't believe it. She hadn't believed it yesterday; she was sure the
BI was wrong. But now . . .

Shot down by an old Marine jet fighter . . . It was the sort of thing
ee might have dreamed up.

She pulled back onto the highway and continued her search,
olding her imagination in, not daring to think, unable to stop.

She found one of the old airfields shortly after eleven o'clock. She drove down a long dirt road leading off the highway, through a thi‹ grove of evergreen trees, and there it was: wide, open, level, covere‹ with grass in need of mowing—and deserted.

She checked it out carefully, then drove back up the dirt road. T‹ next airfield she knew about was fifty miles away, deeper in th Everglades, near Glades City. She decided to stop at the next place sh saw for a cup of coffee and a bagel.

"Tourist," the old man said with soft derision as he shuffled down th aisle and scraped the remains off the plate into the open garbage ca›

"Huh?" Ronnie Joe asked.

"Tourist," the old man repeated, nodding his head to indicate the gi‹ who'd just left the diner and was walking to her car. "Wanted a bag with her coffee." They didn't serve bagels here; they didn't get enoug‹ tourists to make it worth their while having them sent up from Miam‹ The closest thing they had was a Danish made in a factory somewher upstate that came in twice a week wrapped in cellophane. The girl ha taken two bites and left the rest. "Spoke nice, though," he said. Mo‹ of the tourists who got lost and stopped here spoke with harsh Yanke accents. "Southern girl," he mumbled. "Carolina, Virginia maybe.

"Huh?" Ronnie Joe asked, looking up from his newspaper. Wh‹ had old Frank said? But the old man was already shuffling back up th aisle to his radio crooning softly in back of the counter.

*Spoke nice, though,* he had said. *Maybe Virginia.* Ronnie Jo looked out through the dusty glass window to the girl getting into h‹ car. Tourist, all right; the car had a rental agency tag on the bumpe‹ He was remembering the all-points notice that had been broadca‹ yesterday afternoon. A girl in a rental car. A girl from Virginia . . No. He shook his head. It couldn't be anything, and he hadn't had h‹ second cup of coffee yet. But he read off her license number as sh drove out in a cloud of dust, picked up his Florida state trooper's ha‹ walked out to his patrol car, leaned in the front door and looked at th list of wanted numbers.

*Goddamn,* he thought, and got into his seat and started the ca‹ picking up his radio microphone and clicking it on as he drove off afte the tourist girl with the nice Southern accent.

\*   \*   \*

radar umbrella that protects the United States is designed to pick
high-flying craft; it is not capable of covering anything flying low.
s leaky umbrella is in fact regularly penetrated by drug smugglers
ing in from Central and South America and from the Caribbean
nds. To plug these leaks, and in response to requests emanating
n Werther that were transformed into demands from FBI
dquarters and finally into orders from the Pentagon, the Air
ce's 552 AWACS Wing put their Boeing E-3A aircraft on
ding patrol over the Gulf states. Equipped with look-down
ppler pulse radar, the E-3As could see and identify anything in
tion, no matter how low it flew. Shifts of National Guard
ntom and Air Force F-16 fighters were put on call to investigate
aircraft the AWACs spotted leaving the continental United States
hout filing a flight plan, and any plane filing such a flight plan was
ng checked out before departure by hastily assembled teams of FBI
nts.

y midday Werther and Melnik were setting up operations at
mestead. The Coast Guard had all its cutters at sea, their spinning
omes searching for any high-speed ships leaving the Florida
stline for open water. The Miami Air Interdiction Branch of the
toms service had put their AWACS-type P3As at Werther's service;
se are converted navy turboprop Electras, equipped with the same
nketing look-down radar as the Air Force AWACs fleet. Helicopters
m Homestead were crisscrossing the southern Florida swamps
king for the 707 that Werther was sure lay somewhere under the hot
. He sat at a circular desk, spinning from one phone to another,
rdinating, ordering, begging, demanding. He'd had no idea of the
er volume of unauthorized air and sea traffic in and out of the
rida peninsula, both honest and dishonest, smugglers and fisher-
n on their way to and from the Bahamas and the Caribbean islands.
matter how sophisticated the radar equipment and determined the
toms officers manning it, it was clear in the first few hours of
light that there was no way to clamp an iron-tight curtain around
American borders. Now he sat chewing his lip, drumming his
gers on the table, then picked up the phone again. "I want a
rricane," he muttered.

*       *       *

Hardy stood outside the hangar looking up at the helicopter as it swu across the grass airstrip, hung in the sky for a moment like a dragon then tipped and flew over again, more slowly this time. As Ha waved at it, it flew away.

Mason was waiting by the hangar as Hardy walked back. "Did t mean anything?" he asked.

Hardy shook his head; it couldn't possibly. Air Force One was do in the Rockies, and they couldn't have flown a chopper in to it. would take a couple of days to reach it overland. They couldn't kn anything yet; there was no point in panicking because of o sightseeing helicopter that could be looking for anything from drugs a runaway teenager to the nearly extinct Florida panther. He shook head again; just the same he didn't like it. At best it was a bad ome But the sun was drying out the grass nicely.

"Let's check out the weather," he said, and they went into the off and flipped on the radio. The Miami Weather Advisory forecast cl visual flight conditions throughout the Caribbean. Hardy nodd "Soon as it gets dark," he said.

He stood for a moment, thinking about the President. The drug h worn off, and the man was bearing up remarkably well. When he'd go in to see him this morning he was awake, though exhausted. Hardy h walked him to the bathroom, and though his legs had crumpled at fi he was steady by the time they'd finished. He'd eaten a small break and had been dozing intermittently through the day, tied to his b Hardy glanced at his watch. They could give him an early dinner no lacing his coffee with a couple of Valium. Between his exhaustion a the tranquilizer he'd be docile enough for several hours.

The problem that faced Melnik and Werther was how to stop Ha once they found him. If they could find Alison and trail her to hi or if they spotted Air Force One on the ground somewhere a followed his trail from it, they'd have a chance to grab him before tried to get out of the country. But as they soon became aware, Florida wilderness country into which Hardy might have dropped a into which Alison had disappeared was awesomely vast. The Ev glades alone covered more than five thousand square miles, and wouldn't take much to make an airplane hidden there virtua undetectable. They had the Air Force and the Civil Air Pat crisscrossing all over in the hope of finding something, but the chances were small. As for Alison, she had simply vanished.

More likely was the hope of catching a radar glimpse of Hardy trying to leave the country, which led to the basic problem. If he tried to slip the President through their radar net by boat, the solution was obvious: fast Coast Guard cutters and helicopters could intercept anything on the surface. But if he chose instead to try to fly through, what could they do? Whatever plane he flew would be faster than a helicopter, and while the much faster Air Force jets could catch him, what could they do when they did? Shoot him down? Their only choice would be that or let him go.

Then Melnik thought of the Harrier.

Colonel Joe Foster commanded VMA-228, a Marine air-to-ground attack squadron based at Cherry Point, North Carolina. In 1985 the squadron had made a transition from Douglas A-4 Skyhawks to the new Hawker/McDonnell Harrier VTOL jet, the initials standing for Vertical Take Off and Landing. Designed in England and built under license in the States, they were the first and the most successful jets designed for guerrilla warfare in the jungles. Instead of requiring long landing strips, they could swing their jet exhausts from the horizontal to the vertical axis and land, take off or hover like a helicopter; then, swinging the exhaust back to horizontal, they could soar away with a jet's normal speed.

When Colonel Foster received word to move his squadron for temporary duty at Homestead Air Force Base as soon as possible, he didn't know why. But he was a Marine, and as far as he was concerned "as soon as possible" meant yesterday. Within three hours of receiving the telephoned order, he had twelve planes in the air, and while the Florida sun still stood high over the Gulf they were circling into the landing pattern around Homestead.

Melnik had suggested the Harriers not for their VTOL capability but because they could VIFF, a technique he had learned when he flew Harriers with the Royal Air Force in 1973. The acronym stands for Vector (thrust) in Forward Flight, and is a compromise between hovering and full-ahead flight capabilities, in which the pilot changes the direction of the jet thrust for greater agility in air-to-air combat. With this capability the Harrier can change from a near-supersonic fighter to a near-helicopter, flying slower and with more maneuverability than any other jet fighter ever made.

Of course the Miami-based National Hurricane Center refused Werther's strange request, so he had to decide between telling them the reason or going through official channels. He had no choice, really; if word got out that they were on Hardy's trail their only chance would be gone. The man would disappear down a rabbit hole and leave the President to die tied up in an abandoned building or buried alive; there was no limit to the possibilities and no possible way to find him unless Hardy thought that no one was looking. So Werther called the Director of the Bureau and sat fiddling while his request bounced around Washington for what seemed like eternity. Not knowing Hardy's exact plans, he was frustrated and nervous as time was wasted. Finally his request came back to Miami in the form of an order to the Hurricane Center.

The next weather advisory spoke of a sudden buildup of tropical storm Diana between Cuba and Cat Key, and the Center was immediately flooded with calls from people who hadn't even heard of the existence of Diana. In self-defense the center had to take the phones off the hook. The *Miami Herald* sent reporters; the chief of the Hurricane Center put his phone back into operation long enough to call Washington and warn them of the fuss down here that would surely increase and explode when the truth came out. If this weren't fully justified by the most important circumstances, a lot of people would be awfully angry at being lied to by a service they relied on for life-and-death information. The answer came back immediately: Stay with the story.

With that the Center admitted to reporters that they had goofed; they had simply missed the developing storm. The next weather advisory raised it to the status of a hurricane, sweeping westward between the southern tip of Florida and Cuba. All boat and aircraft traffic was prohibited from entering the area. The radar plots began to dry up immediately. By the end of the day the P3As were cruising around with nothing to do, and the Coast Guard captains were able to slacken their speed and even have a cup of coffee. As night fell and the "hurricane" increased in intensity, the radar screens would be empty of blips.

Except for one.

## 80

The Harrier is normally a single-seat fighter, but Melnik had thought to tell Werther to request that the Marine attack squadron fly down one model TAV-8B. The TAV is a two-seater trainer version, and Colonel Foster piloted it himself when he flew his squadron down to Homestead. He was ushered directly into the operations room, where he found Werther alone. After introducing themselves, Werther explained the mission to him and told him that he would fly with Foster in the TAV if the radar planes located Hardy.

The colonel shook his head.

Werther pointed out that since he was in charge of the operation his presence on the scene was mandatory.

Colonel Foster was polite but adamant. "No, sir," he said. "You're not a pilot, so you don't understand. The Harrier is not a passenger-carrying aircraft. She has a full set of controls in both seats, and she's trimmed like a neurotic greyhound. If any one of a dozen handles, switches or buttons is even touched at the wrong moment she'll rear up and be gone. No, sir. Nobody steps into that cockpit unless he's a trained jet fighter pilot. I don't care what operation he's in charge of."

"But—"

"Negative. The subject is not open for discussion. I will follow whatever orders you give, and carry them out to the best of my squadron's ability, but I carry them out; you don't."

Werther thought of calling Washington, but he knew that no one would overrule a field commander. The debate was threatening to become acrimonious when Melnik walked in.

Foster turned at the sound, and immediately gave a snort of welcome. He and Melnik shook hands warmly. "Shee-it," Foster roared, his language undergoing a sea change from the stiff formality with which he had addressed Werther. "Look at what the cat done dragged in. Where you been all these years, boy? You part of this operation?"

"Knocking around, and yes," Melnik answered. "We flew together in the RAF," he explained to Werther.

"Goddamn right," Foster said. "Checked out in Harriers together, this little Jew and me. What kind of bird you flying now?" he asked Melnik.

"Got just a bit old for jet fighters," Melnik said. "Which makes me wonder what you're doing here. We asked for somebody with operational experience, but not with rheumatism."

"Marines don't get old, boy. Old soldiers fade away, and old sailors turn to sea piss, but Marines fly forever. So what are you now? A rabbi?"

"Mossad," Melnik said, and Foster's eyes opened a little wider. "Oh," he said. "So you're in on this FBI crap?"

Melnik nodded.

"That solves our little problem," Foster said to Werther. "I'll take him along."

It didn't solve anything as far as Werther was concerned, but just then the Florida State Police called in to say that Alison Mason was heading southeast on route 41 and was now just twenty-five miles west of Miami. She was being discreetly followed and seemed unaware of it.

Werther made a quick decision. "Okay," he said to Melnik. "You stay with him," indicating the colonel. Then he grabbed his hat and was gone, trailing in his wake a scurrying school of FBI agents like remora fish trying to hook onto a speeding shark.

It was all Ronnie Joe Corklin could do to keep his foot off the accelerator, but the message had been clear. *Don't lose the girl or your ass is in a sling.* That would have been okay, except the next thing his chief had said was *And don't let her see you or your balls are in a vise.*

Goddamn, he was in a Florida state patrol car with lights on top, the whole works. And there she was, driving along deserted side roads with no one else around, so how was he supposed to keep out of sight? All she had to do was look in her mirror. . . .

He eased off the accelerator and let her pull ahead around the bends in the road. They were godawful lucky it was Ronnie Joe on her trail, that was all. He knew these 'Glades like the back of his hand; he had fished and hunted them since he was six years old. So he was able to hang back out of sight of the rented car, letting it disappear in front of him for miles at a time because he knew just where the long stretches without a turn leading off them were. He also knew when a turnoff was oming up; then he would ease forward, catch a glimpse of her and ack off again.

He trailed her in this way deep into the 'Glades, and when she nally did leave the highway he knew it without even seeing her. He ided to a stop a half mile from the turnoff, watching the dust rise ver the trees as she bounced down the dirt alleyway between the angroves. He called in that she had gone to ground, and then he aited.

oon it would be getting dark. Alison had come south down route 29 ast Glades City, and had been searching between there and Choko- skee, one eye on the sun and the other on the forested swamps shing past, knowing that if she didn't find the next airfield before the n went down she'd have to wait another day. But finally there it was, track leading from the road into the mangroves, flashing past before e even saw it. She braked, backed up and turned in. Twice she ran to dead ends and had to backtrack, each time finding an offshoot she ad missed before. Suddenly the track opened up into a clearing, xpanding as she drove through it into a wide grassy veranda and then to a flat plain, and there stood a small hangar with a shack beside it. he had found another of the airfields.

This one was inhabited. She could see a car sitting beside the angar, and on the other side, where the shallow waters of the swamps cked against the grass, an airboat leaned at a slight angle.

What the hell is that?"

There were a couple of cots inside the shack, and Hardy and Mason ere resting on them. Suddenly Hardy sat bolt upright, listening. He hought he'd heard something, and as he listened again he was sure. He umped out of the cot, slipping into his shoes as Mason pulled himself p and fell into the wheelchair beside his cot. Hardy ran to the door and pened it, looking out across the airfield.

As he watched, the nose of a car poked out of the dirt track like a nole appearing among the trees. It stopped for a moment, then ontinued toward them, splashing water from the wet grass as it umbered across the field. It wasn't a cop car, and it was alone, so aybe it wasn't trouble. Maybe it was one of the locals out for a

Sunday drive, maybe somebody lost in the Everglades, maybe . . . A
it came closer, he could see the driver's head.

"Jesus Christ," Freddy said, wheeling up behind him. "It's Alison.

"You son of a bitch," Hardy whispered softly, "you told h
where—"

"I didn't, Gee! I swear I didn't. I don't know what she's doing here.

The car pulled up in front of them, the door opened, and Aliso
tumbled out. "Thank God I found you," she gasped, running up t
Gee and hugging him.

"Yeah, thank God," Hardy said.

Releasing him, she looked from him to Freddy. "You're all right?
she asked.

They nodded.

"You dumb bastards!" she shouted, and began to tremble violentl

They led her inside and poured coffee. When Hardy handed her
cup she slapped it out of his hand. It fell onto the wooden floor an
shattered, splashing their feet. "How could you do it?" she aske
"How could you do such a thing?"

"I don't know what you're talking about," Hardy said.

"Oh, don't you?" she interrupted. "Don't you know anything abou
it at all? You haven't even heard that the President's been killed?"

Hardy was trying to figure out what to do. He had to discover wha
she knew, how she'd got here, and who else knew, but he had to fin
out slowly. "What makes you think we have anything to do with that?
he asked.

She slapped him hard across the face, and the sound reverberated i
the nearly empty shack. He stood, not moving, and she hit him again
Then again. "Don't lie to me!" she screamed. "The FBI is after you
They came and asked where—"

As he grabbed her and pulled her tight against him her words brok
off and she began to cry. In his wheelchair beside them, Fredd
reached up one hand to her.

"Why, Gee?" she asked finally. Pulling away from him, she turne
to Freddy. "Oh Freddy, why did you do it?"

"We didn't," Gee said.

Her eyes blazed with anger, but he held her gaze steadily until h
saw them turn to puzzlement. "The FBI says—"

"The FBI is one hundred percent wrong. We did not kill the President."

"But you're involved—"

"As far as I know, *nobody* has killed the President. We are involved with something, but the FBI is all screwed up. They don't know what's going on, and they think . . . Well, you know what they think. But *we* didn't do it. We haven't killed the President. I promise you."

"Then what's it all about? Don't try to tell me you're out here fishing!"

"I haven't lied to you, kid. You always knew something was up. Freddy and I are involved, and it's more serious than smuggling marijuana, and that's why I don't want you to know about it until it's over."

"When will it be over?"

"Tomorrow. Just one more day. Maybe two, if the rain starts up again. At that point I'll tell you everything."

"And you swear you didn't have anything to do with killing the President?"

"I swear."

Freddy nodded. "We swear," he said.

Directed by Sonny Ewbank, the local head FBI agent sitting next to him, Werther drove with the other agents following in three more cars. They found Ronnie Joe Corklin leaning against the hood of his car, alone on the rural highway.

"Where is everybody?" Werther asked as he pulled up.

"Who?" Ronnie Joe answered. "You're the first ones here."

Werther grimaced. He'd called for a SWAT team as they left headquarters, and had hoped they'd already be in place. "Where is he?" he asked.

Corklin told him about the abandoned grass airstrip up ahead surrounded by the 'Glades. "Was used by drug runners till we put a stop to them. Chased them off, that is; we didn't catch 'em. Nobody uses it now." The turnoff was half a mile ahead. Then it was about a mile inland by a dirt road, or maybe half a mile going straight through the swamps. "But you wouldn't want to do that."

"Why not?"

"Well, it's a swamp, ain't it?"

"Any other way in or out?"

Ronnie Joe shook his head. "What you see is what you get."

Werther turned to Ewbank and told him to send two of the cars up ahead. They were to pass out of sight on the other side of the turnoff and blockade the highway up there. The cars here would set up a similar blockade and were to stay out of sight of the turnoff. When the SWAT team arrived, they were to infiltrate the woods and surround the airstrip. "You're in charge," he told Ewbank. "Stay invisible if they come out reconnoitering, but if they try to get away, don't let them. Not under any circumstances, not for any reason."

"Where will you be?"

"I'm going in to see what's happening."

"You'll never find your way through those woods," Ronnie Joe snorted.

"Sure, I will," Werther said, picking up his walkie-talkie and checking to be sure his gun was secure in its holster. "You're going to take me."

Hardy wasn't panicked, but it was hard to know what to do. If Alison had been followed by the Feds, they might be moving into position around them right now. On the other hand, it would be dark in another fifteen minutes, and the plan had always been to wait for nightfall, when they'd be invisible to everything except radar.

He tried to think calmly. He sent Alison out to look around, as much to get rid of her for a few minutes to give him time to think as to find out if anyone had trailed her here. He told her to go back out to the highway and scout around, with the idea that if the Feds had them surrounded they might think the reappearance of her car was an escape attempt and blow their surveillance in order to stop her.

"Christ almighty," Werther whispered when he could talk again, "thanks a lot." He spat the last of the evil-tasting mud from his mouth and tried to wipe his eyes clear.

"I told you it was a swamp," Ronnie Joe said, half apologetically, half trying not to laugh. He was afraid he'd get reamed for letting happen, but what could he do? This smart-ass New York FBI agent

ad insisted on creeping through the swamp, and when he put his foot
own in a mudhole there wasn't anything else for him to do on God's
reen earth but fall face forward into the muck. Ronnie Joe had pulled
im out, but the man's walkie-talkie was still down there. No use
ying to find it.

Werther wiped his hands on Ronnie Joe's uniform, then cleaned
is face as well as he could. "Come on," he said, and off they went
gain.

Night was falling fast now, especially in the swamp, and it was by
e last fading light that, as Ronnie Joe pulled him up short and
ointed, he finally saw the squat hangar not fifty yards in front of them.
t first it seemed deserted, until they noticed the airboat and the car
ound the side. They stood watching, but there was no movement.
hen, in the shack next to the hangar, a light blinked on. Again they
aited, but nothing else happened.

Werther sent Corklin back to the others to report. They were to
filtrate the swamp and surround the clearing on all sides; when they
ere in position they were to fire off a flare to let him know. "I'm going
to see what the story is," he said. "After the flare, nobody is to do
ything until they hear from me—or unless Hardy tries to get away."

"Then what?"

"Stop him."

Corklin waited, but there were no more orders, so he turned and
oved off. Werther began to crawl forward. Through the darkening
rest he saw the car's headlights turn on, and then the car start up and
ive away. He hurried forward through the muck.

Out on the highway the waiting police had just been joined by the
VAT team when they heard the car engine start. They melted back
to the woods out of sight.

Alison drove out onto the paved surface of the highway and stopped,
oking around. She drove a few yards up the road, then stopped and
oked again. Had she driven half a mile further, around the curve in
e road, she would have run into the blockade. Instead she made a
turn and drove a short way in the other direction, again stopping
d looking around. Finally she turned and drove back to the dirt road.
Hardy had frightened her, telling her that she might have been
lowed all this time. She couldn't believe it, but . . . She cut the

engine and listened. She heard and saw no one. Beginning to brea
again, she started the car and headed back to the camp.

Hardy turned on the FAA radio and listened to the latest weather upda
What he heard was so unexpected that at first he didn't take it in.
stood listening, with Freddy at his side, in increasing incredulity.

"I don't believe it," Mason said, switching off the Hurrica
Center's description of the storm now rushing through the Caribb
gap between Cuba and the mainland of Florida.

Hardy agreed. He knew that Freddy had been following the weath
reports every day for the past week; there had been no tropical sto
Diana, and such storms don't materialize out of nowhere and upgra
into hurricanes within hours. It was barely possible that the comm
cial stations were right in claiming, as they heralded this news sco
that the Hurricane Center had missed the storm while it develop
But he knew how good the federal weather people were, and he did
believe it.

"Something's wrong," he said. The helicopter this morning h
disturbed him, but not unduly. The Feds had lots of people to
looking for in the Everglades; drug smuggling was everyday busin
here. But he had heard another copter later in the day, and thougl
hadn't come within sight, the occurrence of two such craft within
distance of each other in one day suggested more than the us
surveillance. Then Alison had shown up, and now this.

Which explained the hurricane. Somehow those bastards had fou
out what they were doing, and were trying to keep them holed up ur
they could find them or could bring in the Air Force and Navy
clamp a secure seal around the borders of the country. Nothing e
would be important enough to make the Feds lie to the public. Th
were hoping he'd stay on the ground until the hurricane blew ov
giving them time to find him or stop him. And now, with Aliso
help, they might already have found him. They had to get the hell c
as quickly as possible. He would have liked to wait another half ho
for complete darkness, he would have liked to give the grass strip a f
hours more to dry out to be sure it would bear their weight, but they
have to take the chance.

"Let's go," he said to Freddy.

"Alison's not back yet."

"I know."

Freddy stared at him, then slowly shook his head. Hardy started to ~~a~~rgue, then stopped. Freddy was right. If they took off while she was ~~g~~one, where would that leave her? Even if the Feds had lost her on the ~~tr~~ip down here, they'd certainly pick her up again sooner or later. She ~~h~~adn't the faintest idea how to evade them, and in any case she wasn't ~~g~~oing to become a fugitive on her own; he couldn't do that to her.

So she had to come along. Shit, fuck, piss and corruption.

He looked out over the airfield, dredging up all the curses of all his ~~M~~arine years and spewing them out, and then he went back inside to ~~dr~~ink.

~~B~~y the time Werther reached the rear of the hangar the sun had set ~~b~~ehind the tall trees, though not yet over the horizon. Long shadows ~~fli~~ckered as he moved cautiously along the hangar wall to the front. He ~~w~~ould have liked to look through the window of the adjoining shack, ~~bu~~t the shade was drawn. Across the grass airfield he saw the car ~~re~~appear, heading back, so he slipped into the hangar.

It was dark, but he could see a plane. He didn't recognize the type, ~~bu~~t clearly it was an old one, twin-engined, squatting with its tail down ~~an~~d its nose high on two wheels. Midway down the fuselage was an ~~op~~en door, with three folding steps leading up to it. He crossed the ~~co~~ncrete floor and climbed in. The fuselage was cavernous; there ~~di~~dn't seem to be any seats. Squinting in the darkness, he made out a ~~lar~~ge box toward the rear, nearly as high as his shoulders. As he moved ~~to~~ward it, suddenly from outside came the bouncing light of a ~~fla~~shlight and the sound of footsteps walking across the concrete floor ~~of~~ the hangar. He moved quickly into the deepest recesses of the ~~fu~~selage, found a door just behind the large crate, opened it and ~~ste~~pped in, closing it behind him just in time. The flashlight beam ~~sh~~one into the plane as the door clicked shut in his face.

~~Ca~~rrying the President slung over his shoulder, Hardy clambered up ~~th~~e three steps into the plane and went straight to the four-by-six ~~wo~~oden crate. He glanced over the edge, then stuffed the flashlight ~~int~~o his pocket. Carefully shifting the President around, taking his weight in his arms and hands, he lowered him into the empty box. Then he took out the flashlight again and shone it around inside checking the box.

Bush lay on his back, his head in one corner, his body stretched ou diagonally, his wrists and ankles tightly taped. The box wasn't quite bi enough, but with his legs bent he fit. His eyes reflected the flashligh beam; he was conscious but dazed. The Valium had done its work. H wouldn't be comfortable, but he'd be safe. There were no norma passenger seats in the plane; they had all been ripped out for more carg space, leaving only a few bucket seats along the fuselage wall, and in hi semiconscious condition he couldn't safely be strapped into one c them. In the crate he might bang around a bit, but he wouldn't be hur

Hardy stood for a moment looking down at him, playing th flashlight beam over his body and around the wooden crate. H reached in and found the President's arm, sliding his fingers down it t the wrist. The pulse was weak but steady. *There he is*, he thought, *th son of a bitch who killed my son*.

Then he began to shake his head sadly. It wasn't true, he realize He *wanted* it to be true, and in a sense it was, but in a small sense onl The truth was more complex, and the burden he himself carried coul not easily be dumped on that man lying helpless in the crate. H fingers switched off the flashlight and he stood a moment more peerin into the darkness, no longer wanting to see the body down there. The was a faint sour taste in his mouth.

Suddenly he shook himself like a wet dog to shed all his thought Leaning against the crate, he shoved it up against the fuselage on o side and against the lavatory door in the rear. He could hear th President twisting in an attempt to see what was happening and hea his head bump on the floor, bringing forth a dull moan. He waite but there was no further sound. He lifted the heavy wooden cover a put it on top. There was enough separation between the wood slats provide air circulation. He tied the crate down, wrapping a heavy ro around it and along the aft bulkhead, then looping it over th lavatory-door handle. He tested it to be sure it was taut and would ho the crate securely during takeoff, then walked down the steps just Alison walked up.

"We're leaving," Hardy said. "You'd better come with us."

"Where are you going?"

"Colombia. Their extradition process is a joke, and from there we an disappear to anywhere in the world."

Her mouth dropped open. "You mean you're not coming back? ver?"

Hardy smiled. "Ever is a long time, but we won't be coming back oon."

"What did you do? If you didn't kill the President, what did you do hat's so serious?"

"I'll tell you in Colombia," he promised.

She shook her head. "Now."

He could be just as obstinate. "If anything goes wrong, I want you o be able to claim truthfully that you didn't know anything about it. )therwise you're an accomplice before the fact."

"*Before* the fact? You mean you haven't done it yet?"

He scowled irritably. "Or after the fact. I don't know; I'm not a oddamn lawyer."

"What *are* you, Gee?"

"Right now a man on the run. Tomorrow king of the world."

Vell, that was interesting, Werther thought. He heard their footsteps eceding across the hangar floor, and he was alone. He thought again ith longing of the flashlight he hadn't brought along. If he were still moking, he'd at least have had a few matches. He turned around in e small space, feeling with his hands. He bumped his knee as he urned, and reaching down he felt what was obviously a toilet and a nall sink.

He turned back to the door, listened again to be sure they had gone, nd pressed lightly against it. Then he pressed again. Oh, Jesus. He'd eard the scraping sounds and had realized that Hardy must be shoving e crate into place. Now he realized where; it must be tight against is door. The way the door was built to open, folding in half and ending out, it was now completely blocked, and there was no way he ould get enough leverage to budge it. He sat down on the toilet to ink. It was like a child's nightmare: he was locked in this tiny, amped, dark space with evil people out there. Instinctively, for omfort, he reached into his jacket and drew out his gun, and felt

the mud dripping out of its muzzle. When he had fallen into
swamp . . . Oh, great.

In the darkness they opened the main hangar doors and Hardy pus
Mason in his wheelchair up the ramp into the DC-3, through
fuselage and into the cockpit. Freddy levered himself over the arm
and into the copilot's seat while Hardy secured his wheelchair to
back of the seat. Mason ran through the checklist while Hardy w
back into the fuselage and made sure Alison was strapped into on
the folding bucket seats.

"What's in the wooden crate?" she asked.

"That's for the Colombians."

"You're smuggling stuff *out* of the country now?"

He nodded, checked her seat belt, leaned down, kissed her on
cheek and then glanced around the bay. It was dark, lit only by
darkly diffused lights of the instrument panel up ahead in the cock
Not too comfortable. "Won't be long now," he said, and strode up
long incline into the cockpit. Sliding into the pilot's seat, he glan
at Mason, received a short nod in reply, took a deep breath and
suddenly blinded by a brilliant white flare shooting into the air fr
just beyond the first line of trees outside. "I knew it!" he said,
pushed the starter buttons.

The SWAT team watched from just inside the fringe of trees arou
the airfield as the flare lit up the scene, then faded away. They wai
for a signal from Werther. Instead they heard the coughing rumbl
two engines.

The starboard engine kicked into life, followed by the port. Ha
sat still for a few seconds, only his eyes moving, watching the d
settle in as the engines warmed up. Then he pushed in the throt
and the DC-3 lumbered out of the hangar and onto the grass st

"Move out!" the SWAT leader shouted. "Stop them!"

In the last fading light Hardy could see figures materializing out of
trees in front of them and to the side, but the grass strip led straight fr
the hangar doors, and without hesitation he shoved the throttles w
open. As the DC-3 bumped along the grass picking up speed, he saw
small blurred figures running toward them. The old plane rattled a

bounced, carrying him past them, and as he roared by he saw tiny bursts of light and heard the small-caliber bullets bouncing off the metal skin. Once again he was racing through the Vietnam air, waiting for that one bullet to penetrate, to smash the Plexiglas and shatter his forehead, to pierce the gas line and drain the bird's blood.

Then the wheels gave one final bounce and the rusty old bird clawed its way into the air. The roar of its engines blew away the sound of gunfire, and the next minute they were alone in the empty evening sky, curving around to the south in silence save for the steady roar of the engines, alone in an empty universe, climbing off into that wild blue yonder as it darkened into blackness.

Hardy allowed himself a small, tight smile. It had been close, but they'd done it. They were gone.

The world below and all its complications dimmed and faded as they circled and slipped off into invisibility among the darkening night winds. He curved around south of Miami and headed out to sea over the Florida Keys, bound for Colombia, staying low to keep under radar coverage.

## 81

It was one of the Drug Enforcement Agency's patrolling P-3A radar-station airplanes that first saw the blip. Immediately it radioed in its report and turned to follow, keeping it on the screen.

In the cockpit Hardy sat in the left-hand pilot's seat, Freddy to his right. Mason's wheelchair, hooked around his seat, jittered along with the vibrations. Up here the propellers whirred only a few feet from their heads, drowning out all other noises. Each man could see directly front and to one side, and each continually scanned the dark skies.

There was nothing to be seen. The moon had not yet risen, there were almost no clouds and the stars were sprinkled brightly above the horizon, marking it for them. Below that invisible line there was nothing but darkness. There were no fluorescent wave tops breaking, as there would be if a hurricane had really been brewing out in the Caribbean. The only sound was the steady pounding of the two

air-cooled engines, the rattling of the ancient rivets and the groa
of the metal as the old warhorse pulled steadily through the empty

Suddenly a red light blinked at them from the copilot's side o
control panel. "Radar," Mason said.

Hardy glanced at it. He had been afraid of that. They were f
below the limit of ground-based radar, but if the Feds were onto t
they would have their eye-in-the-sky radar planes searching.
waited, staring at the light, willing it to flicker and go out, as it w
if the radar beam swept on and away from them. Instead the red
settled down to a steady glow. Mason hunched forward over
detector, twirling the dials, and a minute later reported that the r
beam was locked on them and that its intensity was increasing.

*Not now*, Hardy thought, whispered, prayed. *Not now. We're so c
we've almost got it made, we're almost away. Son of a bitch, not r*

Six of the Harriers took off, with Foster and Melnik in the lead, lea
the other six behind in case another blip appeared. The Harriers di
carry on-board radar, but they were vectored directly onto the ta
their quarry by the P-3A, and soon they picked it up on their infr
scopes. The night was clear and they saw the target visually
distance of two miles, first the exhausts and then the black shape of
plane itself at just under a mile. As they approached they shifted f
full forward flight into the VIFF mode, slowing down from
hundred miles an hour to match the lumbering speed of t
objective. Carefully they edged in on him from behind and t
spread out, coming up on him from all sides, surrounding him lik
unseen blanket, slowly coming closer.

In the bare interior cabin of the DC-3 Alison huddled against the w
sitting cramped on her bucket seat. Though they were flying low,
wind screaming through the cracks and openings in the anc
airplane's skin chilled her.

Ten feet behind her the large wooden crate bounced and rattle
place. Inside it President Bush lay huddled on the floor, his mouth
hands and feet taped, his body shuddering to the beat of the t
engines that rattled the plane. He had lapsed into unconsciousn
but now the cool night wind, the shuddering of the old frame and

ouncing of the crate on the steel floor all combined to wake him. He
idn't know where he was; he knew only that he ached, and that he
ouldn't move. With his mouth tightly taped, he could barely breathe.
Ie groaned. The sound, stifled and distorted by the tape, was lost in
ie noises of flight. The plane itself was groaning, its old rivets rubbing
gainst even older grooves, its metal skin aching with years of fatigue.
s engines drove the two oversize propellers in noisy arcs just beyond
ie fuselage, and above that the wind whistled.

The President kicked out, banging his shoes against the inside of the
ate. Alison heard that, and glanced at the box. She wondered what
as loose in there, banging around.

In frustration, anger and fear, the President roared and bellowed,
it the tight tape pressing into his mouth swallowed the sound and let
it only a muted groan. Again and again he groaned, and now Alison
gan to hear the sound. If it had been constant it would have been lost
the general cacophony, but coming as it did at irregular intervals she
gan to listen for it, and was frightened to realize it was coming from
e large wooden box she could barely see in the darkness.

She wanted not to believe it, but again and again the moan
unded, and each time it was clearer that it was coming from that
x. She found a cigarette lighter in her purse. She wondered if it was
fe to light it in here. But surely the wind made it safe? When she
cked it on, its glare reverberated around the fuselage before it blew
it, leaving the darkness blacker than before.

She experimented with shielding it with her body, and was finally
le to keep it burning for a few seconds at a time. By its light she could
e nothing but the box, with its wooden cover rattling loosely on top.
ie released her seat belt and, slipping and stumbling with the
unces of the plane, felt her way along the fuselage to the box. There
e leaned against it, maneuvered her body to block the wind, and
cked on the lighter. It held, but as she shifted her feet in order to
ove the top of the crate, the flame blew out again.

Twice more she tried until finally she got it right. With her right foot
iced against the bulkhead and her left shoulder against the crate top
e lit the lighter again, holding it just below her chin, shielded against
wind. Then she leaned hard against the top of the crate and it
pped, shrieking in protest, and moved an inch, then another and

again another, exposing a small opening. She leaned over it ar
looked down into the crate, and in the flickering light saw a half-dea
mouth-taped face with bulging eyes staring up at her. As she gaped
it, it raised its hands, its fingers groping toward her face. She scream

Hardy looked out into the empty black night. There was still nothi
to be seen or heard, but the little red light stayed on.

He tried a few gentle evasive maneuvers, designed to slip away fro
a casual radar beam without alerting the operators that he was doin
intentionally, but the beam followed tightly. No matter what he
the radar emissions not only followed him but increased in intensity
the source closed in on them. Finally the increase shot off the sca
flooding the capabilities of the detector. He knew what this mea
There was no longer any possibility of doubt: it was airborne radar, a
the mother ship was closing in on them.

He flew along steadily, trying to think. The next moment Mas
leaned across him and pointed out the port window. There, mate
alizing out of the black night, was a Harrier fighter hanging off th
wingtip. In the same moment there was a glow from above, and th
looked up to see the burning exhaust of another Harrier just ab
them, moving slowly forward to settle into place high at twelve o'clo
Other Harriers settled in around them, hemming them in.

Hardy flipped on the radio, switching to 122.5, the comm
air-to-air frequency. ". . . do you read me? Repeating, this is Ma
Harrier commander talking to the DC-3 we have surrounded. Do
read me, over?"

Hardy picked up the microphone. "Reading you loud and cl
Over."

"DC-3, let's make a wide, gentle, gradual turn to starboard. We'l
heading back to Miami."

"DC-3, negative," Hardy replied. "What's your problem, anywa

"Not my problem, old buddy. Your problem is the air-to-air
Sidewinder missile I carry on this thing. We will begin our turn in
seconds."

"Negative," Hardy replied. He glanced over at Mason and shrug
Somehow the Feds had found them, so there was no point in tryin
protest their innocence. Even if they weren't sure who they were,

t the President was on board, there was only one way they could
d out, and there was no way that Hardy could talk them into letting
m go. There was only one way out. "Repeat negative," he said into
microphone. "I assume you guys know what our cargo is here, so
k off. There's not a damn thing you can do to make us turn around.
hat are you going to do, shoot us down with your big bad missile?
n't make me laugh, it hurts my arthritis, so why don't you save the
payers some money and stop burning gasoline? Go home, mister."

"DC-3, this is Harrier Commander. I repeat, make a slow turn
—"

"Look, my friend," Hardy interrupted. "The answer is no, and
re's not a damn thing you can do about it. If you want, you can
low us along, but you can bet your goddamn medals we're not going
land in American territory, so what's the point?"

He waited for a reply, but now the radio was silent. For a long
oment nothing happened, and then the Harriers silently began to
ll in tighter around them, drawing the circle closer in a diminishing
ose until the wingtips of the jets on the side were nearly touching the
C-3 and the exhaust of the one in front was breathing heavily against
 cockpit. The DC-3 began to pitch and toss in the turbulent air.
After another long moment, the radio crackled again. "Sorry for the
lay, Mr. Hardy," said a different voice, a slightly foreign accent.
Hardy was startled at the sound of his name. He glanced over at
ason and frowned.

"I was just instructing my pilots to take up their positions, as you
," the new voice continued. "Allow me to explain the situation. Are
u reading me?"

"Loud and clear."

"That's good. My name is David Melnik. I used to be an Israeli Air
rce jet pilot, and now I'm a Mossad agent. I assume you know the
ossad?"

Hardy clicked his microphone button to acknowledge.

"Right. So now I'll explain. The President of the United States is
ad. The Vice President has already taken the oath of office. It's all
ry sad. President Bush was shot down by a crazy Syrian who thinks
at war has been declared. Oh, well. The Yanks have a new
esident, no war has been declared, and that's the end of the story.

"What we cannot allow is *your* story. To have the President deliv
alive to another country, to be held hostage and to show the w
how helpless the United States is in such circumstances—nei
Israel nor the United States can allow this. So we are now going to
around slow and easy and fly back to Homestead Air Force Base.

Melnik paused. "You don't have to do this, of course. You
continue to fly straight ahead while we turn, but if you do we
continue to turn right into you, and you will die. If you're silly eno
to think you might be able to outmaneuver a half-dozen Harriers v
a DC-3, I will simply point out that I have a hot Sidewinder in
belly, which I will dispatch, if necessary, into *your* belly. That wil
the end of the story, and nobody will ever know anything about it.
Hardy, you now have ten seconds to think. Take your time. N
eight, seven, six . . ."

Hardy tried to talk, but the Israeli voice went on: "I'm not e
taking my finger off the transmit button, because I don't want to h
a word you have to say. All I want is to see your wings slowly dip
begin to turn, or else to watch you burn. We're down to three secon
two . . ."

At the count of zero the Harriers began to turn in unison. Ha
tried one last bluff; he held the DC-3 straight and level as the
escort drifted right up to his wingtip. But the Harrier wasn't bluff
it kept on coming, and at the last moment Hardy turned with h
Carefully his right wing dipped and the left rose as the DC-3 bega
curve around to the right and the Harriers turned with her.

Hardy glanced at Mason and shrugged again.

82

Werther had heard a woman scream, and then the airplane bega
pitch and he was thrown around the tiny cubicle, bashing his face
ankles against protuberances unseen in the darkness. He thought
Melnik and his Marine friend must have caught up with them and
they were being shot down, but then the motions stopped as sudde
as they had begun after the plane banked in a wide turn.

He listened at the door, but could hear nothing. Hardy must be ving the plane. He didn't know where Mason was, but the woman ho screamed must have been the sister. He had to take a chance. He dn't know what else to do. He banged on the door.

Alison was in her seat shivering, staring at the crate and trying to :cide what to do. She hadn't recognized the gaunt, half-conscious ;ure inside, nor had it occurred to her to wonder who he was; it was 1ough that Gee and Freddy had someone trussed up like that. Hud- ing in her seat, she wished that everything would vanish: the FBI, her ght to Florida, Gee, Freddy and the half-alive person in the crate.

Then there was a distinct bang. Only her eyes moved; she was too :rified even to tremble.

*Bang!* Her nails dug into her palms; the man in the crate was anging on the walls. No. At the third bang she saw the narrow door :hind the crate bounce with the blow. There was somebody in there.

"Alison! Alison Mason!"

She must be dreaming. Oh God, if only she were dreaming!

She unstrapped her seat belt, got to her feet and edged her way ound the wooden crate. Putting her face close to the narrow door, e called, "What?"

The sound was lost in the roaring of the engines, and she repeated shouting this time. "What? Who is it?"

"Alison, is that you?"

"Yes. Who are you?"

"FBI."

If it was a dream, it seemed to her, it was a doozy.

und hand and foot, mouth taped shut, dumped in a wooden crate a bouncing, rattling airplane, lost in the dark, drifting into and out consciousness, the President concentrated simply on breathing and ying alive, trying to cling to reality in the teeth of this nightmare. *y name is George Bush*, he told himself. *I am the president of—* Suddenly there were voices above him. He couldn't make out the *rds at first, but they were human; he wasn't alone and forsaken in an rnal dream of darkness. He struggled up out of semiconsciousness vard the voices, straining to hear them, and in little bursts of clarity :y rose above the shrieking of the wind and the groaning of the plane.

"FBI . . . agent . . . kidnapped . . ."

*Yes*, he thought, *yes!*

"FBI . . ."

He raised his hands, scratching against the wooden slats of prison.

Once they were set on the course to Homestead, Hardy handed controls over to Mason and released his seat-belt straps. "Where you going?" Freddy asked.

Hardy didn't answer, only pushed himself up out of the seat started back to the cabin of the DC-3.

"What are you doing?" Mason called again, but Gee sim disappeared back into the fuselage, ignoring the question. A mom later Freddy felt a blast of wet air swirling up from back there, a sude increase in engine noise.

Hardy crouched on his knees, braced himself and lifted the hatch. wrestled it against the sudden swirl of the slipstream, and slid it b out of the way against the side of the fuselage, then stared down i the dark wet night, listening to the throb of the engines, wonder how they had found him.

Then he turned away and felt his way back along the fuselage. T wasn't the time to stand around and wonder; right now it didn't ma how they'd found him; all that mattered was getting away. It was ti to put into operation the last contingency plan, the one he'd ho he'd never have to use. But now it was even worse. With Alison he the odds were terribly diminished, and he didn't know if he could p it off. Still, it was all they had left. Realizing this, he put his doubts of his mind. It would work; he would make it work, as he m everything work.

It was disappointing, of course. They had come so close that it hard to give up now. But he had no choice.

Alison heard Hardy come down the fuselage from the cockpit a hurried back to her seat. She wasn't going to free the FBI agent so t he could arrest Gee and Freddy, but the man in the wooden crate .

She watched Hardy in the dim light bend down amidships a

bble at the floor, and then she felt the sudden blast of air and the
h noise of the engines. She saw Hardy straighten up and edge
nd the center of the floor, which was now even darker than before,
ack hole. He made his way around the opening and passed her on
other side of the fuselage. As she watched he went over to the
den crate, loosened the restraining ropes and began to shove aside
heavy slab on top.

Hardy leaned over the open crate and reached in for the man lying
e. He wanted to look him in the face one last time.

The President was a hundred and seventy pounds of dead weight,
Hardy braced his feet against the crate, grabbed him with both
ds by the shoulders and lifted him up. As he heaved him nearly to
shoulders, the President's face came level with his own, and his
htened, staring eyes reflected his own fury and desperation. *You son*
*bitch*, Hardy thought bitterly. *This isn't the way I wanted it to end.*
denly he didn't know whether he was talking to the President of the
ited States or to himself; he didn't know which one he wanted to

Oh my God, Alison thought, *he's going to throw that man out the*
*ch!* "No!" she gasped, but the sound was torn away by the wind and
ipped out the black hole in the floor. She forced herself to her feet,
rfully felt her way around the hatch, ran to the crate and flung
self on Hardy's back. "No!" she screamed in his ear.

Hardy had forgotten about her, and was startled when she landed on
n. He dropped the President and stumbled backward, twisting in her
ns, pulling away from her, but she came after him, tripping and
ling against him. "You can't throw him out!" she screamed,
apping her arms around him.

'What are you talking about?" he asked, picking her up bodily and
shing her away. "You don't understand. Get back to your seat. I'm
t—"

But she wasn't listening. Panicked, she shouted the only thing she
uld think of to make him stop. "The FBI is here!"

What? he wondered. He peered at her in the darkness.

"In there!" she screamed, pointing at the door.

Which was now ajar a couple of inches. Hardy had moved the crate
ittle when he removed the top, allowing leeway for the door to open,

and now as he stared at it he saw four fingers scrabbling around it edges, trying to push the crate away. He reached out, grabbed th handle of the door and pushed it shut hard on the fingers. There wa a sharp cry from inside. He held the door tightly for a second, the released it and the fingers disappeared inside. Pushing the door shu again, he found the twine cord that had loosened and looped it ove the door handle so that it couldn't open.

"You can't dump them *both*," Alison said.

For the first time he realized what had frightened her. "Don't worry kid," he said. "I'm not dumping them. I'm dumping *you*." He nearl smiled at her startled look. "Never mind," he said. "I have to talk t Freddy. Go back to your seat, and watch out for the hatch."

It was strange, he thought as he walked forward to the flight deck They'd come so close. They'd damn near had it all. When he' planned it, he'd thought that if they got this far, with the Presiden stowed in this airplane alone with them, it would be all over. He ha never thought they'd have to use his last plan, and he sure as hell no wished they didn't. Especially with Alison here; that made it tough. H had never really thought about how things might work out with he He'd figured he and Freddy would fly to Colombia, wait for the Libya airliner to pick them up, and then live the rest of their lives in comfo and peace. Somehow she'd catch up with them later. But now . .

He eased himself between the two pilot's seats and settled into th left-hand one. He thought about the FBI agent locked in the lavator he supposed he would have to die too. Unfortunate. He wondere vaguely if he was the same agent he'd talked to on the phone at th airport in San Francisco ten thousand years ago. Reaching arour behind Mason's seat, he took the Mae West out of its pocket an dropped it on Mason's lap. Then he pulled out his own Mae West an began to strap it on. "Come on," he said, "slip into it. We're gettir out of here."

Mason just stared at him. Hardy reached over and tried to strap tl preserver around Mason, but Freddy pushed him away. "Are you o of your mind?" he asked.

"It ain't much, but it's our only chance," Hardy said. He lean back in his seat, took a deep breath and tried to explain. "I never to you about this part of the plan because I never thought we'd have to it, and anyway I didn't want you worrying. It's a long shot," l dmitted, "but we can make it work. We'll leave the DC-3 on utomatic pilot and go out through the hatch. They'll never see us at ight. I can show Alison how to work a parachute and the Mae West; 's scary, but you know there's nothing to it. We'll be all right. There's a inflatable raft back there and we'll take it with us. As soon as we hit e water we inflate the Mae Wests and I pump up the raft, then pull ou and Al on board. We paddle to one of the Florida keys, hitch a de to Islamorada and snatch a private plane from the airfield there. y the time this thing crashes and they get to the wreck, put out the fire d actually get inside and realize that our bodies aren't on board, we'll e five thousand miles away. Once we make it out of the country we'll e set; the first ten million dollars has already been deposited in the wiss bank in my name."

As he talked, it almost seemed possible. He tightened the Mae West raps and reached back to slip the parachute harness over his oulders. "The first reports released will say that no one survived the ash, so we'll have the money out of the bank and be long gone before e Arabs even start looking for us. It's not as good as we planned, but s not bad, kid. Not bad at all."

"And the President?" Freddy asked.

Hardy simply looked at him. The answer was obvious.

"No," Alison said.

They turned around. She was standing in the doorway clinging to it gainst the turbulence. "You lied to me," she said. "You said—"

"I said I hadn't killed the President." He gestured back toward the ar of the airplane. "I haven't."

"You've kidnapped him, and now you want to kill him, as well as e man in the lavatory."

Freddy looked at Hardy in surprise. "What—?"

"What crashed in Colorado?" Alison asked. "If it wasn't Air Force ne?"

"Another plane."

"They're dead? The people who were flying it?"

Hardy shrugged.

"You killed *them*." She couldn't believe it. "You *killed* them."

"They were a bunch of crazy Cubans. All they ever wanted was to e for their—"

"You killed them!"

"I've killed before," Hardy said quietly. "You knew that. It ge easier, that's all."

"You never—"

"I dropped napalm on a little girl in Vietnam. I burned her eye out." He shrugged. "She wasn't the only one, just the one I happene to see."

"That's diff—" she started to say, and stopped because it was and wasn't. "You can't kill *these* people," she said simply.

He nodded his head. "I can," he said. "I will."

"Will you kill me too?"

He waited.

"I'm not going with you, Gee."

In the blackness, in the crate, in a void, in a hole in space and time the bound and gagged President of the United States lay half deliriou with thirst and exhaustion. He knew only that he was in danger of h life, that he was flying somewhere in the night, that he was trappe and that an FBI agent was locked behind the door held with a rope ju above his head.

*I am the head of the strongest nation in the world,* Bush told himsel trying to focus on reality. *I have flown a torpedo bomber against th Japanese and I have been shot down into the Pacific and survived, an I will not end up in a wooden box like a trussed Iowa steer. I will no* He teetered on the edge of awareness, slipped over again into deliriur fought out of it once more, and somehow—not quite conscious where he was and exactly what was happening—somehow managed focus all his energy and prop his enervated body against the side of th crate, twist his legs, heave himself up, reach with trembling tape hands until the fingers found the rope looped around the handle of th door, grasp it, twist, lift and pull it free.

As the rope fell away the body fell back down into the crate, and th door slowly creaked open.

"She's right, Gee," Freddy said. "We can't just leave him to die. doesn't even make sense. Jumping out of an airplane in the middle the night over the ocean? What are the chances?" He shook his hea "It's no chance, Gee. No chance at all."

Silence. "I'm not going back," Hardy said finally. He turned away
om Mason and looked out the window, watching the exhaust flames
f the Harrier in front of them as it bobbed gently in the quiet night air.
head of them, far out on the horizon, they could see the diffuse glow
iat indicated Miami. "I'm not going back to jail. Not again. I'm not
)ing to be put behind bars again. I'd rather drown."

Mason nodded. He understood, but he didn't agree. "I think I'll
ay," he said.

"They'll lock you up and throw away the key," Hardy warned him.

"What's the difference?" Freddy asked. "I carry my jail around with
ie," he said, slapping his useless stumps. "What am I gonna do, run
ut to the ball game? Play golf? Find a nice girl and get married?" He
irew out a bitter breath. "Shit."

They stared at each other. "You go ahead," Freddy said. "But don't
ike Alison. It's suicide, Gee. She stays on board. No matter what they
iink, she's innocent. She doesn't know anything. I'll convince them,
ie'll take a lie detector, she'll be okay. She stays on board. If you make
, she can always come to you later."

"No," she said. Hardy looked at her. She was crying. She shook her
ead. "No."

Slowly Hardy nodded. Freddy was right, and so was she. He turned
ack to Mason. "Keep flying straight and level," he said. "When you
ind, play along with them, go federal witness, tell them everything,
ut lay the blame on me. Bush will tell them how you and Al saved
is life; you can say I was going to dump him until you stopped me.
'hey'll go easy on you."

"I'm not worried," Freddy said. "Those federal prisons have
elevisions and saunas. It'll be like a vacation, with three square meals
day."

"Yeah," Hardy said. He paused. "Sorry," he said. "Sorry for
verything." Sorry for that day in Vietnam when he'd dropped the
apalm on the little girl with long black hair and he'd held steady a
raction of a second too long and the Cong bullet found his gas feed
nd he ran out of juice and went down and they sent Freddy in on the
)lly Green and . . . Sorry for that day when it all began.

He stood up and tied the leg straps of the parachute around his
ighs. "Sorry, kid," he said, wanting to say more.

Freddy nodded his head.

"Good-bye," Hardy said.

"Lots of luck," Freddy said.

"Put your hands up," Charles Werther said.

They turned at the sound of his voice. He was standing behind the cockpit door in the fuselage. The fingers of his left hand, which had been caught in the door Hardy had slammed on him, were swollen and dangling at his side, but in his right hand he held a gun. Hardy couldn't know that the gun had fallen into a Florida swamp earlier that evening, that the man holding it had wiped it out as carefully as he could and was hoping that no one would challenge him to use it. All Hardy could see was the open muzzle of the gun pointed directly at his gut.

*Oh, no,* he thought. *Oh, Christ, no.* He turned and spoke to the black sky outside. "Thank you, sweet Jesus," he said sadly. "I really needed this." He tried to think. He was not going back to jail. No matter how it all came apart in these last moments, he was not going to be taken back and paraded through the streets in a cage and . . .

There was an automatic carbine hanging on the forward bulkhead, just beyond the cockpit door. If he could get to it . . . He was standing beside Mason, next to the pilot's seat. He glanced at Werther's shattered left hand dangling uselessly at his side, then reached behind him, took hold of the wheel and suddenly yanked it full backward.

The DC-3 reared like a bronco, its nose clawing upward, its floor tilting. Werther fell backward, lost his balance and bounced against the floor, his gun falling away as he clawed for support with his good hand. Alison fell after him, down into the cabin.

Outside, the Harriers also reared like horses, scattering away from the lurching DC-3, then drawing close again. Strapped into his seat Mason tried to right the airplane. Hardy held tight to the wheel for balance, then released it and fell against the cockpit wall, trying to brace himself and reach for the carbine.

Werther was tumbling backward, trying to grab hold and to see where the open hatch lay. Then his legs slammed into one of the bucket seats, and he wrapped them around the stanchion. His mind was racing like a lunatic: his gun was lost, but since it was full of mud and useless, his only chance had been to bluff with it. Now that the bluff was called, he had nothing—

Alison came sliding after Werther, hit the side of the fuselage and bounced off, careening in front of him and sliding toward the gaping hole in the center of the floor. He reached out with his left hand, which was closer to her, and grabbed at her leg, but his fingers were swollen and useless. They felt like cardboard as she slid through them and toward the hole. He twisted around and grabbed her trailing wrist with his right hand, felt her momentum nearly yank his arm out of its socket, felt his legs nearly lose their grip on the stanchion, but held on for one second, then for one more. He could see that she was dangling out through the hatch. Only her chest and head and the one arm he held were still inside the airplane.

His grip slipped. He caught at her again, but again he slipped. He summoned all his strength and pulled, trying to raise her so that she could bring her other arm back into the airplane and grab hold of something, but he couldn't budge her. Again his grip slipped another inch, then another. She was going.

Hardy found the carbine, wrenched it out of its holder and turned to face the FBI agent. There he was, stretched out on the floor, reaching out, holding on to—

Hardy dropped the carbine, dived across the sloping floor and grabbed a handful of Alison's hair. Bracing himself against the riveted floor, he pulled hard. She came up a few inches and he slipped his other hand under her arm. Together he and Werther pulled her up another six inches, and then she managed to bring her other arm into the airplane. Werther grabbed it with his free hand, and they heaved her all the way in.

They all lay sprawled for a moment, their eyes locked. Hardy's eyes flickered away first, to one side, then to the other. Werther realized he was looking for the guns. He pushed himself up, looking around, but didn't see them. Then he saw Hardy scrabble sidewise, and following his line of motion spotted his gun, and Hardy, on his hands and knees now, reaching for it.

Alison was trying to stand, slipping against the bouncing of the plane as Freddy brought it under control. As she rose to her knees Werther saw the carbine under her leg. He reached for it, she fell again onto his outstretched arm, and his numbed fingers dropped it.

Hardy grabbed the gun and brought it around in a sharp arc. Werther dug his shoulder into Alison and shoved her away. His right

hand closed over the carbine as Hardy pointed the gun at hi
Werther knew that he'd dropped it in the mud and that it proba
wouldn't fire, but suddenly *probably* wasn't a very comforting word
he saw Hardy's finger tighten on the trigger as if in slow motion.
brought the carbine up and fired in the same motion. Three stacc.
bursts shattered the air, deafening and blinding him as Hardy sp
backward.

Then it was quiet, and for a moment Werther could hear noth
at all, could see nothing but shaking shadows. Then he heard
roaring of the engines again, and rising above it a shrill scream t
began in Alison's throat and filled the night sky. He could see aga
And Hardy was gone.

# Epilogue

A dark, foggy evening in Vienna.

David Melnik walks down Ringstrasse along the trolley tracks, his raincoat collar hunched ineffectively against the fog that collects in little droplets on his long black hair and drips off inside the neck of his coat, running in soft zigzags down his back. It is a bad wig for this kind of weather.

He comes to the Zum Alten Mann, opens the door, goes in. The air inside is heavy with garlic, sausage, beer and smoke from tobacco and a huge wood-burning fireplace. A large group around a huge round table in the far corner is singing. Smaller tables are scattered around the room. He pauses, loosening his raincoat, shaking off the droplets, looking around the room. Déjà vu. He doesn't know why. This restaurant is nothing like the Werthers' apartment. Perhaps it's because of the fireplace. In the first sudden moment he sees it all happen again, and in the next it has vanished, leaving nothing but a memory and a soft sweet pain.

"I want to marry you," he'd said to Lori. "I love you."

They had come to see her together late in the evening the day after they had rescued the President. They had both wanted to go straight home to her right afterward, but first the President wanted to see them.

They had spent the night being debriefed, and the next afternoon had been ushered into his hospital room. He was sitting propped up in bed, gaunt, haggard, trembling, but smiling. "They say I shouldn't have visitors yet," he said, "but I told them I'm not going to sleep until I shake the hands of the men who saved my life."

"I'm not sure who saved whose life, Mr. President," Werther said. "If you hadn't slipped the rope and let me out of that lavatory . . ."

The President smiled, leaned forward and extended both his hands, clasping theirs. Some flashbulbs went off, and then he made a little speech that despite the obvious staging for the press was undoubtedly sincere. When he finished they shook hands again, some more flashbulbs went off, and then they left the hospital to fly home to New York and to Lori.

They didn't speak on the way. There wasn't much to be said. When they reached Werther's apartment they found her in the living room, the drapes drawn and a fire burning in the fireplace. By this time the news had been on television, though no details had yet been given. It was cold outside, but it was warm in front of the fireplace, the chill hiding in the corners of the room.

They had called from Miami, so she knew that they were safe, and from the little they said and the exultation of the news reports, she knew that they had done something wonderful. When they walked in the door she was startled by Charles's bandaged hand, but as she jumped up he waved her back. "It's nothing," he said. "Got a man here wants to talk to you." Then he stepped aside and gave Melnik center stage.

David opened his mouth twice, but no words came. Finally he smiled apologetically and said, "I love you. I want to marry you."

Well, she'd known it was coming. She had tried to convince herself that their last confrontation two nights before had never happened, but she knew it had, and that they would be coming back to finish it. Now here they were, but she couldn't talk. She stood looking at them.

Charles cleared his throat. "The man wants an answer," he said.

She stood in front of the fire and looked at David, then at her husband beside him, and said, "No. No, love, I can't marry you, I can't leave Charlie." She shook her head. "I'm sorry, David." She shrugged. "I can't."

Charles loved her for that moment, and hated her for all the treacherous moments that had led up to it. He stood silently, unmoving, calm and steady as always, but in his chest was a foaming, roiling turmoil that cut off his breath and suffocated him.

For a long moment they stood there like statues, until finally the turmoil in Charles's chest popped like a soap bubble and was gone. Drained and weak, he held out his arms and she walked into them and disappeared forever from David Melnik's touch.

Werther kissed her hair gently, then reached under his arm, pulled out his gun and dropped it on the sofa. "I guess I'll never know," said, aware that he was being melodramatic but unable to resist, "whether I'd have killed the two of you or not."

He almost smiled at the melodrama. Then, as he held Lori in his arms and buried his nose in the sweet smell of her hair, for one short moment the turmoil bubbled up again in him and was as suddenly gone, leaving him with a bewildering hint of the passion that had hold of him. *My God*, he thought, dazed. *It isn't melodrama. It's real.* It had never been in his nature to talk much about love, or even to think about it. He was not a romantic; he equated such feelings with ephemeral dreams. But now he found that he was dizzied by emotion and bewildered at its power and depth.

Melnik went down the hall, turned once to look at them in the light of the fire, and then walked out of their lives.

A log snapped, sparks shot out and sizzled, and then the fire settled again into a warm, cozy glow. He walked across the room and joined a young woman sitting alone by the wall, hanging his raincoat behind her, nodding as he sat down. She greeted him impersonally, her mind on her work—on their work. Taking a notebook out of her purse, she opened it, flipped a few pages and pushed it across to him. He glanced down, read the page and nodded.

It would never end.

An elderly man paid his bill, pulled on his coat and left the restaurant. A few moments later Melnik nodded to another solitary man, who got up, took his raincoat and slipped into it as he walked across the room and out the door. Through the curtained, rain-streaked window Melnik watched him cross the street and walk slowly after the first man. A minute later the woman got up and left, walking in another direction. Melnik put her notebook into his pocket, then picked up the menu and scanned it. He was hungry.

But never again would he have what he was hungry for. He stared at the menu but saw Lori. God, he missed her. He missed her hair cascading over him as she impaled herself on him and fell forward on top of him. He missed her cool fingers and her warm belly, the fullness of her breasts in his mouth, the weight of her, the deep luxurious depths of her. He was *used* to her; she had become part of him, and then she left, that part had gone too and he was lost without it and without her. For what was life about if not love? Would there be another love someday? Would he ever recapture that sense of belonging to someone?

Slowly he shook his head. Lori swirled away and the rest of the world seeped in again. He had his destiny, and never would it change. Or end. There would always be another enemy. They had saved the President, and everything was back to normal. The authorities had decided not to prosecute Alison Mason, but her brother, Freddy, would remain in prison for the rest of his life. Though perhaps not, things being as they are in the United States.

He didn't care; it didn't matter to him one way or another. Hardy was the dangerous one, and he was dead. When Werther realized he had fallen out of the DC-3, he had radioed Melnik in the Harrier to mark the spot, but of course the water erased all record of where he had landed. Melnik had called in to Miami, and the Coast Guard had immediately set to sea in a search-and-rescue operation, but to no one's surprise they found nothing. They blockaded the Florida Keys and the National Guard joined the Florida State Police in barricading the one road that led up from the Keys to the mainland and in guarding all local airports, but they never found a trace.

They didn't expect to, of course. Even in the unlikely event that Werther had missed from only six feet away with a spray of bullets from the automatic carbine, even if Hardy had jumped through the hatch to escape the bullets, even if he was wearing a parachute . . . Well, jumping into night waters from an altitude of only three hundred feet a hundred miles from land, wearing nothing but a Mae West, was as good a way as any of committing suicide. He hadn't had a chance.

Still, they searched for him everywhere. They found nothing, not in Switzerland where the money was stored, nor anywhere in Europe, nor in the Arab countries. There was no doubt he was dead, drowned in the depths of the shark-filled Atlantic waters, dead and gone forever.

Of course, there have been the usual rumors.

Melnik shook his head, and turned back to the menu.

ABOUT THE AUTHORS

VID E. FISHER holds a PhD in nuclear physics from the Oak Ridge
titute of Nuclear Studies and the University of Florida. He has done
earch at Oak Ridge and Brookhaven national laboratories, the
rvard/Smithsonian Astrophysical Observatory and Cornell Univer-
, has been a playwright and actor, and is currently professor of
mochemistry at the University of Miami's Rosenstiel School of
rine Sciences. He also teaches graduate and honors students in the
ool of International Studies. His dozen previous books include
h novels and works about science and politics; his last book, A *Race
the Edge of Time*, told the story of the development of airborne
ar in World War II; his next, *Fire and Ice*, examines the impending
bal catastrophe. He has one wife and three children; his hobbies
lude flying and fencing.

LONEL RALPH ALBERTAZZIE was born in West Virginia, attended West
ginia University, and in 1943 left college to become an Army Air
rps pilot. When recalled to active duty during the Korean War, he
ved overseas with the Military Air Transport Command. Thereafter,
ause of his outstanding flying record he became a Special Air
ssions pilot in Washington, flying U.S. and foreign officials around
world. In 1967 he was assigned to Vietnam, and in 1968 he
urned to Washington to become President Nixon's pilot and the
nmander of Air Force One, a position he held until 1974.

Colonel Albertazzie is the co-author of *The Flying White House*, the
tory of Air Force One, published in 1979. Currently he is a
inessman in West Virginia, where he lives with his wife.

**Greg Dinallo**

SIX TENSE DAYS IN 1962...The world was a helpless witness to the most fateful showdown in history. Finally, the Soviets withdrew their missiles from Cuba. America thought she had won.

TWENTY-SIX YEARS LATER...A robot satellite tracking a Soviet Foxtrot-class sub in the Gulf of Mexico spots a mysterious supertanker—identity unknown. Children playing on a Louisiana beach find the severed arm of missing industrialist Theodor Churcher. And Churcher's son Andrew, seeing a Soviet link to his father, becomes embroiled in a spyworld gambit that could sabotage—or guarantee—Soviet conquest.

### "SUPERB!"—Dale Brown, author of *Flight of The Old Dog*